PRAISE FOR
CAMP

"*Camp* is the perfect read for anyone wondering if they're too much or not enough of their true self. **It's the must-read book of the summer.**" —Julian Winters, award-winning author of *Running With Lions*

"Joyful, exuberant, incisive, and **terrifically queer**. *Camp* is a rom-com with bite and heart, one that examines the walls we build around ourselves—and promises us we have the power to tear them down. **This is literary wizardry.**" —Adib Khorram, award-wining author of *Darius the Great Is Not Okay*

"A **powerful, yet nuanced**, illustration of every queer person's struggle with identity, presented in Rosen's **trademark blend of levity and wit**." —Phil Stamper, author of *The Gravity of Us*

"*Camp* has everything you're looking for: **a winning romance, a celebration of queerness**, a reflection on what it takes to embrace your most authentic self, and answers to questions most queer boys often don't know how to ask in the first place." —Caleb Roehrig, author of *Death Prefers Blondes*

"*Camp* is a **pitch-perfect, joyfully queer** take on the classic summer camp sex romp." —Tom Ryan, author of *Keep This to Yourself*

"**A romantic summertime joyride** and a thoughtful examination of gay culture." —Cale Dietrich, author of *The Love Interest*

CAMP

BY L. C. ROSEN

LITTLE, BROWN AND COMPANY
New York Boston

Copyright © 2020 by Lev Rosen
Interior camp tent © DMaryashin/Shutterstock.com
Interior sun icon © BullsStock/Shutterstock.com
Bonus content copyright © 2021 by Lev Rosen
Text in excerpt of *Jack of Hearts (and other parts)* copyright © 2018 by Lev Rosen
Illustrations in excerpt of *Jack of Hearts (and other parts)* copyright © 2018 by Neil Swaab

Cover art copyright © 2020 by MDI Digital. Wooden background © 10 FACE/Shutterstock.com. Cover design by Angelie Yap. Cover copyright © 2020 by Hachette Book Group, Inc.

Little, Brown and Company
Hachette Book Group
1290 Avenue of the Americas, New York, NY 10104
Visit us at LBYR.com

Simultaneously published in 2020 by Penguin Random House UK in Great Britain
First U.S. Hardcover Edition: May 2020
First U.S. Trade Paperback Edition: May 2021

Little, Brown and Company is a division of Hachette Book Group, Inc.
The Little, Brown name and logo are trademarks of Hachette Book Group, Inc.

The publisher is not responsible for websites (or their content)
that are not owned by the publisher.

The Library of Congress has cataloged the hardcover edition as follows:
Names: Rosen, Lev AC., author.
Title: Camp / by L. C. Rosen.
Description: First edition. | New York : Little, Brown and Company, 2020. |
Audience: Ages 14+. | Summary: At Camp Outland, a camp for LGBTQIA+ teens,
sixteen-year-old Randall "Del" Kapplehoff's plan to have Hudson Aaronson-Lim
fall in love with him succeeds, but both are hiding their true selves.
Identifiers: LCCN 2019034949 | ISBN 9780316537759 (hardcover) |
ISBN 9780316537742 (ebook) | ISBN 9780316537926 (library edition ebook)
Subjects: CYAC: Camps—Fiction. | Gays—Fiction. | Lesbians—Fiction. |
Gender-nonconforming people—Fiction. | Dating (Social customs) —Fiction. |
Love—Fiction. | Secrets—Fiction.
Classification: LCC PZ7.1.R67 Cam 2020 | DDC [Fic]—dc23
LC record available at https://lccn.loc.gov/2019034949

ISBNs: 978-0-316-53777-3 (pbk.), 978-0-316-53774-2 (ebook)

Printed in the United States of America

LSC-C

Printing 1, 2021

FOR ROBIN,
WHO BRINGS SUMMER WITH HER
WHEREVER SHE GOES

ONE

The smell wraps around me like a reunion between old friends when I step off the bus. That dark soil smell, but mixed with something lighter. Something green that immediately makes me think of leaves in rain, or trees in the wind. I love this smell. I love it every summer. It's the smell of freedom. Not that stupid kayaking-shirtless-in-a-Viagra-commercial freedom. That's for straight people. This is different. It's the who-cares-if-your-wrists-are-loose freedom. The freedom from having two seniors the table over joke about something being "so gay" at lunch.

Several tables are set out next to the parking lot, a big banner hanging over them: WELCOME TO CAMP OUTLAND.

This year, I admit, it smells a little different. Maybe not quite as free. But I knew it would be like this when I came up with my plan. This smell, I hope—slightly less pine, a bit more grass, the barest whiff of daisy, which I could be imagining—this is the smell of love.

"Keep it moving, keep it moving," Joan, the camp director, calls out to us as we step off the bus we've been traveling in for the last several hours, waving her hands like a traffic cop. "Tables are by age—find your age, go to that table to register."

I look for the table that says 16 and wait in line. I run my hands over my newly shortened hair. Until two days ago, it had been chin length and wavy and super cute, if I do say so myself, but I needed to lose it for the plan to work. The line of campers moves forward and I'm at the front, staring down at Mark, the theater counselor—*my* counselor. I think he's in his forties, gray at the temples, skin that's a little too tan for a white guy, wearing the Camp Outland polo, big aviator sunglasses, and a pin that says THEATER GAY in sparkly rainbow letters. This will be the big test. He looks up at me, and for a moment, there's a flash, like he recognizes me, but then he squints, confused.

"What's your name, honey?" he asks.

I smile. Not my usual big grin; I've been working on changing it. Now it's more like a smirk.

"Randall," I say. "Randall Kapplehoff."

"Randy?" He practically shouts it, looking me over again as he stands up. "Oh my god, what happened to you?"

"Puberty," I say, now smiling my real smile. I look around, bring it back to smirk.

"Honey, you were a baritone last summer, this isn't puberty," he says. "I barely recognized you."

Good, I think. That's the point.

"I just thought it was time for a change," I say.

"Were you being bullied?" he asks, concerned eyes peeking over his sunglasses.

"No." I shake my head. "Just…wanted to try something new."

"Well," Mark says, sitting down. "It's certainly new. I hope you haven't changed so much you're not auditioning for the show this summer, though."

"We'll see," I say.

He frowns and flips through the pages on his clipboard. "Well, at least you'll still be hanging out with us. You're in cabin seven." He takes a name tag label out from the back of his clipboard and writes a big *R* on it before I think to stop him.

"Actually," I say, putting out a hand, "it's Del now."

He peeks up at me over the sunglasses again. "Del?"

"Yeah." I nod, chin first. "I'm Del."

"Okay," he says like he doesn't believe me, and writes it out on a new name tag sticker and hands it to me. I press it over my chest, rubbing it in, hoping it will stick. "Well, I'm going to have to talk to my therapist about this later," he says to himself. Then he glances at his watch and turns back to me. "Flagpole meet-up is at eleven. So, go pick a bunk and be there in twenty minutes."

"Thanks," I say.

"Later...Del," he says.

I walk back over to the bus where our bags have been unloaded and pick up the big military surplus bag I bought online. The purple wheely bag with the stickers of cats wearing tiaras on it wasn't going to work this summer. Neither was having my parents drop me off. I think that made them a little sad. Camp Outland had been their idea four years ago, after I came out. Not many other twelve-year-olds were talking about how dreamy and cute Skylar Astin was in *Pitch Perfect 2*, and how I hoped my boyfriend would look like him someday, so they thought it would be good for me to meet some other queer kids, and they found Camp Outland—a four-week sleepaway summer camp for LGBTQIA+ teens nestled in the woods of northern Connecticut.

And let's be honest. It was an amazing idea. Every summer has been better than the last. But this summer is going to be the best. Because this summer, Hudson Aaronson-Lim is going to fall in love with me.

I hoist the military bag onto my shoulder, not flinching as the scratchy, cheap canvas brushes my ear, and follow the other campers down the path through the woods. The camp is built like a waterfall feature. At the top is the parking lot, then follow the stairs down and you end up at the administrative section—Joan the camp director's office, the infirmary, the big meeting hall for movie nights. Then another flight down and you have a big open field lined with cabins. The tier below that is the last one—the real camp—and has the dining hall, pool, drama cabin, obstacle course, capture the flag field, arts and crafts cabin, and a boathouse next to the river. I stop at the cabin-lined field, surrounded by the woods. There's a flagpole in the center of the field for morning camp-wide meet-ups and evening bonfires. Breakfast is at nine, lunch is at one, and dinner is at six, then lights-out at ten. Otherwise, we pretty much make our own schedules. Sign up for pool time, sports, waterskiing, or just drop by the arts and crafts cabin and spend all day gossiping and weaving friendship bracelets. My favorite thing every year, though, has been the drama cabin. Mark puts on a show, and you have to audition but it's not like school where the pretty blond girl lands the lead every year. They don't care about gender or appearance when casting, they just want everyone to have fun, and we always do. Last year, I was Domina in *Funny Thing*, and I got a standing ovation after "That Dirty Old Man."

But this year, no theater. This year…sports. I manage not to shiver as I think about it.

"Hey," a voice behind me says. A voice I know. It's low and a little breathy. I turn around and there he is, Hudson Aaronson-Lim, in all his glory. Tall, with muscular arms bulging in his white tee, and equally appealing bulging in his black gym shorts. He has a broad, square face, shadowed by prominent cheekbones and a little stubble. His short black hair is swept to the side, but messy, like he doesn't care. He is, without a doubt, the most attractive man I've ever seen in real life. And more attractive than half the men I've seen on-screen. He's got a killer smile, and he unleashes it on me now, crooked and a little sleazy, but only enough to make it sexy. I get that feeling I get around him, like I'm filled with stars and can be anything I want, do anything I want—conquer the world. Checking in on his Instagram never really gives me the same feeling. It's a high I've missed all year.

"Hi," I say after too long a silence. I hope I'm not blushing.

"You new?" he asks.

I smirk. He barely noticed me before, so it's not surprising he wouldn't recognize me. Now I have his attention.

"You could say that," I answer, not wanting to outright lie.

He steps closer. I coordinated my outfit perfectly for this meeting. Brown flannel button-down with short sleeves, untucked; olive-green shorts; yellow sneakers that pick out the yellow in the flannel. I've also lost twenty pounds, cut my hair off, and studied the "bros" at school all year. I am, I think, Hudson's dream boy. A masc fantasy. Sure, I watch everything I do now, and I won't be able to be in the show this summer, but it'll all be worth it for love.

I smell him as he steps closer—this sort of faded lightning

smell, like day-old deodorant and maple. I work hard to keep my knees from shaking.

"I'm Hudson," he says.

"Del," I say, keeping my voice low.

"So, what cabin are you in?" He's really close now. I can feel the heat off his body and I wonder if he can feel it off mine, like we're touching.

"Seven," I say.

"Oh." He raises an eyebrow. "So, did you pick that?"

"It's my lucky number," I say.

"Well, I'm cabin fourteen," he says. "So maybe your luck is changing."

"Something wrong with seven?" I ask.

"Nah, they're good people," he says. "But I think you'd have more fun with me—in my cabin. Folks like us." He waves his finger back and forth between us, almost like a question, a "We going to do this?" and I have to take a deep breath to keep from nodding.

"Well, it's just where I'm sleeping, right?" I say.

"Yeah," he laughs, and reaches out and gives my shoulder a squeeze. This is the first time he's intentionally touched me and it's something I've wanted for years and it's hard not to melt right away, but instead I just lock eyes with him and smile. Remember, I tell myself, you want him to fall in love with you. If I just wanted to screw him, I could probably do that right now—but I'm going to be the guy who finally gets Hudson to commit. No one else has done it, but I will. Because I have a plan.

"Well," he says, dropping his hand, his eyes closing just a little, like he's curious, "I'll see you around, I hope."

"I hope so," I say, and he grins, and I wonder for a moment if it was too much, but no, I think, as I turn around and head for my cabin, that was just enough. I look back after a few steps and he's still watching me and smiles when he sees me watching and then heads for his own cabin.

Okay, I say in my head, walking slowly, breathe in, breathe out. My legs feel like jelly, my heart is racing. Okay. Okay okay okay. Step one, done. It worked. IT WORKED. Maybe this whole thing could work? Maybe I didn't give up carbs and cut off my hair and spend hours working on my walk and voice and learning not to talk with my hands or quote a show tune every sentence for nothing. Maybe I can really win my dream guy.

I walk into the cabin and George starts screaming. "OH MY GOD," he says, giving me a hug. "I was watching from the window, and I almost didn't recognize you—I mean, I saw the photos on Snapchat, of course, darling, and everything you texted me, but I didn't think you'd really be going through with the wardrobe and styling changes." He reaches up and pets the air where my hair used to be. "Poor hair," he says solemnly. "But you just talked to him, and he totally checked out your ass as you walked away! Could you feel his dark, sexy eyes just burrowing into you?" He wiggles his eyebrows.

"Hey," Ashleigh says from her top bunk on the side of the room, where she's flipping through a comic.

I let my bag drop, and I take one long dramatic breath.

"I think it's going to work," I say.

George screams again, one big drag queen shriek.

I grin, and look them both over. My two best camp friends. Two best friends, really. It feels sad saying that about people I only see for four weeks out of the year, but we e-mail and text, and watch *Drag Race* together while in a group chat, and it's not like I have other queer friends. There's not even a GSA at my tiny school in eastern Ohio. Like, I'm sure there are other queer kids, and maybe they're even out, a little, like I am, to a few friends and their parents, but no one is talking about it. Once you start talking about it, other people join the conversation, and in eastern Ohio, they don't always say nice things.

My transformation at school didn't go unnoticed, though. I was still a theater kid (always the chorus, never a lead—there, anyway), but suddenly the girls were looking at me differently, asking me to hang out. I pretended to be sick a lot. My parents gave me weird looks a lot, too, and asked if everything was okay, but I just smiled and told them things were great. It was definitely strange. But worth it if I can go back to school with my phone lock screen as a photo of Hudson and me making out.

"So," George says when he's done screaming, "what's the timeline on this? You're still going to be able to hang out with us, right? Mark says they're going to do *Bye Bye Birdie* this year, and I am so excited! Darling, you know I'm going to cut some bitches to play Kim, so don't even think of going up against me."

George spreads his fingers out in front of him, his nails painted in green and gold to spell B CAMP @ CAMP. I've been so focused on my own physical changes over the school year, I guess I didn't notice his on Snapchat and Instagram. He doesn't look that different. He's still "stocky," as we call ourselves (well, called, in my case, I guess), but his face is a little more angular, and the stubble and chest hair peeking out from the collar of his purple V-neck give his sandy-colored complexion more maturity. His black curly hair is still shaved at the sides and big on top, but it looks less like a kid's haircut and more like a man's. He's gone from looking too young for his age to looking a little older than the rest of us. And he's wearing it well. Ashleigh hasn't changed at all. Same denim cutoffs, same black-and-white flannel wrapped around her waist and black tank top. Same rough-looking undercut, one side of her head shaved, the other side's unwashed wavy hair falling over her thin, pale face. She's the ultimate theater techie. Lights, sound, stage managing—she does it all, way better than anyone else.

"I don't know if I can be in the musical," I say, trying not to sound as sad as I feel about it.

"Darling, no," George says, shaking his head. "I know you have this plan and all, but there's always time for the-ater!" He does jazz hands.

Ashleigh looks up from her comic, a worn-out copy of *Deadly Class*. "You're giving up theater for this guy?" she asks. "Really?"

"That's the plan," I say. "And he's not just some guy. He's Hudson. THE Hudson. The perfect man." As I say it, a few more old friends come into the bunk—other theater kids. We say hi, give each other hugs, some tell me they like my haircut. Jordan does a double take and says, "Whoa, didn't recognize you. Cool look, though," with slightly worried eyes before grabbing a bed. I take the bunk next to George's, under Ashleigh.

"I thought you'd be taking the top bunk with that new hair," George says.

"Calm down," I say. "It's just a haircut."

"And no theater," Ashleigh says.

"What are you going to do all summer?" George asks.

"Sports, I guess," I say, not really sure which ones I mean. "Obstacle course stuff, arts and crafts."

"Well, at least we'll have that," George says.

"I just don't get this, Randy," Ashleigh says. "Like, I get you have a crush on the guy, but—"

"It's more than a crush," I say. "He makes me feel...different. He's special."

Ashleigh sighs above me, and I see George stare up at her, exchanging a look.

"And call me Del now," I add. "At least in public."

"Del." George tries it out. "I don't hate it."

"I do," Ashleigh says. "It's not your name."

"It's the other part of Randall," I say, taking out my sheets—plain gray this year, not the rainbow unicorn sheets I usually bring—and making my bed. "It's fine. I'm not forgetting who I am. I'm just changing the way other people see me."

"To be more masculine." Ashleigh says it with disgust. She hops down from her bunk and helps me tuck the corners of my sheet in. "As if that means anything. Gender essentialist nonsense."

"It's a type," George says, shrugging.

"It's what Hudson likes," I say, sitting down on my made bed and smoothing out the gray sheets. They're high thread count, at least. They may look different, but they feel the same.

"And you're sure all this is worth it?" Ashleigh asks.

"Absolutely," I say.

TWO

We gather around the flagpole in a semicircle, staring up at Joan, who's looking at her clipboard and making that face she makes all the time, with her mouth twisted to one side. I sit next to George and Ashleigh. I can still be friends with them—that won't hurt the plan. I decided if he didn't like me being friends with them, then he wasn't the guy I thought he was, the one who believes we're all special and can do anything. He might not know how we're old, close friends, but that's not important. Besides, I'm going to need their help.

I spot Hudson on the other side of the circle and he waves at me. I smile. Next to him is his best friend, Brad—tall, lanky, shaved head, and dark skin. He's like Hudson, in that he's into sports and doesn't wear nail polish, but strangely,

Brad has never been one of Hudson's conquests. No one is sure why—it's one of the great mysteries of camp, like whether someone really died in cabin three, or why the cabins aren't gender-exclusive but the changing rooms by the pool are.

"I'm going to need you to show me the tree later," I tell George and Ashleigh.

"You've seen the tree," Ashleigh says. She's already been down to the arts and crafts cabin and raided it for string and is weaving a bracelet.

"Randy has," I say. "Del hasn't. Del needs to see the tree while Hudson is watching so I can say I'd never want to be with a playboy like that."

"Playboy?" George says. "Darling, this isn't the sixties. We don't talk like that."

"I'm more worried about how he talked about himself in the third person, and as two different people," Ashleigh says.

"It helps me distinguish," I say. "Del is like a role."

"Method actors," George says, his voice dripping disdain. "All right, all right, I'll help you out—but I don't know how you're going to get him to eavesdrop on us."

"Just take me to see the tree when I ask you to, okay?"

"Attention, please!" Joan is standing at the flagpole in the center of the cabins, holding her hand up. "When the hand goes up!" she says.

"The mouth goes shut!" shout about half the campers in

response. Some people keep talking, but Joan keeps her hand raised and eventually everyone quiets down.

"Thank you," Joan says. Joan always seems like she hasn't gotten enough sleep. She's maybe in her fifties, with short curly hair and big plastic glasses I swear she's had since the seventies on a chain around her neck, always in the purple camp polo and cargo shorts. "Hello, and welcome to Camp Outland!" she says with half-hearted enthusiasm and a smile that would probably be big if she had the energy. "I'm Joan Ruiz, and I run the camp. I'll be leading meetings here every morning at eight, and I handle our LGBTQIA+ history activities on Monday nights. Otherwise, you're probably only going to be hearing my voice if you get in trouble, so let's talk about how not to do that. First—no cell phones, no computers, no smart watches or belts or whatever they have these days. We have boom boxes in each cabin, if you need music, but otherwise, no technology. If we catch you with a phone or anything else, you'll be put on kitchen cleanup for a week, and we will confiscate the phone. You won't get it back until you go home. It'll be dead by then, so you won't be able to immediately get on the Internet, where I know you'll want to be. That also means you have to write letters—Real Mail, I call it—if you want to talk to your friends or family back home. Next: food! You have to be at all three meals a day. If you're vegan or vegetarian or kosher or halal, you should have told us already and we're prepared for you, but if for some reason you didn't, come see me after flagpole. You eat what you're given. It's not so bad, I promise. Yes, you can be sent candy and snacks from home, but only things that follow the rules—nothing with peanuts or sesame seeds or anything anyone is deathly allergic to—your counselors have a list. When you get food from home, your cabin counselor will go through it to make sure it meets the rules. Don't leave food out! That's how you get ants. More ants. And if you're going to gamble with candy, just do it over cards. No betting on who's going throw up after eating too much or who's going to drop the egg during the egg race. That's just mean. No drinking! If we catch you with drugs or alcohol, you'll be kicked out. Same if you're caught outside your cabin after curfew."

I pluck the grass as Joan goes on, stealing glances at Hudson, who I'm pleased to see is stealing glances at me. We lock eyes once and I grin. This might be going too smoothly. The issue now is making sure he knows I'm not just going to be another conquest. That's what he does. A different boy every two weeks at camp. A week of wooing, a week of holding hands and sneaking out to the Peanut Butter Pit, and then, inevitably, a breakup with some tears.

They always stay friends, though. Hudson is the master of staying friends—and that makes sense. He's nice about it, he never cheats on them, they always just...consciously uncouple.

But I'm going to knock all those other bitches out of the water. 'Cause Hudson is going to stay with me all summer.

And beyond that, too. We're going to be boyfriends and share a tent on the canoe trip the second-to-last weekend of camp.

When Joan is done talking, she introduces the nurse, Cosmo, a skeletal man in his sixties with long gray hair to his shoulders.

"Just stay healthy, everybody," he says by way of his speech. "Like, water, sunscreen. You know." He waves at us and walks away. Joan frowns a little, then hoists the big rainbow flag on the flagpole, running it up to the top, where it starts flapping in the breeze. Everyone watches in silence, but with smiles. I admit, I grow a little teary-eyed at it every year—can you blame me? This is our special home. The scent of the wind rushes back, heavy with that smell— definitely freedom—and I close my eyes. I can't tear up this year. Hudson is watching, and butch boys don't cry in public.

"Okay," Joan says, after the flag is raised. "Go unpack, make your schedules with your bunk counselors, then there'll be some group time, some free swim, and then dinner. After dinner, the counselors are going to put on a talent show for you folks. Go with pride!" she shouts, the official dismissal.

Everyone scatters up and heads back toward their cabins, but I see Hudson coming in my direction. George and Ashleigh look at me, as if waiting for something.

"I'll see you at the cabin," I say. George gives me some side-eye as they walk away.

"Hey," Hudson says, arriving just as they leave. "So, your bunkmates showing you the ropes?"

"Yeah," I say. "It all seems so awesome."

"It is," Hudson says. "Like, could you ever imagine a place like this when you were closeted? No people calling you names, no people asking if you've tried being straight, putting you down. None of that bullying crap. It's amazing."

"I can't imagine anyone bullying you," I say, looking him over.

"Well, not anymore," he says. "My trick is to beat them at their own game." I don't know what he means, but I nod like I do. "So, anyway, I just wanted to tell you you should sign up for the adventure elective."

"Yeah?" I ask.

"Yeah, I always do. It rocks. We mess around on the obstacle course and hike and stuff. Oh, and I try to take my swim class period before lunch...if you want to see me in a bathing suit." He grins, all wolfish charm, and I feel a heat flash down my spine and legs to my toes.

"Okay," I say.

"And, so, let's try to hang out—just us—when we have some free time." He bites the side of his lower lip as he looks at me, like he's nervous.

"Yeah," I manage to squeak out.

"Cool," he says. "See you later." He jogs off and I watch him go, feeling my heart rise and fall in rhythm to his legs.

"Later," I say, after he's way out of earshot. Then I turn around and head back to my cabin.

Inside, music is playing. A sort of vintage doo-wop vibe,

but no vocals. It makes me think of really old-fashioned dancing, like where they twist their hips with their arms bent. And apparently, I'm not the only one thinking of that, because several of my bunkmates are dancing just like that.

"Randy," Mark says as I come in. He's our cabin counselor. "So nice of you to join us."

"Del," I say.

"Right," he says, "sorry. Anyway, as I was just telling everyone, the musical this summer is *Bye Bye Birdie*, and to make sure we're really living that retro vibe, I'll be playing nothing but fifties and sixties music in this cabin. I encourage you to dance to it." He gestures at the campers, who have managed to get themselves in synch—a semi-choreographed routine with hip swivels and tossing back their heads. "It'll give you a feel for the music."

"And it inspires me!" Crystal says. She's the other cabin counselor and plays choreographer to Mark's director. She has wavy blond hair to her shoulders and always wears loose-fitting skirts and peasant blouses. Right now she's dancing... but not to the music, near as I can tell. Just... to something in her head.

"Okay," I say. And I can feel my feet tapping—I want to join in. I want to dance with the rest of them. I take a step forward. Hudson is in his own cabin. He won't see me.

So I start dancing with them. The swivels, the arms up, the head tosses. We add in a few step-forward-back moves, too. It feels so good. All year I've been making sure my movements are casual, clumsy, rough. I've thought about how apes move, swinging their arms. It's so nice to have a little elegance back in my step. To have some rhythm. To feel like myself.

Mark turns off the stereo as the song ends and claps his hands.

"All right!" he says. "None of you are new, so we don't need to do two truths and a lie or anything. Let's get right to schedules. The theater elective is the first half of the day, and auditions are tomorrow, so I hope you all came prepared. As for what you want to do the rest of the day—that's up to you. You know the drill. Put down your choices and we'll figure it out if there's too many campers in anything."

Crystal hands out clipboards with the various electives on them for us to choose from. I look down at my clipboard. Outdoor Adventure is the first activity of the day—just like theater. I take a deep breath and circle it with my pencil. I miss theater the moment I do it, but I know this has to be part of the plan. I'll miss singing, dancing, backstage chaos... last year floods my mind for a moment, all wild joy in my blood. But I'll have it again next year. This year, I'll give it up for Hudson. Otherwise, I won't see Hudson as much.

George looks over and tsks. "Whatever you want, darling," he says.

"Hudson asked me to," I say.

"And you want to make him happy," George says. "Sure."

I circle the swim class period before lunch and then try to think of what Hudson would circle—sports, probably, which means a lot of touch football and kickball. That's okay, I've been practicing, or at least actively participating in gym class. Luckily there's still room for arts and crafts after lunch—the same time as George and Ashleigh. And the whole camp does a free pool time at the end of the day. When I give my clipboard back to Crystal, she looks at it confused.

"You forgot to circle theater," she says, handing it back.

"I'm…" The words make my throat dry and I cough. "I'm not doing theater this year."

Crystal looks like I've confessed to murdering her pet rabbit. She turns pink and her mouth opens and she looks behind her at Mark, then back at me, then back at Mark, until he walks over and looks at the clipboard, then frowns at me.

"Okay, Del." He pauses, frowning, but then makes his expression soft. He looks worried. "What is…all this?" He gestures at me. "Are you okay? Did you hit your head? Is someone making you act like this? My therapist says sudden changes like these are usually the result of trauma."

"What?" I say. "No. I just…wanted to change."

"He's doing it for a boy," Ashleigh says.

"A boy?" Mark practically shouts. "And based on your makeover, I'm guessing he's one of those 'straight-acting' types? Honey, if he's suck—" He pauses, smiles. "If he's kissing you, he's not acting straight. No offense, Jen," he says

21

to one of the campers. "Bisexual folks can act straight and still be super queer. But we're talking about men who don't want anyone to think they're gay until they have a di—" He pauses again, smiles. Mark's gotten in trouble before for his overly graphic language. "Until they're making out with a boy. They hate themselves, and they hate you, too. They're not worth the time of day, much less an entire wardrobe change." By now his voice is loud enough it can probably be heard outside. "I'm going to need to book a double with Dr. Gruber," he says much softer to himself.

"He's not straight-acting," I say.

"He's masc4masc," George says.

"Oh, what's the difference?" Mark asks. "And who even says that? He tells people that over the campfire?"

"We found his BoyDate profile," George says. Which is true. Last summer, when my parents picked me up, they brought my phone and I turned it on—just to see, just to check if I could find his profile, and save it, and maybe there'd be photos—and there it was: HudsonRocks, five eleven, athletic build, masc4masc. As if we didn't know that from all the boys he'd gotten with at camp.

Mark sighs and takes my shoulders in his hands, bending down to look me in the eyes. "Look, Del, Randy, I don't care what you call yourself. I just want you to be happy. Are you happy? Don't you want to wear that same purple sweater you bring every summer? Don't you want to sing in the show?"

"I..." I take a deep breath. I do. But I also want something else, and I can't have both. "I want Hudson."

Mark lets go of my arms and stands up straight. "Well, it's your choice. But, honey, I've been around the block a lot more than you have, and I promise you, a man who makes you change to be with him isn't worth it."

"He is," I say softly.

Mark ignores me and claps his hands. "Everyone turned their clipboards back in? Great. Now let's get back to dancing!" He turns the music on and everyone is dancing again, but I sit down on my bed, my head in my hands, and try to shake the feeling that even though I know this plan will work, I'm letting everybody else down. I take a deep breath. Hudson is worth it, I remind myself. Everything I'm giving up is worth it for him.

THREE

LAST SUMMER

Normally, I don't care for the camp-wide color wars. Three days when all the usual activities are replaced by relay races and capture the flag and making banners and worthless points stacking up like condom wrappers at the boathouse? Not fun. Mark loathes it—says the break from rehearsal and all the screaming damaging our vocal cords is just Joan trying to sabotage the show. The whole camp is divided up into two teams—no splitting up bunkmates, though, to prevent inter-cabin fighting—and this year, we're Green. Not my favorite color, or one I usually gravitate to, sartorially speaking, but I have a great pair of white shorts trimmed in green lace. That and a black shirt, and I think I'm showing my team spirit in a very fashionable way. And at least I'm not on Orange. I don't know what I'd wear for that.

And besides, Hudson is on our team. Not just on it—he's a captain: one of the eight campers chosen to lead their color into battle, four per team. They're like army generals and cheerleaders rolled into one. Hudson has taken to it like it was a mission delivered unto him by God herself. He's standing onstage with the other three generals, in a bright green polo and not-at-all-matching khaki-green shorts. His face is painted with green stripes under his eyes, like a football fantasy come to life, and he's even sprayed his hair with a light coating of bright green wash-out dye. And he's waving a green flag in the air, screaming.

"Go Mean Green!" he shouts with the other generals. Across the soccer field from us, team Orange glares. Another reason I'm happy to be on green: Nothing rhymes with *orange*.

George sits to my right, in green eye shadow and a forest-green romper studded with gold stars. Ashleigh is to my left, in a black tank top and denim cutoffs. A green bandanna that one of the counselors gave her sticks out of her pocket.

"I feel like we're in a cult," Ashleigh says.

"An army," George corrects. "That means a cult that's openly fighting another cult. As opposed to secretly fighting everyone."

"It'll be fun," I say, watching Hudson jump up and down onstage. "I wonder if his underwear is green."

"If that boy owns anything beyond 'funny' boxers with pictures of bacon or something, I'll eat my own underwear,"

George says. "Though I will say those streaks under his eyes are expertly applied. Perfect edges. I wonder who did them?"

"Green briefs," I say, still thinking aloud. "I'm going to picture him in green briefs."

"Gross," Ashleigh says. "I don't need to hear what you're going to be fantasizing about."

"Sweetie, you were the one who did a five-minute monologue on Janice's purple bikini today," I say.

Ashleigh turns to the grass in front of her and pulls out a few blades. I keep watching Hudson. "He's so pretty," I say. "Even in that outfit."

"Darling, that's his thing," George says. "Pretty, masculine, straight-acting, whatever you want to call it. And he only hooks up with other boys like him."

"I mean, I could go butch."

"Randy," Ashleigh says, "come on. You wear women's tank tops, nail polish, sometimes lipstick. You've got long hair and a soft body. No body-shaming, I think you're perfect, but even if you could do the 'straight-acting' thing all of a sudden, you'd still need to change your wardrobe, cut your hair off, lose some weight, get some muscle...."

"I could devote myself to the part," I say. "Go Method."

"And then he'd break up with you two weeks later," George says. "Just like he does with all the others. So even if you could suddenly go butch overnight, it would be for what, a week of making out and then some screwing at the Peanut Butter Pit before he forgot your name?" The Peanut

Butter Pit was under the rope swing at the obstacle course—dug deep enough to afford some privacy for two horizontal bodies in it, and a favorite spot of Hudson's for being horizontal. Or whatever angles are involved for cowboy and doggie style.

"He's not really like that," I say, plucking a blade of grass and twirling it between my fingers. "I mean, he acts like he is, but he's more than that."

"And you know all this how? From looking deep into his eyes?"

"No," I say. "We were in the same cabin my first year. His grandma had just died and Hudson cried in his sleep, had these sad dreams about her. I woke him up once and we talked a little. About his dream. About how to remember her. About how to be the best versions of ourselves. It was… deep." I look down. I haven't told anyone about that night before. It's a special memory, and I know they'll tear it down, but they have to understand: Hudson isn't just hot. He's the only one I know who can make me feel like I'm not just free to be myself here, where it's safe, but I'm free to be myself anywhere I want, and screw anyone who tells me differently.

"Did he even see your face?"

"The lights were out," I say, maybe a little defensively. "But he's a nice guy. He's just never met a guy who's captured his attention long enough to become a real boyfriend."

"Oh," George says. "Sure. And that's going to be you?"

"Yeah," I say, willing it into the universe. "It is."

"We're gonna kick their orange asses!" Hudson says, taking center stage. "So, I know, you probably think it's just a relay race, just some stupid points for a stupid game. And I get that. But guess what? We're going to rock at it anyway. Why? Because we rock! We, queer people, are amazing. And I know out in the real world, it's people telling you to be like this or be like that, and it's bullying and it's people calling you names and keeping you down. People saying we'll never win because of who we are. But here is where we gather our strength. Here is where we work on being everything they say we're not. Here is where we prove to ourselves how much we rock so that out there we can prove it to them and beat them in whatever contests and competitions they throw at us! How we can be anything we want! How we are special!" he says, and he locks eyes with me for a moment, his gaze so intense, it feels like he's talking just to me. I can be anything I want. I can do anything I want. "And yeah, maybe today that means running with an egg in a spoon and not dropping it, but so what? Succeeding here is just preparing to succeed out there, even if it is at something silly like a relay race. So let's get out there and show them all what we can do!"

Everyone cheers. Me included. I don't know if it's that I'm better around him, or just that he can make me realize it, but it's like all my anxieties—being the only queer kid in school, having no close friends outside of camp, my parents being supportive but also treating me like an alien, always watching everything I say, or making sure no one pays attention to me—all of that is thrown off like a drag queen's reveal, and suddenly, here I am, some new amazing superhero: Queer Randy. And all I want to do when that happens is kiss him. Because no one else has ever made me feel like that.

Ashleigh and George make me feel loved. So do my parents, and Mark and Crystal. But Hudson gives me something I don't really get from anywhere else. He makes me feel *special*. Like who I am here—where I don't close my hands on the bus when some jocks pass by so they don't see the nail polish, and have a comeback for anything anyone says to me—can be who I am out there, too.

And I know Hudson isn't talking to me specifically, but it feels like he is. And I think he would, if it were just me in the audience. I think he believes in me, and that makes me feel like I have a thousand stars—a galaxy—inside me, glowing brightly.

"So get in line, and let's run some eggs!" Hudson shouts, and I jump up and cheer and run to be first in line during the relay.

FOUR

The dancing in the cabin eventually changes into putting on our swimsuits for the camp-wide free swim. I'm proud of the swim trunks I found. They're black with white trim, a little tight. I take them out and Ashleigh does a double take.

"Look," she says, putting her hand on my shoulder. "I'm not saying I approve of this crazy plan, but if you're going to do it, you should do it right."

"What?" I ask. "What's wrong with my swimsuit?"

"Trunks," Ashleigh says. "Your trunks. And your shoes."

"I love these shoes."

"That should be your first clue right there," she says. "You're doing like . . . campy straight. The plaid that matches the shoes? The swim trunks that look like something Sean

Connery would have worn in an old Bond film? It's like you're playing straight in a show."

"You can take the queer out of the theater," George says, coming up to us, "but not the theater out of the queer." George is in a white Speedo with a rainbow over the butt. Without his shirt on, I can see that the hint of hair I saw before is a full-on forest over his chest and belly.

"So how do I fix it?" I ask. "I have these in black and red and blue. That's it."

"They should be okay," Ashleigh says. "But let's see the rest of the wardrobe."

I lead them to the cubby I have for my clothes, where everything has been neatly folded and arranged by color.

"See," Ashleigh says. "This could work. You just need to put it together differently. Less thought out."

"Are we going to have a fashion show?" George says. Everyone else who's been getting ready in the cabin pauses and looks over, wide-eyed.

"Fashion show?" asks Montgomery, a thin redhead a year older than us who, when telling stories of his school year in LA, has already described himself as "that bitch" four times.

"Don't tease," says Paz, also a year older than us, with a shaved head and dark skin.

"Fashion show!" chant the other campers. "Fashion show!"

Ashleigh grins, and she and George start rifling through my clothes, throwing things at me.

31

"Montage!" Montgomery shouts, and for the next twenty minutes I'm modeling different outfits for them, to calls of "Ooh, honey, butch!" and "She almost passes!" Even Mark, who seems annoyed by all of this, eventually gets into it—although it also feels like he's mocking me as he puts on "How Lovely to Be a Woman." But maybe that's just because it's from the show. Even with the counterintuitive soundtrack, though, I'm loving it, modeling each of the outfits with all the masculinity I've been practicing over the year—legs apart as I walk, hips forward, nods with my chin. I even flash my abs and show off the guns I've managed to build up. Some of the boys stare at me a bit differently after that—like I'm someone new. Which, I guess is the whole point.

When the little fashion show is over, I have a different selection of outfits. They're...no fun, frankly. I get it— they're kind of sexy in a threw-it-on-that-morning sort of way. But nothing matches, nothing is neat, everything just feels haphazard. If there's a style here, I don't see it, or at least, it's not for me. Still, everyone assures me that they'll get the job done. And what are clothes, really, next to love?

"Well, now that that's over, let's get to the pool," Mark says. "Come on. No one left behind."

I change into the black swimsuit and grab my towel and follow everyone else down the stairs to the bottom level of the camp. This is where the camp feels huge. I don't know exactly how big it is, but it's got to be a few miles in each direction. You can't see the river—the far end—from the steps, though I guess you can see the dining hall from the drama cabin, which are at the two other farthest ends of the oval that encompasses camp. The pool is right by the stairs, though, and is already filled with campers shrieking and splashing. The water looks great, but as we get close, Ashleigh grabs George's and my arms. I look over at her. She's staring at the lifeguard. I look, too. Then I see who it is.

"Janice," Ashleigh says in a whisper.

"Darling, it's fine," George says.

Almost all the staff at Camp Outland is queer—except the lifeguards and kitchen staff. They need to be certified by the state, and it's hard enough finding local queer staff (at least, this is how Mark explained it a few years back), so Joan uses a company that brings people in. Joan keeps an eye on all of them, of course. "She can spot a homophobe from a hundred yards," Mark says. "Why do you think she looks so tired all the time?"

Most of the lifeguards are straight, though. Even Janice Uncas, with her long lavender curls and lip ring, and who's only a year older than us, so it's totally okay, as Ashleigh has pointed out. Last summer, Ashleigh grew really close with her. Not sexy close, but close enough she fell a little in love. And a little in love with a straight girl, near as I can tell, meant a lot of pain all summer.

"It's okay," I tell Ashleigh. "She's your friend. You're over her, right?" Ashleigh had sent us a long e-mail in November about how over her she was.

"Yeah," Ashleigh says. "I just...didn't think she'd be back. I thought she was going to spend the summer with her grandparents, doing Mohegan Tribe stuff. That's what she said."

"I guess things changed," I say.

"She's waving at us," George says. "Wave back."

We all wave back, and then start walking again.

"I just don't want to do this again," Ashleigh says. "I'm going to keep my distance. Stay polite, but not, like, best friends, like last summer."

"Good plan," I say.

"We'll hold you to it," George says.

"Okay," Ashleigh says, pulling at the straps on her black one-piece, which is dotted with skulls. We walk past the safety fence around the pool and past the changing rooms to the pool itself, where George jumps in. I immediately spot Hudson, in a blue swimsuit—trunks, I mean. I hop in before he sees me, up past the waist so he doesn't see the not-quite-masc-enough trunks. The water is a little cold, but the air is warm, so it's nice, and a moment later I dip down to my neck.

"Darling, show off the abs," George says. "Here he comes."

Hudson is indeed swimming over, his dark hair plastered

across his forehead. Brad is with him, and in a moment they're standing in front of me, George, and Ashleigh. There's a long moment where I check out Hudson without his shirt on—the carved but not too carved abs, the strong shoulders that would probably be perfect for sleeping on—and I realize he's checking me out, too, tracing the trail of hair from my belly button down. I blush and dive under to hide it, popping up again a second later.

"You two done admiring each other?" George asks.

"I was admiring you," Brad says to George.

"You grow a little body hair and suddenly they notice you," George says to Ashleigh. Ashleigh is just staring at Janice, though, oblivious to us.

"I've noticed you before, George," Brad says. George looks a little surprised he knows his name. "But yeah...the hair looks good on you. I'd like to lick—"

"Sometimes less is more, darling," George interrupts. "But thank you." He smiles and bats his eyelashes. Brad bites on his lower lip, smiling.

"You're welcome. How was everyone's year?" Brad asks, and Hudson looks confused.

"Bro, Del is new," he says to Brad.

"Del?" Brad asks.

"Darling," George says suddenly, "why don't you and I go talk more about the wonders puberty has worked on my body over in the deep end?"

"Yeah?" Brad grins. "Sure." I shoot George a thank-you

with my eyes. Hopefully he can keep Brad from ruining the plan.

They swim off, and Ashleigh, still staring at Janice, starts to swim away, too.

"I'm going to go talk to Janice," she says.

"No, you said—" I start to say, but then Hudson has his arm on my shoulder—my naked shoulder—and I can't speak for a moment. I turn to look at him. He smiles. His eyes are dark gray with just a hint of blue, and the water flashes on them like sequins.

"So," he says. "I'm glad they left us alone."

"Yeah," I say.

"Relatively speaking," he says, gesturing at the rest of the camp swimming around us.

I laugh. "Yeah."

"So, did you just come out recently?" he asks, leaning against the side of the pool and sliding down to his neck. I copy him, and it feels more intimate—our heads above the water, our bodies under it, blurred by the surface, so it looks like we're touching.

"No," I say. "I came out when I was twelve." That's the truth. Easier to stick to the truth.

"So, your parents just didn't want to send you to a queer camp, then? Afraid it would be, like, all orgies and drag shows? Mine were freaked out about that."

"Something like that," I say. That's a lie. My parents were great about sending me here. They were the ones who found the camp and suggested it four years ago. But I can explain that later. For now, he thinks this is my first year, and I'm keeping it that way.

"I just told them, it's like any other camp, but no one is going to be afraid to get in a pool with me or anything."

"Afraid to get in a pool with you?" I ask. "Who thinks like that?"

"Just some kids from my school. I came out when I was twelve, too. Outed, kind of, except to my folks. It didn't go well. School in the suburbs of western Virginia isn't exactly super liberal. So here, it's like...a vacation, you know?"

"Yeah. In Ohio, too," I say. "I don't think I have it as bad as that, though. People mostly just ignore me."

"Hard to imagine that." Hudson wiggles his eyebrows, and under the water, his knee brushes mine and I look down to cover my blushing.

"Well, it happens," I say. "I'm sorry you were bullied, though."

"Not bullied, really," he says. "I don't like that word—it sounds so dramatic, or like I'm a victim or something. But let's not talk about it. We're at queer camp now! Everything rocks."

"Yeah," I say, our knees now firmly against each other. "Everything is perfect."

We're suddenly splashed as George does a cannonball a few feet from us, Brad doing another right after him. George swims over to us, narrowing his eyes.

"Where's Ashleigh?" he asks.

"She went…" I remember and it hits me so hard, I think I might sink. "She's talking to Janice. I tried to stop her." But not enough.

"Not that hard, by the looks of it," he says, now swimming to the edge of the pool and hoisting himself out. "Come on, we have to stop her."

"Wait, what?" Hudson says.

"Sorry," I say, following George. "She made us promise."

"Should I come?" he asks.

"No," George says. "You'll just be a distraction."

"Come back soon," Hudson says, crossing his arms over the edge of the pool and resting his chin on them.

"I will," I say. "Or I'll see you at dinner."

"Okay," he says as I follow George around the side of the pool.

"Brad will keep his mouth shut, you're welcome," George says quietly as we walk—no running by the pool. "I told him you hit your head."

"What?" I half whisper, half shout.

"It was what came to mind, after what Mark said," he says, hands up in mock defense. "You have some memories, but not all of them. And reminding you of stuff could make you have a meltdown. So we decided it's best if Hudson thinks you're new."

"Why would you say that?" I ask, but we've reached where Ashleigh is sitting next to Janice, their feet dipped into the very deep end. Janice isn't in the lifeguard chair (some older guy is manning it), but she has sunglasses on and keeps her eyes on the pool. She's focused, but she smiles as Ashleigh talks, and they both laugh at something as we approach them.

"That's so funny," Janice says as we sit down next to Ashleigh. Ashleigh looks over at us and frowns a little.

"What's so funny?" George asks.

"Ashleigh was telling me about this guy who kept trying to ask her out at school," Janice says. "You should tell it."

"Oh, so he just wouldn't get the hint," Ashleigh says. "So finally I just grabbed my closest straight friend and said, 'Can we just make out in front of him until he goes away?' and she was like, 'okay,' and so next time he came over to bother me, I started making out with her and he was all offended! He said, 'You should have said something.' As if repeatedly telling him I was a demisexual lesbian wasn't enough? Then he called us dykes and ranted about me on Instagram—but at least he stopped asking me out."

"Yeah, that's funny," George says, throwing me a look. We both know a story about her making out with a straight girl is probably not something that just came up. "But, Ashleigh, we have to go back to our cabin—remember what we talked about?"

Ashleigh frowns, knowing we have nothing to go back to.

"Remember?" I say. "You made us promise."

"Yeah," she says. "Sorry, Janice, I'd better get back."

"That's okay. See you later."

"Later," Ashleigh says as we get up. We all start walking back to the other side of the pool. I'm about to jump in and rejoin Hudson, but Ashleigh tugs on my arm. "We said we were going back to the cabin. She'll know I'm avoiding her if we don't."

"Right," I say with a sigh. I catch Hudson's eye and frown and shrug, letting myself be dragged away by Ashleigh. He waves at me, a sad look on his face.

We trudge back up to the cabin, Ashleigh frowning. "Sorry," she says. "Sorry, sorry. I know I said I wasn't going to do it, but, like, there aren't many girls here I really click with enough to want to..."

"Darling, you're at a queer camp. Have you tried clicking with the other girls?"

"Well...," she says. "Daphne, two years ago."

"She's gone," I say. No campers over eighteen allowed. Everyone keeps in touch—we just don't see them during the summer anymore. It's kind of sad, but then we hear stories about them going off to college and living every day like it's camp, and it's more like they've escaped than they've left.

"I know, but, like, I need to know someone, really like them, before I want to...you know. I don't just think 'she's hot' about some girl and then try to go after her. And it feels like no one wants to get to know me."

"That's idiotic," George says.

"Hard agree," I say. "Not everyone is demisexual. Plenty of the girls want to get to know you."

Ashleigh laughs. "Yeah, but then what if I don't like them?"

"Then walk away," George says. "But promise me you'll talk to someone besides the straight girl this summer?"

"Yeah," Ashleigh says as we reach our cabin. "Yeah, thanks, guys."

"What was going on with you and Brad?" I ask George as we hop in the showers. The bathroom has four sinks and six showers, each with their own stall and towel hook so no one can see us naked, but we can still talk. We shout over the water.

"That sort of thing has been happening a lot lately," George calls back. "I got hairy, now everybody is into me all of a sudden. The boys at school barely noticed me before; now I've slept with three of them."

"You've had sex?" I ask, happy he can't see me blushing red in the shower. I have not. I mean, made out, sure, and it's not like I don't know how it feels when another guy's body is against yours and he's horny. Two summers ago, Carter Monroe kind of implied he wanted to get naked with me after we spent some time making out, but I want my first time to be special. And with Hudson.

"Mmm-hm," George answers.

"Why didn't you tell us?" Ashleigh asks.

"It didn't seem like that big a deal," George says. "I'm from Manhattan, darlings. Sex is just something you do sometimes."

I blush again and force myself to laugh.

"Oh, don't try that jaded act with us," Ashleigh says. "We know you. You're supposed to tell us this stuff."

"I guess...," George says, his voice a little hard to hear under the water. I finish washing and turn the faucet off, then start drying myself with my towel. "Look," he says, "it was...embarrassing. Like, suddenly I look more adult and people want me and I jump into bed with the first of them who offers? I didn't want you guys to think I was a slut."

"Why would we think that?" I ask, wrapping my towel around my waist.

"Well, you're holding out for Hudson, and Ashleigh is only into girls if she has a real bond with them, and here I am, screwing a guy whose last name I don't remember."

"Was it fun?" Ashleigh asks.

"A little," George says, turning the water off. "The first time was awkward. But then it was fun. Lots of fun. Highly recommended."

Ashleigh and I both laugh.

"I don't think you're a slut," I say, doing my hair in the mirror. Styling it to look like I don't care how it looks is very difficult.

"Me neither," Ashleigh says, coming out of the stall, already dressed in denim cutoffs and a black tank top. She

42

runs her hands through her hair, then heads back into the main cabin.

"Thank you, darlings. But remember, if anyone cute asks, I'm a complete whore." He pushes open his shower curtain and steps out, his huge pink towel wrapped around his chest and still almost hitting the floor.

"How about Brad?" I ask.

"Maybe," George says, tilting his head and shaking a can of hairspray in front of the mirror. "He's cute. But it's only the first day."

I finish in the mirror and go back into the cabin to get out one of the pre-selected masc-enough outfits, this one a white T-shirt and blue shorts, then come back to the bathroom, hop into the stall, and change. When I step out, George is scrunching his hair, and Ashleigh is back, applying dark lipstick in the mirror.

"So," I say. "After dinner, can you show me the tree? Make sure Hudson is following us—but at a distance."

"How are you going to arrange that?" Ashleigh asks.

"I think if we all eat with them, and then after, as we're leaving, you pull me aside or something and you're like, 'We need to show you something,' and head toward the obstacle course, he'll follow."

"He'll follow without being seen?" George asks. "I'm as much for wacky hijinks as the next homo, but this feels like a stretch."

"It doesn't really matter if he follows us—he just has to

43

know we went off to see it. But if he does follow, then I can talk about how I'd never be just another conquest for a man like that," I say, putting my hand to my chest and looking like a Victorian woman who's just been offended.

"Maybe not like that if you want to keep this charade up," George says.

Ashleigh snorts a laugh.

"I just need a reason to be cold to him," I say. "Make it clear I want a real relationship."

"And what makes you think he won't just move on to an easier guy?" George asks.

"Who else fits his profile?" I ask. "Who he hasn't already taken to the Peanut Butter Pit, I mean."

"There might be some new guys," Ashleigh says.

"Or who knows, maybe he'll repeat."

"We have a connection," I say. "He's already made his move. He's not looking at anyone else, and he likes a challenge. He might fake the long-term-relationship-guy thing at first, but he'll take it slow. And slow is all I need to make him really fall in love."

George shoots a glance at Ashleigh in the mirror. They both have the "our friend is nuts" look on their faces. Behind us, the other campers start to come in. Jordan walks in just as George and Ashleigh are looking at each other and giggles.

"Maybe you could tell Brad, too," I say to George. "Let him know I'm a romantic, not just another mark on the tree, and Hudson will have to really woo me. Y'know, since my head injury."

George rolls his eyes. "Well, I do like a bigger role," he says. "Though I usually prefer comedies to outright farce."

"Did you hurt your head?" Jordan asks, hopping in the shower.

"No," I reply quickly.

"It's just part of the plan, darling!"

"The romance plan?" Jordan asks, sticking their head out of the shower. They have very short blunt bangs and the rest of their head is nearly shaved, giving their face a very punk vibe, which always amuses me, because Jordan is a giant softie who has seen every romantic comedy movie ever, multiple times. "I LOVE the plan! It's like *Pillow Talk!*" They pop back into the shower. "Or *How to Marry a Millionaire*, what with the planning. How to marry a masc-ulaire!" They giggle.

"Everyone knows?" I ask George and Ashleigh.

"The cabin does." Ashleigh shrugs. "Did you think no one would notice? Or figure it out?"

I laugh. "Okay. That doesn't matter, because it'll be great," I say. "It will work great." I hope. I've turned over all the ways to do this during the course of the year. Getting Hudson's attention was straightforward, but holding it for longer than two weeks is the hard part. But this should work. Not just saying I'm an LTR kind of guy, but making myself a challenge for him. He's never had one of those before, not really, but everyone knows how competitive he is. Always has to be on the winning team in capture the flag. Always has to run through the obstacle course the fastest. Well, he wouldn't give up on a guy he liked, right? Just another challenge. And a challenge means time, time together, which leads to us falling in love. It's a solid plan, or so I tell myself as George and Ashleigh exchange another look and George goes to change. Definitely not a plan I got watching too many old romantic comedies.

"So I have to be the bad guy, then?" Ashleigh says, crossing her arms and leaning against the bathroom wall. "Lead you to the tree, warn you of Hudson's manizing ways?"

"Yeah, if that's okay."

"I'm not an actor, you know. I'm a techie."

"No acting required," I say. "You clearly think this is a bad idea."

"Look," she says, walking back into the cabin, where George has slipped on a bright green satin robe with big flowing sleeves, embroidered with blue carnations. I have a matching purple one with gold-and-white lilies—we both bought them at the same time when I found the link online and sent it to him two years ago, between summers, and brought them last year. But I left mine at home this summer. "It's not that I don't want you to get with him, if you think that'll make you happy. It's just...this whole plan. Pretending to be someone else. Where does it end?"

"We fall in love," I say, following her.

"And then what?" she asks. "You keep being Del the rest of your life?"

I shrug. "Once we're in love, I'll gradually turn back into Randy."

"The guy he didn't fall in love with," Ashleigh says. "You see where I'm confused? This script is all over the place."

"It's all about how you play it," I say. "Besides, what's the worst that happens? I don't get the guy?" Please let that not happen. Please, please, please. I force myself to smile. "Then all this will be over, and you won't have anything to worry about."

"Except your broken heart," she says.

"Well, then you can say you told me so." Please oh please let her not have a reason to tell me she told me so.

"Darlings, let's not fight. Randy has a plan, and he's asking us to help, and if it all goes sideways, then at least it will be a story to tell people, right? It's only love, no need to take it so seriously."

"Right," I say, but I'm holding my smile so tightly, my jaw aches.

"Fine, fine," Ashleigh says. "I just want it on record that I don't see this ending well, and I don't like you changing who you are just for some guy. You can find a guy who loves you for you."

"But they won't be Hudson," I say. "If you just had to change your wardrobe a little to make Janice fall for you, would you?"

Ashleigh climbs into her bed. "Yeah, okay, I get it," she says.

Mark walks in just as she finishes talking. "What?" he asks. "Pool time too boring for you? Too much gossip you didn't want the camp to hear?"

"Something like that," George says, plucking a sandal-wood fan from under his pillow and opening it. "Plus my hair needs time to air-dry before dinner."

"Well, at least that's a decent excuse," Mark says, going into the counselor's room (we've seen inside; it's miniscule, with two twin beds and a nightstand, but I guess counselors have earned a little more privacy). "Dinner is at six, so be dressed by then."

A moment later, the other campers start coming in, showering off and changing into their dinner best. Even George, after his hair is dry enough, changes into a purple T-shirt with a picture of Ariana Grande as the Virgin Mary on it and a pair of very short black shorts. Someone puts on the *Bye Bye Birdie* soundtrack and everyone sings along, prac-ticing for their auditions tomorrow. I smile and listen and sometimes sing along, even though tomorrow will be very different for me.

FIVE

LAST SUMMER

He is so pretty," I say again, lying in the grass and watching Hudson run across the green. It's capture the flag during color wars, and George, Montgomery, and I have gotten ourselves captured so we can sit on the sidelines and watch. Montgomery is in green cutoffs, so short you can see his ass from the bottom, and a black crop top. George and I didn't want to recycle our outfits, so we're in pink and purple, respectively—but our nails are painted green, and conveniently the silk fan I brought from home is a pretty chartreuse, so I've been carrying it around in my back pocket, and now I'm fanning myself with it. Hudson has his shirt off and he gleams with sweat as he runs across the soccer field. I might be drooling a little. But the fan covers it.

"Darling, you have got to get over this crush," George says. "Or come up with a plan for getting his attention."

"I'm working on it, sweetie," I say. "I have some ideas." I pluck a stray daisy and tuck it behind my ear.

"Oh, really?" Montgomery asks. "Like what?"

"Like I just have to make him want to talk to me," I say, tucking another daisy behind the other ear. "If I can make him feel half as good as he makes me feel, just by talking, I know he won't want to give that up after two weeks."

Suddenly, as if he can hear us talking, Hudson runs over to us. George and I exchange a worried look, but he taps us each on the shoulder, and then runs back to his side. He looks behind him and grins a big goofy smile.

"C'mon, dudes!" he shouts. "I freed you!"

The three of us shrug, then stand up and run over back to his side of the line. I tuck my hair behind my ears and wait next to Hudson, who's smiling at us.

"So, no thank-you?" he says.

"Thanks," I say.

"Darling, it was a waste of a trip," George says. "We're useless at this game."

"Nah," Hudson says, looking right at me. "I know you'll be good at it. Just give it a try." I smile back at him, this stupid, doofy smile, because I can feel this warmth in my chest, this feeling like when I did a tequila shot that one time, and I feel looser and stronger. No one has ever believed I could be good at anything athletic. I'm a theater kid, a sissy, I can barely throw a ball. Even my dad said maybe it "wasn't our thing" the first time we tried playing catch in the backyard and the neighbors snickered at us. And Hudson can see all that. He can see my painted nails and loose wrists, and he can still believe I'd be good at it if I tried.

And then he runs off. I turn to George.

"See?" I say. "He's divine."

Montgomery watches Hudson running. "He's got a great ass, at least," he says, folding his arms.

"I'm going to go for the flag," I say, slapping my fan closed and tucking it in my back pocket. "Cover me?"

"What?" George says.

"Are you nuts?" Montgomery asks, but I'm across the line into enemy territory before I have time to answer, dodging the other campers as they try to tag me, going for the bright orange flag on top of the hill on their side of the camp. And suddenly I realize I CAN do it. I can do whatever I want, really, and I'm close to the hill and I can see Hudson ahead of me, too, and I get close, like we're going to do this together, we're going to steal this flag as a duo, and he looks over and flashes me that smile.

And I trip. Fall on my face. Someone tags me right away, but Hudson manages to steal the flag, and he's running with it before someone tags him, too. He walks into jail and sits on the grass next to me, grinning, sweat pouring off him. He smells like dirt and the sun.

"Thanks for that distraction, bro," he says, raising his fist.

I realize I'm supposed to bump it, and do, though it feels forced and stupid.

"Yeah." I nod. "I did that on purpose."

"You were really going out there," he says, and I can't tell if he believes my lie. "I told you you'd be good at it if you tried."

"I guess so," I say.

He grabs some grass out of the ground in a handful, then puts it back down, patting it into the earth. "You know," he says. "We don't have to be whatever they say we are. We can be athletes and superheroes. We can be strong and fast and kick ass. We just have to put our fingers in our ears and stop listening to them, and just let ourselves want to be those things. Want to be greater. Then we can be anything."

"Yeah," I say, and I feel that warm feeling inside me again, like stars. I wonder if he can sense it. I wonder how I can make him feel this way.

"Come on, losers," Ashleigh says, walking up to us slowly, like she doesn't care, and tagging us each on the shoulder. Ashleigh actually loves capture the flag but says she prefers to be a "spy"—make them think she doesn't care about playing, sidle up to the flag, stuff it in her pocket, and just walk back. It's never worked, but she says one day it will.

"See you later, man," Hudson says, running back to our side before launching himself at the enemy's flag again.

"Later," I say.

"You're smiling like a chorus boy who chugged a Red Bull before the big number," Ashleigh says.

SIX

At dinner, Brad and Hudson sit down with us without my even waving them over. Everything is going so much better than I ever could have hoped. The only disappointment is the actual food—dry hamburgers and weirdly soft french fries, like they're wet. But no one really minds the bad food here—not when there's so much ambiance.

The dining hall is...amazing. There's no other word for it. A huge log cabin from the outside, but inside, every log painted a different stripe of the rainbow. Instead of fluorescent lights, there are strings of rainbow Christmas lights, and then big dangling white lamps that Joan (who's a metalworker) made. They're each the size of a beach ball and look like stars. Sure, the lighting is a little dim, but who wants to see the food too clearly anyway? Under the stars, dark wooden tables are set up in a square and we can all sit and eat wherever we want. Platters of food and pitchers of bug juice and water are passed around, family style, and folks with dietary restrictions can go to the kitchen door and are handed their meals. It's astounding. Every time we eat, it's a family meal under the night sky. And sitting next to Hudson, the dim light making his skin glow, it feels like a romantic date.

"Sucks you had to leave the pool early," he says. The clatter of people talking around us is loud enough that by talking softly, no one else can hear. He pushes his thigh up against mine.

"Yeah, sorry," I say.

"No worries, I get it. So, how are you liking everything?" he asks. "It rocks, right?"

"It really does," I say. "I feel so..."

"Free?" he asks.

"Exactly."

George elbows me, and I turn. He's holding out a tray of fries and I take it, scooping some off onto my plate, and pass it to Hudson, who passes it on.

He sticks a fry in his mouth and I watch his lips close around it and suddenly feel very thirsty. I turn as the bug juice pitcher comes my way, and I pour for myself and for Hudson and then the tray of burgers is in front of me, looking like reheated McDonald's. But it's food. I take one.

"When I first came here," he says, taking the tray and a burger, "it was just...like I could breathe? But I hadn't known I'd been holding my breath? And there are so many different types of queer people here, too. I'm the only one I know at home. Before here, I thought that aside from me, they were all like the ones on television."

I laugh. "What, *Will and Grace* reruns?"

"And *Queer Eye*," he says. "That teen rom-com that came out a few months ago didn't play anywhere near me, so I have to wait until it's on Netflix. Maybe they'll show it here, actually. We do movie nights when it's raining."

"Yeah?" I turn away from him so he can't tell I already knew that, and bite into my burger. It tastes like cardboard.

"Yeah," he says, leaning into me slightly. "We should go together."

"You asking me out?" I ask.

"Yeah." He grins. "I am. You interested?"

"Yes." I nod, feeling warm all over. "I will definitely go on a date with you next time it rains."

He laughs. "I better find a way to make it rain, then," he says.

I almost choke on the fry I'm eating, suddenly picturing him in a thong, gyrating onstage as dollar bills rain down around him.

"You okay?" he asks, patting me on the back. He hands me my cup of bug juice and I take a sip.

"Thanks, sorry," I say. "You just said make it rain, and I thought of strippers."

"Oh." He smiles, a little tightly. "Yeah, ha."

"Sorry, should I not have said strippers?"

He laughs. "No. You can say strippers. But I'm not wearing body glitter for you. I don't think that's hot."

"Yeah." I nod, though I think it sounds very hot. "That's not what I meant."

He puts his hand on my thigh and squeezes, briefly, then pulls it back. "But play your cards right and I'll tell you what does sound hot," he says, leaning into my ear. I must flush scarlet, because across from me, Ashleigh raises her eyebrows. She's doing what she promised and is talking to Paz, who broke up with her girlfriend over the school year.

"I should tell you," I say to Hudson. "I'm...not...that is, I'm...I think you're really cute, and you seem great, and we click, but a date first," I say. "You know what I mean?"

He leans back slightly, but he's smiling, looking at me a little differently. Before he was almost predatory, but now he looks sweeter. "I get exactly what you mean. I promise, we can take it easy. First I have to work on that rain, right?"

I laugh. "Maybe stripping is the way to do it, though."

His smile changes again, wolfish. His gray-blue eyes narrow and his eyebrows wiggle. "I would have said that, but I thought you wanted to take it easy."

I lean into him, knocking our shoulders. "I do. I'm just offering helpful suggestions. I want it to rain, too."

"So, maybe," he says, like he's just coming up with it, "we try going and hanging out together—a date-like situation—even if it doesn't rain?"

"That's such an interesting idea," I say, playing along. "I think I could go for that. Though, I'm new. What would we do, if we can't watch a movie?"

"We have time after dinner before the talent show. There's plenty to do—people like to hang out at the boat-house, or there's a bonfire at the flagpole, sometimes. Or..." He lights up. "I could give you a tour. Since you're new."

"That sounds nice," I say. "I'd love to see the sights."

He laughs. "In fact, since we wouldn't want it to rain for that—we could do it right after dinner. Tonight. Before the counselor talent show."

"Tonight?" I ask. This is really going way too well. "I..." I glance over at Ashleigh, who's smiling at Paz. "Ashleigh said she wanted to show me something. A tree? But after that, I'm all yours."

I turn back to him, and his perfect skin has colored slightly—the palest of pink. "Tree?" he asks. "A special tree?"

I shrug and use all my acting skills not to smile. "That's what she said."

"You can skip that, though, right?" He turns to his food and starts gobbling it down. I finally found his one flaw: He's not a cute eater. Why does that make him generally cuter?

"Seems rude," I say. "She's my bunkmate, and she's made a real effort to become my friend. You want to come? Do you know what tree she means?"

"Yeah," he says. "I think I do."

I stare at him in silence, and take another bite of my

burger, another fry. To my right, I hear Brad and George cackling in unison at something.

"Something wrong?" I ask gently.

"It's fine," he says. "Just...you should know. The tree. There was this guy, Hal. And he looked kind of like me. And his name is on the tree. A lot."

It takes every inch of training not to let my eyes widen in shock. This is not where I thought this would go. He's actively pretending to be someone else.

Well...that makes two of us.

"There are names on the tree?" I ask.

"Yeah." He smiles, takes a long drink of water. He seems more relaxed. Apparently he's happy with his own plan. "But that's all I'll say. Keep it a surprise. It's really...like, amazing. Nothing you'd see anywhere else."

"Okay...." I try to sound suspicious. But inwardly, I'm freaking out. This is not part of the plan. I take a long drink of juice and finish my burger just as the dessert platter comes around—cupcakes, very slightly burnt.

Our thighs press together as we eat—chocolate is chocolate, burnt or not—and when Joan dismisses us, we walk together outside, where Ashleigh is waiting for me.

"Come on," she says with absolutely no inflection. "I'm going to show you the tree I told you about now." She waves. The acting is far worse than I could have imagined. I glance up at Hudson, worried she's just given everything away, but he's smiling, apparently not seeing anything wrong.

"Okay," I say. "Hudson is coming, too."

"He is?" she asks.

"Yeah," he says. "I know some people think I'm on there. But that was Hal. He looks like me, but he's not here anymore."

Ashleigh starts to laugh. "What?" she asks.

"I'm just saying…" He pauses, sees George and Brad, and waves them over. "Brad, bro, you know me, right? I'm not on the tree, right?" Brad furrows his brow, confused. "But Hal, the guy who isn't here anymore—he is. And he looks a lot like me, so people thought…"

Ashleigh keeps laughing, but she's trying to hide it at least now. I can't blame her. This is what happens when non-theater people try to do improv.

"Riiiiight," Brad says after a long moment of Hudson and Brad staring at each other. "Hal. Yeah. Hudson's never been on the tree."

"What is this tree?" I ask—my acting being the best going on in the immediate area.

Ashleigh stops trying to hide the laugh and bends over. "I can't," she says. "I…George."

George immediately steps in front of her. "I'll show you the tree, darling," he says, keeping a perfectly calm face. "Ashleigh seems to be having one of her moments."

"Yeah," I say, "that sounds great, thanks." It's so nice to have a professional scene partner.

George turns around and I follow him, along with

Hudson, Brad, and a still-giggling Ashleigh. George leads us past the kickball field, and the soccer field, into the woods. We follow a trail and come to a huge tree, wide around enough that four or five people would have to link hands to encircle it. It's dark, but not so dark I can't see what's carved into its bark—what I'm supposedly here to see. Hearts, lots of them, and in the hearts, names and initials. Tom and Steven, Becky and Jessica, LR and CS. Hundreds of them. And lots of them—lots—are HAL and . . . well, some boy. HAL. Hudson Aaronson-Lim. Except nope, not anymore. Now it's Hal. An imaginary person. I walk forward and run my hands over the carvings.

"See?" Hudson says. "All this love. All this queer love. Doesn't it just . . . rock?"

"Yeah," I say.

"I hope one day I have someone special enough to carve my name with," he says, and looks at me in the dim light, his eyes wide and sweet.

Behind him, Ashleigh barks another laugh.

SEVEN

LAST SUMMER

Think if I faked drowning myself, she'd give me mouth-to-mouth?" Ashleigh asks, staring at Janice from across the pool like a cat at a bird out the window.

"I think you'd have to stop breathing for that, sweetie," I say.

"And she'd probably do that thing where she pressed down on your chest really hard," George adds.

"She could press anything she wanted as hard as she wanted."

"I don't know female anatomy well enough to understand that," I say. "But I suspect it's too much information."

"Oh, sure, you can dream about what kind of underwear Hudson wears but one reference to Janice's hand on my clit is too much."

George and I stare at her wide-eyed.

"Darling, let's not talk about anything under the underwear," George says after a minute. "New rule."

Ashleigh chuckles. "Fine. Prudes."

"It could work, though," I say.

"No," George says.

"Not the mouth-to-mouth, but, like, a rescue, adrenaline pumping, bodies intertwined..."

"Don't encourage her," George says.

"It's a good scene!" I say. "A rescue, a thank-you, a look."

"A scene from what? A straight porn?" George asks. "Come on, darling."

"No, no. It's a meet-cute. Now Ashleigh has a reason to try to pay Janice back for saving her life, and they spend loads of time together and fall in love!" I clasp my hands.

"You've sold me," Ashleigh says. "I'm doing it."

"What?" George says.

"Wait, you have to do it safely," I say, but she's already swum out to the middle of the deep end and has started to flail. I sigh. "These things need planning."

"If she dies, I'm blaming you," George says.

I look across the pool at Janice, whose eyes scan the water but don't take any note of Ashleigh's dramatic splashing. But someone else does. Hudson dives in next to us, paddles out to Ashleigh, and grabs her around the waist, then tries to pull her over to us. I suddenly wish I had faked drowning.

"Heroic," George says with a snicker.

"Hey, it really is," I say.

Hudson is trying to pull Ashleigh, but she doesn't want to be rescued by him, so she fights, kicking to get back to the center of the pool. He looks at her, confused. Janice blows the whistle at them.

"Stop roughhousing!" she shouts.

I can see Ashleigh's mortified face even under the hair plastered over it. She swims back over to us, Hudson following her.

"Dude," she says, pushing the hair out of her face, "what was that?"

"I was trying to help," Hudson says, his face all confusion. "You looked like you were in trouble."

"I mean, that was the idea," I say to Ashleigh.

Ashleigh sighs.

"What?" Hudson asks.

"Never mind," Ashleigh says, then grudgingly adds, "Thanks."

"I just...we have to look out for each other, right?"

"Right," Ashleigh says.

"Right," I say at the same time, with much more enthusiasm.

Hudson grins at all of us. This big goofy grin where he knows he's missed something and doesn't care, because he tried to help and thinks maybe he did.

"Stay safe," he says, and swims over to where Brad and some other folks are trying to keep a beach ball in the air.

"Come on," I say. "He just swooped in to rescue you. It's

not even a sex thing, he's just that good a guy. You can't be mad at him."

"I can be mad at anyone I want," Ashleigh says, rolling her eyes.

"It was heroic," George says. "Even I had a bit of a flutter in my pants. But don't worry, darling, he's still all yours."

"Fine, yes, it was very heroic, he's wonderful, he's perfect, and he totally ruined my plan," Ashleigh concedes.

I laugh. "Should have planned it better. Can't try it again now."

"It probably wouldn't have worked anyway, right?" Ashleigh says. "I mean, crazy plans to win someone's heart never work."

"I think that depends," I say, smiling and watching Hudson jump out of the pool to tap the beach ball into the air. "If they're crazy enough, they might."

That night, we have a big campfire and make s'mores and sing songs. Mark has been trying to get the whole camp to sing "I'm Coming Out," but it doesn't work so well with only an acoustic guitar, and we all know it, so we only participate half-heartedly. George is painting Jordan's nails, and Ashleigh has a system going with five sticks speared with marshmallows, all set up at angles, roasting over the fire, which she runs between, rotating.

"Did she really try to fake drowning today?" Jordan asks,

looking down at their nails. They asked if George could do patterns, and George was willing to try, so he's currently painting black hearts over the sparkly pink base.

"The things we do for love," I say.

"See, the faking it is the problem," they say. "In a rom-com, you have to unintentionally almost drown and be saved, and maybe lose your memory in the process. You can't just splash around. They try that in all the teen beach movies, and it never works right."

"Not to be that bitch," Montgomery says from where he sits on a log watching George paint, "but how is it *ever* going to work? Straight people don't go gay because they rescued one. If that worked, I'd set fire to our apartment on a regular basis until I'd worked my way through all the men from the LA's finest firemen calendar."

"Darling, don't make me laugh or I'll screw up Jordan's nails," George says, chuckling.

I grab a marshmallow from one of the bags lying on the ground, wipe the ants off, and impale it with my twig, approaching the fire. Hudson is standing there, roasting two on one stick. His flavor of the week, whose name I've forgotten, is standing nearby, talking to Brad.

"Thanks," I say to Hudson as I stick my marshmallow out over the flames. "Ashleigh won't say it, but what you did was really brave."

He looks at me and grins. "The pool? So, what was that even about, bro?"

I wave my hand. "It wasn't a well-thought-out plan, but suffice to say, it was for love."

"Awww, then I'm sorry I ruined it," he says. "I love love." I notice he does not glance over at his current paramour, and that I've suddenly gotten very warm, even for standing next to the fire.

"Who doesn't?" I ask. "But I think this was love that wasn't meant to be."

"What? Now you're just bringing me down, dude. I only like happy love stories."

"It just seems a very unlikely pairing," I say.

"Aw, don't count her out. If she's really in love, she should go for it, y'know? Get back in there, take out the competition or dive over the obstacles, and win." He pauses and gazes at the fire, the flames reflecting in his eyes. "I think... I think love is special, especially for us queer people, but we have to try harder. Even if it seems unlikely. Because if you feel a connection with someone. If someone makes you feel special... we don't get that so much. We don't get it as much as straight people. So... it has to be worth it. Even if it is doomed or whatever. You just gotta go for it."

I grin into the fire. "Maybe you're right."

"Hey, babe." Hudson's beau comes over. "Is my s'mores done yet?"

"S'more," I say. "Singular."

"Right," he says, rolling his eyes. "I just want something sweet in my mouth."

66

"Well, I can give you that," Hudson says, grabbing his boyfriend around the waist and pulling him in for a kiss. My marshmallow starts to crackle over the fire, the skin turning black. I pull it out.

"Later," I say to them. They don't even notice as I walk away.

EIGHT

Vou are officially in the most ridiculous situation of all time, darling. And I am HERE. FOR. IT," George says, fanning himself on his bed back in the bunk after our visit to the tree. "I mean, I knew this would be ridiculous, but I didn't realize how much fun it would be to watch."

"This is not the plan," I say, grabbing a baseball cap and a sweatshirt.

Ashleigh snorts from the bunk above me.

"Would you stop?" I ask. "It's fine, though. I mean, so, he's pretending he's not this big..."

"Playboy," George says. "I've decided we're bringing it back."

"That just works in my favor," I say. "It means he'll try to get close to me."

"I guess your makeover really made the right impression if he pulled that story out of nowhere," George says. "Who knew little boy butch was a closet drama diva? I mean, can you imagine what he could bring to the stage with those improv skills and that level of commitment?"

"I don't know how he thinks we won't tell you," Ashleigh says.

"After your giggling fit, I wouldn't be surprised if he thinks you're too amused by it," George says. "Or he doesn't think we know about his love life enough to comment."

"Are you really going to go through with this?" Ashleigh asks, her voice a little hoarse from laughing. "I mean, you playing Del, him playing Hudson-not-Hal? Neither of you will get to know each other."

"I already know him," I say. "And he'll know me. Just me in different clothes."

"With different mannerisms and interests," Ashleigh says.

"Plus a very slightly lower pitch to your voice and a slower way of speaking—nice touch, by the way. Oscar worthy."

"Thanks," I say, feeling a little proud, though I'm trying to be annoyed at how much they're making fun of me. I put the baseball cap on. I feel my smile trying to force its way off my face, it's so big. I let out a little shriek and stomp my feet. "It's going perfectly. He can feel how right we are for each other—that's why he doesn't want me to know it's him on the tree."

George and Ashleigh stare at me like I've just told them about the joys of breasts. George nods.

"Look," Ashleigh says. "I don't want to be the downer here, but just keep in mind, he's a player."

"Playboy," George corrects.

"Sure. Playboy. And maybe he's just saying he's not Hal to get in your pants because he thinks you want someone who isn't a playboy."

"Or maybe he just was waiting for someone he felt a real connection with," I say.

Ashleigh sighs. "Sure, maybe. But...you told me not to drive headlong into heartbreak again this summer, so I'm telling you the same."

"It'll be fine," I say, checking myself in the mirror. I brush a stray hair. Do I put on the sweatshirt or carry it? I'll carry it for now. It's not that cool out. "Okay, I have to go. I said I'd meet him by the flagpole after I grabbed my sweatshirt. I'll see you guys at the talent show."

"He probably needed time to tell his cabin about his new identity," George says. Ashleigh snorts again.

"This is great," I say, heading for the screen door out of the cabin. "See you later!" I push open the creaking screen door and run out to the flagpole for my date.

I'm there first, but I'm happy about it. I wanted to get out of the cabin and have just a moment to enjoy what's happening. Hudson already likes me enough that he's pretending to be a romantic! George and Ashleigh might think it's funny, and okay, it is, a little, but it's also sweet. He's being the guy I know he always wanted to be, and would be, with the right guy, and it's like he already knows that that's me. It's not about just trying to get in my pants. That would be way more work than it's worth. He's doing this because he feels something. And that means that this was the right idea, that all the work over the year, skipping the show this summer, it's all exactly what I needed to do. It has to be. It just *has* to.

I look up at the sky. The sun is mostly down now and the horizon is blue and orange and purple, but right above me, the sky is dark and the stars are aligning perfectly in the sky. They wink down at me.

"Hey," comes Hudson's voice behind me, a little softer than it needs to be. I turn around. He's put an old green sweatshirt on over his T-shirt, but it's tight enough that it hugs his stomach and shoulders, almost more revealing than the tee was. I have my sweatshirt in my hand, I realize, and I suddenly wonder if I should put it over my shoulders or my waist, or is that too femme? I should just wear it, so I put it on quickly as he walks toward me, but I knock my hat off, and as I pull the sweatshirt down over my face, suddenly Hudson is close, in front of me, and kneeling to pick up my hat. He offers it to me and I have to bite back a joke about him being a prince and this being a glass slipper, which would definitely result in me singing some *Cinderella* (Rogers and Hammerstein, not Disney).

"Thanks," I say, and shove the hat on. "Sorry, I just got cold."

"Yeah, it can get chilly here at night," he says. "I don't

know if you have that in the summer in Ohio. It's like really hot during the day, but sometimes at night... cool."

"Yeah," I say. We stare at each other in silence and I wonder if he realizes we're just talking about the weather like two idiots or if he's looking into my eyes and wanting to kiss me. I'm feeling both.

"So, tour time," he says, smiling that big, kind of wolf grin he has. When he does it, his tongue is just barely visible, poking between the small gap in his teeth at the top corner of his mouth. "Obviously, this is the flagpole," he says. "There'll be a bonfire here in like fifteen minutes. People will roast marshmallows and make s'mores and stuff. That"— he points, and steps closer to me, to line up his finger with my eyes—"is cabin fourteen. My cabin. Just in case you want to visit sometime."

"We can just do that?" I ask. "Stop by?"

"Yeah," he says. "Until curfew anyway. After that... well, you gotta sneak, so the counselors don't catch you. There's a window at the very back of the cabin, opens onto my bed."

"Top or bottom?" I ask, blushing the moment it comes out and happy that the dark hides it. "I mean—sorry, I don't mean—"

"Vers," he says before I can go on, and winks at me. "Bottom bunk, though. I like being able to just collapse into bed at the end of the day."

"Me too," I say, which is like half true, because who

doesn't like that, but also the first year I took the top bunk and Ashleigh was under me and then I was painting my nails and some dripped on her, so we switched.

"So you can just knock on the window, you know, and I can climb out of it. If there's any reason for that," he says.

I laugh. These are totally the lines he uses every year. I can tell, they're so practiced. But he's using them on me. And it doesn't mean he's still a playboy. He might just know how they work and he wants to connect with me. Ashleigh was being unromantic, is all. I look up again, at the stars.

"Okay," I say. "All good information to have...potentially. But not much of a tour thus far." There. That cooled it down.

"Thus?" he says.

"Thus," I say adamantly.

"Okay, well, thusly, let us commence to the next stop wheretofore is the infirmary," he says, in a terrible British accent.

"Wheretofore," I say.

"Absolutely," he says, walking toward the stairs. The stairs are carved wood stuck into the ground, and they curve up, like mushrooms on a tree. In some places they're narrow, and some wide, and in the dark, they're a little hard to navigate.

"Careful," he says. "These stairs are tricky in the dark. Want to hold my hand for support?"

I take a deep breath before I say, "Sure," and reach out. His hand takes mine and I feel my dick get hard almost immediately. His hand is warm and a little rough—like maybe I should lend him some moisturizer—but also soft, and when he tightens it around my hand, it's just the right amount of squeeze.

"Didn't think you'd go for that," he says as we walk up the stairs.

"I was trying to call your bluff."

"Well, we definitely just skipped ahead, date-wise. Now we're hand holders," he says. "We're the guys who hold hands within the first five minutes of their first date."

"Only because of these very dangerous steps, though," I say.

"Right," he says, and I can hear how happy he is. "Only 'cause of that."

We reach the top of the stairs and neither of us lets go, even when a mosquito lands on my wrist and starts sucking. Hudson looks at it and swats it away for me. I almost expect him to make a joke about how he's the only one who'll be sucking on me tonight, but if he did I would probably burst into a fit of uncomfortable giggles and run away.

We walk down the path a little to a small clearing where he uses his free hand to point at the three buildings. "So, that's the infirmary," he says. "Cosmo is kind of weird, but also really cool, too. You can go there whenever, and you can just lie down, or he can give you aspirin or Band-Aids if you hurt yourself. Nurse stuff. But he's also just cool to talk to, and he has great stories about Stonewall—he was actually there. I mean, if you care about that stuff. I know not all of us do. My mom says it's not important, but it's still like…cool to hear about, y'know? He also has bowls of condoms, and lube, just sort of on the desk for anyone to take."

"Just on the desk?" I ask, like I haven't taken some before.

"He says trying to act like no one is going to screw is the dumbest thing he's ever heard, so he wants to make sure we do it safely."

"So people have sex here?" I ask. "In the cabins with people watching?" If I turn the conversation to sex, then I can scale it back, too. If he is just being a playboy like Ashleigh said—and I don't think he is—then I just have to tease and pull back, tease and pull back, until he knows me and we fall in love, and then tease and NOT pull back. Del is a tease.

"No!" Hudson says, then laughs. "I've heard some people have tried—real quiet, under the covers, people sleeping—but they always get caught. And then made fun of for the rest of the summer."

"Do people come here just to hang out—no romance?" I ask, pulling it back.

"Oh, sure. It's camp. Tennis, swimming, waterskiing… but that's all down the hill. So let me finish up here. I take my tour guide responsibilities seriously."

"Okay," I say, laughing.

"Here's the office." He points at the small white building that I've seen every summer, more like a house than a cabin. I nod as though I'm seeing it for the first time. "Joan is there most of the time. She and her wife live there all year, but her wife is a lawyer, so she's not around the camp much, except for dinner, sometimes."

"Okay," I say, getting a little bored with all the stuff I know already. But I gotta play the part.

"Oh, and this." He runs for the meeting hall, dropping my hand. I frown a little, but I guess we had to stop at some point. "This is the meeting hall." I follow him, trying to act impressed.

"What's it for?"

"Rainy days—movie nights, any outdoor electives that can't meet in the rain might use it, and sometimes..." He swings open the screen door, then tries the heavy wood door behind it. "Oh well. Sometimes they leave it open. This cabin people have definitely had sex in." He grins at me. I grin back, then turn away. Remember, Del is a tease, I tell myself. No pushing him against the cabin and kissing his very soft-looking lips. Not yet.

"But they have to be quiet," he says, "'cause Joan is right there. Last year, these two girls moaned so loud, she heard them and they got kicked out that night."

"For sex?" I ask.

"For being out of their cabins after curfew," he says, closing the screen door and leaning against the cabin wall. It's dark now and the few electric lights have turned on, but most of the light is coming from Joan's place and the infirmary. "It's a queer camp, so they want to stay sex positive, like not shaming anyone for wanting sex, you know? But the rules are meant to make it difficult to find alone time. But the difficulty is half the fun." He does that smile again where his tongue finds the upper corner of his mouth and presses against the gap between his teeth there.

He takes my hand again and for a moment I think he's going to pull me in for a kiss, but instead he leads me back to the stairs, and down them, back to the cabins and flagpole, where some folks are trying to start a bonfire, and then to the other set of steps, down to the main part of camp.

"So let's see," he says as we walk. He drops my hand when we see some other people on the tennis courts. It makes me a little sad, but I get it—we don't want to look too ridiculous on day one. A slow burn is always more respectable. "So those are the tennis courts," he says. "Do you play tennis?"

"Yeah," I say. Tennis had been one of the easier ways to get fit during the year. Dad set up a net in the backyard. "My dad likes to play, too."

"Cool. I'm pretty bad at it, I have an awful serve."

"I can give you some pointers, maybe."

I can see him smile in the dark. "Maybe." He turns back to the tour and we walk along the grass, taking in the camp. It smells so green and the night has made it smell wet, too— the faint fishiness coming off the lake, but not, like, gross fishy. Other campers are running around with flashlights, scaring each other in the dark, and some counselors are around, watching them. By the drama cabin I see Ashleigh watching George and my other bunkmates practicing dance moves for auditions.

"So, you saw the dining hall, obviously," Hudson says as we walk. He points. "That's the arts and crafts cabin. The counselor who runs it, Marguerite, is this weird conceptual artist in the real world. I think she has stuff in museums? I don't usually go there; I have zero artistic talent."

"Zero? Really?" I ask. I don't mention he's wildly understating Marguerite's weirdness.

"I..." He pauses. It's hard to read his face by just the stars and few electric lights, but he looks almost sad for a moment. But then it's gone, and I decide it's just the dark. "Nah, nothing really. But it's cool if you do. I'm super jealous of people with artistic talent."

"Well, I'm not great at art stuff, either," I say. "But I signed up for A and C. I figured it would be a nice way to relax during the day."

"For sure. And A and C. Listen to you! Already got the slang down."

Drat! Did I overplay my hand? "Well," I say. "I've gone to camp before. Just not this one." It spills out of my mouth without me thinking, but then I realize I'm a genius! This will cover for so many things.

"Yeah? What camp?"

"Oh, just a small Jewish camp in Ohio," I say. "Camp Shalom." It's the most generic Jewish camp name I can think of.

"My dad wanted to send me to a Jewish camp!" he says. "But I told him I really wanted this one. I showed him how the outdoors counselor is an Olympian and then he was okay with it."

"Why wouldn't he have been okay with it?"

"Just... he liked the Jewish camp better," Hudson says, turning away. "Here's the boathouse." He does a presenting motion at the boathouse, which is locked up and dark, the motorboat and canoes parked next to the dock that extends out in front of it. There are no lights on the other side of the river, just trees. It smells like fish and faintly of moss. Hudson points out the boats and talks about waterskiing and canoeing.

"But mostly people hang out on the porch." He points at the covered porch that juts out over the water. "It's great to just chill there, watch the water."

"Cool," I say, trying not to laugh. The porch is prime make-out territory.

"Over here in the woods is the adventure trail stuff," he says. "This is where I spend most of the day. Obstacle courses, hiking... it's awesome."

"I signed up for it, too," I say.

"Cool," he says, putting his hand on my shoulder. "Then I'll show you tomorrow. It's kind of dangerous at night."

We turn and walk away from the river, and Hudson points out more—the soccer field, which is also used for touch football, capture the flag. The farm, with the two pet goats and three chickens. The archery field, the kickball field, the basketball court. And the drama cabin, which he points out but doesn't have anything to say about. I wish he knew how special it is. I'm not sure he's even been in it, aside from sitting in the audience for camp-wide stuff, like the end of summer show. Maybe he doesn't even go to that. He could go to the bathroom and then go hang out in the woods instead of sitting through the show every year. It would explain how he doesn't seem to recognize me at all, even after my pretty groundbreaking portrayal of Domina in *A Funny Thing Happened on the Way to the Forum*.

"I'm excited for the show," I say out loud, then wince. I am, and I want him to be, too, but we are FAR too early in the plan to change him into a musical theater lover. "I mean, so many of my bunkmates are in it."

"Yeah. It's usually fun, I guess? I feel like it's so not my thing and it just goes over my head," he says. Which is better than I'd hoped—although that means he doesn't sneak out, and he DID see my Domina last year and I'm just going to take it as a compliment on how into my characters I get that he doesn't know Del is played by the same future Tony winner. "I guess I just don't get spending all your time on the show. You can't switch out if you don't like it, and it takes so much time every day there's like no time for anything else. I just think there are better things to do."

I feel my blood get hot and I look away, worried I might be turning red. Better things to do? I'm aghast at the idea. Musical theater is joy. It's expressing stories and song and dance and a whole community. It's connecting with people—your castmates, the audience—and playing, and getting to see the same scene done dozens of different ways until you find a truth in it you can express. That sounds so pretentious. But it's true. I get to be a version of myself that feels real every time I act and sing and dance, and here it's queer, unrestrained by gender or sexuality or any of that nonsense. Here you get to find out more about yourself in every scene.

But I can't say that. That would give me away. And besides—he's right. There is something better, otherwise I would still be doing theater this summer. The something better is him.

"Yeah," I say, instead of disagreeing. "I see what you mean." He nods. I nod.

"So, anyway, that's the tour," he says. "You want to head over to the talent show?"

"Absolutely."

"You have your talent ready?" he asks.

For a moment, I'm actually caught off guard, and panic seethes through me like the fizz of a shaken soda bottle as you open it. Did I miss something? It's always the counselors' talent show first night. Then I get it, he's teasing me. The new kid.

"What?" I say. "Do I need one?"

He laughs, and takes my hand as we walk toward the drama cabin. And there aren't even any stairs around this time. "I'm kidding. First night the counselors put one on.

Camper talent show is usually a few weeks in. And strictly optional. You have any talents?"

My cabin usually puts on a big musical number from a show we're not doing, but I guess I'll have to sit that out this summer. "Not really," I say. "You?"

"Nothing they'd let me do onstage," he says. I can feel his smile in the dark. "But I'd be happy to show you sometime in private."

I wait a beat too long before I say, "Sometime, maybe, in the future."

"Sounds like a plan. Oh, I should warn you, though. The counselor talent show . . . it can be kind of a lot? Like, it's awesome, sure, yay gay pride, but just . . . be prepared."

"Okay," I say, trying not to smile. I know exactly what he means. The counselor talent show is one of my favorite events of the summer.

NINE

'm Diana Loan. And I've come to terms with that."

Mark winks, his purple eye shadow sparkling like ame-
thyst under the stage lights, his burgundy-painted lips twisted
up in a slight smile. Not Mark, I should say, but Diana, his drag
persona. She's got black hair up in an oversized bun, studded
with a few white flowers, and is wearing a long-sleeved red
gown, showing off her padded curves. It's sequined in some
places, and patterned with white flowers in others. Her makeup
is painted for the cheap seats, and a pair of long earrings flash
as she turns her head in the light and stalks back and forth on
stage. The spotlight follows her. It would be impossible not to.

"Welcome, young queer people, to Camp Outland. For
you first-timers, hello, I promise to go easy on you. And for
you returning campers, well, I guess they didn't want you at

one of the good camps." The crowd chuckles. "Don't worry! We take anyone here, long as they're queer. Just look at Nurse Cosmo!" He points at Cosmo, who's sitting in the front row, grinning. "We let him work here and he's been dead for seven years." Everyone, Cosmo included, laughs, even though she's told the same joke about him since I've been coming here. There's just something about her delivery. Mark might be high-strung, but Diana is cool and confident.

"I'm only kidding," Diana says, waving at Cosmo. "Cosmo is a piece of living queer history. Actually at Stonewall during the riots. He was in a crowd of people who fought the police for our rights. And it made such an impact on him—being right up against all those warriors. You know how some people don't wash their hands after meeting a celebrity they admire? Well, Cosmo hasn't bathed since Stonewall. You can really smell the history on him." That's a new one, and everyone, including me, laughs. Hudson laughs, too, I'm happy to see. I was a little worried after he said it was a lot that it meant he never enjoyed this drag show. And that would be crazy. I don't mind the masc-only thing, but if you can't enjoy a drag queen, you're probably a soulless monster. We're sitting to the left in the back—we were a little late. But I can see George and Ashleigh a few rows in front of us. They glance back once at us, and see us holding hands. George looks impressed. Ashleigh rolls her eyes.

"So, Joan is pointing at her watch, which means 'move it along, Diana,'" Diana continues. "Honestly, Joan always seems in a hurry to get to the next thing and the next and the next. I think if she had it her way, the summer would be over tomorrow at noon. No, no, we owe Joan a lot. She built this place, keeps it running, so a big round of applause for Joan." Everyone starts to clap and Diana immediately says, "Stop," into her mic. "We have to move it along. So, to open tonight's talent show, we have…" She pulls a list out of her sleeve and checks it. "Oh…all right. I'm sorry about this, but it seems Marguerite from the arts and crafts cabin is going to be singing an original song for us. Everyone, round of applause for Marguerite!"

Diana exits, stage right, as music pipes in over the sound system and Marguerite comes on and does what it essentially an imitation of Björk, something she seems blissfully unaware of. The show continues, Diana introducing each counselor's act—Tina and Lisa, who drive the motorboat, do a decent cover of a Tegan and Sara song; Crystal does a tap number; Rebecca, who runs the canoeing trips, does a cover of an Indigo Girls song (she has a long-standing rivalry with Tina and Lisa); Karl, the German twink who runs the farm and usually is in overalls, comes out in sequined short shorts and a crop top to dance to a Years & Years song; and various other counselors do magic tricks, acrobatics, sing, dance, and are celebratorily, unashamedly queer. Some of the audience even starts dancing for some of the musical numbers. It's like being at a dozen gay clubs in one night—or what I imagine gay clubs are like, having never been to one (not many to choose from in suburban Ohio, and with no one to drive me to the ones in Cleveland). Hudson even stands and pulls me up to dance when Pablo, one of the tennis counselors, shows off a ten-minute DJ mix of "the history of Madonna." Hudson puts his hand on my waist and we sway together before I realize that I stupidly never practiced dancing masc, and that I'm shimmying my hips much more than Hudson is. I try to imitate him, a sort of gentle sway side to side, but it feels stiff and awkward, and soon we're out of synch. He laughs and leans forward as a remix of "What It Feels Like for a Girl" plays in the background.

"Not much of a dancer?" he asks.

I bite back a rude response about how I'm actually one of the best dancers at camp, and it's just trying to match his lack of style that's holding me back. This is part of the deal—I can be a bad dancer for Hudson.

"Never danced with a boy before," I say. That's true. Oh my god—that's true! I'm dancing with a boy! Hudson has his hand on my waist and he's bringing me closer. Our stomachs are touching and I have to tilt slightly so he doesn't feel my hard-on pressing against him.

"Here," he says, putting his other hand on my waist. "Just sway to the beat. Put your hands on me."

So I do. I put my hands on his shoulders, resisting the urge to wrap them around his neck, and we sway like ten-year-olds imitating adults at a wedding until we reach the end of "I Rise," and one of the chefs comes on to juggle. But when we sit back down, Hudson puts his hand on my leg and squeezes, and I glance over at George, who wiggles his eyebrows at me. Everything is going so well.

The evening always closes with Diana doing an outrageous lip-synch to a song from the show that Mark has chosen for us every year, and this year, she does a sultry version of "Honestly Sincere." Usually she comes down into the audience and sits in Joan's lap, or flirts with Cosmo, but this year, she makes a beeline to me, wiggling her padded butt between the seats until she's right in front of me, and, singing into the mic, leans forward and brushes my hair back behind my ears—or would, if I hadn't cut it all off.

"'Write this down now,'" she sings at me. "'You gotta be sincere, honestly sincere!'" And then she moves back into the aisle, still singing.

Well, Mark was never one for subtlety.

But I look over at Hudson, who grins at me, thrilled I was chosen, and I don't care what Diana was singing at me. I just feel happy. *Sincerely* happy.

After Diana closes the talent show to a standing ovation, we all pour out into the night, heading carefully back up the stairs to our cabins.

"So, that rocked, right?" Hudson asks me. We're not holding hands as we walk up the stairs, but we're in the middle of a crowd, so that would probably make things harder.

"It was amazing," I say.

"That Madonna mix was so good," he says. "I don't know anything about DJing but it just, like, rocked, right?"

"Yeah, and Diana nailed that lip-synch," I say. "Mark is going to be on top of the world tonight."

"Like, for me, drag isn't something I'd seek out," he says. "But I like it once a year. Sometimes, though, I feel like the normal one in there, but like, in a good way."

"Normal?" I ask.

"Like, to the outside world," he says. "Being queer is normal, of course, but then there's other stuff, like drag queens and musicals that I feel like . . ." He pauses. "I sometimes feel like I'm sort of split down the middle—like there's normal world and there's gay world, and here is the only time I get to experience gay world, and I love it—but I also feel like maybe I don't fit in it? And I wish it were more like my kind of gay world? I don't know, I'm not making sense."

"No," I say. "I think I know what you mean. We're definitely here in gay world now, and it can be hard to accept that this is your world—the one you belong in. Straight world—not normal world—doesn't want you. But here you can be anything you want and no one will care."

"I don't think straight world doesn't want me." He laughs. "I mean, we have to live in it, and I feel comfortable there, mostly."

"Well, yeah. But you should feel comfortable here, too."

"I do. I just don't want to be a drag queen, is what I'm saying."

"I don't think anyone is saying you have to be," I say, my turn to laugh. "Especially not with those shoulders."

He gives me a funny look, then laughs, too. We reach the top of the steps and the crowd of campers around us floods out, heading toward their cabins.

"You're really smart about this for someone who's new," he says.

"I thought about it a lot," I say, not exactly a lie. I have thought about it. The first time I put on nail polish outside of camp, I thought to myself, *This is another reason for assholes to be assholes in my direction*, and then I thought, *They're going to do that anyway, you may as well feel a little joy every time you catch your nails sparkling in the light*. And I thought about the boy at camp who'd told me I was special in the dark, and how I felt like I could be. But that's not a story to tell Hudson. Not a Del story.

"Yeah," he says. "Come over here, I want to show you something."

He takes my hand and leads me to the side of the meeting hall, in the shadows.

"What?" I ask.

"Was this a good first date?" His face is half in shadow, his cheekbones sharp in the light, his eyes bright.

"Yeah," I say. "Really good."

"Good," he says. He turns a little so I'm leaning against the side of the meeting hall to look at him now, and then before I realize it's happening, he leans forward and kisses me. I always thought his kisses would be kind of rough, honestly, almost unpracticed—a stupid thought, considering his history, I know, but his energy is so strong, I thought his kiss would be like a punch. It's not, though. It's soft, but still direct, his tongue carefully opening my mouth as his arms wrap around me. He leans his body into mine and I don't mind he can feel my hard-on, 'cause I can feel his, too. His hands float down to my lower back, pulling me even closer. I know I should be pushing him off—this is more than just a kiss now; this is bordering on making out, and that's too far, that's playboy behavior, that's going to make me just another two-week conquest, but also it's happening and it feels so good. Breath-catchingly good. Singing a solo good. Standing ovation good.

But I call upon the strength within me and I pull away when we pause to breathe.

"Not so fast, now," I say. "Or I'll start to think you have more in common with that Hal guy than you let on."

He looks a little shocked for a moment, and I'm worried I screwed it up, but then he grins.

"Right," he says. "Slow. Sorry. You just . . . you're a really good kisser."

"You too," I say. I'm still leaning against the wall. My knees are too weak to support me. I didn't think that was an actual thing—weak in the knees—but here I am, so I guess it is.

"That's how a good date should end," he says. "Right? That was okay?"

"Yeah," I say. I want to grab him again. I want to feel him pushing up against me again. I want to wrap my legs around him and have him hold me up as we keep making out and pushing against each other and—

"So, want me to walk you to your cabin?" he asks.

"Sure," I say. He takes my hand and my knees don't give out as I stand and we walk in silence to my cabin door, where I turn. I can feel my bunkmates watching from the windows.

"Well," he says. "Good night. See you tomorrow."

"See you tomorrow," I say. And he lets go of my hand and walks toward his cabin, glancing back once to find me still watching him. Then I go inside.

"This should not be working as well as it is," George says, leaning against the wall next to the door so he's the first thing I see when I walk in. "It's like some sort of disgusting meet-cute. If you somehow got a dog together before the end of the summer, I wouldn't be surprised."

"Isn't it perfect?" I ask, grinning.

He rolls his eyes but can't help smiling back. "I guess your ridiculous plan really is getting you everything you want. Maybe I should come up with ridiculous plans. Ashleigh, we need ridiculous plans."

Ashleigh is on her bed, going over what looks like a tech manual for lighting equipment. "For what?" she asks.

"I don't know," George says. "What do you want?"

"I want to be stage manager this year," she says, sighing. "But that's not going to happen. It'll be someone from cabin eight, same as always." Cabin eight is where most of the theater tech kids are. Ashleigh only bunks in seven with us, where the talent is, because of how close we are. "I guess there's the whole falling-for-a-not-straight-girl thing. That's a goal."

"Okay, so...what's a ridiculous plan for that?" George asks. Ashleigh shrugs. George turns to me.

"I don't know," I say, walking over to my bed. "I think it's too vague. Ridiculous only works for really specific stuff. You could try drugging the water in cabin eight, though. Nothing deadly, just, like, make them all so dizzy, they can't read the cues in the script. Then you're stage manager by default."

"I don't want it by default," Ashleigh says. "I'll be happy if I'm just in charge of the lights this year."

"Maybe we need to dream bigger," George says. "I want ALL the parts in the show."

"Over my dead body," says Paz, from the bunk above George's. "I'm going to be a kick-ass Rose. You really want to sing 'Spanish Rose'?"

"A fair point. I want all the parts except Rose, which can be played by Paz."

"I'll still steal the show," Paz says. We all laugh.

The door to the cabin opens and Mark comes in, still in his Diana dress and makeup, but holding his wig. The cabin bursts into applause. Mark bows a few times.

"Thank you, thank you, I think it was a good show tonight."

"Better every year," Crystal says from the wall she's been leaning against, talking to some other campers.

"Help me out of this thing, will you?" he asks, and Crystal runs forward to unzip his dress. "I hope you all had fun. But auditions are tomorrow, so you'd better rest up. Well." He turns a withering Diana look at me. "Auditions are for most of you."

"I wish I could do both," I tell him.

He waddles over, holding up his now unzipped dress with one hand, and sits on my bed. "I just hope the summer doesn't end up being a disappointment for you. You can't join the cast mid-rehearsals, remember. Maybe I could find a place for you on tech, but there's choreography and harmonies."

"I know," I tell him. "I just... haven't you ever done anything crazy for love?"

"So many things," he says, leaning back. The front of his dress falls forward. "There was this one guy, we were doing the chorus of *Funny Face* on a cruise out of Miami. He was beautiful, had a huge—" Crystal clears her throat and he stops, looks at me and the other campers who are listening. "Personality. *Real* big. But he also had a boyfriend—but the boyfriend wasn't on the cruise. So I told him I knew his boyfriend, and that he wouldn't mind if I understudied the role, so to speak. Insane. Got some very angry phone calls when that cruise disembarked. I deserved them, too. I can't work Miami anymore. That's the level of stupid I think this is at."

"But did you love him? Or was it just lust?"

"What's the difference when you're twenty-three?" he

93

asks. "Or sixteen. Look, I don't want to keep having this conversation with you. Lie, remake yourself, whatever. But just make sure you're really happy, and it's not just that you're super unhappy but you finally got what you wanted so now you have to be happy otherwise what was it all for? That's a classic musical theater plot, and I just won't have one of my actors—even if he is...on sabbatical—play that part in real life. This isn't *Follies*."

"Or *Merrily*," Crystal says.

"Any Sondheim." Mark stands, the dress falling almost to his waist now. "Just be happy, Randall," he says. "You only get four weeks a year. Don't waste them."

I almost laugh. "I won't. I have a plan. And I'm ahead of schedule. I didn't think Hudson would kiss me until the end of the week."

"Kiss?" George nearly shouts.

Ashleigh's head drops over the side of the bed, staring at me. "You didn't mention a kiss."

"There may have been some lip-to-lip contact," I say, looking coy.

"This is not my business," Mark says, going into his room.

"But it's ours!" George says, now staring at me from his bed, stomach down, head propped up on his hands, feet in the air. "Who kissed whom?"

"He kissed me," I say.

"Where?"

"Against the side of the meeting hall."

"When?"

"Just now, after the talent show," I say, laughing at his questions. "It's no big deal."

"Isn't it?" Ashleigh asks. Her head is gone, so she's just a voice above me. "I mean, to you, anyway."

"It was a real kiss. Tongue and everything."

"Hands?" George asks.

"No hands in my mouth, no," I say, confused.

"I mean where were his hands, darling?"

"Oh! Lower back."

"No ass squeeze," George says. "A gentleman."

"Or a playboy who knows the right moves," Ashleigh says. "He kissed you on the first date. Even you said you're ahead of schedule. I thought the point was not to be one of his two-week flings."

"It's fine," I say. "It's going perfectly. I'm holding back enough. He can have my mouth, but not my..."

"Darling, don't finish that sentence. Everything about it is wildly inappropriate."

"Yeah," I say, regretting it.

"Was it a good kiss?" he asks.

"It was," I say, trying not to sigh and failing.

"Did he pin the pin on?" Paz asks from her bunk, quoting a *Bye Bye Birdie* lyric. "Or was he too shy?"

"No pins," I say. "We're not going steady...yet."

"At least not for good," Ashleigh says.

"What's the story, Morning Glory?" George sings, continuing the song.

"What's the word?" Montgomery responds from across the cabin. I bury my face in my pillow.

"Hummingbird!" Paz responds. And within ten seconds the entire bunk is singing "The Telephone Hour" from *Bye Bye Birdie*, all of them on their beds, miming telephones and doing stylized dance-in-place movements. Mark peeks out, now wearing pajamas, and nods approvingly.

"More head tossing," he says to Jen. "Kick more, Jordan!" He goes around directing as everyone sings. When they finish, he applauds. "Very good start. Now save your voices. Auditions are tomorrow. Lights-out in twenty."

He goes back into his room, nodding to himself.

"It's going to be such a good show this year," George says, standing. "I'm sad you won't be in it, darling." He grabs his toothbrush from his kit and goes into the bathroom. Honestly, I'm sad I won't be in it, too. But this is worth it. It *has* to be worth it.

Which means it *has* to work.

"Going steady for good!" one of my bunkmates sings from the bathroom.

TEN

FOUR SUMMERS AGO

'm woken by crying. It's gentle, almost haunting, and at first I'm worried that maybe there was some truth to what that older camper said about the ghost on our first night, but then I shake my head. Ghost stories are part of camp. Ghosts are not. Though if they were to haunt a queer camp, they'd have to be fabulous, so maybe that would be pretty cool, actually. I sit up in the darkness. The lights are out in the counselors' room, and there's no moon, so it's really pitch-black. I listen.

Yeah, definitely crying, slightly muffled. From right under me.

I'm on the top bunk because I'd never had a bunk bed before and grabbed the first top I could see. Bed, that is. And it's fun literally climbing into bed. Under me is another new camper, a cute boy named Hudson who everyone is already crushing on. I carefully climb out of bed. It's definitely Hudson crying. I kneel by where I think his head is and I whisper.

"Hudson, are you okay?"

He keeps crying, softly. I reach out and carefully try to touch his arm. I think I graze his cheek instead and pull my hand back quickly. The crying stops for a second.

"Hello?" he asks in a whisper.

"You were crying," I whisper back. "Are you okay?"

He sniffs, the crying apparently over now that he's awake. "Sorry. I was dreaming."

"About what?" I ask, leaning against the leg of the bed.

"It's not important."

"I just want you to feel better," I say. And I do. Because these are the first queer people I've ever met and I want us all to feel better. Better than other people make us feel. I want to be his friend. I want to be everyone's friend. "If you talk about it, you might feel better."

He sniffs again, and I think for a moment he's fallen back asleep.

"It was my grandma," he says. "I dreamed she was back, but in the dream I remembered she wasn't, and..." He sniffs. I think he's crying again. Stupid Randy, making it worse.

"She died?" I ask.

"Yeah," he whispers. "Just before I came here."

"What was your favorite thing about her?" I ask.

"What?"

"It's what my mom asked me when my grandma died. She said if you hold on to your favorite memory of her, it means they're still with you."

"Oh." I'm sure he's crying again now. I hear his hand wipe his cheek. "She was... really cool. She sent me here."

"Really?" I ask. "I never even came out to my grandparents."

"She was the first person I told. She gave me this big hug and told me I should always be myself and be proud of who I was."

"That's a good memory."

"Yeah." He sniffs again. "She wanted me to come here so I had friends like me."

"Well, now you do," I say, and I reach up and put my hand on the edge of his mattress. He must feel it, because he puts his hand lightly over mine.

"Thanks," he says. "You won't tell anyone I was crying, right?"

"Not if you don't want me to," I say.

"I just really miss her."

"I know."

The darkness seems to pulse for a second, and he sighs.

"I just wish I could be better at this," he says.

"Better at what?" I ask.

"I don't know... all of it. Being gay."

"I don't think there's a better way to be gay," I say. That's what Mark, the drama counselor, had told us all during auditions last week. That the show was going to be very gay, but that didn't mean what we thought it meant, that it just meant it was going to be very proud. That there was no better gay. I'm not sure I understood, but it feels like something worth repeating now.

"I don't know," Hudson says.

"I think we just get to be us. We don't have to worry about the outside where we need to hide who we are so people don't bully us. That's all we have to do to be good at being gay."

"Yeah," he says. "I like that." We sit in silence for a moment. "Hey...will you do me a weird favor?"

"What?"

"Will you rub my back for a few minutes? My mom always used to do it to help me sleep."

I smile in the dark. "Sure," I say.

"You're right, you know," he says as he turns onto his stomach. "We can be anyone we want. Not just here, even. My grandma would have wanted that for me. To be... better."

He takes a deep breath, and I feel his hand reaching blindly in the dark as it smacks my forearm. He holds on to it and then runs it down to my wrist, making goose bumps rise like the bubbles in seltzer. He finds my hand and grabs it, squeezing. I squeeze back.

"Thank you," he says. "You're really special." His voice is so soft, I can barely hear him, but suddenly, I can feel stars exploding inside me.

I rub his back softly for a few minutes until his breathing turns deeper, and then I get back into bed. I realize he probably doesn't even know it was me. If he's like my dad, he won't even remember it in the morning. But that doesn't matter.

I close my eyes and try to go to sleep, but it feels like a galaxy is forming inside me, and it's morning before I know it.

"Hey, you okay?" I ask, hanging my head over the edge of the bed to look at Hudson.

"Why?" he asks. "Did I snore?"

He doesn't remember. "Just talking a little in your sleep."

"Oh..." He rubs his eyes. "I don't remember. I think it was good dreams, though."

I smile. "I'm glad," I say. He looks at me funny, and I pull my head back up, staring at the ceiling. He had good dreams, because of me. He said I was special. And he's right—it's not just about being ourselves, about being who we can't be out in the rest of the world. It's about being who we want to be.

One of my new friends from drama, George, was wearing some cool nail polish yesterday. I liked it. Maybe today I'll ask him to do my nails. I think I'd like that. I think that's what I want. I like the way shimmery nails make it look like you're magic under the skin. Like you're filled with stars.

Hudson gets up and walks over to the bathroom, his hair adorably disheveled. I have a sudden memory of the way it felt when he squeezed my hand last night, and I think about how, if my nails had been painted, they might have sparkled in the dark. I think he would have liked that. I know I would have—our fingers linked together, glitter winking out of every other nail. How it almost was like that anyway, because he knew I was special—he knew I had stars under my skin already, even in the dark. Even not knowing who I was.

I like this camp. I like deciding to be someone different. Someone special. I climb down from my bunk and go get ready for the day.

ELEVEN

Normally, I'd be auditioning today. No one auditions for specific parts (though I'm sure George is campaigning hard for Kim), but everyone gets up and sings a solo of their own choosing, and then Crystal does a few rounds of choreography to see who can move like they want. Then there's like a half hour where everyone hangs out outside, resting after the dancing, or reviewing the scripts. Then come call-backs. Singing songs from the show, people dancing together, acting together until lunch. Then, later that day, Mark and Crystal hang the cast list in the cabins of people who tried out.

It's a fun day. Stressful, but fun. Hearing everyone sing, dancing together, going over parts and practicing. It could be terrible, I know, with everyone backstabbing and saying nasty things to psych each other out, but it's never like that. Everyone just wants the show to be great. I don't know if that's because it's a queer camp and we're all excited, or because Mark and Crystal don't tolerate meanness, or if it's just some magic summer thing, but auditions are always fun here.

But I'm not auditioning today. Well, kind of.

"First thing we're going to do is one run of the obstacle course each," Connie says. We're all lined up in front of her, like army recruits or something, but Connie wasn't in the military. She's a former Olympian. Track. Two silver medals, one bronze. She's the most famous person who works at the camp, which is probably why she's on all the promotional material and doesn't have to live here for the summer, like the other counselors. She drives in. She's tall, narrow, with dark skin and long, straight black hair. If she hadn't come out as trans, she might have had a career as a great coach. If there wasn't a more famous trans Olympian, she might have gotten a TV deal, or her book would have sold better. Being black probably makes the world overlook her, too. But she seems to like it here. She's a gym teacher during the rest of the year. She likes working with kids.

At least, I think she does. She's hard to read. She looks us each over, appraising. She raises one eyebrow when she comes to me, and one corner of her lip twitches up. Is it funny I'm here? I mean honestly, yes, it's hilarious, but also, no it isn't. I can do this. It's just an obstacle course. Hop through some tires, crawl under a net, run up a steep ramp, get across a rope ladder suspended between trees, then go down the slide, hop from rock to rock over the small (but waist-deep and freezing cold) stream, get across the monkey bars and the wire-walk, dive through a tire swing into a sand pit, which you then need to get across for the big finale: the Peanut Butter Pit, a rope swing that hangs over a deep pit. Swing across that, and you've made it to the end. The trouble with the rope swing is it stays perfectly still, hanging over the pit—it's not waiting for you to grab it. You have to jump for it.

So it's just that. Sure, it's hard. But so is hitting the high note in "That Dirty Old Man," and I did that last year.

"If you fall or fail, don't worry about it. Just get back up and keep going. If you want to skip one of the obstacles completely, that's all right, too, just run around it. No judgments. I just want to see where you're all at. But by the end of the summer, you're all going to be running this, easy." A few of the new campers turn pale at that. I probably do, too.

"The wire-walk is new," Hudson whispers to me, excited. Our shoulders are touching and I'm so aware of his body, I feel dizzy. "That's going to take some crazy balance." I'm doomed.

"I'm more worried about diving through the tire," I whisper back.

"There's a mat under the sand. You can't hurt yourself."

"That almost sounds like a challenge. Which, to be clear, I will not be rising to."

Hudson laughs and Connie glances over at us, that eyebrow raising again.

"Don't worry," she says. "We're not just going to be doing this. We'll go for hikes, climb trees, and learn how to build tents and start fires. All the good woodsy stuff. But the obstacle course is a challenge. And I want to show you that you're all up for a challenge—'cause life is going to throw them at you. And maybe swinging across that pit at the end isn't going to make some asshole stop calling you names, but it is going to make you feel really good, I promise. So, who wants to go first?"

Hudson and a few others raise their hands, and she starts sending us through, one by one. We all watch, but it's like auditions—this isn't a competition. I'm rooting for each and every camper. Hudson is the fifth up and watching him move makes my whole body shiver a little. He's in low-slung beige shorts and a blue T-shirt that isn't tight but rides up a lot, showing off his stomach and hips. Watching him climb the ramp, then cross the rope ladder, I can see the muscles in his arms working. His calves flex as he jumps from stone to stone. He is the most perfect human specimen I have ever seen.

And I kissed him last night.

No, he kissed me.

What is even happening?

"Randy," Connie says, and I realize it's the second time she's saying it. "You sure you want to do this?"

"It's Del," I tell her. Luckily, Hudson is on the other side of the obstacle course now, so he can't hear. "I go by Del now."

She nods. "Okay, Del. You're up."

I couldn't train for this in Ohio. I lifted weights and ran track, but the only thing we had at school that's on the obstacle course is the tire hops—which are first. I get through them easily, and quickly—there's a pattern to it, like dancing. Crawling under the net isn't hard, either—just use your body to slither, like a snake—that's something Crystal makes us do to warm up sometimes. But then comes the ramp, and my training for that was running up the steepest hill I could find—which in Ohio was maybe forty degrees. I looked at the physics of it, though, and it's not that difficult. Not like Donald O'Connor running up the walls in *Singing in the Rain*. Just a really steep hill. I can do this, I tell myself as I hop up after the net. Just charge.

So I charge, and it works. I grab on to the top to pull myself the rest of the way, which isn't great—Hudson didn't need to—but it's allowed. The rope ladder isn't so bad, either, just crawl across a swinging rope ladder slowly and carefully. I've helped move lights in the theater at school, and it's kind of like that, I decide, as it rocks back and forth under me. Scary, sure, but doable. The slide is just a slide, and hopping from rock to rock isn't actually that hard as long as the stream isn't flooding over them, and it's not today. I'm shocked by how well it's going, honestly.

The monkey bars I should have practiced. There's a park near me with them, but they're for little kids and I felt silly going there. I figured if kids could do it, so could I. What I didn't figure was that it burns! I hang in place from one arm and stretch out the other for the next bar, my own weight heavy and pulling painfully on my arm. I'm sweating, too, so I try to go quickly, or else my hands will slip. One kid before me failed the monkey bars, so it's not the end of the world, but I don't want Hudson to think I'm the second-worst one here.

Maybe it IS a competition. But just for me. Win the course, win Hudson. In fact, was the kid who fell one of his exes? How many of them are here? I tried to never pay much attention—George said it made me mopey—so I only half know their faces, like blurry people in the background of a photo of Hudson. I think the guy who fell was one of his conquests. And maybe the one who went first and got through everything but the Peanut Butter Pit.

It goes slowly, but I make it across the bars, and I can feel my shirt sticking to my back with sweat now. If I still had my old, longer hair, it would be plastered across my forehead. When I drop from the monkey bars, my hands clench closed involuntarily, and my palms feel like they're burning. But I have no time to check. Next is the wire-walk—a wire tightrope, but only a foot off the ground. I didn't prepare for it at all because it wasn't here last summer. But I pull myself up onto it by the tree it's tied to, and focus. The good news is, no one has done this one yet. Everyone has fallen, only Hudson kept hopping back on where he fell, taking another step and then falling again. Everyone gave up after their first or second fall.

But actually, it's not that hard. It's not easy, don't get me wrong. The wire flexes and bounces under me and I wish I were barefoot so I could grip it, but walking a perfectly straight line is something we need to do for chorus choreography. Sway too far to the left or right, and you'll whack the person next to you with your jazz hands. So I do what I do when dancing, and I focus not on my feet, but the tree at the other end of the wire. I stretch my arms out for balance, and then, not too slowly, I walk.

I make it halfway before I fall, farther than anyone else. But I don't land on my feet, like they all had. Instead, I tumble, landing on all fours. That's...not good. I glance up, but Hudson isn't laughing. He's cheering me on.

"Come on, Del! Get up! You can do it!" I love him.

I give the wire a look from the ground, then push myself up and move on. I already proved enough. The tire hoop is next—suspended horizontally, four thick ropes holding it in place. This is about tumbling, I remind myself. You just have to jump through the hoop. Then land in a somersault, and ideally roll to your feet and keep moving.

I leap, and my stomach slams into the tire. I didn't leap high enough. I hear someone let out an "oof" from the sidelines, but it doesn't actually hurt much. It's rubber. But that sound—someone thinking I've screwed up, because I have—that makes me feel like an idiot. That hurt. That floods me with stupid feelings of "Why are you doing this?" and "This will never work when Hudson sees how not-masc you are" and "Don't you wish you were auditioning now?" I feel my skin burning bright red. I hope it wasn't Hudson, but I can't see and I need to focus on finishing, but I'm half through the tire, arms in front of me like Superman, feet swinging just off the ground. I grab the bottom of the tire and pull myself through that way, landing inelegantly on my back in the sand, which smells like feet.

I stare up at the sun through the trees for a moment. Ever notice how trees against the sun looks like the Milky Way? George and I like doing this after auditions—lying in the shade, staring up and blurring our eyes just enough that the light between the trees becomes huge rivers of stars, and the leaves become empty black. Day into night, back into day again.

"You can do it, Del!" someone shouts. Hudson.

I push myself up.

There's only one thing left: the Peanut Butter Pit. Why peanut butter? I almost ask it out loud. The rope is in the middle of the pit, far out of reach. I back up and take a running leap. I make it pretty far, too. My hands scrape the rope as I fall into the pit. Luckily, there's a mat down here, too. And this I don't feel bad about. Only Hudson has made it so far.

I climb out of the pit at the other end, and Hudson immediately gives me a hug and every bit of pain in me evaporates. My hands go from being on fire to...well, still being on fire, but in their desire to pull him into me. My body, which ached a moment ago, feels fine now. My muscles go from stiff to soft...except for that one part of me that goes the opposite. He smells like earth and sweat, which I know makes it sound like I have some sort of fetish, but I think it's just his sweat. His sweat smells good. Sweet and dark, and a little salty. I wish I could bottle it or make it a fancy scented candle to keep in my room and only burn on special occasions.

Who am I kidding? I'd have it burning 24/7.

"You did really great," Hudson says. Over his shoulder, I see the other campers who have gone staring at me. One of the guys, one of Hudson's exes, I think, smirks and looks away. I hold him a little tighter.

"I screwed up the tire, like I said I would."

"But you did well on the new wire. That thing is impossible, too. How'd you make it so far?" He lets go of me, but keeps one hand loosely around my waist, resting on my hip. It's like all the nerve endings in my body have migrated to that hip and are sending lightning bolts to my brain, and it takes a moment for me to realize he's asked a question.

"I focused on the end of it, not my feet," I tell him.

"Smart," he says. "I'm going to try that next time. Oh, Brad's up."

Brad messes up on the wire-walk, too, but he's the second

person to handle the Peanut Butter Pit. When he lands, he high-fives Hudson.

"That tightrope is a bitch," he says.

"Del handled it pretty well, though," Hudson says, pulling me a bit closer. I have a sudden urge to giggle, but restrain myself.

"Yeah." Brad nods, looking at me. "You've got great balance."

"Thanks," I say, smiling and desperately hoping he's not going to give me away. George said not to worry about it, and I trust George, but maybe George shouldn't trust Brad.

"From dancing?" Brad asks. I do my best confused face as my mind empties of replies.

"Ha," Hudson says. "Nah. We were dancing last night, and he's . . . not a dancer. No offense, babe."

BABE. He called me babe and now my mind is blank again. I'm just a blow-up doll here, as these two men talk about me, shoving me back and forth between delight and fear.

"No?" Brad laughs. "That's funny."

"I'm awkward," I finally say, though I have no idea why I decided to say it, or why I've said it in such a high voice.

"Nah, just a little stiff," Hudson says. "It's 'cause you're new. You'll loosen up."

I laugh, a little forced, and swallow; my throat is dry.

"At least you didn't say you'd loosen him up," Brad says, rolling his eyes. "Don't let him use lines on you, Del. He might seem smooth, but he's just as awkward as you, underneath."

"Yeah?" I ask.

"I don't think either of us are awkward," Hudson says.

"Mmm." Brad nods, looking unconvinced. "I was wondering, though, Del...is George single? He have a guy back home or anything?"

"Who's George?" Hudson asks.

"My friend," I say, a little annoyed he doesn't remember. "In my cabin, Middle Eastern, wears nail polish all the time, and sometimes eye shadow?"

"Right," Hudson says, then turns to Brad. "Really? Nail polish and eye shadow?"

"And a hairy chest, and I'm guessing a hairy ass," Brad says, wiggling his eyebrows. "And he's funny. But..." He turns back to me. "Is he single?"

"Yeah," I say. "He's single."

"Cool," Brad says, and nods a few times to himself.

"All right!" Connie shouts, walking over to us. The last of us have run the course, and she's carrying a cooler of water bottles. We each eagerly grab some. The water feels almost as good going down my throat as Hudson. His hug, I mean. "You all did well. Looks like everyone had trouble with the wire-walk, though. Balance is important! Balance is what helps with every activity—hiking, sports, dancing, getting things off high shelves. So let's go work on that. Everyone gather around and spot."

We all head toward the wire-walk and stand on either side of it. Our water bottles are empty and we throw them back in the cooler, then put our hands out, like walls for people to lean on as they try to cross the wire.

"Now," Connie says. "I put this in because even though yes, the obstacle course is a race, and yes, I will start timing you next time we do it, you still need to be patient. So every step you take needs to be careful, and you need to find your balance before you take your next one. Del, you did pretty well at it, you want to try again?"

"Sure," I say, not feeling like I have much of a choice. I pull myself up onto the wire again and find my balance, like I would before a high kick, and I take a step, focusing on the end of the wire. I go slowly. I slip once, but someone's hand catches me, and pushes me back upright.

"Thanks," I say, without looking at them. Then I keep walking. When I make it to the end, everyone claps, Connie included.

"Well done," Connie says. "Your breathing before each step, and how you lifted your leg from the hip, not the knee, was very good."

"Thanks," I say, suddenly feeling very embarrassed. "And thank you, whoever caught me."

"That was me," says the guy who smirked at me before. Maybe he's not so bad.

"Thanks," I say.

"That's what we do for each other," he says.

"Okay," Connie says. "Next up ... Brad, how about you?"

"Aw, come on, I barely tried this one," Brad says.

"Exactly," Connie says. "Up you go."

I take my place spotting and Brad gets up, trying to find his balance. He looks down at his feet and takes a step, almost falling, but is caught by a few of the other campers.

"Look ahead," I say. "To the end of the wire."

Brad raises his head and takes another step, walking carefully across the wire. He stumbles a few more times, but never falls completely off when people catch him. When he gets to the end, he looks very relieved. We all applaud again.

"It's harder for those of us who are taller," Connie tells him. "Find that center of gravity." Brad nods. "And nice advice, Del."

"Thanks," I say, and I put my hands out to spot the next person.

"Jane, you're up next."

So I screwed up the tire...but Hudson still likes me, and now maybe Connie does, too? Maybe this plan isn't just going to work, it's going to earn me respect. Maybe all these jocks are going to become my friends. Wouldn't that be a laugh?

TWELVE

After the outdoors elective, we have instructional pool time, where we're tested on our swimming and put into classes—sadly, I'm not with Hudson. And then it's lunch. Hudson and I walk in together—not holding hands, but closer than two friends would walk—and I spot George and Ashleigh right away and head toward them.

"Babe, you don't want to sit with everyone from the obstacle course?" Hudson asks.

"They had auditions today," I tell him. "I want to know how they went."

"Okay, sounds important," he says, especially when Brad walks by us, heading right for George. He laughs. "I swear, Brad doesn't get crushes often, but when he does, it's like he doesn't know what to do with himself. He goes total puppy dog."

"That's cute, though," I say, watching Brad sit next to George. George grins at him.

"I guess we're going kind of puppy dog with each other, too," Hudson says. He takes my hand, and I grin as I sit down across from George and next to Ashleigh.

"So?" I ask. "How'd they go?"

"I sang 'Let Me Be Your Star,' from the fictional musical *Bombshell* from the hit TV show *Smash*, and I knocked it out of the park," George says.

"He really did," Ashleigh says. "People applauded."

"I'm worried he's going to get Rose after all," Paz says, from the other side of Ashleigh. That's interesting, them sitting so close. Paz is cool, she's a friend, but first the bunk over George and now sitting with us . . . I look at them, then look at George, who shrugs slightly.

"I just want Kim," George says. "But I don't know how well I did at the dancing. And she is a dance role."

Hudson leans into me. "Dance role?" he asks.

"A character with a lot of dancing," I say. "I mean, most roles dance some, but Kim has a dance solo in one song and usually dances in other parts . . ."

"You know the musical?" he asks.

"Darling, it's a classic," George interjects. "There's a movie, mostly the same aside from the stupid thing with the turtle. Netflix it when you get home."

"Um, okay," Hudson says, looking at me confused.

"It's a good movie," I tell him, but without too much enthusiasm, remembering that musicals aren't his thing.

"Sure." He narrows his eyes at me, but I can't tell what it means.

"I bet you're a great dancer," Brad says to George.

"I know how to use my body," George says, batting his eyelashes. Then he frowns. "But that's not the same thing. I screwed up some of the steps."

"Hey," I say. "Don't go over it in your head. It's done. And you said yourself you sang great. Mark knows what you can do."

"Yeah," George says, nodding. "Thank you, darling. I feel better."

"How about you?" I ask Ashleigh.

"They put in some new lights. Mark showed all the techies some design schemes, and it looks fun this year. I think I'll probably be the ASM on the lights again. We'll see."

"You always run an amazing lighting set," Paz says.

Ashleigh turns to me, away from Paz, so Paz can't see. She widens her eyes. I smile and nod. She frowns, anxious.

"So, I feel like you guys are old friends," Hudson says to me. "Not like you're a new kid."

Everyone is silent for a moment.

"Ah," I say. "Well…" I can feel my brain spinning through lies, trying to figure out the best way to distract him from this idea. Do I just kiss him? That works in movies. I'd like that.

"We are," George says before I can try my plan. "We met online. I told him about this camp."

"Oh," Hudson says. "In one of those, like, coming out support groups?"

"Yeah," I say, grateful to George for being as good an improv-er as I am. "George has really helped me."

"Well, I'm glad." Hudson grins, then goes to fist-bump George. "Good mentoring, dude."

George looks at his fist suspiciously, then pats it like a wet dog.

"I'm a delight, darling," George says.

The platters of food start passing around and we each take heaps of the pasta with canned tomato sauce and powdered cheese and eat hungrily. After my workout this morning, I'm starving. As we eat, we break off into little couple pairs— Brad and George flirt, though George keeps him at arm's length. Paz talks to Ashleigh, who seems horrified anyone would want to talk to her. And Hudson talks to me. About the obstacle course, mainly, about how to get through the tire dive—it's about your knees, apparently—and the Peanut Butter Pit—which is about your knees, too, but also about trying to grab the rope earlier than you think you'll need to. I nod and tell him how the obstacle course was for me, and the whole time, our thighs are pressing together and he's smiling at me, and this is everything I've wanted every summer to be for the past four years.

After lunch, he gives me a kiss on the cheek before

heading off to archery and I go to A&C. I stand there, outside the dining hall, just smiling as he walks away, not even staring at his ass, just feeling where he kissed me. Then remembering how he kissed me last night. Then wanting to kiss him like that again.

"Darling, you look like a deer in the headlights," George says, walking past me toward the A&C cabin. I follow him.

"Seriously," Ashleigh says. "You're getting everything you want, you're practically boyfriends already. Stop acting so surprised he's into you. You made yourself into his ideal."

"I've always been his ideal," I say, following them. "Just...now he'll notice, because I ran the obstacle course this morning. Same Randy, new hobbies."

"Mmm," Ashleigh says.

"You should talk," I say as George pulls open the screen door to the A&C cabin with a creak. "Paz wants to get to know you—the way you said you were going to—and you're freaking out."

"I talked to her." Ashleigh rolls her eyes as we sit down at the circular table in the middle of the cabin. It's a big table, taking up most of the cabin, but the walls are covered in cubbies, filled with craft supplies—sequins, construction paper, string, glitter, cardboard, pom-poms, paints...everywhere you look, there's something.

"So?" George asks her. "You talked to her....Any... feelings?"

"It was, like, two conversations. She's cool. I don't know."

"Okay," George says, then turns to me. "Now, tell us about this obstacle course. Did it end in Hudson's pants?"

I laugh. "No. It was awful...but kind of cool? I did really well on the wire-walk—it's new, like a tightrope—and Connie thought I did okay. Missed the Peanut Butter Pit, though."

"Oh please, only like five people at this camp can make that," George says. "But your ruse didn't collapse? Hudson believes you enjoyed yourself?"

"I kind of did." I shrug and smile.

"More than being in the show?" Ashleigh asks.

I frown, feeling suddenly very heavy. "No. But Hudson put his hand around my waist, and he left it there."

"Marking his territory," George says, impressed. "Not bad."

"And he called me babe!"

"The straightest of all pet names, of course."

"Okay!" Marguerite says, entering the cabin in a sudden burst. Other campers are sitting around the table with us now, some I know, some new, but none from the obstacle course, thankfully, and we all look expectantly at Marguerite. Most of the counselors wear T-shirts and shorts, but not Marguerite. She's in a red dress with large white polka dots, and since last night, she's braided some red beads into her short brown bob. "Today, we're going to make what are traditionally called God's Eyes. But what is God, really? Do you believe in her? I want you to use sticks and yarn to think about the way the world watches us—especially those of us who identify as queer. Who is watching you? Is it out of protection? Or is it the cruel eye of the patriarchy?" She clasps her hands together, as if praying. "And do you watch back?" She smiles, then nods. "Go, find two sticks, about the size of your forearm, and pick out some yarn from the cubbies. You can use things besides yarn, too, if you want. Or you could use white yarn, and we could dye it with flowers!" She claps her hands. "Think about it."

She steps aside from the door, leaving us to go outside to look for sticks.

"It's cool that I'm better at all this outdoors stuff than I thought I would be, though," I say as we walk into the woods. "It's like Hudson said when he captained color wars—we can do whatever we want, if we try."

"I don't know if he means it that way," Ashleigh says, leaping up and pulling a thin twig off a branch. "Think Marguerite would be okay with a smaller God's Eye?"

"Sweetie, just tell her you think God has small eyes, which is why she can't see all the suffering in the world," I say. "She'll eat that up."

"Cool," Ashleigh says. She grins at me.

We gather our sticks, and back inside, Marguerite shows off her own God's Eye, which she calls "Panopticon" and is made of knitted wires and extension cords around sticks. We start working on our own God's Eyes as Marguerite walks the room, nodding and giving us tips.

"Thanks for that save at lunch," I tell George as I weave

glittery pink yarn around the two birch sticks I have. "Pen pals. Smart."

"Now we don't have to pretend not to be friends," George says.

"I was never going to do that," I say.

"No?" Ashleigh asks. "What if he wants you to sit with his friends at lunch tomorrow?"

"I can sit away from you guys every now and then," I say. "It's only fair we sit with each other's friends. Maybe we can join the groups. Brad likes you, George."

George sighs. "He does, doesn't he?"

"So?" I ask.

"So, he's cute. I don't know what I want. I was thinking the summer would be relaxing, that you would have enough romantic shenanigans for both of us. I just want something simple. Easy. And I don't know if Brad is it."

"Why not?" I ask.

"Different worlds. I'm not going to strip my nail polish off for him, like you did."

"Maybe he likes your nail polish," I say. "When Hudson asked about it, he said you were hot, and you made him laugh, and he didn't care about your makeup routine."

George smiles as he weaves some purple string around his sticks. "Did he?"

"Yeah," I say.

"He said he liked George's nail polish?" Ashleigh asks. "How did that come up?"

"Oh," I say, and suddenly my throat feels dry. I stare down at the sticks. "Just, Hudson thought it was funny that Brad would be into someone who wears nail polish."

"Mmmm," Ashleigh says. "This is the guy who you think will like you for who you are by the end of the summer?"

"It's only day two," I say, maybe a little too loudly. "We have to get to know each other first."

"Okay, okay," Ashleigh says. "Sorry."

"Just...it'll work," I say. "I really like him. He really likes me. We just have to talk more." I pause. "And maybe kiss more."

George laughs. "Magic lips, with lipstick that spreads the power of femme to even the butchiest among us!"

"Funny," I say, trying to sound dry, but I'm laughing, and so is Ashleigh.

"But darling, your plan is working. I'm so impressed. So is most of the camp."

"Most of the camp?" I ask.

"You think your makeover went unnoticed?" Ashleigh asks. "Do you know how many guys have asked me if you're single? And how many girls asked if you're okay?"

I laugh. "No way."

"Oh, darling, very yes. We've initiated a whisper campaign to make sure no one interferes, though."

"So everyone thinks I was hit on the head?" I ask, horrified.

"No...they know something closer to the truth than

Brad." George suddenly focuses on his yarn and sticks. "Sorry, but there were a lot of questions. But everyone is sworn to secrecy, I promise."

"And these are just the people who really recognized you," Ashleigh says.

"Oooookay," I say, taking a deep breath and looking at the center of my God's Eye, which makes me very dizzy. "Everyone knows my plan, sort of, then." Part of me is nervous—that means anyone could tell Hudson. But no one has, yet. And then part of me warms up a little. It's like I'm the star of a show everyone is watching. Better not mess up my lines, then.

"There's a betting pool over if you'll pull it off," Ashleigh adds.

"What?"

"Darling, she's kidding."

"George bet two packs of Junior Mints on you messing it up."

"I did not. She's making that up." George's eyes are wide with horror.

I look at Ashleigh. She's stone-faced, weaving her thin string over the sticks. We're silent for a minute and then she cracks a smile.

I laugh.

"That was so mean," George says, throwing a ball of yarn at Ashleigh, who laughs and throws it back.

"Art shouldn't be violent," Marguerite says calmly but

loudly. We all turn our attention back to our God's Eyes in silence for a moment.

"So what's the plan, anyway?" George asks in a low voice. "If you're already holding each other's hands and kissing?"

"Boyfriends next," I say definitively. "Then we talk more—get to really know each other. Parents, music, coming out. Everything. Then maybe more kissing. No sex, though. Not yet. Soon, though. Soon."

"You really want to get naked with him, don't you?" Ashleigh asks.

"So badly," I say.

"Four years of built-up sexual desire," George says. "Darling, I'd be impressed if you make it past tomorrow."

"Better grab some condoms from Cosmo tonight," Ashleigh says, smirking.

"And lube," George says. "More than you think you need, if you want to do anal. And clean up beforehand. In the shower, you know?"

"Unless you want to top," Ashleigh says. "Does he bottom, though?"

"He made a joke about being vers," I say. "I don't know. I'm up for anything."

Ashleigh rolls her eyes. "No erection puns, please."

I chuckle. "Whatever we do, it'll be next Wednesday. Not tomorrow." I realize my voice has become regular volume again and Marguerite is staring at me.

"What does a God's Eye see, Del?" she asks. "And what does your counselor hear that she really doesn't want to?"

"Sorry," I say.

We spend the rest of the period making our God's Eyes. George's is purple and red with bright pink sequins dotting it like stars. Mine is pink and blue, but with the glittery yarn, and Ashleigh's is tiny, made with thin string for bracelets, in every available color. Marguerite compliments our work before hanging them all from the ceiling at different heights, some low enough for her to hit her head on. "See you tomorrow," she says. "We'll be dyeing silk scarves with plants!"

After A&C, I have sports as George and Ashleigh head to the boathouse for their nature elective.

I show up just as Ryan, the sports counselor, is blowing his whistle and barely have time to say hi to Hudson before we're divided into opposite teams.

"Capture the flag, boys! And girls! And non-binary folks!" Ryan says, handing out bandannas in red and blue for us to wear to show what team we're on. Ryan thinks his baby face lets him get away with trying to be "cool" and "on our level." It's tragic. "Camp classic. You all know the rules?" He doesn't wait for anyone to answer. "Good. Let's play!" He blows the whistle again, and I scramble away from him, wondering where the border is. I watch the other campers, clearly used to Ryan's rules, and figure out it's the center of the soccer field we're on. Hudson stands on the other side of it, smirking at me, far too sexy.

"Hey," he says. "So, you gonna try stealing my flag, babe?"

I walk up to the border. "With the way you're watching me, I'm not brainless enough to try now," I say.

"But if you come over here, I can tackle you," he says, winking.

"If you want to get physical, why don't you come over to my side?" I ask. Flirting is getting easier. Maybe because, like Ashleigh said, I know he's into me, so it's not like I'm risking anything.

"It's hot," he says, and starts peeling off his shirt. His bandanna is hanging from his waist, and I try to stare at it, instead of the way his shirt peels away from his abs like it was vacuum sealed. I'm definitely licking my lips and doing that cartoonish loud swallow. He has just a little hair on his chest, and his chest and arms are defined, but still soft looking. They'd be nice to push up against.

"That's cheating," I say, when his shirt is off.

"What?"

"Causing a distraction."

"That's not a distraction," he says with a grin. "This is," he says at the exact same moment he tosses his shirt at me, covering my face as he runs by me. I laugh, but it works. I take the shirt off my face, trying not to obviously inhale his sweat, and drop it on the ground before taking off after him, but he has too big a lead. Then one of my teammates—a girl from the obstacle course—comes at him and Hudson swerves. I take a sharp turn and gain a little ground. He looks back once, both me and my teammate chasing him now, and smiles, before veering to the left, toward where our flag is lying unceremoniously in the goalie net. But even once he has the flag, he has to get it back to his side, so I go wide, anticipating where he'll have to run once he has it.

And I'm right—he grabs the flag off the ground in one swoop and turns, heading now right for me. He sees me and tries to turn, but I pounce and tackle him. He falls backward, with me on top of him.

"Ooof," he says. "Rough."

"You said there'd be tackling," I say with a shrug, sitting up so I'm straddling him, and plucking the flag from his hand. "Isn't this how the game works?" I should get up. But I don't. Hudson puts his hands on my thighs, his fingers creeping just up inside my shorts, and I can feel his body press upward between my legs.

Then Ryan whistles. "Save that for your private time, boys," he shouts at us. "And this is a touch game. No need for tackling, Kapplehoff."

"Sorry," I say, blushing furiously as I get off Hudson. A few of the other campers are staring at us.

"I need some water," I tell Hudson. "You're in jail." I point to where caught campers are waiting for a teammate to free them.

"Yes, sir," he says with a smile. "So, where's my shirt?"

"Back over there. You can come get it later."

"I will," he says, walking to the jail. I walk off the field and go over to the nearest water fountain, where I let the water spray on my face before actually drinking. I was ready to pull down his shorts right there. No wonder he always gets laid by the end of the first week. I shake my head. I can't do that. I can't be just another conquest. I didn't give up the show for a lay, no matter how pretty he is. I gave it up for love. And that means no sex. For... at least two weeks? That seems a long time. Maybe ten days. That sounds fair.

I know I should be more nervous about losing my virginity, too, but if I'm losing it to Hudson, I don't feel nervous at all. It feels right.

Once my face has cooled down, I head back to the field, where Hudson waves at me from the other side, having apparently already escaped. I smile back.

Eventually, our side wins, but it's by the end of the period, and there aren't any more tackles, sadly. After that, Hudson and I head to the free swim, where we can just swim and play in the pool, and don't have to take lessons. The water feels amazing after running around all day. Hudson and I lean against the wall, holding hands under the water.

"So, you have a fun day, babe?" Hudson asks.

"Yeah," I tell him.

"Awesome. I'm glad. And after this, we have some free time until dinner, if you wanted to hang out or something."

"Yeah," I say as George and Ashleigh hop into the pool next to us. "I'd like that."

"Awesome," Hudson says again, nodding.

"Oh, hey," Ashleigh says, looking at the other side of the pool, "Janice is on duty."

"And you're not going to talk to her," George says as Ashleigh waves at Janice. Janice waves back.

"Hey, Paz," I say, spotting her walking by us. "Come get in."

"Okay," Paz says. She hops in. She's in a black one-piece with a low neckline. She smiles at Ashleigh. "What's up?"

"We didn't ask you how you thought your audition went," George says, stepping around Ashleigh, so she's closer to Paz.

"Oh." Paz nods, her shaved head gleaming. "I mean, I think it was okay. You heard. 'Big Spender' from *Sweet Charity*. Maybe a little on the nose, but I think I did it well."

"You did," Ashleigh says, after George elbows her. "You sang really well. If they don't cast you as Rose, it'll be, like, the worst decision."

"Thanks." Paz grins, and Ashleigh smiles back, not even paying attention to Janice anymore.

George nods at me.

"So, what's that about?" Hudson asks.

I swim away a little, Hudson following. "Ashleigh has a thing for one of the straight lifeguards. We're trying to redirect her affections somewhere they'll find more ground."

"Oh," Hudson says. "That's cool. Crushes on straight people are the worst. Like... I get it. I've had a lot. But I think that's 'cause there's just more of them, you know? I don't get crushes on straight guys here."

"I don't think I've ever had a crush on a straight guy," I say, considering it. "Except for celebrities."

"Oh yeah? What are your celebrity crushes?"

"You first."

"I asked first."

"Fine... Taron Egerton," I say. I don't mention it's from seeing him in *Rocketman* with the makeup and amazing sequin jumpsuits.

"Okay," Hudson says, nodding. "Respectable choice. Little short, but cute."

"Yours?"

"Oh man. Chris Evans probably."

"Kinda basic, but understandable," I say.

"Basic?" Hudson laughs, then splashes me. "This from the guy who chose the little white dude. At least my guy sometimes wears a beard."

"Yeah, but it's not exactly original. His ass is a meme."

"So my opinion is shared by many," Hudson says with a shrug. "That just means it's a respectable choice."

I laugh. "Okay. Well, if Chris Evans ever shows up at camp, I'll make sure you don't know about it."

"Oh, what? You trying to land me?" he asks, smiling as he swims a little away from me.

"I feel like I'm doing a good job," I say, chasing.

"Maybe," he says, wiggling his eyebrows. "Maybe I really liked being tackled before."

"Yeah, I felt that."

He grins, and maybe even blushes slightly before diving underwater. Next thing I know, his arms are around my waist, and he pulls me under. I open my eyes to the chlorine-blue world of feet and bubbles and Hudson holding me close to him. I know he just pulled me under, but I'm not worried. When he kisses me, his breath is warm in mine, and the water between our lips tastes of chemicals. Then we both pop back from underwater.

"Did you two just kiss underwater?" Ashleigh asks. We're right by them again. "Gross."

I laugh and look away, and Hudson throws his arm around my waist again. "I don't think he's gross," he says.

Ashleigh rolls her eyes, and George raises an eyebrow at me.

"Oh no," I say, suddenly realizing it. "We're that couple."

Hudson turns slowly to me. "Couple?" he asks.

I feel myself turning bright red. I did just say couple. Well, that was stupid. I mean, was it, though? We're kissing and holding hands, right? But no, that's wrong. We're just kissing and holding hands. Couple is not a thing we've discussed. Except in my head, for the past four years, where I imagine him getting down on one knee and asking to be my boyfriend and everything is perfect, and later maybe we have a house in New York and I'm a Broadway star and I think maybe we have a cat and a dog, 'cause I like them both. George kicks my knee under the water, and I remember what just happened and my mouth is dry again.

"I didn't mean, like, couple couple," I say. "I just mean, like, that couple of guys who are engaging in PDA that makes everyone around them roll their eyes."

Hudson laughs. "Okay. We're that couple, then, yeah, maybe a little."

"Maybe a little more than anyone wants," Ashleigh says. Paz covers her mouth as she snorts a laugh.

"So who do we think is going to be Birdie?" George asks, trying to defuse the situation. "Jen?"

"I think Jen is going to be Albert," Paz says. "I think Montgomery for Birdie—or you?"

"Me? Darling, I don't have that sort of swagger."

"That's why I like it," Paz says. "Birdie with a fan, Birdie as a drag show."

George tilts his head, considering.

"Is that how it is in the movie?" Hudson asks, confused.

"More Elvis," I say.

"Technically, Conway Twitty was the original inspiration," George says. "But yes, it reads as very Elvis. Which is sort of a drag show itself."

"How is Elvis drag?" Hudson asks, looking like he wants to roll his eyes.

"Performative masculinity," Paz says. "Exaggerated ideas of what maleness is..." She looks at Hudson, whose brow is furrowed. "Acting butch to make fun of what masculinity is."

"I thought Elvis was just…like that?" he says.

"I think we all act a little," I say.

George raises an eyebrow at me.

"Well…okay," Hudson says, his voice getting hard. "But, like, being butch isn't drag. It's just being…like what you want to be."

"I think it has to do with how exaggerated it is. Or who it's for," Paz says. "At least, that's what we talked about in my women's studies class this year."

"I don't get it. I feel like drag and stuff like that is what straight people think gay people are, not what straight people think other straight people are."

"I don't think sexuality has to do with it, necessarily," Paz says.

"I think what straight people think queer people are shouldn't matter," Ashleigh says.

Paz barks a laugh. "True."

"Well, maybe not here," Hudson says. "But out in the regular world…" He frowns, then spots Brad across the pool. "I'm gonna go say hi to Brad," he says to me, giving me a quick kiss on the cheek before swimming away.

I frown. Did the conversation drive him off? I turn back to the three of them, who are staring at me, waiting for a reaction. I feel…angry? I shouldn't, I know. They were just saying stuff, but it felt like they were fighting with him at the end. Or maybe he was fighting with them—or was about to?

"You sure this plan is going to work?" Ashleigh asks.

"Maybe if we don't try to thrust gender theory on him on day two," I say, crossing my arms.

"Sorry," Paz says. "I know what the plan is, but I don't know the rules."

"You don't need to apologize," Ashleigh says.

I sigh and lean against the side of the pool, slinking down. "He'll come around. We just need to ease him into it. This was good. We gave him some ideas. Ease him into it."

"Are you talking to us, or yourself?" George asks.

"Both?"

I look across the pool to the deep end, where Brad and Hudson are splashing each other.

"If it makes you feel better," Paz says, "it's all nonsense, right? Butch, femme, masc, whatever...it's meaningless."

"Not to him," I say, watching Hudson.

THIRTEEN

George, Ashleigh, and Paz get out of the pool early when they spot Mark walking from the drama cabin back to the cabins up the stairs, clipboard in hand. I swim over to Hudson, and we spend the rest of the swim period splashing each other, the conversation that maybe upset him forgotten. We even kiss underwater one more time.

When the lifeguard blows the whistle, signaling the end of pool time, Hudson hoists himself out of the water next to me. We grab our towels and walk up the stairs to our cabins.

"So...," he says. "Want to hang out after dinner? Before Joan's class tonight?"

"Sure," I say, smiling. Good. Everything is still going according to plan.

"Cool," he says. "I'll see you at dinner?"

"Yeah," I say, grinning.

"Awesome," he says. At the top of the stairs, he looks around quickly, then kisses me on the lips, pulling me tight against him by the waist. I feel my mouth start to open, dying to go further, to pull off my clammy swimsuit, to pull him close, but before I can even think about any of that, he pulls away. "I'll meet you at your cabin. We can walk to dinner together."

I know I'm still grinning like a moron as I walk into my cabin. The casting sheet is hanging where it always is, next to Mark's room, and I see it before I see anything else. I even instinctively start walking toward it, wondering what I got, what my role is—maybe I'm Birdie!—before I remember I'm not on it, and turn away. George is stretched out on his bed, Paz and Ashleigh sitting on the end of it in what space he hasn't taken over.

"So?" I ask.

"I have sad news," George says, suddenly snapping open a bright pink fan and fanning himself with it. "Let them go first." He leans back dramatically onto his pillows, still fanning himself. "I'll need time to tell my tale of woe."

"Okay," I say, worried. He clearly didn't get Kim. "So..." I turn to Ashleigh.

"I'm stage manager!" she practically squeals, a huge smile of delight opening across her face. Delight does not come

138

often to Ashleigh's face, and it looks uncertain on her, nervous. I wrap her in a hug, lifting her up from the bed and into the air. "I didn't think I would. But Mark says he trusts me, and we're talking the designs he wants to implement, and I might get to make some changes if I want, and I'm just so excited."

"That's amazing," I say. "Congrats."

"I'm going to boss all those cabin eight kids around so hard."

I laugh. "I bet." I turn to Paz. "And you got Rose?"

"Of course," Paz says, brushing her shoulder. "Mark says we can even try to throw some Portuguese in, really bring some of my Afro-Brazilian-American Girl Magic to the role."

"But...," I say, turning back to George. "No Kim?"

"No," George says, still fanning himself, pouting. "He went with Montgomery, though I think casting the tall redhead is a little OBVIOUS." He shouts the last word in the direction of Mark's closed door. "I'm Harry. The dad."

I sit down next to George in what little room is left and lay my hand on his shoulder. "Maybe it's an excuse for people to call you Daddy?" I ask.

He frowns. "You're the third person to make that joke," he says, his eyes darting to Ashleigh and Paz. "It didn't make me feel better the first or second time, either."

"It's not a bad role," I say. "Lots of comedy. Two songs."

"I know, I know." George sighs. "I shouldn't be complaining. It's a nice part. Just...not the part I wanted."

"You can complain to us. We're your friends," I say. "That's what we're for."

"I just...wanted to be the ingenue, you know? Here is the only place I even have a chance at playing that, and I know I'm...this big hairy guy now. I knew it was a long shot. I just wanted to try it this year, because I feel like I'll never have the chance again. I wanted to try it. To play with that—get to bat my eyelashes and do the big innocent eyes for laughs. I think I'd be good at that."

"You would be amazing at it. And you'll get a shot, I promise," I say, squeezing his shoulder. "When we're in college, in the summer, we'll create a touring theater company, and you can be any ingenue you want. Sandy in *Grease*? Cinderella?"

"Promise?" he asks. "You're still going to be doing theater even if your butch boyfriend doesn't approve?"

"He'll approve," I say. "And yes, I promise."

George stops fanning himself, and I realize he'd been drying his eyes, fanning them to keep them from getting too teary.

"Hug?" I ask. He nods, and sits up and hugs me. After a moment, Ashleigh wraps her arms around us, too. And then Paz, which is new, but okay. Then Jen from across the bunk, and Caroline, and everyone else—a big group hug around George. I laugh.

"Okay, darlings, stop it," George says, pushing us off and snapping open his fan again. "I'm fine. And we are all going to be amazing in this show. Especially you, Montgomery," George says, pointing his fan. Everyone smiles and returns to their beds. I sit across from George, Ashleigh's feet dangling down in front of me.

"So what's the rest of the cast? Who got Birdie?"

"Jordan," George says, nodding across the cabin, at Jordan, who's talking to Jen. "Non-binary Birdie. Mark says we'll be using 'they' pronouns for Birdie and that Birdie will be a 'Ziggy Stardust type pansexual genderfluid object of lust.'"

"That's pretty cool," I say.

"Jen got Albert. That new guy, Lyle, got Hugo. Mattie got Mae, though honestly, I was sort of hoping Mark would do that role as Diana. But Mattie will be good."

"Oh yeah," I say. "That's a great cast."

"It would be better if you were in it," George says. "I bet you would have gotten Mae if you'd tried out, and we could sing 'Kids' together."

I smile, imagining it for a minute: George and I onstage, maybe George in suspenders and a cardigan, me in a fur-collared coat, back to back, complaining about the youths today. It would be fun—George and I haven't gotten to play together much onstage. Domina didn't interact with Hysterium much in *Funny Thing*, and before that we were both in the chorus. We play in exercises, of course, but never onstage. And we'd be so good together.

I feel a lump in my stomach sort of like nausea and also getting punched. I wish I were in this show. I wish I were onstage, singing my heart out with George. I want it so badly that I almost want to rush up to Hudson and tell him the truth now so I can have him and the show this summer. But that's not the plan, and the plan is in place because it's what will work. Telling Hudson I'm a crazy stalker before the week is up probably won't.

Mark's door opens and he steps into the cabin. "Everyone feeling okay about the casting now?" he asks. His eyes linger on George. Everyone nods. "I was sad not to write your name on that cast list, Del," he says to me. "But I was on the phone with my therapist for an hour last night, and he says I have to let other people make their own mistakes. I mean, decisions."

"Sure," I say, trying to smile, but I can't. Maybe it was a mistake. "It's fine."

Mark looks at me a moment, pursing his lips, before looking up at the whole cabin. "We only have a few weeks to do this, people, and you know your parts, so start learning your lines, your notes, your dance moves. I expect you to come by after dinner to rehearse, too, and use all your free time to make this the show I know it can be. Everyone excited?"

Everyone shouts yes, in unison.

"I better shower off this chlorine," I say, and go to the

bathroom to wash while they talk about the show. I can hear laughing and a little singing as I rinse my face. I try to wash away the regret, too. I knew this would happen, I should have prepared myself. It's really hitting me—I'm not in the show this summer. And I'm going to miss it. But this was part of the plan. This is to get Hudson. This has got to be worth it.

I dry off and get dressed, and by then, Mark has put on the album of *Bye Bye Birdie* and the overture is playing loudly, my bunkmates singing snatches of lyrics that go with the melodies as they pop up. Some of them dance. They're all so happy. And I'm happy for them. Just a little sad for myself.

"Um, hi?" I look over at the front screen door to see Hudson walking in. He stares at the cabin filled with campers singing and dancing, and his expression is so confused and cute, but then he spots me and he breaks into a big smile and never mind, I think. It's all worth it. And I know that sounds so dumb, but then he reaches out his hand and I wave goodbye to everyone like we're not all about to walk to the same place, and Hudson and I walk down the stairs together, just holding hands, like we've been gone for so long when it was maybe half an hour and yet in that half an hour, he missed me. He missed ME. He might finally start to feel about me the way I've felt about him for four years and who cares if I can't be in the show one summer just for that.

"So, your cabin is crazy," he says as we walk.

A swarm of tiny bugs flies by and I laugh and dodge them. "I know, they're great."

"Are you going to be able to sleep? Will they let you?"

"Of course, they have to rest their voices. And Mark is strict about them getting enough sleep."

He laughs. "Okay, so I guess you don't want to sneak into my cabin for some shut-eye, then?"

I feel a spark jolt through me at the suggestion. "I don't think we'd get much sleep that way."

He laughs again as we go into the dining hall. "We can sit with my friends tonight, right? They're mostly from the obstacle course."

"Sure," I say. "We can all sit together, maybe. I know Brad would probably appreciate sitting next to George again."

He rolls his eyes. "I still don't get that, but yeah, okay."

We find a seat with his friends and when George and Ashleigh come in, they sit next to me, blending our groups together—at least spatially. Brad and I are the only two who really talk to the theater kids and the jocks. No, that's wrong. I'm a theater kid, and Hudson talks to me, so it's only Hudson and Brad. Or I guess it's me? I guess it depends who's asking. But I try to talk to Hudson's friends, too. There's the one named Drew who I think might be his ex, but spotted me on the wire, and Sam, the girl who chased him with me during capture the flag. They seem cool. They talk about sports that I don't pay attention to, and training routines, which I can talk about but find boring. They're nice. I can hold a conversation with them. Hudson seems to like them, and he wants me to like them, so I try. And it's fine. But it's not like talking to George and Ashleigh. But why would it be? They've been my friends for years. It's easy with them. It's normal for it to be harder with new people.

Besides, they don't need to be my best friends, I remind myself. Just friendly. And we are. So it's fine, and by the time dinner is over, Hudson seems happy. We've blended our groups enough that Hudson and I can sit, thighs pressed together, and still talk to our friends. Which I think is all he wanted.

After dinner, my friends go off to the drama cabin to rehearse some more, and Hudson takes me by the hand and leads me to the boathouse porch. We're the first ones there, and no one else tries to follow us in, though we can hear people walking by below us. The porch has a love seat that faces the water but is out of sight from anyone walking by because of how far back it is, and we sit down there, holding hands.

"So," I say after listening to the water for a while. "About that 'couple' thing I said during pool time..."

"Don't worry about it, babe," he says, leaning his head on my shoulder. "I mean, between last night, and the obstacle course, and capture the flag, and two dinners, and all the time in the pool...this must be like date five by now. Totally normal to call us a couple."

"Oh?" I ask. "You saying you want to be my boyfriend?"

"Maybe," he says, lifting his head and grinning at me. He kisses me softly on the lips. "What benefits would I get as your boyfriend?" He kisses me again, deeper, our tongues coming out, his hands around my waist, pulling me on top of him.

He must do this every summer, he's so good at it. Five dates in one day, making out, me already crouching over his lap.

"So we can be boyfriends," he says. "We're ready for that, right? I mean, really, we haven't done enough making out, considering we're on date five. I mean, that's a good date to get naked on, right?" His hand slips up my shorts—farther than it's ever been, and I gasp as he finds my briefs. His thumb slips under those and touches my hip bone. I never realized before what a pleasure center the hip bone is, but it's like he just pressed a button and I'm flooded with joy and lust and color—pink, mostly—and I can feel my eyes rolling back in my head. He pulls me forward and kisses my neck, his other hand roaming up the front of my shirt. I want to be naked with him so badly. I've wanted it for years. I want to do everything with him, but this is too easy, too smooth. This is Hal, and I want Hudson. I take a deep breath and roll off him so I'm sitting next to him again.

"That's all true," I say, looking into his eyes. They're gray with flecks of blue, and in the light of just the one bulb over the porch, they glow. "It is like five dates, and I really like you."

"I like you, too," he says, grinning and putting his hand on my leg, creeping it up my thigh again. "I've actually never felt so connected to someone so quickly."

Every part of me wants to believe that's true. And maybe it is. I'm sure it is. That's why my plan will work. Because we have this connection—one that goes through Del, and gets right to Randy—I know we do. But I don't know if he really believes it yet, or it's just a line from Hal. So I put my hand over his, interlacing our fingers and stopping its roaming.

"But we also would have talked more. Gotten to know each other," I say.

"Okay," he says, squeezing my hand. "So...what do you want to know?"

"I don't know...about parents, coming out, your favorite movies or music?"

He nods, thinking about it. "Let's start with those last two, then. I really like the John Wick movies, and before we got here, I was listening to a lot of the new Walk the Moon album. You?"

"Oh," I say, surprised, for some reason, that he's so willing to just talk. And a little disappointed. I was hoping he'd push for more making out. Also, I don't know Walk the Moon, and I'm concerned I will be tested now. "Well, I…" Damn. My favorite movies are all musicals, my favorite music is all show tunes…But I don't want to lie, either. "Do you know Audra McDonald?" I ask.

He shakes his head. "She a pop singer?"

"She does a lot of genres," I say. Not lying.

"See, the thing that sucks about camp is no phones. I can't look her up to play some. At the end of the summer, when you have your phone back, you'll play her for me?"

I grin. He just said end of the summer. Like we'll still be together at the end of the summer. Everything is working.

"Yeah," I say. "So now you come up with a question."

He smiles and squeezes my hand in his. "Okay…what do you want to be when you grow up?"

The words *an actor* almost come dancing out of my mouth from sheer muscle memory of that being the answer I've given to this question since I was six. I laugh instead, to give myself time. What does Del want to be? I shouldn't say athlete. I shouldn't lie that much.

"I'm not sure," I say instead. "I think…" Don't lie too much. "I want to tell stories."

"Like a writer?"

"No, I don't think I'm good enough at writing for that. I like to read, but…I don't know. I'm hoping I'll figure it out later."

He nods. "I get that. And I like to read, too! My favorite

book is *Shoeless Joe*. It's like...older than I am. By a lot. But my dad gave it to me when I was little and I just loved it."

"What's it about?"

"Baseball...America. The way sports can sort of live on, I guess? Or players can, and plays and games?"

"That's cool." I grin. Sports can live on the way good theater does, I think but don't say. "I think my favorite book is probably *Finishing the Hat*. It's an autobiography by Stephen Sondheim."

"Who's that?"

I do my best acting to date by not slapping him. He'll learn, I remind myself. I'll teach him.

"He's a storyteller," I say, though that's barely scratching the surface. "But you never answered your own question—what do you want to do after school?"

"So, I don't know exactly," he says with a shrug. "I want to try to be an Olympian, maybe, like Connie was. Track and field. But I know that's a long shot, and I know it wouldn't be, like, a career. But maybe I could coach after or be a trainer in a gym? I know it doesn't sound like much, but I like encouraging people."

I nod. That sounds perfect for him. "Like when you encouraged me on the obstacle course," I say.

"Yeah." He grins. "I like doing stuff like that. I like helping people...be better. Making people feel like they can do stuff. And I like being physical. So training, coaching...I think I'd like that."

"Well," I say, "since you answered some questions, I think maybe we can get a little more physical ourselves now." I lean closer to him.

"Oh yeah?" He does that thing where he smiles and the tip of his tongue finds the space between his teeth.

"You said we had to do more of both, right?"

"Okay," he says, wrapping his arm around my waist, his finger sliding under my shirt. "A kiss per question."

"We'll work out the exchange rate," I say, leaning in.

FOURTEEN

We're late to the meeting hall for Joan's queer history lesson. Not just a few minutes, either, but ten minutes, and she's already showing a PowerPoint presentation. But at least I feel like we're bonding a little more. Yes, we did more kissing and question asking, but we kept our pants on (though not our shirts) and we did talk some. His mom's name is Lois, and she's a real estate broker, and his dad is Sam, a foreman. His mom's parents both came over from Korea when they were kids and met and got married here; his dad's great-grandparents fled pogroms in the Ukraine. He has a dog named Rufus. His favorite TV show, when he's not watching "the game" (I didn't ask what sport this meant, so possibly it means all of them?), is *The Simpsons*. I didn't have to lie about anything—I told him I liked watching old

Parks and Rec episodes on Netflix, and that seemed butch enough, and I definitely didn't make up parents or anything. So all still on track—but with bonus make-out sessions! And I think we're boyfriends now? We never clarified that point, but it feels like we were agreeing to it. I should have asked about that and done less kissing.

And also paid attention to the time. Joan sighs as we sneak in and take a seat in the back.

"As I was saying." She clicks something and the screen behind her, the only light in the otherwise dark amphitheater of a cabin, changes to show people in suits and dressed from the 1950s or maybe 1960s. It's a black-and-white photo and everyone is well dressed, wearing sunglasses, and holding up signs that say things like HOMOSEXUALS ARE AMERICAN CITIZENS TOO and GOVERNMENT POLICY CREATES SECURITY RISKS.

"These are from the first gay protest outside the White House, in 1965. The papers didn't cover it. No one paid attention. But there were queer rights organizations before Stonewall. The one that organized this protest was called the Mattachine Society. They were founded in the early fifties, so don't let anyone tell you we haven't been trying to get equal rights for very long, or that we're a new thing." She clicks and the PowerPoint cycles through more faces, and she talks about the history of the groups. My first year, I thought the history lessons felt a little out of place for a summer camp, but I've come to like them. I wish Mark gave them, instead of Joan, so they'd have a bit more flair, but Joan cares about this stuff, and she finds interesting little details—like today's lecture. The Mattachine Society (which started as all men) and the Daughters of Bilitis, their sister organization, two "homophile" organizations, as they called themselves, that tried to campaign for queer rights with sip-ins, where they went to bars and asked for drinks and told the bartender they were queer—which, legally, meant they couldn't even drink back then. They very politely would drink, and leave.

"The idea was that they would show everyone that queer people were normal and respectable, not terrifying sexual perverts like the newspapers often made them out to be. And to that end, they trained themselves to be 'normal'— there's one story of a meeting at the Daughters of Bilitis where a woman who had previously had a short haircut and dressed in jeans and a leather jacket showed up in a dress and walked in heels, and everyone applauded, so happy they'd changed her."

I swallow and look at Hudson, who's watching the screen. The light makes his skin pale. He nods slightly.

Joan continues her lecture, telling us all about pre-Stonewall gay liberation movements of the fifties and sixties. When she finishes, she takes questions, and Ashleigh raises her hand.

"Was she happy, though?" she asks. "The woman who changed from jeans to dresses?"

"I don't know," Joan says. "Probably she was harassed by

police less, and fit in the straight society more, which would have made life a lot easier, and probably a lot safer from harassment and violence. But safer and happier don't always go hand in hand. It's a choice that a lot of us have to make—when to come out, who to come out to. You've all thought about it, I'm sure. As for her dress... I imagine it might have felt like a costume. You're all at that age where you're trying on identities anyway, so I don't know if you understand what it's like to be told there's a right and wrong way to be queer, and the right way looks just like being straight, yet probably some of you do."

"But there is no difference," someone in front says. "That's the whole point of what we're fighting for—equal treatment because we're all the same."

Joan nods. "Well, we're all people, deserving of respect and equal treatment. But straight people aren't all identical. Some straight women do wear jeans." The crowd chuckles. This is the closest Joan has ever gotten to a joke. "But it's different for a lesbian to wear jeans than it is for a straight woman. So maybe the equality we're fighting for isn't just marriage or the ability to not be fired from our jobs for being queer—which is still perfectly legal in over twenty-five states, by the way—but the ability to be whoever we want, jeans, skirts, makeup, heels, beards, whatever, and still be treated like anyone else."

"Is it possible the woman in jeans was trans?" asks someone else.

"Sure." Joan nods. "Again, I don't know. But I'd imagine that a lot of this idea of 'fitting in' hurt trans people who at the time identified as gay or lesbian because they didn't have the language for it. Of course, trans people existed before Stonewall, too, but the terminology was different...and the subject of next week's lesson, I think, since we're out of time now."

Joan flicks the lights on, causing momentary blindness in everyone as they flinch and wait for their eyes to readjust.

"Have a good night!" she calls out as we start to leave the cabin. "Sweet dreams."

Hudson and I walk out together, hand in hand. I feel like I should ask him about what he thought of the lesson, but I'm also afraid of his answer. I don't want him to say he thinks it was good that the woman could walk in heels. I don't think he will. He's not a bad guy. But I also don't know. I've never thought to ask why he only likes masc guys. George says it's a preference, like having a thing for blonds, or like Brad's love of body hair. A fetish, kind of. And that's okay. It's normal to have things you're into. But hearing about the way they treated that woman made me wonder if he would have clapped for her, too. 'Cause there's a difference between being into something in a person and thinking a certain type of people are better.

"So," he says, when we stop at my cabin. "I'll see you tomorrow, right?"

"Yeah," I say.

"I had a really good time tonight. It was a good fifth date."

I laugh. "Yeah. It was really good. I'm looking forward to dates six, seven, eight, and . . . nine? Tomorrow."

"Nine. That's awfully presumptuous." He smiles at me, leaning back against the wall of my cabin.

"You're right, I'm sorry. Want to hang out again tomorrow night, after dinner?" I ask.

"Yes," he says, smiling so widely, I swear his teeth are glowing. I lean forward and kiss him, and he wraps his arms around me, pulling me closer, his hands straying up the back of my shirt.

"Oh my god, are you two boyfriends yet?" Ashleigh asks, suddenly beside us. Hudson pulls back, looking a little sheepish.

"Yes," I say. "I was giving my boyfriend a good-night kiss," I say, raising my chin a little. Ashleigh rolls her eyes.

"That was more than one kiss," George says. He's next to her, fanning himself with a different fan, this one rainbow. "But if you want to keep going, I'm sure your audience wouldn't mind." He gestures with his fan at the campers walking around us, several of whom are staring at us. I feel my cheeks turning bright red and hope it's dark enough it doesn't show.

"Okay," I say, turning to Hudson. "Good night."

"Good night, babe," he says, pecking me on the cheek before he walks away.

"You two have got to get it under control," Ashleigh says as we walk into the cabin. "You're going to end up screwing in front of the flagpole with everyone watching. Unless that's your thing? No judgment if you're an exhibitionist, but you should probably find some consenting voyeurs."

"I'm not an exhibitionist," I say, maybe louder than I should, as a few of our bunkmates turn to look at me. I flop down on my bed. "And I don't think he is."

"It wasn't on his dating profile," George says, slipping his shoes off and taking out his nightgown. He slips it over his clothes and with a few quick movements removes his T-shirt and shorts from underneath.

"Yeah," I say. "What did it say, do you remember? Just, like, masc4masc, or...was it...worse than that?"

"Having doubts about your dream man?" Ashleigh asks.

"Just...after tonight's lecture. I thought it was a preference, but..."

"It didn't say 'no fats, no femmes, no blacks,' if that's what you're worried about," George says. "It was something like 'masculine guy seeking the same.'"

"Okay. So it's just a preference," I say.

"If it said *no* something, that would be bad," Ashleigh says, getting out her toothbrush. "That's exclusionary. Like, 'no fatties' is bad, but 'prefers fit women' is okay, I think?"

"Feels like a fine line," Paz says, hopping into her bunk. "What if it said they like 'white guys'? That's not far from 'whites only.'"

"Yeah," Ashleigh says. "You're right, sorry."

"But what about, like, guys into body hair?" I ask. "That's not bad, right?"

"Historically, people with body hair haven't had to use separate water fountains," Paz says dryly.

"Right," I say. "Sorry."

"When I see a profile that says they prefer skinny twinks," George says, "I know I won't ever stand a chance with that guy. But when it says 'no Middle Eastern guys,' then it feels like I'm being rejected for who I am, my identity. Hairy isn't such a huge part of my self-worth. But being Middle Eastern, being Jewish? That's about me. And saying you're rejecting all that preemptively because it doesn't get you hard? That's racist. Your dick is racist, and so are you, and you really shouldn't be putting that online. It's tacky."

Paz laughs. "Yeah, what he said."

"Okay," I say. "But that's not about masc or femme. That's behavior. That's mutable. I mean, I changed, right? Like the woman putting on heels. So…it's not bad, right? Like…would Hudson have applauded when that woman walked in heels? Or would he have said it's better to be herself, even if I—the lesbian version of Hudson, I guess?—am not into her in a leather jacket and jeans?"

"You mean if you were here, where it was safe to wear the jeans and not get harassed for it?" Paz asks.

"What he means," Ashleigh says, "is would he think it was okay you went butch for him, because that means it'll be okay when you drop it later." She turns to me. "But we don't know him as well as you do." She sticks her toothbrush in her mouth and starts to brush. "You ashk him."

"What do you think?" George asks.

"I think...," I say. "I think it's just a preference. I think he'd tell that woman to be herself, because being herself has nothing to do with attracting femme-only women or something."

"So you think he'd tell you to be yourself," George says.

"Only if I was willing to give him up," I say quickly. Maybe defensively. "And I'm not. But he wouldn't think putting on the dress made her a better person. Just more attractive to people who like girls in dresses. And there's nothing wrong with that, right?"

"I mean, we could say you should be attracted to a person's character, not their wardrobe," Paz says.

"Oh please," George says. "I judge men entirely by the contents of their closets. And their drawers," he adds, wiggling his eyebrows.

I snort a laugh and stand up and take my toiletries into the bathroom. I brush my teeth and wash my face and stare in the mirror for a moment after, my face wet. I look different from last year. I look like what Hudson is attracted to. That was the point. I put on heels for him. And it's worth it. Tonight definitely showed me that—he's kind and fun, and I want to keep kissing him forever. It's just a preference, him liking this me, and not the chubby, long-haired Randy with flowers in his hair and lace on his shorts. After all, he likes me. Not just my face, body, wardrobe. We've talked. He thinks I'm special, that we have a connection. And if a haircut was what it took to show him that, then it's worth it. And once he sees it, he won't mind if my hair grows back or if I love musicals or paint my nails. Heels or jeans, maybe Paz is right. It's about falling in love with a person—preferences are just things that make us think we're more or less likely to fall in love because of what our dicks react to at first. So I made his dick hard. Now we can fall in love. And love is more important. And I'm falling wildly in love with Hudson.

The next day goes by like the last one: We hike instead of doing the obstacle course, Hudson and I holding hands when we can, we eat lunch together, and I hear about rehearsals from Ashleigh and George during A&C (George has already mastered his song and is having fun with it, Ashleigh made suggestions about changing the lighting scheme that Mark liked, and apparently Crystal's choreography is panic-inducingly ambitious this year), and then we play kickball during sports. Then we all swim together, Hudson wrapping his arms around me and putting his head on my shoulder to talk to Brad in the pool. Then Hudson and I steal some time at the boathouse to make out, our hair still wet and smelling of chlorine, before running back to our cabins to change and head down to dinner, which we eat thigh to thigh before it's time for that night's activity: a campfire by the flagpole where we all take turns telling ghost stories and making s'mores. I sit on a log, and Hudson sits in front of me, and I wrap my arms around him like he did to me in the pool, and I feel warm and happy.

True, I am ready to get naked with him already. And I know he is, too. But that's not part of the plan. So we stick to making out—though we're learning to hide it better, to avoid the eye-rolling from other campers.

The day after that, at the boathouse, his hands slip down the back of my swim trunks as I straddle him, and I feel his hands squeeze my bare ass for the first time. The day after that, lying down on the love seat, I feel our erections press against each other, instead of just our legs, for the first time. Every new thing our bodies do brings with it a heady light-ness in my body, like I'm being thrown out of my own body because it's so crazy it's happening—really happening. Hudson Aaronson-Lim is my boyfriend. Hudson Aaronson-Lim is falling in love with me. This is better than a musical. A musical is just pretend. This is real.

Except that I'm not. Which I remember the next night, after dinner, when he turns to me, our hands interwoven as we walk out of the dining hall, and asks, "So what do you want to do?"

"Me?" I ask. "I don't know. What do you like doing?"

"Oh, come on, you've been here a week, you're not new anymore. You pick the date-night activity."

I smile on the outside, but inside I am feeling the sheer panic of being onstage when a spotlight pops on and you've forgotten the opening lyrics. I was not prepared for this—he's supposed to be the one showing me the ropes, doing butch stuff. I know what I'd want to do—go hang out at the drama cabin and maybe paint each other's nails, but that is definitely not what he'd want to do, and not what Del would want to do. What do butch guys do on dates, anyway? It's been mostly wandering around camp and him showing me stuff, then going to the boathouse to make out so far, and I've been enjoying that quite a bit, especially the latter part. I suppose I can't just say "Let's go right to the boathouse," though. Or "Let's go watch sports," 'cause there's no TV, and there's not even a game going at the kickball field.

"So?" he asks.

"I was looking to see if there was a game." I nod at the kickball field.

"Nah, let's keep it just us," he says.

Right. Sexy butch date. Intimate butch date. I go through the sporty camp things to do that aren't team related—archery, hiking, tennis. TENNIS.

"How about I show you how to play tennis?" I say. This could be terrible, of course. He said he was bad at tennis, and I've gotten okay at it, but I suspect his definition of *bad* and mine of *okay* might be on completely different scales. "We can work on your serve."

He grins. "Okay."

We walk over to the tennis court, me going over serving form in my head. He gets out the tennis equipment.

The court is empty, so we stand next to each other on one end, Hudson looking at me expectantly in the light from the lampposts around the court.

"Right," I say. "So...this is, um, a..." And the name for the long stick with the round bit with the grid of wire or string or something is completely gone. I shake it like I'm doing jazz hands, like it's all very exciting.

"Racket?" Hudson asks, raising an eyebrow.

"Yes. That. And this is a ball!" I bounce the tennis ball on the court and it flies upward at an odd angle before I can catch it, rolling away to the other side of the court. Hudson eyes it suspiciously.

"I thought you said you were good at this," he says.

"Well...I don't know about good," I say. "I mean, I can hit the ball with the..." I swallow. "Racket." Phew. "Sometimes."

Hudson laughs. "Are you messing with me?" he asks, stepping closer and putting his hands on my hips, his thumbs finding the space between my skin and my clothes, just under the waistband, and gliding back and forth.

I look down at his hands and my mind is blank. Well, not blank. It's just been invaded by one thing. And it isn't tennis.

"Maybe we should just go to the boathouse," I say, my voice breathy.

He laughs, stepping back. "Uh-uh. You're showing me how to improve my serve. Come on." He takes a ball, throws it into the air, and slams it—right into the net. "See? I always do that."

"Okay," I say, stepping behind him and letting my hands run over his shoulders. He presses his back into me, his whole body warm, my body warm. I have a sudden urge to just start nibbling on his ear, to lick down his neck, to keep going, taking his shirt and pants off so I can have him right there on the tennis court.

But no. I have to hold back! I won't be a two-week conquest! He's not going to be Hal for me.

"So, do you like tennis?" I ask, adjusting his shoulders and the way he holds the racket. "Do you play much?" Turn the conversation less sexy. Then I won't be as quick to give in. Get to know him, get him to fall for me. That's the plan.

"I don't know. I think I like stuff where I'm really competing with myself more," he says. "That's why I like the obstacle course. I actually really love track and field. I'm on the varsity team."

"Yeah?" I say, impressed, as though I don't already know this. I try to bend his arm for a volley, keeping it raised. His skin is so warm, it's intoxicating. I pull my hand back.

"Yeah. So tennis always seemed less my thing. How about you? Why did you get into it?"

"They have dogs that retrieve the balls," I say without thinking.

He laughs and turns to look at me. "What?"

"There are these videos online, they train dogs to retrieve

164

the balls when they go out of bounds," I say. It's the truth. It was my second-favorite discovery when googling sports, after some of the really fun uniforms they have out there. Well, third-favorite, if you count the men in the uniforms. Fourth-favorite if you count the men out of the uniforms. But a top five, for sure.

"So you're into tennis 'cause of the dogs?"

I shrug. "I mean…sort of?" *I'm into tennis because I wanted a sport because I'm into you!* I almost tell him, but that would give it all away. "I like the way you have to watch, I think," I say, trying to come up with something. "You have to read your opponent, find out what they want to do, and then give them a variation on that—something where they think they know what's happening, but then it goes all sideways." There—that's kind of like theater, like how actors play. That's true. That's Randy…through a Del filter.

"So you like competing against people," he says.

"I guess." I shrug.

"That's cool. I think they're both good ways of improving yourself, you know. Making yourself better."

I nod. "That's why you got into sports?"

"I mean…sort of," he says, stretching his arms up and looking at the sky. "So, I always liked running around and stuff. I was always an active kid. And my dad loves sports—they were always on. Not just baseball and football, but like track meets, the Olympics, snowboarding. And he was always trying to get me into them, too, and I had all this energy, so, like, being in Little League was fun, sure, but it also was something to do and my dad would always cheer from the stands—'That's my boy' kinda crap, y'know?"

"Yeah." I nod.

"So I just did it. But I never loved Little League like I do track. Baseball, you have a team, other guys you have to rely on to throw you the ball..."

There's a long pause as I can sense him swallowing something.

"They don't like a queer kid on their team?" I ask.

He shrugs. "Kinda. I mean, they never called me a fag or anything, but...they used that word a lot."

I shake my head. "I don't like that word."

"Yeah," he says, looking up again so I can't read his face. "Me neither." His voice is weird, a little cold. But then he looks back at me, all charming smile. "Did you have trouble when you came out?"

I shrug. "I mean, some. Mostly people just ignore me."

"You said that before, and I still can't imagine it," he says, his eyes running up and down me.

I blush. "Well, I'm quiet at school. I mean, I'm out to some people, and I don't lie when people ask, but...people figured it out. Not much changed, though. No one was careful to stop using *gay* as a bad word or anything. Once someone wrote *fag* on my locker. My parents got so mad, stormed the principal's office. They found out who did it and suspended him. Since then, mostly they leave me alone. Dirty looks, laughing...as long as I don't stare at anyone, keep my head down, though..."

"Wow, that's cool your parents were so...good."

"Your parents aren't?"

"Well, there was that thing with a swim class once. None of the other guys, a lot of them from the baseball team, would get in the pool, said they'd catch my gay, didn't want me staring at them or copping a feel underwater, stuff like that. This is when I wasn't really out yet. Like, I knew, and someone had caught me looking at pictures of Instagram thirst traps on my phone in study hall, so everyone else kind of knew, but no one was talking about it to me. Until this swim class. And then everyone knew. I could have denied it, I guess, but I didn't. I told them I was just going to swim alone, then, get my gay all over the water as I practiced for the swim race at the end of the semester. That was my coming out to the school. Kinda like yours. Oh, but I came in first place in the race."

"And your parents didn't care? Were you out to them?"

"Yeah, I was. But they just asked me what I'd done to get those guys' attention. Told me not to flaunt my sexuality."

"They blamed you." I feel myself glaring at shadows behind him that could be his parents.

"Not blamed," Hudson says quickly. "I mean, they're not bad people, just...." He sighs. "They're parents. They want to protect me."

"Yeah."

"Anyway, that's part of why I run alone. Challenge myself. Make myself better. No one to let you down with homophobia if you run alone. And they don't get to win as many games as they would if I were on the baseball team."

"Serves them right," I say.

"Yeah. And speaking of serves . . . aren't you going to help me with mine?" He turns around, sticking his ass out at me. "Is this the right form?"

I step up behind him and reach around, taking his arm and pull him back a little, our bodies flush. He feels so good against me. He smells so good.

He pushes his ass into me. I grab his hips and push back. He takes in a sharp breath, lets out a soft half moan.

"That doesn't feel like the right place to hold your racket," he says, and I laugh and step back. What were we doing? Serving, right. Tennis serving, not serving looks or anything. 'Cause we're masc.

Actually, I am good at serving, I remember. It's a dance move, hands over the head, then bring them down, but wrist at an angle, like when you want to show jazz hands to the audience.

"It's all in the wrist," I tell him, reaching around and taking his wrist in my hand. I lean my head on his shoulder and lower my voice as I shape his arms. "You want to keep your wrist higher, so the angle isn't so severe, like this," I say. Our bodies are pressed together, and he keeps pushing further back into me.

"Okay," he says. We both stand there for a moment, interlocked, before I take a step back.

"So try," I say.

He serves, this time whisking the ball over the net. "I did it!" he says. He takes another ball from the ground and serves again, and again gets it over the net. "Wow. Babe. That... actually really helped." He turns around, smiles at me. "I thought you just suggested it so you could wrap your arms around me."

"Can I not do that without a tennis lesson?" I ask.

He smiles, stepping toward me. "You can do whatever you want," he says in a low voice, before kissing me. His arms wrap around me, and our tongues find each other. He bites my lips slightly—new, but surprisingly enjoyable. I gasp and he moves away from my lips to my ear.

"Want to go to the boathouse?" he asks in a whisper.

"Absolutely."

On Friday, we run the obstacle course again, and I make it through the tire swing, and even grab on to the rope swing over the Peanut Butter Pit—though I don't make it across. Hudson says I did a good job, though, and kisses me on the cheek. I've been trying to get myself ready for today. The end of the first week, the time when Hudson usually invites his boyfriends to the Peanut Butter Pit after dark, where they finally get naked, and I would love to finally get naked with him, but I know I have to say no. I have to show him I'm more than just a fling. And I have a plan figured out. When he asks me if I'm ready, I'm going to say I want to talk more first—and then ask him about the most unerotic thing I can think of—coming out to his parents.

"Hey, Del?" Brad taps me on the shoulder as we watch the other campers run the obstacle course. "Can I talk to you for a second?"

"Sure," I say. Is this where he warns me what Hudson means when he invites me here tonight? Tells me to bring condoms? That would be quite a system, but it wouldn't surprise me.

He pulls me away from Hudson, who shrugs and goes back to watching the other campers.

"What's up?" I ask Brad, when we're out of earshot of everyone else. Has he finally figured out I didn't bump my head?

"It's about George," he says.

"What?" For a moment, panic floods me like cold water. Did I miss something with George? Is he angry at me? Did he lose his voice? "What's wrong with George?"

"Nothing." Brad grins. "At least... I don't think anything. But I feel like we've been flirting now for a week, and he's funny, but he's not like... I don't know if he's really into me. I mean, look at you and Hudson—you guys have been boyfriends for the entire time he and I have just been flirting. Is he really into me? Or should I give up on this?"

"I know he thinks you're cute," I say carefully. No one has ever come to me for romantic advice before. But I guess having a boyfriend makes you an expert. Especially when you came up with a plan to get him. "George wants something easy," I say. That's what George had said.

"I can be easy," Brad says, smiling.

"Not like that," I say. "He just...he wants someone he can be himself around, and I think he's worried that you'd want him to..."

"Be someone completely different?" Brad raises an eyebrow at me, and puts his hands on his hips. "Wonder where he got that idea."

"So you know it wasn't a bump on the head," I say. I take a deep breath. He hasn't told Hudson yet, so that's good.

"I'm not an idiot. And hey, you do what you want. I thought you were cool before. You killed that song last year, what was it? 'Dirty Old Man'?"

"Yeah?" I find myself smiling, remembering it.

"But if this is the new you, that's cool, too. As long as you're not doing it to mess with my friend."

"No," I say quickly. "No. I just wanted him to notice me."

"Well...you got that. Now how do I get George to notice me?"

"You won't tell Hudson?" That would throw everything off. He likes me now, he's into me, and maybe he could even see me under the glittery trappings if he knew, but it would be too much, too sudden. I need to make him love me first.

"I'm not blackmailing you," Brad says, looking annoyed. "I'm asking. If you don't want to tell me, that's fine. I get it."

"No." I shake my head. "Sorry. George thinks you're cool, and cute, and I think you just need to show him you like him for him, and you don't care if he wears makeup or has an extensive fan collection. Or just tell him that. Ask him out. Stop flirting, and make a move. Make it easy for him."

Brad nods. "Okay," he says. "Thanks, man." He goes in for a hug, and I hug him back. "And for what it's worth, Hudson really likes you. But maybe he's the one person at camp who really has a right to know who you used to be?"

"He will," I say. "Once I know I'm not just one of his two-week romances. Once we're . . ." I let the sentence fade.

"Oh." Brad nods. "Playing for keeps. Okay. Good luck."

"Thanks. And there's no real difference, you know. Between Randy and Del. I'm still me."

Brad looks me up and down before nodding. "I get what you mean, but if you really want Hudson . . . if you want him to fall for you—for Randy—then you have to tell him, right? Because if there's really no difference, he won't mind."

"Right," I say. Which is true. Except . . . not yet. Playing for keeps, like Brad just said. And that means winning first, getting Hudson to fall. Then it won't matter. Then he'll have seen me—the most important parts of me—and the other stuff, theater, glitter, sports—all of that will be unimportant and he'll love me with nail polish or without. I'll tell him, and he'll laugh and say, "None of that matters. I know *you*. And you're special."

If I tell him too soon, though, he'll tell me I'm a liar and never want to speak to me again. So I have to go slow.

"Thanks," I say to Brad.

Brad runs back toward the group and I follow slowly. Hudson turns to me and grins, extending his hand for me to take when I'm close.

"So, what was that about?" he asks quietly.

"He just wanted some advice."

"Advice? On what?"

"Looooooove, obviously. From me, the looooooove expert."

"You're such a nerd, babe." He laughs, resting his head on my shoulder.

"A love nerd."

"So he's still into George?"

"Yeah."

"What did you tell him?"

"To tell George he's not just flirting, that he really likes him."

He lifts his head up and looks at me. "You think they'll really work?"

"Sure."

"They're so different."

"So what? We're not the same."

"We're more similar than them."

I shrug. "I don't know."

"Please don't start wearing nail polish," he says, and it's like a sudden punch to the throat.

"Why not?" I ask, my voice coarse.

"I dunno. I just...like you like you are. A regular guy."

"Would nail polish really make a difference?" I try not to make it sound like begging. I know it's early in the plan, but this has to work. All of it, including turning back into Randy. And it will, I tell myself, closing my eyes for a moment. It will, it will, it will....

"Nah," he says, leaning his head on my shoulder again. I sigh, relieved. "I don't know. It's not like you're going to start wearing it, right?"

"Right," I say, watching one of the first-year kids leap for the rope over the Peanut Butter Pit and miss. Not yet, anyway.

FIFTEEN

H onestly, I'm a little offended," I tell George and Ashleigh that night after a camp-wide scavenger hunt, where cabins were teams, so I wasn't with Hudson, sadly. "Isn't the first Friday when he normally asks a guy to go to the Peanut Butter Pit with him?"

"But you said you wanted to take it slow," Ashleigh says.

"Well, yeah," I say.

"Darling, your plan is working. He's treating you like a real boyfriend, not a fling. You said you wanted to wait until week two, right?" George lies on his stomach, painting his nails a new color he found over the year. It's called Unicorn Trampoca-lypse, and it's prismatic glitter with pink, purple, and navy, and I have never wanted anything on my fingers so badly. He already promised he'd paint mine with it when I start wearing it again.

"Maybe ten days."

"Isn't that closer to his schedule?" Ashleigh asks. "His usual one?"

George snorts. "Getting a little tired of waiting?"

"Yes," I say, leaning back. "Really tired of waiting."

"Well, the next step in your plan is love, not sex, so you'd better take the scenic route as you get into his pants. Can you do my right hand?"

"Sure," I say, moving to his bed and taking the nail polish from him. I carefully fill in the nails on each of his spread fingers, watching the polish sparkle in the light. I look at my own hands—unpainted nails, skin rubbed raw from rocks and the rope swing. I'm a little proud of it, of how well I've adapted to this role, and how well I'm playing it. But I do wish I could sparkle again like Unicorn Trampocalypse.

"Besides, we don't know for sure it's Friday," George says. "Maybe it's tomorrow. Maybe he sneaks into your cabin tonight to whisk you away."

"Yeah," I say, moving on to his next nail. "You're right. I'm being silly."

"You're being horny," Ashleigh says.

"Who's horny?" Paz asks, coming back from having brushed her teeth in the bathroom and launching herself into her bunk, then immediately wincing.

"No one," I say at the exact same time as Ashleigh and George say, "Randy."

"There's a terrible pun there," Paz says, rubbing her shoulder.

"Which thankfully no one has made yet," I respond, my voice arch as I paint the last of George's nails.

"What's wrong with your shoulder?" Ashleigh asks Paz.

"I fell during the choreography for 'Shriners' Ballet' today. Crystal has me literally jumping over two of the Shriners' outstretched arms to be caught by another. He didn't catch me very well today."

"Ouch."

"I mean, I'm happy the dance isn't a bunch of dumb sex jokes, and now it's more about me beating them up, though. And at least I don't have to run up a wall, like Jordan does during 'Honestly Sincere.' I think Crystal was high when she came up with the dancing this year."

"I'm actually sort of happy I didn't get Kim," George says softly. "Montgomery has to walk along the edge of a raised bedframe at one point. It's like an inch wide. While singing."

"It's more Cirque du Soliel than musical theater, honestly," Paz adds.

"Sounds like the obstacle course," I say with a laugh. "Sweetie, this is going to be at least two coats." I point at George's nails with the polish brush.

"I know. It's quick drying, though. We have at least ten minutes before lights-out." We both blow on his nails to get them to dry faster. "What are you doing tomorrow, since you don't have rehearsals all day like us?" Weekends are mostly free time. Counselors are around, so we can drop into the A&C cabin or get in line for waterskiing at the lake, but there's nothing scheduled, no planned stuff.

"Hudson wants to go on a hike, just the two of us."

"See, so that's when he'll probably ask. A lovely hike, he kisses you, he says he wants to see you again tonight, in private, and so on. I'm sure he has this down to an art."

"Probably," I say. George takes the nail polish back and does his left hand. "Yeah, you're probably right. And then I'll say no, and ask him deep personal questions so we connect even more."

"Sure," George says. "Sounds like a plan." He carefully finishes off the last of his left nails, then hands the nail polish back to me and spreads out his right hand again. I start painting. "You know, I have a date, too. Brad is going to come hang out at the drama cabin, and when rehearsals are over, we might go hang out at the boathouse or something."

"Oh?" I ask. "Finally giving him a shot?"

"It's funny, it's like he knew exactly what to say." I focus on carefully spreading the polish of George's nails, but I can feel his stare.

"I didn't coach him. He just asked why you seemed shy about taking it to the next level, and I told him. Should I not have?" I look up. "I'm sorry."

"Darling, no, it's fine. I had to make a decision about that sooner or later, and when he told me he liked me—the whole package, not just the body hair—that helped a lot. He seemed to mean it."

"He did," I say, going back to his nails. "He says you make him laugh."

"Darling, I make everybody laugh."

"Eh," Ashleigh says from above my bunk. "You're okay."

"Thanks," George says. "I think so."

"So you're like a love guru now," Paz says from above us. "Randy with the romance plan."

"I mean . . . maybe a little. My plan is working, right? So I must know something."

"Darling, you know one thing. Don't get ahead of yourself."

"Yeah, Paz, don't say stuff like that, it'll go right to his head."

"Randy, the romance king," I say, handing the nail polish back to George. "Has a nice ring to it."

"If my nails weren't wet, I'd hit you with a pillow."

"Mine aren't," Ashleigh says, hopping off her bunk, grabbing my pillow, and knocking me on the head with it in one swoop.

"I'm kidding, I'm kidding," I say, blocking her with my arm. "I'm no romance king."

"Good," she says, throwing my pillow back and looking at George's nails. "That's a cool color."

"You want some?" George asks.

"Nah. It'll get chipped while I'm playing with the light rigs. Don't waste it unless your folks are sending you more."

"Maybe not this color, but they'd better be sending more nail polish," George says. "I only brought two bottles."

Paz dips her head down over the top of the bed and looks. "Oh, it is pretty."

"You want?" George asks.

"If you're offering..." Paz hops down from the bed and stands next to Ashleigh—much closer than she needs to. Ashleigh glances at her, nervously, then gets back into her own bunk.

"Sit," George says, patting the space next to him. Paz sits next to him and stares up at where Ashleigh is, like she's trying to look through the bed. "Spread your hands," George says. "We might only have time for one coat before lights-out, though."

"That's okay," Paz says.

George starts to paint her nails and I stand up, stretching as an excuse to stare at Ashleigh, who is frowning, and flipping through a comic without really reading it. I raise my eyebrow at her, not wanting to ask what's going on with Paz while Paz is sitting right below us. She looks at me and shrugs. Well, that doesn't clear anything up.

"Lights-out in five," Mark says, coming out of his room in pajamas. "So you'd better have brushed your teeth. Remember, plaque can lead to throat infections, and I won't have any of you taking time off to rest your voices just because you couldn't be bothered to have good dental hygiene. Plus we want those teeth to sparkle under the lights."

"Are you really giving us a lecture on brushing our teeth?" Montgomery asks. "We're not seven."

"You all look seven to me," Mark says. "Everyone under thirty looks seven to me. My therapist says it's because of my anxiety over aging, but I think it's just my brain protecting itself from getting emotionally invested in children."

"Oh, sweetie, you mean you're not invested in us?" I ask.

"If I were emotionally invested in you, Randall Kapplehoff, I would cry myself to sleep every night until your hair grew back and you started dressing well again."

"You have been crying a lot," Crystal calls from inside the room.

"Be quiet, Crystal."

The entire cabin giggles.

"Laugh all you want," Mark says. "Lights-out in five."

I lie down in my bed as George finishes the first coat of Paz's nails.

"You want another layer on yours?" I ask him.

"Nah," he says. "It can wait until tomorrow. He closes the bottle up and puts it in his cubby. "Besides, I want to save some for when you can wear it again. It'll be your un-masc-ing nail polish."

"Oh my god, why have we not been calling it that all the time?" Ashleigh asks. "The Grand Un-Masc-ing. And right now, you're masc-ed." She pauses. "And you want to go to a masc-ed ball. Or two."

"Gross, no, be quiet," I say, but everyone is already laughing and I start laughing, too. A minute later, Mark shuts out the lights, but we all continue to giggle quietly in the dark.

SIXTEEN

want to show you the best view in camp," Hudson says, taking me by the hand and leading me into the woods.

"Okay," I say. "How much of a hike is this?"

"It's not too bad, promise. You have bug spray on, right?"

"Yeah."

"Good."

He leads the way, and honestly, I have no idea where we're going. I've always stayed out of the woods in past years, except during color wars, when we have the nighttime Spy Wars—the two teams split the whole camp up and each try to get as many people as possible to "safety" in the other team's territory (usually the boathouse and meeting hall) without getting spotted by anyone on the other team. We have flashlights, so sneaking across the camp in the open is out of the question and usually people try to make it through the woods. George and I always joke it's a disaster waiting to happen, but no one's gone missing yet.

But just hiking around the woods in the day hasn't been anything I'd done before a few days ago, and then Connie had taken us on a pretty easy trail. Hudson is already leading me up something much steeper than that. And with much thicker woods. And bushes.

"Is this really a trail?" I ask.

"Kind of."

"Do you know where we're going?" I squeeze his hand.

"Yes."

"And how to get there?"

"Pretty sure."

I laugh. "How do you know it, then?"

"Connie took us there at the end of last summer, as a treat, and I just thought it was really special." He squeezes my hand back. "And you're really special. So I wanted to show it to you."

My heart melts a little when he says that, and any anxiety I have about walking deep into the woods with no trail and no idea where we're going fades.

"Then I guess we should find it," I say.

We have to break hands as the trail gets steeper and we pull ourselves over rocks. We both have backpacks, with water and some snacks—he'd told me to bring them—and we stop a few times just to drink. Sweat is pouring down our faces, and there's a perpetual hum of insects. I'm pretty sure something is crawling up my leg at one point, but I just swat it away and keep walking. We chat a little about favorite old movies (his is *The Fugitive*, 'cause his mom loves it, mine is *Bringing Up Baby*, because of Katharine Hepburn, but I tell him 'cause it's funny), but we're panting and it's hard to talk too much.

It's been nearly an hour by the time Hudson says, "Okay, we're almost there." The sun is high above us, and even though we're shaded by the trees, I can feel my shirt sticking to my back with sweat.

But then the trees part a little and we come out into a glade on the top of a cliff. It's grassy and covered in daisies. A small brook runs through it to the edge of the cliff, where it turns into a thin waterfall off the edge. The air smells amazing here. Green and floral, like freedom and love.

"Wow," I say, in a half whisper.

Hudson takes my hand and walks me to the edge of the cliff, where we can see the camp below us. We're not actually as far up as I thought we'd be. I can still hear people calling to each other, and we can't see as far as the drama cabin, but we still feel far enough away that we're in our own little magical glade. Hudson drops his backpack on the grass and sits with his feet hanging over the edge, and I do the same, sitting next to him, then lie back on the grass. The bubbling of the faucet-thin waterfall makes a sweet sound. The trees shade us, and when I squint my eyes, they turn into galaxies.

It's just Hudson and I, alone in this most magical place he's brought me.

He leans back, putting his head on my chest, and I wrap my arm around his shoulder.

"Like it?" he asks.

"It's perfect," I say. "Thank you."

I look at him and reach my mouth down to kiss him, and in moments he's straddling me, his mouth pressed into mine, biting my lower lip a little. My hands are up his shorts and boxer briefs, grabbing his ass. He leans back, chewing on his lower lip, and peels off his shirt, then pulls mine off, and tosses them on the grass. Then he dives back down into me, kissing not just my lips but working his way down to my neck, and then my nipples. I've never felt a mouth on my chest before, and gasp at the way his tongue draws circles on me, then moves farther down, to my belly button. I run my hands through his hair, and then he unbuttons my fly.

Oh. He's moved on from the Peanut Butter Pit, I guess. Or I'm special enough he wanted someplace new for me.

He tugs my shorts off, leaving me in a pair of black briefs, my hard-on visibly straining against them, and he puts his mouth over it and I toss my head back, spilling out half-slurred words as a thousand new sensations sing into me like a chorus.

No. Not yet. Stop. This is exactly how I become another two-week fling.

"Wait," I say, so softly he doesn't hear me, his mouth now on my thighs. "Wait," I say again, and he looks up.

"I have condoms in my backpack," he says, then kisses my stomach.

"No," I say, practically pant, "it's..."

"Too much?"

"I'm sorry," I say, trying to scoot away from him even as I want him to keep doing what he's doing. I pull my shorts back over my underwear. He leans forward and kisses me on the mouth again.

"It's okay," he says, adjusting himself so he's lying next to me, propped on one elbow. "You told me you wanted to go slowly...I just...I should have checked before pulling your clothes off."

"I mean...I wanted you to. I'm just...I don't want to dive in too quickly."

"It's okay, babe. I get it." He leans forward and kisses me again, his tongue slipping into my mouth. Then he pulls away suddenly. "But maybe we should cool down for a bit." He laughs and grabs for his backpack, pulling a bottle of water from it and chugging it. Some of it flows out of his mouth and runs down his neck and chest, and I need to look away or I will be naked with my mouth on whatever part of him he wants in less time than the most frantic backstage costume change.

I had a plan for this, I remind myself. Something to kill

the sexual mood, improve the emotional one. To make us bond. Right. Coming out.

"Why don't we talk?" I ask.

"Yeah," he says, wiping his mouth. "That's a good idea." He comes over and sits next to me again. "What do you want to talk about?"

"Who did you come out to first?" I ask, maybe sounding a little too prepared.

"Oh. So, this conversation. I guess...well, it ain't sexy."

I laugh. "I mean, only if your coming out led immediately to something sexy."

He shakes his head, laughing too. "Yeah, no. So, I did know one guy who came out to his best friend, though, and then they had sex right there, in their basement. So it can be."

"Oh. Well, yeah...that's sexy. Not what happened to me, though."

"Or me. Apparently they never spoke again after that. He was really sad about it."

"Oh." I look out at the camp and scoot up so my legs are hanging off the edge again. Hudson scoots beside me and hands me the bottle of water. I drink from it deeply.

"So, can you go first?" he asks, leaning against me. "Since you brought it up and everything."

"Yeah." I smile and put the water down between us and wrap my arm over his shoulder. Thinking about this almost immediately dispels the lingering tingling in my body. "Sure.

It was my parents. It wasn't bad, actually. I mean, I'd always sort of known. Like, I feel like there was never a time I thought I was straight, just a time I didn't really think about sex, if that makes sense. And then, I was twelve, and people were talking about sex and crushes, and we had health class, and I guess I realized that this was something my parents needed to know. So at dinner, I just told them. I was like 'So you know, I'm gay,' and they stopped eating and looked at me for a while, and looked at each other, and then my mom nodded and said, 'Well...all right.' And I don't know what they talked about themselves, but, like, a week later, Dad asked if there were any girls in my class I wanted to take to the end of school dance. And I was so confused! 'Cause I'd told them. And so I looked him in the eye and said, 'You mean boys. I'm gay, remember?' and then, that night, Mom and Dad asked me a bunch of questions—how could I know? Wasn't I young? Did someone else tell me I was gay? And I guess I just answered them well enough that they said okay, and that was that."

"Wow," Hudson says, taking my hand and squeezing it. "That's pretty easy. But it's cool you were so direct, and, like...insistent, I guess?"

"I mean, my parents were pretty great about it. They read up on everything, Mom joined PFLAG and apparently went in with a lot of questions. But then they were on board. They love me, you know, and that means all of me. That's what Mom said a few weeks later when I asked if she and Dad were angry about it. They love me, all of me."

"That's kind of amazing."

I smile, because this is Randy he's talking about. Randy who was direct and insistent. This is working just like it should—he's getting to know the real me.

"Were your parents bad about it?" I ask him.

He takes a deep breath. "No," he says softly. "I mean. They weren't that cool. But they were fine. But I told my grandma first. We were really close. And she was one of the most amazing people I ever met. She came over from Korea when she was like five? Was a teenager in the sixties and seventies and just loved that style. Had one of those round, like, big hairstyles so long, it came back into style. I showed her a picture of Amy Winehouse once and she was thrilled. And she always wore, like, neon and glitter. She was never afraid to be loud and herself. She was always happy, and she could always make me laugh. Kind of like you."

"I'm like your grandma?" This is more "not sexy" than I was hoping for.

"You make me laugh, I mean." He nudged me hard with his shoulder. "You know what I meant." He takes a breath. "She died a few years ago." He looks out at the camp, his legs swinging over the side of the cliff.

"I'm sorry," I say. "If you don't want to talk about it…" Though we already have, only he doesn't recall it.

"No. I was just remembering. I've tried not to think about her for a while, but now…it feels good actually? She was just this amazing person. She watched me a lot after school when I was little. I went to her house and we...would just hang out. Or we'd go to the movies. I remember once, and...I haven't thought about this in years. But once when I was really little, we went to see some movie, and it was kind of scary and I screamed at one point—I don't remember what it was. Teeth, I think? Like an animal? Anyway, I scream, and burrow myself in her arm, and some guy behind us leans forward—and this is an adult—and he says, 'Hey, don't be such a girl about it.' And my grandma, she just turns to him and says, 'Don't be an asshole about it,' and he snorted and leaned back, and she said to me, 'You scream whenever you want, baby.' She was so great."

I look at him and I can see his eyes are wet, like he's trying not to cry, so I clasp his shoulder tight and he leans against me, wiping one of his eyes.

"Sorry," he says. "I haven't talked about her in years."

"That's okay."

"When I was like ten, my parents said I could start going straight home instead of taking the bus to her house, and I saw her less. But when I was twelve, and I knew—like knew I was gay 'cause I just really wanted to kiss this guy in my grade. And I didn't want to kiss any girls. And I knew it was...not great to be gay. I knew people didn't like it. And this was on top of being like one of five Asian kids at school. Not a good combination for popularity. So, anyway, I snuck out of the house and walked a few miles—in Virginia heat— to my grandma's place. Just so I could tell her."

"She take it well?"

"Yeah. I mean, that's why I wanted to tell her, I think. I knew she'd love me no matter what."

I want to tell him, suddenly, about our first summer, talking about her in the dark. But I don't, of course, because it would give everything away.

"She gave me a big hug and said it didn't matter to her at all, and yes, it would matter to other people, but who cared about them? I cried so hard, and she hugged me for what seemed like an hour, but when she let go, I felt so much better. She said I should be proud of myself for knowing who I was and what I wanted, and to never let anyone tell me that anything about myself that made me happy was something to be ashamed of. I've tried to keep that in mind."

"That sounds great. So she was fine with it."

"Yeah. My folks weren't as cool....So she drives me home, and they didn't know where I was, so they're freaking out, and she sits us all down and tells them I have something to say, and I tell them, 'Mom, Dad, I'm gay.' And Mom says Grandma is putting ideas in my head, and Dad says I'm not and we can worry about it when I'm older, and that was it for a while."

"But they sent you here. They must believe you now, right?"

Hudson shifts uneasily in my arms, pulling away and lying down on the grass to look up at the trees. I lie back, too, but he's farther away now. "My grandma died a little after that." He takes a deep breath. "A lot of stuff happened. We were all upset. But I told them about it again, and I'd found out about this camp with Grandma—she'd wanted me to go, so I could make queer friends, have fun. And I told my parents that, and I told them it was like her last wish for me. So...I came."

"That's really great, though," I say, taking his hand and lacing our fingers. "That she could still do that for you."

"Yeah." Hudson sniffs. I look over and he wipes his eyes with the back of his arm. He turns his face away from me. "Sorry, I shouldn't do this."

"Do what?"

"Crying. It's not...I don't like people seeing me cry."

"I don't mind," I say, turning my whole body toward him. I take him by the hip and turn him toward me, too. His face is a little wet from tears. "It's okay to have emotions."

"No, it isn't," he says with a half-hearted laugh. "You ever cry in front of other people? They will give you a hard time about it. I remember I got hit in the nose with a soccer ball once in middle school, and the guys on my team all yelled at me to stop and called me crybaby for the rest of the year. It was already hard enough to get them to realize I wasn't, like, a math nerd, and then I screwed it all up by making them think I was, like, a girl. That's sexist, I know, but that's just how guys talk about other guys who cry. So I don't do it."

"Well, you don't have to worry about that with me," I

say, wiping a new tear away from his face. "You can have whatever emotions you want around me. That's what boyfriends are for, right?" I squeeze his hand.

"I don't know. I've never cried in front of a boyfriend before."

"Well, you can cry in front of me. I don't mind. I'd rather you feel okay having emotions in front of me than hiding them or something."

"That's nice to say, but..." He brings his hands up and wipes away his tears, and leaves them there for too long, covering his face.

"Really," I say, pulling his hands down. His tears are mostly gone.

He smiles. "Okay."

"Your grandma sounds like she was amazing."

"She was."

We lie there in silence for a few minutes, staring at each other. The tears stop running down his face.

"Have you ever done the trees into stars thing?" I ask him.

"The what?"

"Here, turn onto your back and look up at the trees and the light coming through." We both shift onto our backs. "Now unfocus your eyes a little, and imagine that the leaves are actually the background. They're the darkness, and the light coming through is stars. Like full galaxies, not just little winking ones far away. Like you're right under the Milky Way."

"I...oh," he says, gasping slightly. "I see."

We lie there, staring at full galaxies that don't exist, our hands intertwined, until Hudson sits up suddenly. "We're going to be late for lunch," he says.

"Oh, right." Attendance is required at all meals. Last summer someone slept through lunch on a Saturday and the whole camp had to go on a search for him. He ended up getting teased pretty mercilessly once he was found, and Joan was very angry.

We quickly put our shirts back on and start hiking back. Downhill goes faster than uphill, but we still go quickly enough that we're not talking, and still burst into the cafeteria five minutes late. The whole camp looks up at us. Joan glares. George, Ashleigh, Brad, and Paz all snicker.

We quickly take seats that, thankfully, George saved for us, and grab at the grilled cheeses going around before getting up and washing our hands.

"So...were you busy?" George asks.

"It was a hike," I say. "We lost track of time."

"I'm sure," George says seriously, nodding.

"How were rehearsals?"

"Good!" George says.

"George has already mastered his dance for 'Kids,'" Paz says. "I still can't leap high enough to get over the Shriners' arms."

"Crystal added a thing where Jen has to swing on monkey bars during 'Put on a Happy Face,'" Ashleigh says. "I think Crystal has finally lost her mind."

"It's going to be really cool looking, though," Paz says. "They're doing it in a playground, so there are slides and stuff that Jen is trying to get me to go on and I keep turning away. And Ashleigh can get some happy-face lights, which is going to be so cool. Mark said he'd thought of it but assumed it wasn't possible."

"I'm not sure it is," Ashleigh says quickly. "I'm still figuring out if I can get it just right."

"You will," Paz says.

"I watched part of it," Brad says. "The rehearsal. It's hard, man. I didn't realize, like, I've just always seen it at the end of the summer and it's like done and perfect. I didn't realize all the work that goes into it."

"You didn't see all of it, though," Paz says, her face radiating mischief.

"C'mon," Brad says.

"I caught them making out in one of the prop closets," Paz says to us, grinning.

"I had some free time between calls," George says with a shrug. "You were the one who walked in on us."

"I didn't know you'd be in there. Next time lock it, or put a sock on the doorknob or something."

"In the drama cabin?" I ask, a little scandalized.

"It was just kissing," George says. "No worse than what you do in front of our cabin every night."

"Okay," Brad says, looking very embarrassed. "I learned my lesson. We can move on."

George giggles and puts his hand on Brad's thigh.

"How was your hike?" George asks.

"Good," I say. "Hudson showed me a great view."

"I'll bet," Ashleigh says. I glare at her.

"You're all terrible," I say.

"No, it really was amazing," Hudson says. "We just talked. I..." He pauses. He looks at me, and then looks away suddenly, his brow furrowing. "It was great," he says, quieter.

I look at Hudson, but he focuses on his food. His thigh moves away from mine and I can feel my heart racing. Did I just do something wrong? Did he suddenly remember me, or something, like real me, not Del, from last summer? Something about the light, or my voice? Talking about his grandma?

I put my hand on his leg, and he doesn't pull away, but he doesn't lean into me, either. We all keep talking, and no one but me seems to notice that there's a sudden wall between me and Hudson, when just an hour ago we'd been closer than ever. After lunch, Hudson says he's going to go shower and write his parents and takes off, so I walk with George, Ashleigh, and Paz to the drama cabin.

"Was he acting weird?" I ask.

"Hudson?" Paz asks. "No more than usual."

"I feel like he got cold all of a sudden."

"Did you finally screw?" Ashleigh asks.

"No. Really. We just talked. We made out a little, but that was it."

"Maybe lunch didn't agree with him," George says. "But he seemed fine to me. I wouldn't worry about it. Your plan is still very much on track. You going to come watch rehearsals? We're going to learn the big group number for 'A Lot of Livin' to Do.' Crystal will probably have us literally making human pyramids and jumping off them.

"She did have me bring in some trampolines," Ashleigh says.

"Please tell me that's a joke," Paz says.

We walk in nervous silence long enough that Paz's eyes get huge with worry before Ashleigh cracks a smile.

"You are so mean," Paz says, shoving Ashleigh's shoulder. Ashleigh's smile gets bigger.

"You going to watch?" George asks me.

"Sure, for a bit."

I watch the rehearsals for a while, but it feels bittersweet. I love watching them. I love seeing the theater develop amid a bunch of falls and misplaced feet. I love hearing the half-singing that goes on in a dance rehearsal, and watching Crystal move her arms in ways that make no sense as she directs the choreography, or hearing her wacky names for moves—"Now bunny spin, hug yourself, worm wiggle, keep worm wiggling as you hop to your next position, good...now exploding star! Great. Montgomery, your solo now, so you kick to the front of the pack, and cross kick, cross kick, hands on hips, wink...no, wink a little more angrily. This is about your rebellion, remember."

After an hour, they have the basics down, and it's going to be a cool dance number. Jordan's Birdie radiates some serious swagger, and Montgomery has the ingenue sex kitten thing down. George and Paz are in the background of this one, too—as different characters—just so the stage feels really full of dancers. And it is. The entire company just out there, working together, dancing and singing. I miss it so much. I wonder if they'd let me just get up there and dance with them. Only for rehearsals. Just so I could feel that again. I wouldn't have to be in the show—though that would feel even better.

Damn, I miss this. And now Hudson is being weird, and maybe the plan isn't going as well as I want, and I don't want to give up on Hudson, but...Maybe if I came back now, they'll let me be in the chorus. I'm a fast learner. I could pick up some steps. Or just work backstage, at the prop table or something. I'd rotate every other day with Hudson or at the drama cabin. I could tell him I was sick. Like rotating your heart back and forth between two bodies. That's what it would feel like, I think. Slingshotting my heart back and forth until it got vertigo. No. I need to find a way to get my heart into both of them at once. That's what the plan is for.

They finish "A Lot of Livin' to Do" and move on to the

"Shriners' Ballet," the cast rotating off stage, lights flickering on and off. Being back in the drama cabin feels like home. It smells like rubber and wood and the cigarettes Mark quit two years ago but still has one of on opening night. I want to press myself into the stage, and I almost wouldn't mind if it was right now, with everyone dancing on me.

Maybe the issue with Hudson is that we really bonded today. I got too close, and even with everything I've done, remaking myself, holding back, maybe he's just not able to connect with someone like that. Or maybe he just needs time, and I'm spiraling because I want everything to work with him, but I still miss this so much, it feels like I haven't been breathing until now.

"Well, well," Montgomery says, sitting behind me as I watch Paz and the Shriners onstage. "Look who dragged his ass back to the theater."

"You were so good up there," I tell him, turning around. "You nailed it, really."

"Of course I did," Montgomery says, trying to act cool, but I can tell he's pleased with the compliment. "But what are you doing here? Shouldn't you be off pretending to be butch for your butch boyfriend?"

"He's writing his parents," I say. "And I missed you all."

"Really?" Jordan asks, sitting next to Montgomery.

"You were amazing, Jordan," I say. "You radiate that David Bowie vibe that Mark wants."

"Aww, thanks," they say, swatting at my shoulder.

"I still don't get why you're here," Montgomery says. "Won't it blow your cover? Aren't you above us now that you've ascended to the heights of masculine masturbatory fantasy?"

Jordan snickers.

"Oh please," I say. "Hudson knows I'm friends with you. Don't be a—"

"Drama queen?" Montgomery interrupts. "Like you used to be?"

"That's not what I was going to say." I roll my eyes. "And I'm still a drama queen. The whole camp is my theater."

"That's true." Jordan nods. "He is putting on quite a show."

"I've never been a fan of one-man shows," Montgomery says with a sigh. "They always seem so self-involved."

I laugh. "Are you really mad at me?" I ask. "Just for not being in the show?"

"I don't know yet," Montgomery says, crossing his arms. "And it's about more than the show."

"Montgomery," Mark shouts from the front of the theater. "Where are you? We need you for 'What Did I Ever See in Him?'"

"Coming," Montgomery calls, standing and walking to the front of the theater.

"He just feels like you abandoned us for a hot guy," Jordan says.

I nod. I can see their point. "Not just any hot guy,

though," I say. They have to understand that. They've known how I've felt about Hudson for years.

"Look, I love a rom-com, and you are making. It. Happen." They snap between each word. "Which is super impressive. But no one likes being a background extra in someone else's show. Is this the first time you've even been in the drama cabin this summer?"

"No, I was here for the talent show."

"Okay, first time you've been here for you?"

"I mean...I've been busy." I look down. I feel like I'm being grilled in a police station.

"I get it." They stand up. "But you can't act like nothing has changed, either."

"I'm still with you at night. I dance in the morning."

"My dad had this really big job when I was a baby," Jordan says. "Left for work before I was up, home after dinner. I was just starting to talk. Knew the word *dada*, though. Then I forgot it. My mom made him quit, take a job that had him home enough I knew who he was." They shrug. "Anyway, that's just a fun story my mom likes to tell me. I gotta go get measured for a costume. Good seeing you!"

They smile and walk off. I get what they mean, and what Montgomery is mad about, but it'll all be fine soon. Either Hudson's about to dump me anyway, and that's why he's acting funny, or in a few weeks I'll be able to tell him the truth. And then everything will go back to how it was.

I watch the rehearsals until I'm just up there, with them,

in spirit. George comes out once to say hi, but Mark quickly makes him run backstage for a costume fitting. Ashleigh sits next to me sometimes, making notes, asking me if I think a scene needs a follow spot or not, and then she vanishes again and the lights go a little bluer and she comes back and asks if the stage feels more "suburban" now, and I say yes to everything, because I think that's what she wants.

When Mark dismisses everyone, we go back up to the cabin together and change into our swimsuits and then go back down to the pool, where Hudson is nowhere to be seen. I feel sad in a way I haven't since camp started and Hudson said hi. I feel like I'm missing something I love, and without Hudson next to me, kissing me, resting his hand on my hip, I'm forgetting why I did it in the first place.

We only have ten minutes in the pool before they kick us out to get ready for dinner, and we make the most of it, cooling off in the water.

"You seem sad," George says, toweling himself off as we walk back to our cabins. "I'm telling you, he's probably having stomach issues. Living in the bathroom."

"Or he's jerking off. If you two really did just talk, he's probably feeling frisky," Ashleigh says.

I grin. Hadn't thought of that. "Maybe. But it's more just watching all of you onstage. I'm sad I'm not up there."

"Oh, darling," George says, sad for me. He wraps one arm around me as we walk, hugging me. "You made your choice, though. And you're happy, right?"

"I just wish I could have both, I guess," I say.

"Next summer, right?" Ashleigh says.

"Yeah," I say.

At the cabin we all shower off before heading down to dinner, where Hudson sits down next to me, but I still feel a strange distance between us.

"You okay?" I ask in a low voice. "I didn't see you in the pool."

"Sorry," he says, squeezing my leg. "Fell asleep writing my parents a letter."

"Okay," I say.

"I'm kind of groggy." He offers me a half smile before turning back to the watery lasagna in front of us.

We talk about the show a little more, and practice our stories for tonight's scary story bonfire, and Hudson seems fine, just a little distant, and I want to know what's bothering him but don't want to be a nag, but I also wish if something was wrong he would just tell me so I could know what's happening. I want to fight for him, but I don't know how, because I don't know what's wrong.

I barely pay attention to the scary stories around the campfire that night, not even Ashleigh's, which is always the most horrifying. I feel like my life is scarier than any ghost or whatever right now. Hudson stands next to me, roasting a marshmallow and smiling and laughing, but he's not calling me babe or putting his hand on my hip like he usually does, so I know something is wrong and it's a pile of dirt in my stomach. I want him so badly to just pull me close and to feel that electricity between us again, that desire to run off and kiss in the dark, but he's somber now. I've gone from rom-com to drama, and it's not cute.

When we say good night, I kiss him on the mouth, and he kisses me back, but it's not like last night, or any of the previous nights. It's soft. It's quiet.

After lights-out, I lie awake for a long time, wondering what I did wrong, and how to fix it, or if I can fix it, or if I should bother fixing it if not fixing it means I get to be in the show again. Does he know? If he does, and he didn't outright end it, that's good, but it feels like my plan is failing, and if it's failing, what am I even doing anymore trying, when I could go back to theater? Was Hudson worth it if this is all going to crash and burn tomorrow?

No. Of course Hudson was worth it. Is worth it. I just feel like suddenly, with Hudson being distant and not being in the show, I have nothing. Like it's all slipped through my hands like glitter. I stare at my hands in the dark. I miss my nail polish. I miss Hudson. And for the first time this summer, I don't have a plan for getting back either.

SEVENTEEN

Astrud Gilberto, 'Fly Me to the Moon,'" Mark announces by way of waking us up. "Technically it was written in the fifties, but Gilberto recorded it in 1964, the same year as Sinatra, though they'd both been performing it for a while. Of course, Sinatra's version became the famous one. People associated it with the Space Race. Couldn't do that with a Brazilian woman, I guess. I find her version to be much more romantic, and frankly, superior."

He presses PLAY as we all begin getting out of bed, barely having listened to his lecture. The music, though. The music is...amazing. I've heard the song before—Sinatra, I guess—but this version is flowing and rhythmic, and makes me think of posing in silky robes that flow out like wings. And apparently I'm not the only one. George is up, already making wings with his nightgown, and everyone else is following him, throwing their sheets over their shoulders and using them as capes. I hold back for a moment, wanting to join but also knowing it doesn't fit the Del character. But I don't have to play Del here. Here I can be Randy. And besides, maybe Del was a failure. Maybe Del is about to get dumped. I grab my sheet and start dancing with the rest of them, the smooth music moving me and making me feel like some sixties starlet.

The screen door creaks open and I turn dramatically to see who it is. And there's Hudson, staring at me, confused.

"Hey," he says.

"Hey," I say, in my matching pajamas and with a sheet around my shoulders like a dressing gown. This is probably very bad, but I keep smiling.

"What are you doing?" he asks. Everyone around me is still dancing, but I can see Mark watching us with a raised eyebrow. I drop the sheet on my bed and walk to the door, then outside. Hudson follows.

"I was just dancing. We start the day with music," I say, hoping I sound nonchalant.

"Like that?" Hudson asks.

"Actually, that kind of dancing is great for flexibility," I say. "My soccer coach taught me some of those moves." He stares at me for a moment, and I can't tell if he buys it. Change the subject, Randy. "So why did you stop by so early?" I smile up at him. His hair is wet. He must have been up early and showered.

"I wanted to see you," he says, shrugging. He grins for a second but it falls. "You know, just because you share a bunk with them doesn't mean you have to act like them."

"Them?" I say.

"I mean..." He frowns and we walk around to the side of the cabin. I can still hear the music from inside. "Sorry, that sounded bad. I just mean, you know, you don't have to be a stereotype."

"Stereotype?" I ask, my body feeling chilly. Inside, the music stops. A new song comes on.

"Like, all girly and stuff. I know plenty of queer people do that, but...that's the thing everyone expects us to do, right?"

"I don't know," I say. "As opposed to what?"

"Showing people that you're more than just gay, you know?"

"I don't," I say, genuinely confused. "You're being weird."

"Sorry," he says. He takes both my hands in his. "I'm nervous."

"Why?" I ask. Is he about to break up with me? Is that why he'd been weird last night? What did I do wrong?

"So, I wanted to tell you something. And...I'm afraid of what you'll say."

"Okaaaay...," I say, clutching his hands now, not minding that my palms are sweating. "Now I'm nervous."

"So..." He takes a deep breath, looks up, looks back at

me. "So, okay. You know that first night? When we went to the tree?"

Oh.

"Yes," I say carefully.

"I lied." He lets it hang there, and I do my best performance of serious/concerned/confused because inside I am jumping up and down. He's telling me the truth? Already? This is going SO well.

"About what?" I ask, a slight, Oscar-worthy tremor in my voice.

"I...I am HAL. Hudson Aaronson-Lim. So, all those hearts on the tree, those were me and my previous boyfriends."

"Oh," I say, all stunned silence. "Why did you lie?"

"Because." He drops my hands and turns away. "I liked you, like a lot, right away. You are so hot, and I felt like we had a thing, like, immediately." He turns back, and I nod a little so he can keep going. "And you said you wanted it slow, and so, I guess I just wanted you to think I wasn't some...slut. I mean, like a romantic slut. I've had a lot of boyfriends. But they never last long. I always liked the...fun parts, but then that's all it was, and I would get bored, and, I mean, I liked them, we stayed friends, but I never clicked with them. And I was worried maybe that was me. 'Cause I really wanted to click with someone. And then you were there and I thought it could be you, but I didn't want to ruin my chances before they started, so..."

209

"You lied."

He nods. "I'm really sorry," he says, reaching for my hands again. I let him take them. "I know it was a terrible thing to do, but the thing is, the reason I'm telling you is that yesterday, on our hike, with any other guy, I would have just given you a few lines and then coaxed you into making out some more—hopefully sex. But with you, it was different. I told you about my grandma. I mean, I cried in front of you! That's crazy! I've never done that...and I thought I'd feel stupid after, like I'd shown you something I shouldn't have, and you were going to leave me. But I didn't. I felt...really happy. And at lunch, sitting next to you, I looked at you, and it was like I knew I could be my best self with you. Like... there were stars inside me, galaxies like the ones we saw in the leaves. And I realized you did all that for me, and, so, I just...couldn't stand that I was lying to you anymore. It felt gross." He takes a deep breath. "So...that's why I'm telling you. I'm sorry. But I also think I might be really...falling for you."

I let the silence hang for a moment, and look down at my feet.

"What do you think?" he asks. "Are you angry?"

I look up at him, now not hiding my grin or the giggles starting in me.

"You knew," he says, his mouth falling open in shock.

"I mean..." I shrug. "Ashleigh's laughing that night told me something was probably up."

"So she told you?"

"I asked. They didn't, like, offer it up," I say, raising an eyebrow before he gets mad at them.

"So, why did you keep...seeing me, then?"

"Like you said," I say, stepping forward and wrapping my arms around his waist. "I felt like there was a thing between us...and you're really hot." I kiss him.

"So we're good?" he asks. This would be the moment to tell him. He just told me about his secret identity, maybe it's time to unveil mine. I take a deep breath.

"We're great," I say. Not yet. It's not time yet, that's not the plan. It's too soon, I haven't shown him enough of Randy yet; it would ruin everything if I told him now. Stick to the plan.

"'Cause I just said a lot of things I've never said before."

"That's why we're great." I kiss him again. He puts his hands one the small of my back and pulls me into a hug.

"Your pajamas are really cute," he says softly.

"Thanks," I say.

Everything is good again. Better than.

"You want to come dance?" I ask. Maybe now I can start showing him more of Randy, not just Del.

He grimaces and shakes his head. "Not my scene. But I'll see you at breakfast." He kisses me again before going back to his cabin. I walk back into mine. New music is playing.

Mark raises an eyebrow at me. "Everything okay?"

"Everything is perfect," I tell him. I start dancing with

everyone else again, floating light as air as I brush my teeth and get dressed. Everything is better than perfect. I don't know why I felt so down last night.

At breakfast, Hudson and I are back to how we were, sitting close, a hum of something unnameable between us, like we're passing one heart back and forth faster than light so we can both use it. Maybe it's even better than before. I'm aware of every slight glance in my direction, how even when he smiles at a joke someone else told, he looks at me, so we can share the smile. We're our own little universe.

There's a big game of soccer that we join in for the morning, and after lunch, we go to the pool and spend the afternoon splashing each other and stealing underwater kisses. We talk, too, all day, when we can. About stupid stuff—comic book movies and hot actors, and books we have to read over the summer for school.

We duck out of the pool early and go to my cabin, where we make out on my bed until we hear voices about to come inside and quickly separate as Montgomery and Jordan walk in to me pulling my shirt back on. Montgomery stops in the doorway and puts his hand on his hip, staring at us.

"Don't stop on my account," he says. "I like to watch."

Jordan snorts a laugh and heads over to their bunk, ignoring me.

"I'm gonna go," Hudson says, eyeing Montgomery nervously before pecking me on the cheek and heading for the door. Montgomery doesn't move, so Hudson slips past him. Montgomery turns to watch him go.

"Can you not scare him?" I ask.

"But I like watching him run away," Montgomery smirks.

"Really?"

"Oh, come on," Montgomery says, rolling his eyes and going over to his cubby. "You used to have a sense of humor."

"Used to?" I ask.

"Well, maybe you still do, but you're too busy sticking your tongue down Hudson's throat to say anything funny anymore."

"That's not fair."

"I know I'm being that bitch again," Montgomery says from his cubby, where he's toweling his hair dry. "But it's fair."

"What do you mean? I thought you weren't really mad at me."

"I said I wasn't sure yet. And then you spent all of today with him again. It just feels like there's *us*, the theater gays," Montgomery says, taking shampoo and conditioner down, "and there's *them*, the..." He waves a hand. "Jocks or whatever. And now you're one of them."

"C'mon, we're all queer. It's not like we're in *West Side Story*." I turn to Jordan. "It's a rom-com, right? I'm in a rom-com."

Jordan shrugs. "Sure! But I told you, no one likes being

an extra...and like Montgomery said, after we told you that...you just went right back to him. We went back to being extras in your life."

I sigh. I was never as close with either of them as with George and Ashleigh, but I've always thought of them as my friends. "I'm sorry," I say. "I'm just really happy. Can't you be happy for me?"

"Sure, fine, whatever," Montgomery says, heading for the bathroom. "I'm sorry I said anything, just relax." He doesn't even look at me before he leaves. I hear the shower turn on a moment later.

"I'm still your friend," I tell Jordan.

"I know," they say. "Don't worry, he's probably just jealous he's not getting any yet."

"Yeah," I say. "And you?"

"I'm happy for you," they say with a shrug. "Just maybe a little sad for me."

"We'll hang out tonight, then," I say.

"Cool." Jordan smiles, then goes into the bathroom with a change of clothes.

So maybe I'm a little caught up in Hudson. But that's because it's all part of a plan. And that means work. They understand. They just miss me is all.

I make it a point to sit with them at dinner (Hudson on my other side), asking them about their parts—Jordan is exhausted from the running up walls but loves their costume, Montgomery was "born for this." Everything is much better afterward, I think.

That night is the camp-wide water-gun fight. We each have to wear white shirts and are given water guns and balloons and access to blue-colored water. If your shirt gets stained, you're a ghost, able to walk around and shout at people but not shoot anymore. Hudson and I make it pretty far before ghost Ashleigh leaps out of nowhere and Paz shoots us both. But we get her back by being ghosts who warn her targets early.

When Hudson kisses me good night, it's around the side of the cabin, so people can only see us if they're looking. We make out against the wall of the cabin and my hands slide up the back of his shirt and pull him closer to me. I want to consume him, I want to join with him and never stop feeling the heat of his body wrapped around mine, his hips against mine. We only stop when I hear Mark, in the cabin, say, "Ten minutes to lights-out."

"That's my cue," I say.

"Cue?"

"To exit," I say. Does he really not know what a cue is? Is that just a theater person word? It can't be just a theater person word.

"Oh, right." He frowns. "I didn't want to understand."

"Sorry," I say, kissing him once more before walking for the cabin door. "Good night."

"Good night," he says. I watch from the window as he

walks back to his cabin. I think I might even sigh. Thank god no one notices.

"Del, darling, could you be Randy for a minute and help me show Paz how to properly snap open a fan?" George asks from his bed.

"Crystal has me doing it a lot for 'Spanish Rose,'" Paz explains. "But she says I'm not doing it with the right oomph."

She demonstrates, wildly gesticulating while she opens her fan, which only opens about halfway. It's an American flag pattern on one side and the Pride flag on the other.

I sit down next to her and reach for George's fan. He hands it to me and immediately produces another from under his pillow.

"First off, sweetie, your hands should be farther down, like so." I show her. "And then don't try to move the fan with your arm. Think of it as throwing one side of it." I snap open the fan, put it in front of my nose and mouth, and flutter it alluringly while batting my eyelashes at her. That feels so good. I've missed that. "Now you try."

She tries again, getting the fan all the way open, but without the satisfying clacking noise a good, dramatic fan opening has.

"Better!" George says. "Don't worry, darling. I wasn't very good at it at first, either, but I knew I had to be able to do this for all my dramatic moments," he says, snapping his fan open, widening his eyes and fanning himself. "Randy taught me."

"You're still using your arm too much," I say. "It's in the wrist. Here, can I hold your arm?"

"Sure."

I hold her forearm steady so she can't move it. "Now try—just your wrist."

She tries moving her arm but can't, and the fan barely opens. I close it for her. She tries again, this time just with her wrist, and it flies open with a clatter.

"YES!" George says. "Now flutter and say something dramatic!"

I let go of Paz's arm and she makes her eyes huge, fanning herself. "I hope it's pizza for dinner tomorrow!" she announces in a voice so booming, Jordan looks over, raises their eyebrows, and says, "Yeah...wish it into the universe," nervously.

"A-plus delivery," George declares, "but we need to work on your content."

"I'm not an improv person," Paz says, defensive. "But no, I know that was bad."

"The fan was good, though!" I say. "Try again?"

She opens the fan again with an even faster snap, and says loudly, "I AM your mother!"

"Better," George says.

"Oh...you're doing a bit," Jordan says from their bed. "You should have said."

"I think you have the snap down," I say.

"Me too. Thanks, Randy. Del. Sorry."

"I'll answer to anything," I say, winking. "But I gotta brush my teeth," I add, noticing Mark staring at me and tapping his watch. I laugh as I grab my toothbrush and get ready for bed, managing to sit down just as Mark turns the lights off. It's been the perfect day. And as I go to sleep that night, I only feel a little guilty that Hudson has told me his truth and I haven't told him mine.

The next day we're back on our regular schedule and in Outdoor Adventure, and Connie has us practicing the Peanut Butter Pit. I actually manage to get across once, though only after a few tries. But I'm getting better. I can almost always at least grab the rope. Sometimes I grab it too low, and I need to get more momentum, but I tell myself I might need this one day—there are plenty of shows with swinging: *Peter Pan*, some versions of *Candide*. True, they have the rope waiting for them, but leaping isn't so bad.

When we're done, Hudson comes over to me and puts his hand around my waist, kissing me on the cheek even though I'm pouring sweat.

"So, babe, I was thinking," he says softly. "Maybe tonight, after curfew, you and I could come back here..."

"Oh?" I say.

"Del." Connie comes over and Hudson immediately goes quiet. "I want to talk to you for a second." She looks at Hudson. "Alone. You'll see him later, I'm sure."

"Later," Hudson says, giving me another kiss on the cheek before heading toward the pool.

I look up at Connie nervously. Why does she want to talk to me? "Am I in trouble?"

Connie smirks. "No. Come on, let's go somewhere quiet."

I follow her away from the obstacle course a little farther into the woods. When the sounds of the camp have faded slightly, she stops and turns to me.

"I've been really impressed with you this summer, Del."

"Oh. Thank you." What is happening?

"I'm not going to say I understand your makeover, or what your intentions were with it. I've heard things, but honestly, your life is your life, and your choices are your choices. But, because of those choices, this is the first summer I've spent real time with you, and I think you're a leader."

"Oh. Thank you," I repeat. Still no clue what's happening.

"You put in the work on the obstacle course. You help the others learn the parts of it they don't understand. You're encouraging, positive, helpful." She pauses and I'm waiting for her to say, "But you're not fooling anybody, go back to theater," or something. Instead, she says, "I think you'd make a great captain for the color wars."

"What?" Can you have no feeling in your body? Is that a thing? All your nerve endings shut down as you reboot with new information? 'Cause that's what's happening.

"The teams this year are Blue and Red. I think you'd be a great Blue team captain. We start on Friday. You'd have to spend some free time planning stuff—before dinner, usually. But your job would be to organize your team, decide which cabins are participating in which games, and generally be a cheerleader for everyone. Encourage them. Show them what a proud queer person can do. You up for that?"

"I..." Me. A color war captain. My body has rebooted and feelings come flooding in. Pride and shock and the realization that maybe, in some way, I've become Hudson. I can be to people what he was to me—outside of the sexy stuff, of course. I could make other queer kids feel like they can do anything. Like they can be the best versions of themselves, or at least find the best versions of themselves here at camp, and then go back to the world outside and unleash them. That's what Hudson always wants us to do.

I feel stars inside me exploding, making new stars. "You really want me?" I ask.

Connie nods.

"I'm honored. Thank you so much. Not just for this." I clutch my hands to my chest. "But for all you've taught me, that helped me become this. And of course, I need to thank Hudson, and my parents, and my friends George and Ashleigh, and even Mark, who gave me a hard time about this, but has always been an inspiration to me. I feel—"

"Okay," Connie interrupts flatly. "This isn't accepting a Tony. You want to be captain?"

"Yes!"

"Great. You and your other team captains and I will meet after pool time in cabin four, up the hill." I nod. Cabin four is one of the empty ones, and each team on color wars has four captains. "Don't let anyone see you, if you can help it. And no telling anyone. It has to be a surprise when we all come out."

I nod, waiting for more.

"That's it. See you then. Go to your next activity."

"Okay," I say, nodding. "Thank you again. It means so much to me that you would—"

"Del. Go."

I nod again and walk away. My heart is so light, it might fly out of my chest like a butterfly. I might join it. Maybe this whole summer wasn't just for Hudson. Maybe it was for Del, too. For the people Del can inspire. Del is a leader. Del is someone people look up to. A Stella Adler, but, like, for sports or something. Randy was never any of that. And it feels amazing to know I could be, well, like Hudson. That I could be up on a platform, and the people staring at me could feel inspired somehow. Could feel like they could do anything, just because of something I said. I bet I could use it for theater stuff, too. It'll give me gravitas. I could take on some serious roles—*Death of a Salesman*, starring Randy Kapplehoff! *Glengarry Glen Ross*! That would be something different for me. I always assumed I'd end up in *Who's Afraid of Virginia Woolf?* someday, though.

I barely pay attention in swim class, and at lunch, when Hudson asks what Connie wanted, I just tell him she told me my form on the obstacle course was getting better, and that must be enough to account for my dazed look, because he doesn't ask anything else. I giggle more than I should at things that aren't that funny. The lightness continues all day, through making "friends from stones" in A&C to touch football in sports and through free swim, where I keep wanting to pick everyone up and spin them around, I feel so happy.

After swim, I tell Hudson I can't hang out because I need to write my parents, and he nods and says he doesn't mind, he has to do something, too. We walk up the hill and I leave him in front of my cabin, and then, when no one is looking, I walk over to cabin four and casually pull the door open and go inside.

There are several empty cabins on the hill—the camp is only a hundred or so campers, and the cabins hold a dozen each, so we don't need all twenty of them—but I've never been in an empty one before. There are no beds. Connie has brought a plastic folding table and five folding chairs and has set them up in the middle of the cabin, but I can see where she dragged them through the dust on the floor.

"That's two," Connie says. She's sitting at the head of the table. Next to her is a camper a year older than me, but whose name I don't remember. He's got unwashed black hair and a goatee, and is wearing a torn T-shirt that's too big on him and cargo shorts. "Del, you know Jimmy?"

"Sure," I say. "I've seen you around."

"Yeah, man," Jimmy says, extending a hand. "Jimmy Mendoza. Del, is it?"

"Yeah," I say, sitting opposite him.

It occurs to me suddenly that Hudson must be a captain, too. Sure, he was one last summer, but people can be captain twice in a row. That must be why he didn't mind my not spending time with him. He's going to be so surprised to see me when he comes in.

The door swings open, but it's not Hudson who enters. It's Charity Levine, from cabin eight. Charity is usually in charge of the costume department. She's in A&C almost all day long. Everything she wears she handmade, including, I'm assuming, her current outfit, an A-line summer dress in pink-and-white check, with lace at the square neckline and a matching pink ribbon choker. Her brown hair is parted down the center and falls in perfect glossy sheets to her shoulders. Seeing me, she smiles brightly.

"Randy," she says. "I was wondering where they'd hidden you away. Cabin four, I guess."

The thing with Charity is I can never tell if she's being mean or if her voice just sounds like that, so I don't know if that's a joke or an insult.

"Wait," Jimmy says. "Is it Randy or Del?"

"Del," I say to him, then turn to Charity. "It's Del now."

"Right." Charity nods and sits next to Jimmy, smiling at me in a way that again—is she friendly or a bitch? I try to assume it's friendly, but something about her eyes makes it so hard to tell. "Sorry. The plan, the plan. Del, not Randy. It's very exciting. Is it going well?"

"Yeah," I say. "Haven't you heard me talking to George and Ashleigh in A and C?"

"Oh, I try not to eavesdrop. Especially not when people are talking about sex and relationships. I have no interest in those. I just focus on my crafting. And you." She turns to Jimmy. "Jimmy, right? Tom's boyfriend, but he was too old to come this year?"

"Yeah, it sucks," Jimmy says. "I miss him. And now I gotta get my T injections from Cosmo. I mean, I'd do them myself, but I can't stand looking at needles."

"I can do them," Charity says. "I'm great with needles."

"But, like, you mean sewing needles, right?"

"It's about sticking the pointy end in the right place either way, right?"

"I guess..."

"Charity, it's generous of you to offer," Connie says, "but I think Cosmo should be handling any injections at camp."

"Yeah," Jimmy says, looking relieved. Charity shrugs.

The door opens again, and Paz walks in. She looks at everyone, her eyebrows raising when she comes to me. It's not Hudson, but I'm still glad to see a friendly face. She sits down next to me.

"Hey," she says. "So, this is our crack team?"

"It is," Connie says, standing. "We are the Blue team.

You'll meet the captains of the Red team tomorrow so you can plan your big entrance together. For now I want to show you how the cabins will be divided and the schedule for the weekend so you can start planning which cabins should participate in which activities."

So no Hudson. I bet he's on the other team. I can't imagine he's not a captain. I hope he won't be jealous if he isn't. Maybe he'll be on my team, though, and I can be his captain, make him do some push-ups, maybe do a dance for me....

"So here are the teams," Connie says, her voice taking me out of my daydream. She hands out clipboards to each of us with a list of cabins and campers on our team, and then the schedule. Friday is the big opener, which starts with a game of capture the flag after dinner. Then on Saturday we have the egg race, swimming races, a pie-eating contest, a relay race through the obstacle course, and a kickball game. Sunday is queer trivia and a talent show before the final ceremony, where the judges add up the points we've earned in each challenge and present the award—which is a plaque that goes up in the dining hall for the rest of the summer, and bragging rights, mostly. I look over the list. Hudson's cabin is on the other team. Oh well.

"Oh, my cabin should do the pie-eating contest," Jimmy says. "We're, like, always hungry."

Connie raises an eyebrow at that. "Remember, you get points for team spirit, too. So you'll need to lead your team in cheers and songs, especially when they're not the ones participating in the event. So start thinking of rhymes."

"True Blue," Charity says. "Don't be Blue, we're better than you. Kill Red dead."

"Let's try to keep away from violence," Connie says.

"Put Red to bed?" Charity tries.

"Good." Connie nods. "But let's look at the activities and make sure you get them so you can start figuring out which cabin to assign to which game. . . ."

We spend some time going over everything, and trying new cheers ("We're Blue, we're Blue, guess what we're gonna do? You're Red, you're Red, we're putting you to bed" was my favorite, probably because I constructed it from Charity's slogans). By the time Connie tells us to meet back here tomorrow at the same time and sends us down to dinner, I'm even more excited, but also kind of nervous.

"This is wild," I tell Paz as we walk down to dinner. "Right?"

"Yeah," Paz says. "I think it'll be fun."

"Can I ask you something?"

"Sure."

"Does Charity hate me?"

Paz laughs. "Nah. She's like that with everybody. Super friendly, but with those intense eyes. And I think she's a little defensive here, because there's always one kid who tells her it's a queer camp, and being ace and aro isn't queer."

"What? It's literally in the acronym on the website."

"That's what I say, but some people are rude. Charity doesn't even report them, either. I do, though. Joan takes them aside for a special lesson on inclusivity as punishment."

"So you're close?" I ask. We're almost at the dining hall, but I decide it'll look normal walking in with Paz; no one will know we're captains.

"We bunked together our first year. She's cool, trust me. If she's freaking you out, or you think she's being mean, just tell her—she'll immediately apologize and try to make it up to you by crafting you something."

I laugh as I push the door to the dining hall open. "Okay. And Jimmy? He's in cabin nineteen?" Nineteen is the stoner cabin.

"Oh yeah," Paz says. We sit down with our friends, though Hudson only comes in a few minutes later. He grins at me and sits down.

"Wait," George says. "Why did you and Hudson enter separately? Did you not spend this time together? Did Andrew Lloyd Webber finally write a good musical?" His eyes go wide. I resist the urge to point out that *Dreamcoat* isn't bad.

"I had to write a letter to my parents," Hudson says.

"Yeah...," I say. "And I was checking on something at the obstacle course."

"I thought you were writing your parents, too?" Hudson asks.

"At the obstacle course," I say. "I wanted to try to draw the distance of the Peanut Butter Pit for them."

227

Hudson laughs, but George looks at me curiously, able to see right through my lies. Luckily, he doesn't say anything until after dinner, when he pulls me aside as we walk to the queer history lecture.

"I can't tell you," I say. "But it's good. And Hudson doesn't know."

"Darling, what on earth?"

"Let's just say I'm going to help make camp more… colorful."

George raises his eyebrows. "Well, how exciting. I look forward to your outfits. Having to resist making them into drag fantasy costumes around the color of… yellow?"

"Blue."

"Ah, a missed opportunity. You'd like swimming in blue glitter eye shadow, maybe blue lipstick. Now all you can do is some football player lines under your eyes."

"Yeah." I shake my head. "Think I could get away with it? Team spirit is kind of butch, right? Like all those guys who do the tacky full body paint at football games. Lipstick and eye shadow aren't a huge leap from that. I'll say it's all for team spirit."

He looks at me pityingly and pats me on the arm. "I'll doll it up enough for both of us."

I laugh. "You'd better. I'm going to miss the opportunity to wear a full blue sequin jumpsuit, with, like, pink stars all over it."

"Do you have that?" George asks, suddenly serious. "If

you have that, you need to get your parents to ship it to you priority."

"I don't, I don't. I was just making it up."

George sighs. "Too bad."

The queer history class picks up where the last one ended—discussing pre-Stonewall trans people and organizations. Joan shows us some clips of a female impersonator named Julian Eltinge, who was in Hollywood movies in the twenties, and Christine Jorgensen, who underwent sexual reassignment surgery in the fifties and then worked as a nightclub singer.

"Though it would be an overstatement to say trans people were accepted," Joan says, "they weren't invisible, and they weren't all persecuted for being who they were. Though some, like Lucy Hicks Anderson, definitely were."

Joan tells us about Lucy Hicks Anderson, arrested for marrying a man. She'd been raised as a girl since a young age—had convinced her parents and doctors that was the right course of action in the late 1800s—but was arrested for signing her marriage certificate. That she was black also made her an easier target for persecution. Then Joan goes on to various people who seemed to have more fluid gender. Many drag cabaret singers in the thirties, forties, and later, female impersonators who preferred to stay identified as women, and just men who wore dresses when they wanted to, or women who wore pants.

"We've been playing with gender and sex forever. The

idea that stepping outside your society-defined gender was somehow perverse, while it existed to a degree, didn't really get codified until women started trying to take equal power."

At the end of the lecture, I walk back to the cabins, holding Hudson's hand.

"So, when you meet my parents at the end of the summer," he says, and I feel a little thrill—I'm going to make it as his boyfriend until the end of the summer, he wants me to meet his parents!—"don't mention this lecture to them, okay?"

"Sure," I say, keeping my tone cool. "Why not?"

"Just...they're cool, like, mostly. I don't think they'd have a problem with trans people, maybe. But the more, like, gender-bendy stuff? They might not like that. When my dad gets really mad at me he tells me I should be ashamed of myself 'as a man.' I don't think they even know what non-binary is."

"Well, the title character in the musical is non-binary this year, so...they'll be introduced to it," I say.

"They are?" Hudson asks, a concerned look growing on his face and then turning to concentration. "Okay. I'll explain it in a letter. Or maybe we'll just skip the musical."

I stop walking, which he doesn't notice until his hand pulls on mine. Then he turns around, confused. "What?"

"You can't skip the musical," I say. "Our friends are in it. It means a lot to them."

"Yeah, but, my parents..."

"Will deal with it. This is important." I tug on his hand.

"They're your friends, really."

I cock my head, confused. "No, they're our friends. Brad is...dating George, maybe? Kissing at least. We have lunch with them every day."

"Well, yeah, but...you're closer with them."

"So?"

"So, look, it's just about my parents, babe. I don't want them to think they've sent me to camp where I'm going to turn all...different." A mosquito lands on his neck and he swats at it. The way he bends his neck slightly to the side is so strangely sexy.

"You've been coming here for years. They won't think that. Come on, you have to go to the show."

He grins at me. "Okay. I can't say no to you." I feel my body get warm all over and start walking again. "I'll try to explain it to them in a letter, so they have time to prepare."

"Prepare?"

"You know. Old people."

"Sure," I say. We're at my cabin, and we go around the side to kiss good night for a little while.

"This week, we should go by the drama cabin. So you can see what *our* friends are doing all day. So you can feel like they're *our* friends. Okay?"

He shrugs. "I mean, if you want."

"I do."

"Then sure," he says, kissing me lightly on the lips. "So, I'll see you tomorrow?" he says. I nod, and kiss him again. He pulls me closer by my ass, and I shiver as our bodies collide.

"Hey, wait," I say, suddenly remembering this morning, before I was made captain. "Did you want to talk to me about something? You said something about going to the obstacle course?"

"Oh," he says, as if remembering, too. Honestly, I'm a little offended he hasn't been thinking about it all day. "So, yeah...I thought maybe, if you wanted some alone time, we could sneak out after curfew...but now I don't know. I don't want to get in trouble."

That's never stopped him before. "Oh."

"I mean...I'd love some alone time with you, babe," he says, sliding his hand up my shirt. "But maybe this weekend?"

"Yeah," I say, leaning forward to kiss him again as his finger makes a crescent moon under my nipple. "This weekend would be good."

"You'll be ready?" he asks. "I mean...what I'm saying is—"

"Yes. I know what you're saying." Honestly, I'm ready now. He's opened up to me, he's actually said he's falling for me, and he's talking about the end of the summer. The plan is working. And besides, I want it. If he asked me to strip right here I'd probably do it, but two weeks was the original plan anyway, and now I have the color wars stuff eating up my time, so this'll be perfect. Sunday, after Blue wins.

He smiles, his tongue against the gap between his teeth at the corner of his mouth, a little gesture I've only noticed this summer and am already obsessed with. I think it means he's happy, but also turned on. It turns me on, anyway.

"Cool," he says, like I didn't just say I want him naked and against me in so many words.

"Cool," I say back to him.

"So, good night," he says.

"Good night."

I float into the cabin and get ready for bed, barely paying attention to everyone around me, and when I fall asleep, I dream of Hudson, in a blue sequin jumpsuit covered in pink stars.

EIGHTEEN

The next day goes quickly—a hike, hand in hand with Hudson, swimming, lunch, softball, more swimming. I love every moment with Hudson, but when I have to go to meet up with the other color war captains, I get excited about that, too. I'm the first one in cabin four after pool time. Connie comes in a moment after me, then Jimmy, Paz, and Charity, who's carrying perfectly folded squares of fabric tied with curled ribbons.

"I made us matching rompers!" she says, handing one out to each of us. I look at Paz, who shrugs. "I know you're doing this butch thing this summer, Del, so I did them in black-and-blue plaid. Pretty butch, right?" She grins. I nod. "I'm good at eyeing people's measurements, but let me know if anything doesn't fit. Oh, and I put a little black lace down the front of mine. I can do that for any of yours, too."

"Cool," Jimmy says, taking off his shirt.

"Jimmy, I don't think here is—" Connie starts, but Jimmy has his shorts off before she can finish, and is pulling the romper up over his candy-cane-printed boxers. It's unbuttoned to the waist, and he makes no move to button it up, but it does fit him perfectly. Charity has a great eye. And she's right, it may be a romper, but I don't feel like I'm going to look too femme in it. Just shorts and a button-up shirt—as a one-piece.

"These are great, Charity," I say. "Thanks."

"Try it on and make sure it fits when you have a moment," she says.

"Thank you," Paz adds, looking hers over. "We'll be pretty cute, all of us in these at once."

"It'll be so cute," Charity agrees as the door opens behind her.

We turn to see the Red team captains. First is Ryan, the sports counselor, and following him are Sam, who was on my team in capture the flag, Brad, and Jasmine Khatri, who's a year older than me and spends most of her time waterskiing and canoeing, and is always the first in the audience to stand up during the musical and clap. Behind her is Hudson. I grin at him when he comes in and he smiles back.

"I knew it," he says. "You wouldn't be sketching the obstacle course for your parents."

"I thought it was a perfectly good lie," I say.

"All right," Connie says. "Let's all sit down."

There are more chairs and we all sit around the table, Hudson scooting his chair up to mine.

"First of all," Connie says, "I want to emphasize that this is a FRIENDLY competition. No pranking each other, no cabin raids, no chants about the other team dying or being hurt or crybabies or anything like that. This is about fun, and part of fun is good sportsmanship. As the captains, you have to demonstrate that, and if you see anyone being out of line, even if they're on your own team, call them out for it."

"Yeah, people," Ryan adds, "play nice."

"Now, let's plan the big entrance on Friday night. Usually we do this at the end of dinner. Some kind of sketch with the captains leading into a big reveal as you run around the room, cheering, getting people hyped up. Any ideas?"

"We should use Del and Hudson," Paz says.

"What?" I ask.

"You guys are the most public couple this summer. You should have a big fight or something, and be like, 'There's only one way to settle this—color wars!' and then the rest of us come running out and do our thing."

"We're not the most public couple," Hudson says. "What about Lillian and Daphne? Or Dave and Dimitry? They've been together for years."

"No, it's you," Jasmine says. "You guys are waaaay into the PDA."

Everyone around us nods and I stare at my feet to hide my blushing.

"I dunno," Hudson says.

"I'm okay with it," I say, turning to him. "Could be fun." And my only chance to do some acting this summer.

"Yeah?"

I turn back to the group. "But the fight has to be over something really dumb."

"How about food?" Sam suggests.

"Oh yeah," Paz says. "Pepperoni or sausage pizza or something."

"Not sausage," Connie says quickly. "Let's see if we can make it color associated. And I'm not sure what the menu will be."

"Bug juice," Jimmy says. "The powdered drink stuff. Can you make sure there's blue and red that night?"

"Yes, I think we can." Connie nods.

"So I say the blue is better? And Hudson says the red is better?" I ask.

"Yes," Paz says. "It works because they all taste the same. Like sugar."

I turn back to Hudson. "You okay with this? I don't want to pressure you into it."

Hudson shrugs. "I just don't know if I'll be good at it. I'm no actor."

"It'll be short. We can practice beforehand." I lay my hand on his thigh. "I think it'll be fun."

"Okay." He shrugs. "I mean, if my acting is bad, at least that's part of the joke, right?"

"Yeah," I say.

"So just start shouting 'Red,' 'Blue,' 'Red,' 'Blue,' and that'll be our cue to come rushing in," Paz says.

"Great," Connie says. "Then Ryan and I will announce the start of the games and how the teams are divided. Now let's go over the scheduling and make sure you all understand what the events are, and where you'll be leading the non-participants in cheers and songs."

We go over everything, figuring out cheering sections and when we march our teams from location to location. The Red team leaves after a while and we start trying to figure out which cabins to assign to which activities. We have five cabins in total, and five activities. We give Jimmy's cabin the pie eating, and Charity's cabin the egg race. We give cabin five, with mostly younger kids, the kickball game. But then there's just the swimming races and the obstacle course relay race, and cabins eighteen and seven. My cabin.

"Hudson's cabin is definitely going to be our competition for the obstacle course relay," Paz says. "They run that thing every week. I don't know how we can beat them."

"I do," I say, smiling. "We'll take them on. Cabin seven." I point to our cabin on the list.

"Are you sure?" Connie asks.

"Positive."

"All right," Connie says. "Then we have it all set. All we

need are some good cheers…and I was going to say some good blue outfits, but I think we have that covered," she says, looking at our rompers, mine still expertly folded and tied with ribbon.

"Did you want one, too?" Charity asks. "I can make one. What are you, six-two and three-quarters?"

"I…yes," Connie says. "But no need to make me anything. Focus on your fellow captains' outfits. I'm just your supervisor. But for now, we should get to dinner. See you all tomorrow to work on cheers."

We leave the cabin and head down to dinner, Paz walking next to me.

"Hey," she says. "Can I ask you something?"

"Sure."

"It's about Ashleigh."

"Okay."

"So, I know she's demi, but…I mean, we've been hanging out a lot. I think she's really funny, and really hot, but if she's not feeling it, that's okay. But is it that she won't feel anything for me in that way, or just that we haven't clicked enough yet?"

"Oh," I say. This is not easy like the George one. "Honestly, I don't know. I'm not demi. I have no idea what it's like, aside from how she explained it to me."

"How did she explain it to you?"

"Well, this was years ago, but she said that non-demi people can go to a movie and see a movie star and be turned on by them and want to get with them. She doesn't do that. She doesn't feel anything for someone she doesn't know. A character in a movie, maybe, though usually not, 'cause she knows they're just a character. But for her to get turned on by a person, she has to know them."

Paz sighs. "So you really don't know?"

"Just ask her," I say. "Tell her you're into her, and you're hoping she's into you, or will be, but if she's not, you don't want to spend the summer pining over someone with no interest. She'll get that, trust me."

"That sounds so awkward."

"Yeah."

"Can you ask her for me?"

"No," I say quickly. "I mean, I can, but I wouldn't tell you unless she said she wanted me to tell you, and then it's just passing notes in class, right? Just ask her."

"Yeah." She sighs again. "Okay."

When we go into the dining hall, Hudson is already there and I run to take a seat before helping myself to the chicken nuggets going around.

"Hey," he says. "So, I'm a little nervous about...the thing we agreed to." He looks around and speaks softly.

"Don't worry about it. It'll be silly and fine. We can practice later, if you want."

"Yeah, if that's okay. I don't want anyone to think it's for real, either. I don't want anyone to think I'm mad at you, babe."

My heart melts a little, and I run my hand down his arm. He doesn't want anyone to think the fight is real! That's too adorable. I'm so, so lucky.

"I think if they do think it's real," I tell him, "they'll figure out it's not the moment everyone else comes running in in costume."

"Yeah." He squeezes my thigh. "And, so, you're cool with this? Being on opposite sides?"

"Sure." I dunk my nugget into some ketchup. "It's just a game."

"And you'll be cool when we kick your ass?" He grins and wiggles his eyebrows.

"You can try," I tell him, staying cool. "But I'll be fine if we lose. You'll be okay, too?"

"I mean, that's not going to happen, but yeah, I think I'll be okay."

"Confident man," I say, licking my lips.

"I have some experience."

"Maybe I'll give you some new ones."

"So, are we still talking about the thing... or a different thing? 'Cause I thought we said this weekend. I meant when the first thing is over, by the way."

"That's what I meant, too. And yeah, I think that'll be perfect timing."

His hand inches up my thigh, his fingers under my shorts.

"I don't know which thing I'm more excited about," he says.

"You don't? I'm a little offended."

"Okay," he says, leaning in so I can feel his breath on my neck. "I know."

I swallow.

He pulls his hand back. "So we can rehearse a little after dinner, before the night swim?"

"Perfect," I say, happy he's pulling back. I didn't want to be sporting this hard-on when I stood up after dinner. I make a point of asking for the blue juice, just to seed our act a little, and spend the rest of the night hearing about the rehearsals and planning our skit in my mind.

After dinner, as everyone goes up the hill to the cabins to change into swimsuits, I take Hudson aside behind my cabin to practice our performance. He picks it up quickly, not that there's much to it. I open with a comedic monologue on why blue juice is better than red, he disagrees, I disagree, he shouts *red*, I shout *blue*, repeat until people run in. It's simple. But his acting could use a little work.

"Be more forceful," I tell him. "Make me believe you really think red juice is better."

"Um...okay. The red JUICE is better."

"You don't need to emphasize the word *juice*."

"Right. So, you learned all this stuff from your bunkmates?" he asks, leaning on the wall next to me.

"From our friends, yes. Try it again."

"The RED juice is the best!"

"Good. No, you're wrong, blue is clearly superior," I say, giving him my most heated look.

"So...you look kinda hot doing that."

"Doing what?" I say, smiling.

"Just, being so forceful."

"Oh. Well...the blue juice is better," I say, and grab the collar of his shirt and pull him toward me for a kiss.

"Is this part of the sketch?" Hudson asks in a whisper.

"Del!" Mark calls. "Come on! We're headed down and I have a cheap disposable underwater camera to give you, which Joan is going to mail away to get developed because no one uses these anymore except for underwater photos."

"I'd better go. But I think you have the sketch down."

"I never realized being on opposite sides could be sexy," Hudson says.

"Don't say that when I'm leaving. That's just mean." I grab him, and pull him in for another kiss before running back into the cabin, where Mark hands me a camera and I quickly change into my swimsuit. They give us the cameras every year for the night swim, even though the photos never come out. Mark says Joan wants a cool nighttime underwater shot for the website but is too cheap to hire a real photographer to get one.

At the pool, Joan, who is not in a swimsuit and will not go into the pool, loudly reminds everyone to wind the camera between shots before we all dive in. The sun is low, so most of the light comes from the few lights set up around the pool and the underwater lights. Everyone dives under, snapping selfies or shots of their friends with bubbles coming out of their noses, hoping for a shot that isn't blurry. I take one of Hudson kissing me on the cheek above water, and one underwater. Neither of them will come out, but it's fun to do this couple-y thing, the taking of the selfie, the posing, the being willing to display it…if not on our phones, then maybe on our bunks when we get the prints, and at the end of the summer, we can download the photos with a code they send us.

So that's neat.

I spot George and Brad doing some cute, couple-y photos, too, and Paz and Ashleigh doing photos together, if not kissing ones. But Paz does put her arm around Ashleigh's waist, so maybe they've talked. I should check in on that.

After pool time, Hudson and I kiss good night, and in the cabin, I try on the romper Charity made me, which fits perfectly. And, which, when left unbuttoned most of the way, showing off my somewhat hairy chest and treasure trail, looks perhaps too sexy. I'll have to remember to unbutton it for Hudson.

"Darling, you look amazing. Where did you get that? If we had real cameras, I would take a photo of you for your dating profile right now."

"I don't need a dating profile anymore," I say, grinning and turning around from the bathroom mirror I've been admiring myself in. "And from the looks of you and Brad, neither do you."

"Oh." George waves me off and starts brushing his teeth. "It's just a fwing."

I shrug. "Whatever. It's cute. I'm glad you're having fun."

"I'll have more fun when we can have some awone time." I laugh.

"What's funny?" Ashleigh asks, walking in. I look behind her—no Paz.

"George. But I want to know..." I lower my voice. "What's going on with you and Paz?"

"Oh." Ashleigh looks behind her at the bathroom door. "I don't know. She's nice."

"And?" George asks, foam dripping from his mouth.

Ashleigh shrugs. "I could be...maybe...thinking she's kind of hot."

"YESH!" George says, spitting foam everywhere, though thankfully not on my romper. He spits into the sink. "Good."

"But that doesn't mean she likes me," Ashleigh says, putting toothpaste on her own brush.

George and I roll our eyes at each other and I go back into one of the stalls to put on my pajamas.

"Of course she does," George says.

"She's friendly, I don't know," Ashleigh says.

"Just talk to her," I say. I don't want to betray Paz's

confidence, but if neither of them speak to each other all summer, it's going to be ridiculous.

"Maybe," Ashleigh says. I step out of the stall, changed. Ashleigh is brushing her teeth, and George shrugs at me. I go to put my romper away, and George walks with me.

"You never said where that came from," George says, nodding at the romper.

"Uh . . . someone made it for me. For a thing," I say.

"Oh." George nods. "Blue. Right. Good. I just got a package with blue nail polish and eye shadow. I'm set."

I smirk and get into bed, not wanting him to show me the makeup I won't be able to wear.

"Oh, and I think there's some glittery blue lipstick in the drama cabin. I bet Mark will let us use it."

"Probably," I say, getting under the covers.

"Sorry, sorry, I know, shouldn't talk about it. But I'll be prepared. I have a blue fan, too. I'm excited for the looks I'll be working."

I don't say anything, feeling sad about the two streaks of blue under my eyes being the closest I'll get to makeup of any kind this summer. The closest I get to expressing my real style. Maybe I can put some glitter on them. I can get away with that, right? And besides, what am I even worrying about? Hudson is falling for me. I could probably wear a full face and he'd be fine.

The next day, when I meet with the other captains, we finalize all our cheers and go over which cabins are on what games again. Everyone is still skeptical of my cabin taking on the obstacle course, until I explain my reasoning to them, and then everyone gets excited, like maybe we have a chance.

"You'll have to convince everyone, though," Paz says. "I mean, I'll help, but this is your idea, and theater kids are great at self-esteem when they know they're going to be good. But if they think they're going to come in second place...well... you know how we are."

"I think it'll be good," I say.

That night, the camp activity is stargazing. We've shut out all the lights in camp and are lying in the middle of the soccer field while Karl, the nature counselor, points out constellations and planets, his accent making it all sound very academic. Hudson and I lie in the grass holding hands.

"So, tomorrow, we're not meeting before dinner," I tell him. "Are you?"

"No. We have everything worked out, so we're not worrying about it again until Friday."

"So, maybe you want to visit my friends in the drama cabin? Mark is running rehearsals before dinner now."

"Oh," he says, as though he'd forgotten we were doing that. "Yeah, okay. We're just going to watch rehearsals?"

"And go backstage, maybe. It's chaos, but fun, relaxed chaos."

"Have you been already?"

"Yeah," I say. "They invited me." And I want to tell him how it felt like home and how I felt sad to be there, but not REALLY be there, but I can't, and holding all that back makes me cough suddenly, and feel like I've been hit in the throat.

"You okay?" he asks, turning onto his shoulder to look at me. I sit up and cough again and he pats me on the back.

"Yeah." I wipe away at a tear gathering in my eye. "Just swallowed funny."

We lie back down and look up at the stars. They're not as good as the imaginary stars you see when you look at trees. The stars you can make yourself see. Those are a flood, like diamonds spilled over black velvet in a heist movie. These are like pinpricks in black canvas, a Fresnel light shining through them. You can see each of them individually, and you can see how they run together.

"Each of them is really millions of kilometers away," Karl says.

"That's like miles," Joan says quickly.

"Ya," Karl says. "Millions of miles. And they're millions of kilo-miles from us, too."

"I like the stars you showed me better," Hudson says, taking my hand in his.

"Me too," I say as our fingers interlace.

NINETEEN

When we go into the drama cabin after pool time the next day, it's still perfect. The smell, the lights, the sounds of it—people dancing onstage, people murmuring in the audience, watching, people backstage trying to figure out cues, stage makeup, costume changes. We go in through the back, but I check the call sheet and see George is probably onstage, rehearsing one of his big numbers: "Hymn for a Sunday Evening." The Ed Sullivan number, performed as a kind of church choir hymn, hence the title.

"Come on." I take Hudson's hand. He's looking around at the chaos of backstage, kind of nervous. I'm thrilled he's getting to see it, though. This is part of the plan, the easing him in—although I guess backstage is never easing of any kind. But he's getting to see what Randy is into now. And

he's seeing that Del is into it, too. That Del is Randy...a least
a little.

"What is all this?"

"It's backstage," I say. "You think people just wait calmly
in lines to go on?"

"Yeah, I did."

I laugh, quietly, and pull him through the doors that lead
to the audience. "Be quiet here, they're rehearsing."

Onstage, George and Mark are talking. George is in a big
rainbow choir robe, along with the actors playing the rest of
the family. In the audience, I see Brad waving at us. We go
over and take the seats in front of him.

"You come here?" Hudson asks.

"Yeah, to watch George. It's pretty cool."

"That is a big crush you have," Hudson says.

"Right back at ya," Brad says.

Hudson snorts as Mark runs back to the audience. Montgomery and David, who plays Mrs. MacAfee, take the rainbow robe off George, revealing George's own T-shirt and
shorts.

"They don't have his suit ready yet," Brad whispers.

"Okay," Mark calls from the audience. "Crystal?" Crystal, at the piano, gives the thumbs-up. "All right. Don't
destroy that dream," he says, the last line before George's.

"Me, on *The Ed Sullivan Show*?" George says, turning to
the audience, his face moving from astonished to a manically

pleased grin. Crystal starts playing the piano and George starts singing.

It's a hilarious performance. George is playing it not just like he's obsessed with Ed Sullivan, but like he wants to get in Ed Sullivan's pants. Like he's finally being given the opportunity Kim has been given—to kiss his celebrity crush. It's a smart, super queer, and amazing move, and reminds me again of how much I miss being in this show—being in Mark's vision of the show especially. George keeps singing as the rest of the family comes forward and places the rainbow robe around him, and George lets his hands trace down the front of the robe—zipping it closed, but also very sexy—as he sings. When he cries out "Ed, I love you!" at the close of the song, it feels romantic and sensual. David, playing George's character's wife, even looks at him, a little hurt, but shrugs, as if he understands, and maybe shares the crush. And George does it all perfectly. The notes, the face, the way he makes it funny, but also into an aching love song. He's brilliant. I stand up and applaud when he's finished. He spots me in the audience and waves.

"We're working here," Mark shouts at me—or us, rather, since Brad is standing and applauding, too. As he sits back down, he grabs the seat in front of him—the one next to Hudson, and Hudson does a double take. Even in the dim audience lighting, I can see why: Brad is wearing nail polish. Unicorn Trampocalypse.

"What is that?" Hudson asks, grabbing one of Brad's hands.

Brad pulls his hand away. "George put it on me. It's fun, right?"

"What?" Hudson asks. "I get you have a big crush, but you're going to let him change you like that?"

"Hudson," Brad says, "it's just nail polish. What's the matter?"

"It's not... that's not..."

Brad looks at me, asking for help, and I take Hudson's hand.

"It's just nail polish," I say.

"You too?" he says, and he looks at me like I've stabbed him in the back. The look I'm afraid he'll give me if he ever finds out the truth.

"Dude," Brad says. "What's going on? You're being an asshole."

"We're trying to rehearse here!" Mark yells at us from the stage. Hudson frowns and walks out into the aisle, heading for the exit. Brad crosses his arms and leans back in his seat. Onstage, George is staring at us, confused. I sigh and run after Hudson.

He pushes open the door to the cabin and walks outside. The day is bright.

"Hudson." I catch up to him. "What's wrong?"

He sighs and sits down on the grass. He starts pulling out blades of it. "I was being an asshole, wasn't I?"

"I mean, it seemed like a big reaction to a little nail polish."

"But what's after that? Eye shadow? Does he start carrying around a fan?"

"So what if he does?" *George does all that*, I don't say. Does he have a problem with George?

Hudson lies back on the grass, and I sit down next to him. We're silent for a while. Something is going on, and I can't tell what it is. Does he just really hate anything even mildly femme? Every summer he's been telling us our queerness made us powerful, that we could do anything we wanted. Every summer he's been making me feel like I really could. I could understand if it didn't turn him on, but I can't believe he really has a problem with men wearing makeup or using fans. That's not the Hudson I know.

"I just..." He looks at the trees over us, and I can tell he's unfocusing his eyes. I reach out and take his hand, and he squeezes mine. We sit there for a while, holding hands. "Remember I told you I stopped going to my grandma's after school for a while? It wasn't because my parents thought I was old enough to stay home alone. It was because my dad walked in on me doing my grandma's makeup."

"Oh," I say. I know I shouldn't smile right now, but I want to. Little Hudson, carefully applying lipstick to his grandma! It's so cute, right? But it's shocking, too. Not so masc after all, I guess. But I like that. I like that maybe he's more like me—the real me—than I knew.

"I know, it sounds weird."

"No," I say quickly. "I was thinking it was cute, actually."

Hudson refocuses his eyes and looks at me and smiles. "Yeah?"

"Yeah. But I don't get why that would make you angry at Brad for painting his nails."

Hudson frowns and looks back at the sky. "So, I used to watch her do her makeup in the mirror every day. And I thought it was, like, so pretty and so cool, so one day I asked her to show me how to do it. And she just taught me. Didn't even question it. So, then I start doing her makeup for her when I come over, and she let me play—crazy colors that don't go together, drawing butterflies, sports team logos. A lot of really awful stuff, not pretty, but some of it... Anyway, so I put some on me, too, sometimes, but Grandma always wiped it off really quickly.

"So, then one day, my dad got off a job early and he came to pick me up—he had a key, and he walked in on me putting purple eye shadow on Grandma. And he stared at me, like he was really shocked, and I didn't get it. Like at all. And even Grandma went kind of weird and immediately put the makeup away and got my backpack and sort of sent me away with Dad.

"I didn't get what was happening at all. I just knew something was... off? And then that night, Mom came into my bedroom and she said that makeup was for girls. And I said okay, because I kind of already knew that. I wasn't going to wear lipstick. I just liked putting it on Grandma. And she said that meant I shouldn't do Grandma's makeup anymore. So then I sort of understood. And I asked why. And this was before I even knew I was queer, but Mom said that boys who do makeup are a different kind of boy. 'And those boys aren't what you are.'" He pauses and says the words not in his mom's voice, but solemnly, like a commandment. "And I didn't get it, but I got it, you know? It felt a little like she'd been yelling, but she hadn't. She was speaking in a soft voice and stroking my hair and she told me she loved me and tucked me in and I went to sleep. And so the next day, Dad said I could take the bus home and just hang out, and gave me a set of keys. Which seemed so cool! I didn't even put the two together—me being home alone meant me away from Grandma."

"Okay," I say. He's been just staring at the sky as he said it, and I'm doing my best to hold back tears for Little Hudson having this special thing he did with his grandma taken away from him. "But you know better now, right?"

"I mean...I get it, yeah. I know it's just makeup, and here, at camp, it's fine, right? But out in the world? My parents have met Brad. They know he's one of my best friends. I think they think we'll get married someday."

"Oh." I swallow, suddenly nervous and jealous and my body is shaking.

Hudson laughs. "Babe, don't worry. I am not his type. But, like, Brad is one of the reasons my parents let me keep coming here, I think. Because there's another gay guy like me. Who doesn't have the makeup or the fans. And if he starts that, and he has makeup on or anything when my parents come to visit..."

"You're afraid if he changes, your parents will think this place will change you," I say. "And then they won't let you come back."

There's a long pause.

"Yes."

I lie down on the grass next to him. The sky has a slight haze in it as it gets later. It's not dark, just grayer, and when I unfocus my eyes, the fake stars aren't as blinding as they usually are. I try not to show the relief I'm feeling. He doesn't hate makeup and fans and femme—he's just afraid of his parents. He still thinks we can be whoever we want here...just not out there. Which is funny, because he always talks about being who we want out there. He's made me braver. But when it's your own parents, it's different, I guess.

"I get why it freaked you out," I say. "But also it's Brad's choice. And I don't think nail polish means he's changing. He's still Brad. Just like if you took all the makeup off George, he'd still be George." Just sadder George, I think. Although, isn't that sort of what I've done to myself? Am I sadder? I would be if I didn't have Hudson.

"I get that. I just...I saw it, and I thought of my grandma, and I thought of how I didn't get to see her as much, and then

I thought of my parents, and them seeing Brad, and them telling me next summer I should just stay home, and not seeing Brad again, or you... and it was like it all suddenly leaped into my head at once and I freaked out. But I was an asshole."

"Yeah," I say. "You kinda were. You should go apologize to Brad."

"I will." He laughs and turns onto his side, and I turn onto mine to look at him. He kisses me on the lips. "Thank you."

"For what?"

"Just for listening. I've never told anyone any of this before, but with you, it's like, when I say it, I can deal with it."

"That's what boyfriends are for, right?"

"No." He shakes his head. "Or if they are, I've never had a boyfriend before."

"Well, you haven't. That was Hal."

He smiles and kisses me again, deeper this time, his hands around my back pulling me into him. Then he rests his head on my shoulder, still squeezing me.

"I love you," he whispers.

My heart actually stops for a minute. I'm positive. I'm a medical marvel for one instant as every cell in my body freezes up, blood stops flowing, lungs stop breathing, brain stops... brain-ing. And then it all starts up again.

"I'm sorry if it's too soon to say that," he says.

"I love you, too," I say quickly. I don't add: *I've loved you for years.* Later, I'll tell him later, when I reveal everything to him. He loves me. He said so. That's the part of the plan I never thought would work, really. The next part. The part that means now I CAN tell him, but he won't mind, because he loves me, and maybe I should tell him right now...but why ruin the moment? Right? It would ruin the moment. I'll tell him later. Not now.

I kiss him instead.

TWENTY

By the time color wars starts on Friday, I haven't told any-one about our I Love Yous. I wanted to keep it private, hold it close, not to be shared for George and Ashleigh to make fun of, even if it would be the friendly teasing, the kind I deserve for getting what I want. At least for a little while. But my moments alone with Hudson—holding hands at dinner, kissing good night—feel so much more special now. So much more intense. This isn't a summer fling. This isn't just hormones. This is fate. This was meant to be. And everything I've done, my crazy scheme, all of that was what needed to happen for Hudson to finally love me the way I love him.

Honestly, I'm pretty proud of myself. I made a plan, and it was hard work, but I executed it. Sure, it's not quite done—I still haven't gotten all the way naked with Hudson (at least outside my imagination in the showers sometimes), I still haven't told him the truth, or worn nail polish, or clacked a fan open in front of him, but I'll do those things soon. Sunday after color wars, we already have plans to find some alone time at the Peanut Butter Pit. And if that doesn't work, we signed up to share a tent on the canoe trip next weekend. Though the idea of waiting that long makes me kind of crazy. I'm willing to sneak out after curfew just to finally have sex with the man I love—and who loves me. Even if we get caught, it would be worth it.

Which makes the fake fight even more fun. I know he loves me, and he knows I love him, so when I tell him, in a louder-than-usual voice, that his choice of the red powdered fruit beverage is "disgusting. It tastes like candy that melted in someone's shoes," it's almost hot, the way he turns to me, nervous about the acting, but happy to be doing something with me—his boyfriend whom he loves.

"Oh please," he says. "Blue is the gross flavor. And it stains your tongue so you look like a corpse!"

"Nice improv," I whisper. He grins at me.

"Really? This is how we're doing this?" George asks, across the table from us.

"Better a blue tongue that those red lips!" I shout, going full drama now. "It looks like you have a harlot's disease. Red is the color of blood, but blue is the color of peace! Red is small, limited anger—blue is the endless sky! Throughout time, red has always been the color of villainy, and blue the flag of heroes! Blue is clearly the superior juice!"

"Ha!" Hudson says, standing and knocking my glass down to the floor. Color me impressed—he's getting really into it. "Blue? Blue is the color of sadness. Blue is for people who can't appreciate red."

"You red-tongued monster!" I declare, standing up and then standing on the bench and pointing down at him. "Blue juice is better!"

"Red is!" he shouts, standing up on the bench next to me, his face close to mine.

"Blue!"

"Red!"

"Blue!" As I shout, Paz comes marching in with Charity and Jimmy behind her. They're all wearing the rompers, and wearing blue makeup on their faces (Jimmy and Paz like war paint, Charity more like she's doing a mermaid photoshoot for her Instagram). Paz is carrying a blue flag and raises it up, chanting "Blue" in unison with me as everyone around us rolls our eyes, aside from a few of the younger campers who either look confused or excited. Then the other Red captains march in with their flag—and much less well dressed— and Hudson and I get down and join our teams, me tearing off the faux T-shirt I'd been wearing over my romper for just this purpose (Charity is a FAST sewer, made it in a few hours). I love a good reveal.

We all march in place at the front of the dining hall,

shouting our colors at each other for what feels like far too long before Joan jumps up on a table and shouts, "Color wars!" without nearly the amount of passion as is required by the moment. Luckily, Mark is there and he gets up, and starts screaming, "Color wars!" jumping up and down, circling the room until everyone is also screaming, at least half-heartedly. A brave and powerful bit of acting from him, considering how much he hates color wars.

Joan puts her hand up and the room quiets, and she starts telling us which cabins are on which team, and everyone is forced to sit on the left or right side of the room for dessert—chocolate pudding with strawberries or blueberries, respectively. Connie addresses our side of the table, telling us which games each cabin will be playing for the Blue team.

"We're doing what?" Ashleigh asks when she hears we've been assigned the obstacle course.

"Trust me," I say. "We're going to beat them."

"Darling, did you hit your head? For real this time?" George asks.

I grin. "I'm telling you. I have a plan."

They lean in, and I tell them. They look skeptical, but nod.

"Maybe," Ashleigh says finally. "I mean . . . if nothing else, we'll surprise them."

"I really think we can win," I say.

"And Hudson won't mind if we do?" George asks.

"Nah." I wave him off. "It's just a game. Besides. He loves me." I couldn't keep it in anymore.

George's eyebrows shoot up. "Oh, does he now?"

"He does. He said so and everything."

"Wow." Ashleigh's eyes widen. "I'm genuinely impressed. You really tricked him into loving you."

I stare at her, not trying to hide how much what she said hurts. It wasn't a trick. It was a *plan*. And it worked. He *loves* me. Not just Del, but *me*, underneath it all.

"Ashleigh," George says, slapping at her hand. "Don't be mean."

"Sorry, that came out wrong."

"It wasn't a trick. He knows me," I say. It feels wrong in my mouth, though. "I'm going to tell him everything. After color wars. And he'll still love me."

"Of course he will, darling," George says, nodding. "Right, Ashleigh?"

"I hope so," Ashleigh says.

I frown. There's no need to hope. It'll work. Love doesn't just go away, right? I shake off this sudden jitteriness in my legs and go back to telling people about how I know we can beat the obstacle course.

The first color wars event is that night: the Spy Game. We're given little red or blue vests to wear and then the whole camp is divided down the middle, from the cabins to the river. Blue team starts at the meeting house and has to get to the boathouse, and Red team vice-versa, with the line down the middle being at the tennis courts. While in enemy territory, if you're spotted by the opposite team, you go to jail. We're all given flashlights.

Paz takes control outside the meeting house, assigning some people to patrol and some to try to get to the other side. Then we begin. I honestly don't know how this game is allowed, it's so dangerous. A bunch of us sneaking around the woods with no one able to watch all of us? Seems like it's asking for trouble. But that might be what makes it more fun? Even previous summers, I've always loved trying to sneak across camp in the dark. And this summer, I feel like I'm extra prepared for it. I rub mud on my face and arms. I pull my black socks all the way up. And I take off into the woods behind the cabins.

The woods that extend around camp aren't so thick you can't find the camp again pretty easily just by looking for light. They do go pretty far out, but I think most of us are too scared of getting lost to get too deep. I have a few other campers with me: Montgomery, who I make wear a black hat to cover his red hair, and Jordan, who is prepared in a black ski mask and black pants and long-sleeved shirt under their blue vest. I'm supposed to lead them across the camp, though honestly, I feel like Jordan should be in charge. I tell them to keep low to the ground and move quietly. Getting down the hill is easy—the woods have a gentle slope, and besides, we're still on our side of the camp. But I don't want anyone to see us going into the woods.

"Last year," Jordan whispers, "they had people patrolling the woods by the border, but there's a stream there that looks like the one from the end of *Funny Face* that covers the sound of rustling bushes."

"You lead the way, then," I say.

"Okay," they say. "But keep up. I'm going to get there before Ashleigh this year, so help me."

Montgomery and I follow Jordan deeper into the woods, and sure enough, there's a small brook nearby. It murmurs loudly enough to create white noise. We walk along it, keeping low and in the bushes. A few times we spot beams of light, but they swing over us. I'm not sure how far we get, but soon we see two figures right in our way. Jordan holds up their hand, and Montgomery and I stop, hiding in the bushes.

"The teams are so unfair this year," says one of the figures. I think the voice is Drew's, from Outdoor Adventure. "I mean, we're going up against cabin seven for the obstacle course? Did you see that? Hudson laughed when he read it."

"Don't be an ass," says the other voice. Sam, from sports.

"I'm not being an ass. I'm just saying. They're not the most athletic bunch. They're theater kids. They'll win with the cheers and stuff, for sure, but that's not enough points to even make a dent."

"That doesn't mean you have to gloat. Let them try their best and have fun. That's what this is about. Fun." They're quiet for a minute. I try not to breathe too loudly.

"Think this'll break up Hudson and Del?"

"Jealous?"

"I mean, he's at the two-week point. That's when it usually ends. And Hudson will need someone to get together with for the last two weeks."

Jordan puts their hand on my wrist, and I realize I'm clenching my fists.

"He's not getting back together with you, Drew," Sam says, walking off. Drew follows her. "If you're horny, just hook up with Derrick. He's easy."

"Not as hot, though," Drew says, sounding resigned as he walks after her.

"Trouble in paradise?" Montgomery whispers to me. "If you're feeling lonely, you know..."

"Shhh," Jordan says.

I roll my eyes in the dark. Hudson and I are fine. Though I don't like that he laughed at my cabin taking his on in the obstacle course. If he did. Drew might have been lying.

We follow the stream through the woods until it hits the river. No one is patrolling here, but we see some flashlights swinging around in the distance, and we're out of bushes here, so we keep very low to the ground—Jordan slithers on their stomach. There are two Red team guards outside the door of the boathouse, though. Luckily, there's the porch. I boost Jordan up and they climb onto the porch. Then I lift Montgomery, and once he's up, he and Jordan extend their arms. I jump and grab their arms and they lift me up onto the porch, where we collapse in a gasping pile.

I look out over the rest of the porch. Ashleigh is relaxing on one of the chairs. She turns to us and nods.

"S'up?"

"HOW?" Jordan asks, standing. "How did you beat us? I was timing us. We went fast along the safest possible route."

"That's your trouble right there," Ashleigh says, lying down in the chair and crossing her legs at the ankles. "Safest."

Jordan makes a noise like a growl and goes into the boat-house, where there are stickers to put on our vests, to prove we made it. Wearing those, we can walk freely to the jail and release everyone there, as long as we go back to our side with them, and give up our sticker in the process—giving up our win to free everyone so we can all try again. It's a risk, though—the team with the most people who've made it across wins. So giving up one person to try to bring more over is a gamble.

"You should wait half an hour so the jail is more full," Ashleigh calls.

"You're going to make them crazy, you know," I say to Ashleigh, sitting down next to her.

"Jordan is too careful. They'll beat me next year, though. Or I'll take them with me and show them how it's done."

"Now," Jordan says, appearing in the doorway.

"What?" Ashleigh says.

"You'll show me now," Jordan says.

"I'm waiting half an hour," Ashleigh says. "But then, sure, I'll show you. If you can handle it."

Jordan narrows their eyes and sits on the floor of the porch, cross-legged.

"I'm just staying here the rest of the night," Montgomery says, settling into one of the chairs.

"Hudson is one of the guards if you wanna go make out for half an hour," Ashleigh says to me.

"Or ask him why he laughed at our cabin being the one going against his on the obstacle course," Montgomery adds. I roll my eyes. No way Hudson did that.

"He did?" Ashleigh asks.

"If he did, and I don't think he did, it's out of context. It wasn't, 'They're ridiculous for trying to take us on,' it was, 'Ha! I know exactly how to defeat them!' But he's underestimating us," I say. "Only because we don't know the obstacle course, is all. That'll be our advantage."

"I still don't think we have a chance," Montgomery says. "I mean, they're like an army that does that course every day. Or did you choose us 'cause you wanted Hudson to win and feel big and strong?" He raises an eyebrow at me and purses his lips, mocking me.

"No," I say, crossing my arms. "I chose us 'cause we'll win. You just have to trust me."

"Trust you? You're not even in the show this year,"

Montgomery says. "You're barely in the cabin. All you do is make out with Hudson. We get it, you did it, yay you," he says flatly, doing unenthusiastic jazz hands. "But look at you—all butch and playing sports. Do you even care about the show this year? Do you care about anything besides Hudson? You want us to trust you, but I don't even know you."

It's like he's slapped me across the face, and my mouth hangs open, my eyes watering a little. I thought it was better with him and Jordan, after that one time they said I wasn't around enough... that one dinner we talked... and then they said it wasn't much, and I just... forgot about them. I haven't been a good friend, I realize.

"Of course you know him," Ashleigh says.

"We do," Jordan says. "But we haven't seen him much this summer. It just feels like you're not really part of the bunk anymore, Del."

"I'm sorry," I say softly. "I know I've been wrapped up in my relationship, but..."

"You can't say you're one of us and then not be," Montgomery says. "We've spent rehearsals together waiting for our cues, practicing dance moves, we've done the chorus together and had inside jokes and been part of... something. And now you're not. And then you swoop in and ask us to do this thing that you just KNOW we can do that none of us want to do, that we all know we're going to be awful at, and the person in front of me is like... I don't know him. I don't trust him. And I don't want to embarrass myself in front of the camp so he can look good for his boyfriend."

Jordan nods. "It just doesn't feel like you're one of us."

"I still am," I promise them. "I'm just working on something else, too."

"Is that what they call it these days?" Montgomery asks, raising an eyebrow.

"Look." Ashleigh sits up and puts her hand on my shoulder. "I get it. You're still you. Del is a role. And you're still our friend. But it's hard to follow you into what looks like a losing situation for us—one that'll totally humiliate us—when you've only spent a fraction of the time with us this summer that you usually do. When we see Del more than Randy. That's all they're saying, I think." Jordan and Montgomery nod.

I look over at Ashleigh. Her, too? I thought out of everyone, she really understood what I was doing, what it meant to me. Maybe not approved, exactly, but was hopefully for me. Was supportive. But if I'm letting even her down...

"You don't look like Randy," Montgomery says, his hand waving up and down my body. "I only see Del."

I nod, slowly. Okay. Yes. I've let them down. I've spent too much time being Del, not enough being Randy. So they don't trust me.

But I can fix that. I just need another plan. And one comes to me almost immediately.

"Okay," I say. "I get it. But we're going to win tomorrow. I have a plan, and I'm going to show you I'm still one of you."

"In one day?" Montgomery asks.

I stand up.

"Going to your butch boyfriend now?"

"No," I say, giving him my sassiest smile. "I'm going to free the jail and then get ready for tomorrow." I grin. I have an idea.

I run out of the cabin, past Hudson, who waves at me. I run back to give him a peck on the cheek, then take off for the prison. There are only a few kids there, but I free them and run back to my side, looking for Charity. She usually plays guard.

I find her by the A&C cabin, shining a flashlight around. I'm out of breath from running when I stop in front of her, and have to bend over for a moment before I can talk.

"You all right, Del?"

"The A and C cabin is open?" I ask.

"Yeah, they don't lock it up in case we need glitter or something."

"Great. How fast can you sew?"

TWENTY-ONE

When we march toward the obstacle course the next day, we are feeling pumped. After some frantic sewing last night from Charity and a talk with my cabin, I decided to show them that not only was I still Randy at heart, but it was Randy, not Del, who was going to lead them to victory. So, that morning, after a rushed breakfast, we'd raided the costumes of the drama cabin and shared all our makeup, and made ourselves into a team.

Paz and Montgomery are practically matching, in sheer blue stockings, blue briefs, blue bras, and nothing else. George has a blue feather boa and fan. Jordan is in a blue sequined flapper dress. Even Ashleigh is wearing a blue tutu and has her hair pulled on top of her head and tied with a blue bow. We're all dragged out in our own way. Lipstick, glitter eye shadow, and earrings, all in shades of blue, paint our faces in different ways. And I'm in the pièce de résistance: a blue sequined jumpsuit covered in pink satin stars, and on the back, like a sports jersey, the number 7 with a big lipstick kiss over it. I also have huge false eyelashes, blue glitter lipstick and eye shadow, and the jumpsuit is unbuttoned to my belly button.

I know this is a risk, but I don't think it's too big. Sure, after Hudson's freak-out about Brad's nail polish, maybe he won't love this. He won't think it's hot, like I know it is. But we talked about that, and we said I love you. He loves me! What's some makeup and sequins going to matter? Maybe he'll even kind of like it—I do look pretty hot—and this will be the way I can show him who I really am. And even if he doesn't like it, isn't turned on by it, then I can just say it's for team spirit. To bring us together, to win the competition. It's like those guys at football games who paint their bodies to match the team colors. He'll understand that. He has to understand that, right?

And besides, he loves me. So everything will be fine. You can't take that back over a jumpsuit and some makeup.

We march up to the front line, Mark trailing behind us with the boom box. The way Hudson's bunk looks at us, we may as well be walking in slow motion. Mouths drop, eyes go wide. The entire Red team cheering section goes quiet for a moment, cowed by our fabulousness.

Connie raises her eyebrow at me. I blow her a kiss. Joan seems unfazed.

"Take your places," she says, and goes to wait at the Peanut Butter Pit, the finish line. Me and my team take our places at each of the obstacles. I'm last—the Peanut Butter Pit. Right next to Hudson.

"What are you wearing?" he asks.

"My team needed a morale boost," I say. "This is it." I grin. He doesn't grin back. "I know it's a lot, but it made them feel good." And me too, I don't add.

"You look ridiculous."

I force a laugh, even if that feels like falling off the wire-walk. "Come on, I look pretty hot."

Hudson turns away from me, but before I can say anything else, Joan blows her whistle. The moment she does so, Mark hits PLAY on the boom box. A song from *Bye Bye Birdie* rings out over the course. The opening one from the movie, which technically isn't in the show, but felt right for the moment.

From where I'm standing, I can see each of the events. George is on the tires. George isn't the most elegant dancer, but he can land a step, and these are some of the simplest steps he's ever seen. He keeps pace with the Red team no problem.

He tags Jordan, who immediately is on the ground, crawling under the net at top speed, and then, at the end of it, running up the wall with practically zero effort. They've been running up walls in rehearsal all day, so I knew this wouldn't be a problem for them, just like I know Ashleigh, whom Jordan tags, will have no trouble walking over the rope ladder and taking the slide down. We're in the lead by the time she lands and tags Daniel, who handles the rock hop as easily as any chorus boy would.

Jen is up next on the monkey bars. She's been doing this for the "Put on a Happy Face" routine, so she handles herself well, but not as well as Brad, who manages to catch up with her. When they land, we're neck and neck.

Luckily, next is the wire-walk, and Montgomery is our secret weapon. Jen tags him and he hops up and walks across it at a decent clip, not falling once. He does lose a few seconds with a fancy dismount, and a wink at his opponent, though, so when he tags Paz, she only has a slight lead. She'd been nervous about the tire dive, but I explained to her it wasn't any different from diving through the Shriners' arms for the "Shriners' Ballet," so she backs up, runs, and flies through the tire, landing in a somersault and rolling up to me with much more grace than I've managed all summer.

When she tags me, we're a little in the lead, but if I screw this up, we lose, end of story, no redos. I've gotten across a few times. But now it's all on me. Not just winning, but proving...something. To my cabinmates, to Hudson and his friends, to me, maybe? To show that Randy can do what Del can do. To show that maybe they're actually sort of the same person.

So I back up and I run and I leap for that rope and catch it, and even though I can feel Hudson swinging next to me, I jump and hit the ground like he's not there.

"Blue wins," Joan says with very little excitement. I leap in the air, and my team, seeing my reaction, starts screaming.

Hudson crosses his arms. "What was that?" he asks, staring at me.

"That was us winning," I say with a grin. "What do I get for winning?"

"Points," Joan says, still deadpan.

"I mean...," I say, walking up to Hudson and running my Unicorn Trampocalypse–nailed hands down his chest. "Do I get a kiss?"

"Not like that," he says. "I can't believe you won. With them. Looking like that. It's like you...it's like you spit in my face."

"What?" I ask, taking my hands off him. "It's just a game. We dressed like this for morale. It's just makeup, clothing. Your parents aren't here. Why does it matter?"

"Just..." He looks up at me, and I've never seen his face like this. He's angry. Really angry. I feel a thousand things at once. Hurt, that he'd be angry. Afraid, that my plan has failed, and now he doesn't love me anymore. Stupid, for ever putting this makeup on. Stupid again, for thinking he loved me enough not to care what I wore. And stupid a third time, for ever thinking this plan would work. That he would ever love *me*.

All the emotions are forming a chorus line in my chest for their big tap number, their feet working in perfect unison, and it's like one of those big routines you see in movies from above, where they spiral and make different loops, mixing, mingling, but all putting their foot down at the same time, and stomping down into me.

He walks away into the woods, and I follow him. It's just like when Brad wore the nail polish, right? He just needs to talk it through. He LOVES me. He's not going to change that because I beat him in an obstacle course in sequins. What, he can't handle me winning and looking fabulous?

Or maybe it's just the looking fabulous. I don't know. He sits on a rock in the woods, hidden from everyone else by bushes. I sit down next to him.

"What's the matter?" I ask him again, more serious. I put my hand on his leg.

"I...look, if you'd won, it would have been embarrassing, 'cause this is my thing, the obstacle course, you know. But you did it in makeup and whatever you're wearing now."

"Sequin jumpsuit," I say quickly.

He sighs. "I just think that you're better than that."

"Better than what?" I ask.

He doesn't say anything, but I feel like I'm starting to understand, and now a new emotion joins the chorus in my chest. Anger.

"Every year," I say, "you tell us we can be better. You stand up and tell us that no matter what straight people think, we're just as good as them. We just showed you that." I take my hand off his leg. "I don't know why you get to be angry about it."

I go to get up, but he puts his hand on my leg, and I stay.

"I lied about my coming out," he says softly. "My parents. They didn't actually handle it that well. I mean, they seemed to, at the time, but later... right after my grandma died, I was in the mall with my mom. I don't remember why. And she was looking at makeup, and I was with her. And I found this eye shadow. Blue..." He looks up at me, but he's not smiling. "Sort of like what you're wearing now. I picked it out, and I showed it to my mother. I said, 'This was Grandma's favorite shade. Can I buy it?' Don't know why I asked permission. No, I do. Because I knew I shouldn't want it. Or, like, I wanted her to say it was okay to want it. Or something. And she took it from my hand and put it back in the little sliding tray it came from, and then she grabbed me by the wrist and pulled me around the corner, where it was empty, and then she pushed me up against the wall—not hard, but hard enough I can remember my head kind of knocking on the wall. And she held her hand against my chest, like she was pinning me there, and she said in this low whisper voice, 'I don't care what your sexuality is, but I won't have my son wearing makeup like a faggot.' And then she let go."

"That's awful," I say. I knew his parents weren't super comfortable with the queer thing, but calling your kid that word... that's something else.

"Her mom had just died. She was upset. And she apologized right away. I remember, I just stood there, and I felt like she'd carved my chest out, like I was just empty, and hollow, and like, if I spoke, it would echo because of how there was nothing inside me, and she walked away, but then she turned around. Like, not even five steps, and she said, 'I'm sorry, I shouldn't have used that word. Come on, we're going to be late.'"

"That's all she apologized about?"

"And that night," Hudson says, not having heard me, "my dad came into my room, and he sat on my bed and he said he heard Mom had used a bad word, but she'd apologized, and he asked if I was okay. And I told him I thought I was, but it was also kind of shocking. And he said to me, 'Hudson, you need to understand. You're special. Your mom and I . . . we don't really get gay people. When you told us you were homosexual, we thought that maybe that was it—that you weren't really our son anymore. We worried. But we came to terms with it. It's not what we wanted for you . . . but it's fine. But, stuff like makeup, drag queens, dancing in their underwear on parade floats with feather boas and stuff isn't you. That's . . . being a freak. And it's weak willed of them, I think. I mean, that's what society tells them they're supposed to be—these fairies prancing around in their short shorts. But you're not like them. You're stronger than that. You look at society and say, "Yeah, I'm a homosexual, but I'm no sissy." I'm proud of that. I'm proud of you for being like that. And I think that's all your mom was saying. That we're proud of you. Okay?' And I said okay, and he left."

"But that's not okay," I say. "That's terrible."

"The thing is," Hudson says, taking his hand off my leg. "I liked that he said I was special. And...I think he's right."

The chorus line stops dancing for a moment, and then starts up again, but the orchestra is out of tune. Off tempo.

"Right how?" I ask.

"I think it's weak willed to be a stereotype. Being what everyone tells you you should be. I think being more...masculine, I guess, is strength. I think it's better."

"That's ridiculous," I say. "My team just kicked your ass in high femme."

"That's why it made me so mad," he says. "But...I know what you're going to say. That clothing doesn't matter. Makeup doesn't matter. And maybe here it doesn't. But back home? You know what would happen to me if I wore what you're wearing in my hometown? Or held hands with someone dressed like that?"

"I think if you hold hands with a boy, homophobic assholes won't care what that boy is wearing."

"Maybe. But maybe all they want is for us to be like them."

"Screw them for wanting that. You said we could be better. But being like them isn't better. We can do everything straight people can do, you're right, but what makes being queer special is we don't have to if we don't want to."

"I...don't know if I'm that brave," Hudson says. And when he says it, the dancing in my chest stops. The dancers are collapsed in a heap. My heart breaks for him.

I take his hand. I squeeze it. "Sweetie, you are."

"With you..." He looks down at our hands linked, my nail polish peeking out between his fingers. "How did you know?" he asks suddenly. The forest goes quiet. Not a bird is chirping.

"Know what?"

"What I've said every year? How I always say people can be better?"

Well. Jig is up. Now or never. Time for my big number. Deep breath, Randy. Like before your solo.

"Because you always said it to me. Every year," I say.

"What?"

I stand. Revealing monologues can't be given in a sitting position. I stand in front of him and I take both his hands and I try to look loving and sincere. This isn't part of the plan. I was going to ease him back into it. I was going to show him all the sides of me he hadn't seen yet and then tell him everything, when we were happy and in love. The jumpsuit was supposed to be safe, because it was a costume, a preview, but not something he would take so seriously. I don't know if he's still in love with me—I think so—but right now, we're not happy. Not like we've been before. And I haven't eased him into anything.

"My name is Randall Kapplehoff."

"I know," he says, looking confused.

"And this is my fifth year at Camp Outland."

He pulls his hands back. "What?"

"Every other year, I went by Randy," I say, walking a little away from him, then back. "I looked different, too. I had longer hair, I was chubbier. And I was in the show every year. I've always been a cabin seven kid. Last year, I was Domina in *A Funny Thing Happened on the Way to the Forum*."

He looks up at me, brow furrowed, and I can see the recognition pass over his eyes. And then pain.

"Why?" he asks.

"For you." I step closer to him and kneel in front of him. "Every year, being around you, the way you talked to us—even if it was just a crowd during color wars—made me feel...special. Like stars inside me, galaxies. You said we could be anything, and I believed you, even if you didn't mean it the way I thought you did..." I pause, wondering for a moment as I say it if that means everything I loved was a lie, and I only really knew him, really fell in love with him this summer. "It made me feel like I could do anything. You made me feel that way. And...I wanted to do the same for you. I wanted to be with you. So I..."

He stands up and walks away, anxious footsteps, his back turned to me. "So you lied?" he asks.

"No," I say quickly, standing and going to him. "No. I changed my hair, my clothes, lost some weight, and I did different activities this summer. But I never lied. I just...didn't show you everything about me."

"You lied," he says again, not a question this time. His eyes are wide, looking at everything but me.

"No," I say. "Hudson. I'm still the same guy. I really liked the obstacle course. I like being color wars captain, I like sports and hiking... it surprised me that I liked them, but I do. I just also like musical theater and dancing and singing and wearing makeup and nail polish. And I love you." I reach out for both his hands but he pulls them away.

"So this," he says, pointing at my outfit, his hand moving up and down in disgust. "This is the real you."

"Yes," I say. "But it's still the same person you know and love."

"No." He shakes his head, backs away from me. "I don't know who this is. And you've been lying to me all summer. From the moment we met and I asked if you were new. Lying. Does anyone else know?"

I can feel the tears starting. They stream down my face as I nod. This isn't going to work. This was never going to work.

"Who else? Brad? People in my cabin? I mean... who doesn't know?"

"It doesn't matter," I say.

"Everyone has been laughing at me this whole summer? Tricked by... by some theater kid in makeup. Role of a lifetime, I guess."

He's crying too now, but he wipes it away with the back of his clenched fists.

"I'm still the same," I tell him, though I know it's pointless now. "I'm the guy you fell in love with."

"No." He shakes his head. "You're what my mom would call a faggot."

The word shoots out of him like a bullet and hits what was left of my heart, and just like that, it's gone. I don't feel sadness anymore. The waterfall ache of our relationship collapsing in front of me like a glacier refreezes. Everything freezes. I can see it on his face, too, how this instant is being etched into our brains, how neither of us can even breathe in it.

And then it ends.

And I walk away.

"Del, wait," he says, coming after me. "I didn't mean to use that word."

I turn around. "It's not about the word. You think I haven't been called that before? Heard it whispered about me by girls in the hall at school, or just hurled at me by guys on the street? Hell, Montgomery calls people faggot as a term of endearment sometimes. I know that word, Hudson. I know what it means, and I know what you meant when you said it. Even if you hadn't used that word, you would have found a way to say it. Because it's what you think, isn't it? We can be better. You said you meant it as be less of a stereotype. Act more like the straight people. You thought I was better. Just like you—special. I am special, Hudson. I am better. And I am a faggot."

"Del, I'm sorry, I was angry, I don't know who you are, and—"

"Yes, you do," I say, turning my back on him. "And my name is Randy."

I find Mark at the egg races, still playing the *Bye Bye Birdie* soundtrack.

"Where were you?" Mark asks. "Blue needs some cheer power. Oh, your makeup is running. Are you okay?"

"Can I come back to theater?" I ask. My voice sounds hollow, so I try to smile, make it seem better. "I know I can't audition. I'll work backstage, make sets, run the prop table, whatever. I just want to come back."

"Are you okay?" he repeats. He looks sad.

"Just...please, can I come back?"

He gives me a hug suddenly, arms wrapped so tight around me, and me crying blue makeup onto his shirt.

"Of course you can. You can always come back."

TWENTY-TWO

LAST SUMMER

The lights are so bright, I can feel myself sweat under the makeup and my toga the moment I set foot onstage. The audience's energy is eager, but not anxious. It's the top of act two, and it's been a good show so far, so they're willing to go along with what happens next.

And what happens next is my big number.

Mark and Crystal have crafted quite a dance for me, as if booming and holding the notes and the tongue-twisting lyrics weren't enough. The stage is an amphitheater, a coliseum, steps all around me as I walk onto the stage, look out at the audience, and sing.

The great thing about "That Dirty Old Man" is that it's a song I can go super dramatic on, and Mark has encouraged this. "Golden Age of Hollywood Elder-Diva," he said.

"Think Norma in *Sunset*, Davis in *All About Eve*." And so I've mastered the slight head tilt back, the wide eyes. I'm not in drag, but we put false eyelashes on me anyway, just to get that vibe. And now I have to keep it all while singing about the man I love—who is the worst, and I know it—and how he cheats on me, and how victimized I am, and how I don't know if I want to kill him or kiss him.

And while I sing, I'm walking up and down the steps of the amphitheater. Not walking. Dancing. And then giving poses. It's tricky. Singing is most important, then acting, then dancing, at least according to Mark, so if I miss a step, I shouldn't worry about it. But I don't want to miss a step.

And I don't. As the melody builds and I sing, I can feel the audience getting into it. I can feel them trying not to laugh for fear of interrupting, feel them hanging on my words, my faces, my steps. Up and down the steps, just like my character's relationship with his husband. Every new affair a challenge, every moment I keep loving him a downfall, and the only compromise anger. Funny anger, of course. The poses, the faces, the wide, high steps, the fluctuating between rage and lust. As I sing I can feel the audience laughing quietly, but also feeling for me. I can feel us having a conversation, playing with the idea of this character, and who he is and what he wants. How lonely he is. And we can all relate to that.

I finish by holding a high note, then a flourish and a bow, and then the applause. It hits me like a strong wave in the ocean, almost knocking me over. And as the lights go out, I see Jasmine, in the crowd, stand while clapping. I smile, but Jasmine stands for everything. But then, shockingly, other people stand. Other campers. My parents. Other campers' parents. The whole audience, and I can feel tears prickling in my eyes as I clasp my hands together and bow, and blow some kisses—staying in character—before sweeping offstage.

"Listen to that applause!" George says, hugging me the moment I'm hidden from the audience.

"They were standing!" I say when he lets go of me. My voice is nearly a whisper.

"WHAT? A standing ovation?" George says, hugging me again. "Darling, that is amazing and you deserve it!"

"Shhhh," Mark says to us. "But that was fabulous, Randy. You should be proud. Now get ready for your next cue."

After final bows, the entire cast and crew is backstage hugging and laughing and crying. The most bittersweet thing about the show is it's the last day. After this, we go clean up, finish packing, have a late lunch with our parents, and then we all leave. Our proudest moment is also our good-bye.

But for the moments after the show, the happiness overwhelms the sadness. I hug George and Ashleigh and Paz and Montgomery and everyone else. When we're done celebrating, Mark and Crystal have us all hold hands in a circle on the stage (the audience has cleared out by now) and Mark gives a little speech.

"Thank you all for being part of this show this year. We really created something special and amazing and I hope you all know that. My therapist says that theater is a way for us to play with different identities without losing who we are, to try things on, to let go and not care what people think. And maybe he's a little right, but he's also wrong. Because theater is who we are. Those identities aren't different costumes we try on—they're different facets of us, different bits of truth. And it takes bravery to show those truths to the outside world. So I am SO proud of you. All of you." He sniffs as tears start to run down his face, and Crystal lays her head on his shoulder. "For showing not just the vision I had, but yourselves. We are a family. A crazy, dramatic queer family. And I'm so glad we had this summer together and this show." He shakes his head, trying not to cry any more, and that makes me cry a little, too. "I will e-mail you all the video from the show. I know I won't see you all over the year, but I will be thinking of each and every one of you, and our show next year. Now...will the people whose last summer it is here please step into the middle of the circle?"

Five campers step into the middle of the circle, and Mark starts to name them, but just ends up bawling. Crystal takes over.

"You will always be part of this family," Crystal says. "You will always have a place in this theater. And we will always e-mail you back or call or video chat or whatever if you need us. I know it'll hurt not to come back next summer, but you're going to go out there and have amazing queer theatrical lives. And next summer, you'll come back and sit in the audience and tell us afterward about everything you've done at college. We'll be proud of you forever. And we'll miss you, too."

"But not a lot because you can always, always e-mail," Mark says quickly.

The outer circle closes in on the leaving campers, a big group hug with more than a few of us crying. Then we break, and wipe our faces, and change into our normal clothes to go back out into the world.

Outside, my parents are waiting.

"Honey! You were amazing!" Mom says, running up to me and hugging me.

Dad slaps me on the back. "You were great, kiddo."

"Thanks," I say.

"Were you wearing fake eyelashes?" Dad asks. I nod. "Wild. Theater is so kooky."

I laugh, and my mom spots George and Ashleigh walking over with their parents, too.

"Hi, George, you were amazing," my mom says. "And Ashleigh, those lights were beautiful."

"Thank you, Mrs. Kapplehoff," they say almost in unison.

Their parents compliment me, too, and then we take a short walk around camp before heading to the cafeteria.

"Darling, I don't know how I'm supposed to go back to school after this," George says to me at lunch. "What a summer! And now, back to New York, where my high school will no doubt put on some perfectly straight version of some perfectly straight musical, and me and all the other kids will be fine in it, but not... transcendent. That's what today was. Transcendent."

"We'll have next summer," I say.

"That's true," George says, reaching out for my hand, which I take. Ashleigh looks over at us and we look at her until she sighs and lays her hand down on ours, too.

"It's not like we're not going to be texting all the time," she says. "But sure, next summer. It'll be amazing."

TWENTY-THREE

t's easy to slip back into theater. It's almost like I never left. Backstage jokes, learning cues, watching rehearsals from the audience. Everything feels natural. My nails are Unicorn Trampocalypse, my wardrobe has been rearranged into its most stylish version, and I have a fan in my pocket for when I get warm or need to make a STATEMENT. If I weren't just working backstage, it would be like the first two weeks of camp never happened.

Well, that and the pitying looks. And the strange heaviness in my stomach that I feel like I have to hide all the time.

No one knows exactly what happened. I told them it was over, and that I was coming back, and that was that. We played through the next day of color wars—Blue won, and I knew I felt proud of that, but I felt it the way you feel something through a thick sweater. It never really touched my skin. But I performed proud and happy, and danced with my fellow captains onstage in our matching rompers. And then that was over, and I went to the drama cabin and everything just sort of slid back into what it had been before. What it was always supposed to be, if I hadn't been so stupid.

Hudson ignores me, just like I ignore him. I don't look at him the way you don't look at the sun. I'm always aware of where he is, just so I can avert my eyes.

"Do you want to talk about it?" George asks on Monday night as we're getting ready for bed.

"There's nothing to talk about," I say. "The plan failed. I told him the truth, and it turned out he wasn't who I thought he was, either."

"Okay, darling, but we're here, you know."

"Yeah, what George said," Ashleigh says. "I'm happy you're back in theater...but I hate that you're hurting."

"Not hurting," I say. Which is true. More numb than hurting. "I just feel stupid."

"Not stupid," George says. "A romantic, maybe. A dreamer."

"A theater kid," Ashleigh says.

"But never stupid," George finishes.

I smile, lying in my bed. "Thanks."

"Whatever you need," George says.

I'm really lucky. I shouldn't complain. So my dream guy ended up being just a dream. It was a long shot anyway, right?

Mark turns the lights out, and I can feel tears prick their way out of my eyes and I don't know why. I don't have anything to be sad about. Everything is back to the way it was.

So I don't feel like I'm filled with stars anymore. So what? Space is mostly just emptiness. Miles and kilometers between them.

I feel worse for Brad. Hudson and I splitting has led to the two groups splitting up at lunch, but he wants to sit with George, too. So he splits—breakfast and lunch with Hudson, dinner with George.

"Dinner is more romantic," he explains. George rolls his eyes, but smiles when Brad kisses him on the cheek. I look away. I'm not going to be that friend, the one who can't handle his friends being happy in a relationship because his just ended. Because if I did that, I'd be alone, with the way Ashleigh and Paz are holding hands all the time now. Ashleigh hasn't said anything, but on Tuesday, George spots them making out behind the drama cabin before rehearsal.

"Ashleigh had Paz against the wall and was practically doing a vampire impersonation," he whispers to me backstage right after spotting them. "If Paz vanishes mysteriously and then becomes a night person with a pale complexion, we'll know why." A few minutes later, they come back into the theater, a hickey already forming on Paz's neck.

"I guess they talked," I say, giggling and looking away.

I really am happy for her, and for George. I genuinely mean that, but for some reason, looking at them being happy is hard.

After they all go backstage to get into costume, I go watch from the audience. Mark hasn't found anything for me to do yet. I'm watching Paz and Montgomery rehearse "One Boy" from the audience when Mark, sitting in the front, calls back to me.

"Randy—what did you think?"

"What?" I call back.

He waves me up and I walk to the front and sit next to him. "Congratulations," he says. "You're my new assistant director. Crystal and I decided we could use your input. So what did you think?"

What? I'm what now?

"Of the song?" I ask.

"Yes, of the song, Randy," he snaps. "Come on, keep up."

"Oh..." Deep breath. "Okay, so I think since the lyrics switch up a lot anyway, you can switch the genders every other verse. Guy, gal, boy, girl."

Mark nods. "Good. But the performances?"

I look up at Paz and Montgomery. I don't know if I want to critique them.

"I know they're your friends, but they want to do their best," Mark say. "Right?" Paz and Montgomery nod. "And we all know you have a bit of director in you. All you've been doing for the past two weeks is starring and directing in your own show. So...this is a song where they're talking about how they love one person, how they want to settle down now. What's wrong with it?"

"It's too performative," I say, without thinking. "Sorry."

"No," Mark says. "Go on."

"They're looking out at the audience, like they're trying to prove their love, but when you feel that, I think it's more inside...you don't need to show it off, don't need to prove anything. They should look up more."

Mark scratches his chin. "I like it. Let's try it. Don't look at the audience this time. Look at the stars."

Crystal starts playing again, and this time it looks much more romantic if I do say so myself. When it's done, Mark is nodding.

"Good! I like it. Crystal, I want more movement, though. What do you think?"

Crystal stands and gives them some new steps and I turn to Mark as they work.

"Are you doing this because you feel sorry for me?" I ask.

Mark raises an eyebrow, then looks sad for a second, sorry for me—but not the way everyone else has been looking at me. He doesn't feel sorry for me for losing Hudson. He feels sorry for me for some other reason.

"I'm doing this, Randy, because you're a talent, and it might be too late to put you onstage, but I'm going to use your talent the best way I can. And that means your eye. This isn't a pity position. I want you working with the actors, making sure they really convey feelings, like you just did. Got it?" I nod, and he smiles, putting his hand on my shoulder. "Of course, all final decisions are mine, though."

I laugh. "I wouldn't have it any other way."

I sit with Mark the rest of rehearsal and give a few notes. I might not be onstage, but I actually love helping in this way. Maybe this is my future. Randy Kapplehoff: Broadway director. Well...director/actor/dancer—Triple-Threat Randy, they could call me. I like a slash, I realize. I like how they add to your identity instead of replacing it full cloth. Just the thought of it makes me open my fan and cool myself off as I watch the rest of the show.

When rehearsal is over I go backstage, where George gives me a hug. I wave to Ashleigh, who is up in the stage manager's box behind the audience.

"Darling, you are so good! That note you gave me about the sneer during 'Kids'? It felt so much better after that."

"Yeah?" I ask. "You don't mind me giving you notes?"

"Not at all," Paz says, walking up to us. "Not when you do it so well."

Ashleigh creeps up behind Paz and puts her arms around her. "So Randy is a director now!" she says. "That fits."

I grin. "Thanks."

"I liked it, too," Montgomery calls from across the room. He walks toward me. "Very authoritative and butch. Hot. You know, since you and Hudson are done, maybe you and I..."

I turn away. The mention of Hudson feels like being pushed offstage.

"Really, Montgomery?" George asks. "There's shameless, and then there's you."

"Oh whatever. He's hot. Every boy at camp who isn't trying to screw Hudson is going to try to screw him now. I just want to throw my hat in the ring."

I swallow at the mention of other people screwing Hudson. Or I try to. My throat is too dry, though.

Montgomery walks by me, trailing his hand down my arm as he does so. "Think about it. You've seen how flexible I am."

He walks out the door, swaying his hips a little. Ashleigh, arms still around Paz, asks, "Are you okay?"

"I'm fine," I say, and walk toward the door out into the hot air of the summer. I squint against the light.

George and Ashleigh run out after me. I walk away from the cabin, but they follow, and I love them for it.

"For what it's worth," George says, "I don't think Hudson will be hooking up with anyone else this summer. Brad says he's...really confused. And heartbroken, Brad thinks, though Hudson won't admit it."

I feel a little ping inside me, like my heart is beating again after not for who knows how long. "Heartbroken?"

"I don't think that means he wants to get back together," George says quickly, and I nod. Of course not. Why would he? Why would I, after what he said? Why did my chest leap at that thought? "But maybe you should try to talk to him? He keeps looking at you at lunch like he wants to, but you won't even look at him.... What did he do that's so awful?"

"It doesn't matter," I say. He said what he's been saying for the past four years, I just never understood. That he's better than me. Better than my friends. Because our makeup makes us queens. Because we're just weak-willed stereotypes.

"Darling, I only want you to be happy. And you don't seem happy."

"What do you mean?" I ask, putting on a perfect face of joy. "I'm happy."

"Randy, you're an amazing actor, but don't try that with me. You're unhappy. I heard you crying last night."

"We both did," Ashleigh says, sitting on the ground next to me.

"It'll pass." I let the happy face drop. "There's nothing to be sad about, really. He...wasn't who I thought he was."

"Okay," George says. "So who is he?"

"I don't want to..." I sit in the grass next to Ashleigh and lie back. George lies down next to me, and Ashleigh, too, all of us looking at the trees. "If I tell you what he said, you won't tell? I don't want people to hate him."

"Okay," George says carefully.

"Fine," Ashleigh says, sounding annoyed about it.

"He said that when he means 'better'—when he says every year that we can be better, better than straight people think we are, that he means less of a stereotype. He thinks it's weak willed to wear makeup, or like musical theater. He thinks we're just..." I don't want to say the word. "...Queens," I say instead.

"He said that?" Ashleigh asks.

"Yeah."

"And what did you say?"

I stare up at the trees and try to make them stars, but trees are just trees. "I said that that was a terrible way to think. And he told me why he thought it...but said maybe he was wrong." I can feel an ant crawling on me and look down. He's marching carefully over my forearm. I let him keep walking.

George props himself up on one arm, staring at me. "Wait...so you changed his mind? You got masc-only Hudson to say he was wrong about masc being superior queerness? So what went wrong?"

"Wait..." I close my eyes. "Did you know Hudson thought like that?"

"I always guessed," Ashleigh says. "I mean...that's usually where masc4masc comes from, right? Masc is better. I don't want to date a woman, that's why I'm gay. Men are better and women are gross. I are manly and only suck on the manliest penises. Grrr."

George laughs and nods. "What she said."

I laugh and it feels good, like my heart is singing. "I wish you'd told me that's what he meant."

"Would you have believed us?"

I'm silent for long enough that we all know the answer is no.

"But I'm still confused, darling. You won him over, I thought. That was part of the plan. You got him to love you, and next you were going to get him to appreciate the finer things in life, like nail polish and Broadway, and then ease back into regular Randy before you told him."

"I...accidentally let something slip, and he asked about it, so I told him everything. The plan."

"Oh," George says. Ashleigh makes a tsking sound.

"And then it was like everything I'd just said was undone." I lower my voice, afraid to say it. "He called me a faggot. Not in the nice way."

"What?" George sits up. "I'll go kick his ass. Show him what a good manicure can do to that pretty face of his."

"If I get to him first there won't be anything left," Ashleigh says, already on her feet.

"No," I say, pulling them both back down by their arms. "No, don't do that. That's why I don't want to tell anyone."

"Fine," Ashleigh sighs.

"And really, he said his mom would call me a faggot. But...he was saying it, you know?"

"His whole family sounds messed up, then," Ashleigh says.

"Yeah, they are. I feel bad for him. They really made him hate himself, I think."

"That's all straight people ever make queer people do,"

Mark says suddenly as he steps into our sun, hovering over us. "You're late for lunch."

"Sorry," I say as we stand up. "Sorry. And you didn't hear all that, did you?"

"More than you wanted me to," Mark says. "George, Ashleigh, why don't you get to the dining hall? Randy and I need to talk about the show."

George and Ashleigh nod, and start walking away.

"You did a good job today," Mark says when they're out of earshot, walking slowly toward lunch. "I'm very proud."

"Thank you." I look down at my feet. "You won't tell anyone what you heard, right? I shouldn't even have told George and Ashleigh."

"You had to tell someone. You can't keep that sort of thing buried. My therapist would say trauma like that needs to be shared."

"It wasn't trauma," I say, rolling my eyes. "It was just a fight. He said something mean. I was the crazy one. Cutting my hair, treating this like a role."

"Don't do that," Mark says. "Don't say the thing that happened to you wasn't a big deal, or you deserved it. Someone you loved said something terrible to you. That's trauma."

"He said it because of what his parents have said to him for years, though."

"That's not an excuse," Mark says. "Terrible things happening to you are never an excuse to do them to someone else. But maybe it's a reason to forgive him…if he's willing to apologize. And change."

"I don't know if I want to."

"Because then you'll still be in love with him and he'll still be mad at you for your playing out a rom-com for the entire camp without telling him?"

I sigh. "Yeah."

"Sounds like you need to apologize, too."

We're at the dining hall, and Mark pulls the door open so we can walk inside. It's crowded and I glance over at where Hudson has been sitting. He's staring right at me, and our eyes meet, and I feel a thousand things rise up inside me like a zombie horde clawing its way out of the graveyard. I'm hurt and angry and guilty and sad and still so in love with him. All I want to do is go to him and hold him, because I can see he's feeling his own zombie horde of emotions.

But I can't. So I look away instead, and the emotions quiet. Not gone. Just easier to ignore.

"What do you think of Paz's costume for 'Spanish Rose'?" Mark asks, not noticing the little war that was just fought inside me. "I feel like we should make it more Afro-Brazilian, but I don't know what that is, honestly."

"Ask Paz," I say. "She'll know."

"You do it," Mark says. "And then get Charity to do adjustments, if needed. I trust you."

"Thanks." I smile, but I feel Hudson's eyes on my back

and it's like everything else is quiet because of that. I smile and laugh through lunch, but it's all just acting again.

I talk to Paz about her costuming during lunch and take her suggestions to Charity during A&C. Charity, blissfully, does not give me the same pitying look the rest of the camp does. Instead, she wants to focus on the work, adding stripes of red-and-gold-patterned fabric and red feathers to Paz's dress for the number.

After A&C, I go back to the drama cabin instead of going to sports. Technically, it's not theater elective now, but everyone still comes and goes, doing optional dance rehearsals with Crystal, or blocking scenes with Mark. The second half of the summer is crunch time for the show, and everyone crams in as much rehearsal as they can to get it right. It's good to feel like I have a purpose. Every moment I'm working on the costume with Charity or watching scenes with Mark, I forget about Hudson. There's still a hollow part of me, a place that used to be filled with stars that I can feel like an ache, but I don't notice it as much when I have so many other things to focus on. So many new stars to add, like Mark nodding with approval when I tell him about the changes to Paz's costume, or Jordan saying, "Yes, I get that, I love that," when I suggest they think of "A Lot of Livin' to Do" as not just about going out and partying, but about going to the one queer club in this small town. It changes their whole performance, too, from a dance number to a real scene, and Mark squeezes my shoulder and says, "I am so smart for making you an AD." Each moment like that is a star, and they start to fill me up.

When pool time comes around, Mark sends me out to go play in the water. "You need to relax after a long day," he says to me, and to all the other campers who are backstage. "Go swim."

Hopping into the pool, I realize how right he is, too. The water and sun feel amazing, and I don't even mind Brad and George flirtatiously splashing each other, or Ashleigh and Paz standing shoulder to shoulder against the wall. I don't even know where Hudson is anymore.

That's a lie. He's by the diving board. I don't look.

Instead I try to relax. I sink under the water and let it surround me, let myself float in a little cocoon where the rest of the world is far-off splashes. When I pop back up, George splashes me and I splash him back and soon all of us are chasing each other around the pool trying to splash each other.

We stop when Janice blows her whistle at us and shakes her head. I laugh and swim back toward the side of the pool with George. Paz and Brad keep chasing each other, with less splashing, and Ashleigh goes over to Janice.

"Should we worry about that?" George asks, looking at Ashleigh, popping out of the water onto the side of the pool like a mermaid to talk to Janice.

"Nah," I say. "She's got Paz now, right?"

"That doesn't mean the old crush is gone."

"She hasn't said anything about Janice in weeks." As I say it, I look over at them. Ashleigh laughs at something.

"I don't know, darling. This worries me."

"They can be friends, maybe."

"Like you and Hudson?"

"That's different," I say, my voice a little too quick and flat. "They're not exes. It's just a former crush."

"Former might be overstating it," George says as Ashleigh swims over to us.

"She hooked up with a girl," Ashleigh says in an excited whisper when she's next to us.

"What?" George asks, his voice monotone. He looks at me like I should have known better.

"Janice. She went to some party this weekend and she ended up making out with a girl, and she says it was cool! She might be bi!"

"Might?" I ask.

"Heteroflexible, three-beer queer," George says, "whatever. But none of them are relationship material, darling."

"Why not?" Ashleigh asks. "We click so well, and now she might want to make out a little, like I've always wanted. I should tell her, right? I should ask her to hang around when she's off duty and we can go somewhere private."

George and I exchange a worried look. "First," I say, "that would get her fired."

"How do you know that?" Ashleigh asks. "She's a life-guard, not a counselor."

"Darling, don't you have Paz now?"

Ashleigh sighs and looks at her reflection in the water. "I like Paz. I do. Enough that I've been getting a little . . . friendlier with her."

"We know," George says with a smirk.

Ashleigh glares at him. "And she's pretty. And funny, and really smart. But Janice is . . ." She looks behind her at Janice. "She's the dream."

"But she's a real person, too," I say. "And when you meet one, the other goes away."

"Just because you and Hudson didn't work out—" Ashleigh starts, and I shake my head so violently, she stops.

"Yes," I say after a moment. "That's part of it. But, sweetie, I'm just saying. You don't know how it could go. You could give up Paz for her, and lose them both. That's what happened to me, with the musical, kind of. Do you want to risk that?"

"You did," Ashleigh says. "Wouldn't you do it again?"

I sigh.

"It's not the same," George says. "She will reject you, Ashleigh. She has to keep her job. And then you'll be awkward together. Just . . . keep being friends. And see where it is when she's not a lifeguard anymore. If you and Paz aren't together, I mean."

Ashleigh sighs. "I just . . ."

"I get it," I say. "She seems in reach. But George is right. You can't force it. You can wait a week and a half to talk to her about this, right?"

"But then she'll be here and I'll be back in Boston."

"Not so far, really," George says.

"Yeah, okay." She nods, looking sad. "And I shouldn't do that to Paz anyway. I should see where it goes. And she's a great kisser. I bet she's good with her mouth other places, too. . . ." She smirks as George and I roll our eyes. "But I am going to invite Janice to the show."

"Oh yes." I nod. "Do that for sure."

Ashleigh takes off, swimming back to Janice. Across the pool, I see Paz watching, too. I frown a little in sympathy.

"You know, just because Hudson wasn't what you thought he'd be doesn't mean you can't have a dream guy," George says.

"I know," I say. "I just have no idea who that would be."

"Hudson in nail polish?" George asks.

I laugh. "Something like that."

It starts raining during dinner, so for the evening activity we all go to the meeting hall and Joan puts on *The Miseducation of Cameron Post* so we can all sob for a while. George and Brad sit on one side of me, and Ashleigh and Paz sit on the other, and sometimes I catch all of them giving these worried "Are we being too cute next to him?" looks to each other and me, but I just watch the movie and think about what was missing in the "Honestly Sincere" number today. I'm actually pretty impressed with how well I'm handling it all. I mean, sure,

I'm not happy, but I'm putting on a good show of it—I'm not spending the day in the infirmary bawling my eyes out over a broken heart, or being betrayed or anything.

I'm sad. But I'm happy, too.

After the movie it's still pouring outside, so we all run to our cabins, T-shirts lifted over our heads in a futile attempt to keep our hair dry (also—why? We're going in the pool tomorrow, right?), screaming and laughing as we get soaked anyway.

Except Hudson is standing at the door to my cabin. He's already soaked, his white T-shirt plastered to his body, hair falling over his forehead in rivers, eyes squinting against the fury of the raindrops. He waves, sheepish, when he sees me, and I know I can't just walk away, not when he's getting soaked, some romantic puppy dog gesture or preamble to a speech in the rain about how I "done him wrong" maybe? Some kind of monologue in the rain, surely. And I thought I was supposed to be the drama queen.

"What?" I ask him.

"Can we talk?"

"Not now. It's pouring."

"So maybe tomorrow?"

"I'm getting wet," I say, and then immediately flinch at the flirtiness of it. Nice job being cool and aloof, Randy. "I'm going inside."

"But—"

I don't let him finish, I just open the door to my cabin and go in. I want to peek out the window, see if he's waiting, looking up at me, getting wetter and wetter, hoping I'll come back out, but I shouldn't, and besides, George is doing it for me.

"He's leaving," George says after a minute. "You didn't want to talk to him?"

"In this weather?"

"It would make quite the scene," George says.

"I've dealt with enough scenes today," I say. "I'm going to sleep."

George shrugs and I only glance out the window once as I'm getting ready for bed. Hudson isn't there. Why would he be?

I fall asleep to the sound of the rain on the roof. It has a rhythm to it, somewhere in between a heartbeat and the overture to a show.

TWENTY-FOUR

t rains all the next day, too, which is fine, because it gives us an excuse to spend all day in the drama cabin, working on scenes, costumes, dancing. We're having our first run-through of the entire show tomorrow: a full performance with costume changes and lighting cues and a million other things that can go deeply, horribly wrong. Two years ago, during the first run, a sandbag fell and almost literally killed a chorus boy. Not me. But that kid never came back to camp after that. Probably for the best. He was unlucky.

But I don't want any sandbags this year, and as few mistakes as possible, so I go around asking people what they need, and making a list, which I give to Mark, so we can practice all the bits that feel off. We spend the whole day doing that, breaking only for lunch. It's busy and exciting and frustrating. And I don't think about Hudson even once.

Thursday morning, though, I realize I have to.

"This one is cheating a little," Mark says as he wakes us all up. "The song itself—'It's in His Kiss,' sometimes called 'The Shoop Shoop Song,' was released in 1963, first sung by Merry Clayton . . . but this cover is from 1990. It's Cher! How can I not use Cher? I won't apologize! In fact, I will say that Joan not letting me show *Mermaids* during movie night is a gay travesty!" He nods as if having made his point, and hits PLAY.

The music starts playing as we get out of bed, and it's impossible not to dance to. Or sing into a comb or hairbrush to. Or do little coordinated backup dances to, as George and I quickly start doing, tossing our heads and lip-synching to the backup singers. Montgomery takes it upon himself to lip-synch to Cher until Mark comes back out of his room and takes over. It doesn't take long for the entire cabin to have a dance routine worked out, a virtual music video, and it feels so good to be dancing and shooping and being myself, and not caring if Hudson is going to walk in and see me like this. George grabs our fans and when the song goes on to another (another Cher, definitely not from the 1960s, but we'll give Mark a break) we start voguing and catwalking down the cabin.

Mark hops in the shower, and when he comes out we're all still dancing.

"Get ready! Come on! Don't make me turn Cher off!"

He laughs as we all scramble to get dressed and brush our teeth. "And don't forget to pack up what you need for the canoe trip. We leave tomorrow."

The canoe trip. Right. Oh.

Oh no.

I turn to George, wide-eyed, no longer dancing. George is lost in the song, flapping his fan in one hand, brushing his teeth with another, still dancing to the music.

"Trade tents with me?" I ask him.

He turns to me, his eyes going wide. "Oh...," he says, toothpaste dripping from his open mouth. "Fuh."

I nod in agreement. "So you'll trade?"

He shakes his head and spits the toothpaste out. "Sorry, darling, but Brad is really excited for this. We haven't really had a chance to..." He wiggles his fingers. "Perform a duet. The kind with a climactic high note." He tilts his head. "Actually, he's a bass, so it won't be that high. But it'll be loud and long, so help me."

"Okay, but I can't share a tent with Hudson," I say.

"Sorry, darling, I feel for you, I do, but you'll survive a couple of nights of sleeping next to the boy. You can ignore him up close."

"Please?" I beg.

He gives me sad eyes. "Do you really need this? Because if I say yes, it'll break Brad's heart."

"I..."

"I'll talk to Brad about it," he says, but he looks sad. And now I feel terrible. I should have remembered this earlier. What if this is what Hudson wanted to talk about the other night and I acted like it was some big weird emotional thing and did the cold walk away. I was the drama queen after all.

"Oh!" Mark says. "And I forgot to give these out last night." I pop my head back into the cabin and see Mark putting little packets of photos on each of our beds. "From pool night. Printed photos. There's a link where you can download them on the package, too."

As if today didn't have enough unpleasant reminders.

Mark throws a pack of photos on my bed and Ashleigh swiftly grabs it and puts it on hers.

When she sees me watching her she shakes her head. "You don't need those right now."

I nod. She's a good friend.

Hudson doesn't try to approach me at breakfast, so maybe he figured something out with the tents and George won't have to trade. Maybe Hudson found someone to trade with and I'll be in a tent with Sam or someone whom I wouldn't mind sharing with. Even a stranger. That would be fine.

Maybe he burned the photos of us from the pool.

I try not to think of any of it as I go into the drama cabin. I push aside guesses as to where Ashleigh could have hidden the photos—why do I want them anyway? I can see myself sobbing over them in bed, and I still want them. I shake my head. I could ask Mark if he can make someone trade tents with me, but that would be stupid and childish and he would roll his eyes and tell me to deal with it. And he would be right. I shouldn't even have asked George. I can get through it. I don't want those photos. I can do without.

The first run-through goes really well. The show is Mark's best I've seen. It's gay and funny and campy and filled with real love in a way that shines above the source material—which was already one of the best musicals of all time. But Mark has made it his own. No, our own. Everyone does an amazing job. A few cues are missed, some costume changes go wrong, but nothing we can't work out. After lunch, Mark gives notes on everything and we run a few more scenes before he lets us go swim.

The moment I get into the pool, Brad is there, glaring.

"I am not giving up a night of eating that hairy ass just so you don't feel weird sharing a tent with Hudson," he says.

"Hi," I say. "That's a lot of information."

"Come on, Randy. Tell George he doesn't have to trade."

I know he's right. "Did Hudson find someone to trade with?"

Brad rolls his eyes, shakes his head. "You're so...You really need to talk to him. Just...don't trade, okay? I really want to—"

"You've already explained."

"Hey, don't kink-shame me."

"Sorry, you're right. I will...share the tent with Hudson. And I hope you have fun with George."

"Oh, I will. He is so my type and I cannot wait for him to have my legs in the air while he pounds—"

"You really like to share, don't you?"

"Sorry." Brad shrugs. "Just looking forward to it."

I laugh. "It's fine, but George is like my brother."

"Oh," he says, eyes wide. "Yeah, sorry. But thanks for being cool about it. And just...look, Hudson is upset, too, y'know? He's not a bad guy. You really kind of messed with his head, the way he sees the world. But...I think he needed it. But now he's feeling unbalanced and you left, and..." He leans against the side of the pool, next to me.

"I'm not going to help him," I say. "He doesn't want me to."

"Are you sure?"

"He said something—"

"He told me. And I told him that wasn't okay, even though he already knew. And he wants to apologize. For real. You should let him."

"Why?"

"Because you're not the one on the high ground, Del," he says, raising an eyebrow at the name. "You both screwed up."

I cross my arms. Maybe he's right, but I did what I did for love. Hudson can't say that. "So what good will talking about it do?"

"What will it hurt?"

"What will what hurt?" George asks, hopping into the water next to Brad.

316

"Apparently, Brad's ass will hurt after the pounding you'll be giving him—"

"Hey!" Brad says. "Come on, you just said I shouldn't talk about him that way 'cause he's like your brother."

"Oh, you absolutely shouldn't. But I'm going to tease you about it anyway. George, he has both nights of the canoe trip planned out. There's going to be twenty-three minutes of sixty-nineing—"

Brad splashes me as I laugh and swim away. They chase me, still splashing, until Ashleigh comes to my aid, cannon-balling in front of them, and then it becomes an all-out splash war until the lifeguard blows the whistle at us.

"So I don't have to trade with you?" George asks when we're sitting on the edge of the pool.

"No. I'll be fine. You should get to ... see what Brad has planned."

"Oh, I intend to. What do you think you and Hudson will do?"

"I don't know. Maybe we'll try to talk. Maybe we'll just fight. Maybe we'll lie there in silence and sleep. Or maybe he swapped with someone at the last minute. But it's not the end of the world, and I shouldn't take something away from you just so I don't feel awkward."

"Thank you, darling. You know I'd trade if you need me to."

"I know. Thank you."

George hops back into the pool, and I watch him and Brad

dive underwater to sneak a kiss. I spot Hudson watching them, too, and then looking up at me. He tries to smile, but looks frightened. I look down at my nails. The nail polish I put on for color wars is chipped now. I should put on a new coat.

I dive into the pool.

Very few of us actually enjoy the canoe trip. It tends to be more busywork than fun. After lunch, we all go down to the boathouse and get in canoes and then we paddle upriver for about an hour to a small island where we set up tents and camp out for two nights before heading back. Rowing, fire building, tent-setting-upping, cooking (barely). It's more survivalist than entertainment. Maybe Joan thinks it'll serve us well if ever have to run away and hide in the woods because we flee a conversion camp or because we escape a heterosexual society where conversion camps have become mandatory. Or maybe she just wants a weekend off—she doesn't come with us. Connie takes over as boss, leading us all in songs (Mark, begrudgingly, comes along, and Crystal plays guitar), showing us how to set up tents, dig firepits. Karl takes us foraging in the woods for berries and mushrooms. We swim in the river. It's all VERY dirty. Not in the fun way. Well...the sharing tents without counselors certainly makes it dirty in the fun way, too. But only if you're sharing your tent with the right person, which I, obviously, will not be.

Connie says a weekend in the woods is what camp is all

about. I say the point of camp is to be able to be near enough to the woods to appreciate them, but not live in them.

"I do not like the look of those clouds," Ashleigh says as we row downriver. It's three to a canoe, so naturally George and Ashleigh and I are sharing one. George is at the back steering, and I'm at the front. I look up at the clouds she's talking about, and I don't like the look of them, either. They're thick and there's no end in sight.

"I thought we were done with rain," George says, swatting at a mosquito on his neck.

"I think we're following it," Ashleigh says. "It's the same rain."

We all groan in unison. We've only had one other summer when it rained on the canoe trip, but it made the whole thing that much worse. A ramshackle awning over the fire that means the smoke gets everywhere, and no hiking in the woods, foraging, or swimming. Just hiding out in your tents or getting blasted with smoke as Crystal has a coughing fit trying to sing the next verse of "The Rainbow Connection." At least that's how it was last time.

"Connie," I shout. She's in a canoe with some twelve-year-olds, practically handling the canoe alone, but within shouting distance. She's bringing up the back, while Rebecca, Tina, and Lisa try to race each other to the island up front.

"What's up, Del?" Connie shouts back, smiling at me. I realize I kind of missed her this past week. She was fun to hike with, encouraging with the obstacle course.

319

"It's Randy again," I say, realizing we haven't really spoken since I left her elective. "Are you worried about those clouds, too?" I ask, gesturing up with my chin.

She looks up and purses her lips. "It should be okay," she says. "Might be a little wet tonight, but we'll be good by morning." She nods while looking at the clouds, like making sure they've understood their orders. Weirdly, that makes me feel better.

"Well, there you have it," I say.

"I hope those silver medals made her psychic," Ashleigh says.

"Sweetie, if I were to trust anyone at this camp about the weather, it would be her. Or maybe Karl," I say, looking around and finding his canoe a little ahead of us. He's also looking at the sky. I look back at Connie, who is still staring at the clouds.

"Darling, I think they're worried, too."

TWENTY-FIVE

The he storm breaks almost the exact moment we pull our canoe onto shore. Thankfully, it's not heavy at first, just a drizzle, but it quickly turns to real rain as the other campers pull their canoes up.

"A snake!" one of the young boys from Connie's canoe shrieks, hopping out of the water.

"Okay," Connie shouts to the group. "Get with your tent buddy, take one of the tents, and set it up. Karl, help me get a tarp up so we have somewhere to try to make a fire."

"Use Tina and Lisa," Karl says. "I'm going to collect firewood before it all gets soaked."

Connie nods and motions for Tina and Lisa to help her. They lift the tarp out of one of the canoes as the campers line up in front of Mark and Crystal, who are handing out tents.

"Del." I hear the voice call to me, and I don't want to turn, but I know I have to. Ashleigh and George give me pitying looks, then turn away. "Del, I have our tent."

Hudson runs up next to me, holding a tent. I turn and look at him. He's smiling. I want to smile, too, but then I remember everything and I can't.

"Okay," I say.

"Maybe over there?" he says, pointing a little out of the way.

"Sure," I say, without much enthusiasm. I follow him to the spot where he unfurls the tent and he starts putting pegs in the ground while I assemble the rods that hold it up.

"So, I'm glad you didn't switch," Hudson says. "I mean, I know you wanted to. But I'm glad you didn't. I was hoping we could talk."

I don't say anything. I work on getting the rods straight and then threading them through the tent itself. It's tricky, but Hudson pulls them through on the other end and we latch them into place.

"So you don't want to talk?" Hudson asks, sounding angry. "All that work you did, all those lies, and now you just want to drop it?"

"You lied, too, *Hal*," I say.

He nods, then sets the tent into the ground. "So, I thought about that. A lot, actually. But you knew I was lying. That must have been funny to you."

I don't say anything. The rain gets heavier. Hudson

stamps the pegs farther into the ground on one side, I hit them with a rock on the other.

"No?" he asks.

"No," I say. "I didn't think it was funny."

"Your friends were laughing."

Hudson unzips the tent and throws his backpack inside. I throw mine in, too, and then we both try to get in at the same time, bumping shoulders. I step back and motion for him to go first. He does.

It's not a bad tent, as tents go. Big enough for way more than just the two of us. Mesh panels for airflow, which Hudson starts zipping halfway up to keep the rain out. I roll out my sleeping bag, checking it's still dry. It is. Good thing I brought a fancy camping one this year, not my soft pink one.

I sigh and lie down on the sleeping bag. The rain is loud enough now I can't hear anything else.

"So, was it funny to you?" Hudson asks, rolling out his own sleeping bag on the other side of the tent.

"No." I shake my head. "It was sweet." I sigh and turn onto my side, away from him. "This is why I didn't want to share a tent. I don't want to fight. I get it, I was wrong, I lied or whatever, I tricked you. I'm terrible. I'm crazy. I get it. You're angry. Fine. Let's just not talk."

"We could do plenty without talking," he says, in a tone I hadn't expected to hear from him again and which immediately makes all the nerve endings in my body stand at attention.

I turn around to face him, and sit up. He's smiling,

naughty. "Oh," I say. "Is that what this is? Going to reward me for my successful masquerade with a nice tumble in the sleeping bags? Or is it an apology?"

He looks confused. "No, look, Del—sorry, Randy. That came out wrong."

"Let's just not talk," I say again, lying back down, away from him.

"Okay, everybody," I hear Connie shouting through the rain. "We need some help building the fire, if you want to come over here, under the tarp."

I wait to see if he'll go. If he does, I'll stay, but if he stays, I'll go. He doesn't move, but then we get up to leave at the same time.

"You want to help build the fire?" he asks, surprised. I narrow my eyes. We went on the same hikes, did the same activities with Connie, but now that he knows I'm a theater kid, it's like all I am to him is some nature-averse princess, and I would be an amazing princess, don't get me wrong—I rock a tiara—but I can do anything he can do and be a princess while doing it.

"What, you don't think I can?" I ask.

"No," he says quickly. "Come on, let's go help."

I follow him out into the rain, which is getting heavier by the minute. Soon it'll make the world invisible.

We trudge through the thankfully only slightly muddy ground to where we see a bright yellow tarp slung between the trees. It's big, but probably not big enough to cover everyone sitting around a fire. The ground is sandy here, dotted with stones, but it looks like the tarp went up quickly enough that it's not soaked. Karl is in the center of the dry ground, putting stones around a shallow pit. A pile of dry and dry-ish wood is next to him. Other campers stand around, watching him, but it looks like most have stayed in their tents.

"We need more stones," he shouts. I run out into the rain, away from Hudson, looking for stones. My clothes are wet against me pretty quickly, my shoes start getting uncomfortably cold and squishy. The ground is mud, and I admit, I'm not being as careful as I should. The rain makes it hard to see, and I can feel the ground trying to suck my shoes up, so I lift them high and hard, marching...but then I put them down just as hard. Which might also just be because putting your foot down hard feels good when you're angry. And I'm angry. Angry at Hudson for what he said, angry at myself for my whole stupid plan, angry at the weather for raining, at the world for making us share a tent, and angry again at Hudson for his weird little flirting. What was that about?

And maybe I'm so caught up with how angry I am that I'm not careful, which is how I slip into the ditch.

It's not a big ditch, but it's a bit of a mudslide, and at the bottom, my ankle hitches on a root and I fall over it. I don't hear a pop or snap or anything, but in this rain, what could I hear? All I know is it hurts. A lot. Tears-mingling-with-rain a lot. I get myself into a sitting position and try to stand, but the ground is slippery and putting too much pressure on my foot makes it send up big, blaring, painful alarms. So I'm stuck.

"Help!" I shout. I can't hear anything over the rain, though. I doubt anyone can hear me. I'm going to die in the rain in a ditch. Hudson will go back to our tent, I won't be there, and he'll think I've gone off to crowd into someone else's, or maybe he won't care at all, just be happy I'm gone, and no one will tell Connie I'm missing, and I'll sit here all night in the rain, sinking into the mud, dying of hypothermia. I can already feel myself shiver.

"Help!" I try again.

"Hello?" comes a voice through the rain.

"Yes! Hi! I tripped, please, can you help me get back to the main camp?" I shout out, trying to keep the rain out of my eyes to see who it is. "Be careful, it's a pit."

He comes closer and then gently climbs down into the pit.

It's Hudson. Because of course it is.

"Whoa," he says, looking at me. I'm covered in mud, I know. "What happened?"

"I slipped," I tell him, really wishing it were someone else. "Can you go get Connie?"

"Nah, come on." He kneels next to me in the mud and puts my arm around his shoulders.

"Just get Connie," I say, but he's standing, lifting me up. I lean on him as we walk, and he finds a gentle slope out of the pit. "Thanks," I say softly, angry now that he had to be a nice enough guy to save me.

"Of course," he says. "You okay?"

I try putting some weight on the bad ankle, now that we're out of the mud and the land is firmer. It doesn't feel so bad. Just a twinge now. A half-hearted "please don't," which I happily ignore as I take my arm off Hudson and walk back to camp.

"Randy, wait," he says. I can walk but not very quickly, so he keeps pace. "You'll fall again."

"Oh right, 'cause I'm just some fairy who can't even put one leg in front of the other unless it's a runway sashay, right?" I say.

"What? No. I just mean, you slipped the first time, so be careful."

"I can handle myself. I know you think I'm some limp-wristed, weak-willed stereotype, but I was on all those hikes you were." I'm not yelling. I'm talking loudly so he hears me over the rain.

"I know, Randy, I just mean . . . it's slippery."

"I'm fine." I walk ahead and he lingers a step behind me until we're back at camp, and then I sit down close to the fire.

Connie sees me covered in mud and comes up. "What happened?"

"I slipped."

"He twisted his ankle," Hudson says, standing behind me. "He couldn't get up."

"Okay, go get the first aid kit," she says to him. "And some towels to get this mud off you." Hudson runs over to

327

the Black Bag—infamous for holding endless condoms, dental dams, and lube (the counselors know what happens on these trips), as well as first aid kits, and being open all weekend, just left there for folks to use.

Connie has me lift my leg and puts it on a cooler to keep it up and then touches it in a few places. I wince, but only a little.

"Just a little turned, I think," she says as Hudson comes back with towels. He's wiping himself off, and when he sees a cut on my knee immediately starts wiping that off as well.

"Thanks," I say, trying not to sound friendly.

"Sure," he says, taking out a Band-Aid and slapping it over the cut.

"You'll be fine by morning," Connie says to me. "Just keep it up for a while. No more rock gathering, okay?

"And Hudson, help him back to the tent later, just in case, okay?"

"He doesn't have to—"

"Yeah," Hudson interrupts me. "Of course."

Connie goes back to the firepit, which is starting to liven up. Smoke is pouring out and getting stuck under the tarp, making my eyes prick a little.

"Thanks for helping," I say to Hudson.

He sits down next to me. "What did you think I was going to do? Just leave you?"

"I don't know."

"You really think I'd do that?" he asks.

I sigh. "No."

"Good."

We sit in silence for a moment.

"So, I'm going to go help with the fire. Don't head back to the tent without me, okay?"

He puts his hand on my shoulder, and for a second I think he's going to kiss me on the cheek, like he used to, and I can see in his eyes that he thinks of it, but he turns and heads toward the fire instead. I watch him build it up and think maybe I was being an ass. I mean, he was helping. I fell. It was human. It was the right thing to do.

But it doesn't mean anything, I remind myself. He was just being decent. And besides, I don't want it to mean anything. I want to go to sleep and not think about him anymore.

"We got hot dogs!" Connie shouts to the campers still huddled in their tents. "Hot dogs and s'mores. Come and roast yourself some dinner!"

People come out of their tents, shrieking as they try to cover themselves and dash under the tarp. More than a few slip in the mud. Everyone gathers around Connie, grabbing hot dogs and sticking them on the ends of sticks they've plucked from the woods before lining up to roast them over the fire. Mark and Crystal hand out buns and soon there's a decent line going as everyone roasts and eats. George and Ashleigh see me sitting and bring me a stick and then, when I tell them what happened, help me closer to the fire.

"So he came to your rescue?" Ashleigh asks, raising her eyebrows. "In the rain?"

"He heard me yelling. It was what anyone would have done."

"It's just very...Jane Austen?" Ashleigh says. "Heathcliff? Something."

"Darling," George says, gently telling her to stop.

"Sorry, right," she says. "It wasn't anything. Want me to roast a weenie for ya?"

"Yes, please."

George and Ashleigh act as my roasters, cooking my hot dogs and then marshmallows for s'mores, since there's nowhere to sit that's close enough to the fire.

Crystal gets out her guitar and tries to play some songs, but she's difficult to hear under the sound of the rain on the tarp.

"If I catch a cold from this," George says next to me, licking chocolate and marshmallow off his fingers, "I'm going to be deeply angry."

"Mark is handing out chewable vitamin C to everyone in the show." I nod at Mark, who's carefully going around, looking for his actors and crew and making them take chalky orange-flavored tablets (he got me first).

"Hey, Randy?" Hudson calls to me. "You ready to go back to the tent?"

"You're not going to stay up?"

"For what?"

I shrug and nod and let him help me up—though it barely hurts now. I grab a few bottles of water as we head back to the tent. We're both totally soaked by the time we get inside and Hudson takes out a towel from his bag and starts drying himself and the tent where we've dripped. Then he takes off his shirt.

I swallow as I look at his damp naked skin and quickly turn away. Romance may be over between us, but lust definitely isn't, at least not on my side. He's still top-name-on-the-marquee gorgeous, his body still carved from some stone I don't know the name of. I pull my shirt off, too, and lay it flat in the corner to dry. I hear him unzip his shorts, the sound impossibly loud over the rain. I stare out the window, even though there's nothing I can see. There's some rustling behind me.

"You can turn around now."

I turn, and he's in his sleeping bag. In his corner of the tent, his shoes, shirt, shorts, and underwear are all laid out to dry.

"You could have turned around before, too."

I glare. "Why are you flirting?"

"What?"

"Before and that, what you just said. You're flirting."

"I don't know...we used to flirt before."

I put my hands on my hips and cock them to one side. "Yeah, but now I'm not your type, right?" I lift a hand and bend my wrist at him. "Now I'm just some faggot," I say, giving myself a lisp. "Some weak stereotype, right?"

He frowns. "No," he says. "And I'm sorry for what I said.

He sits up a little, his sleeping bag sliding around him to his stomach. Did he put on clean underwear? "Randy, I need you to know that. I am really so, so sorry for that."

I let my arms drop and I sigh. "I know. But you still said it."

"I was angry, embarrassed that everyone, the whole camp, knew everything and had known the whole time, and I....I wanted to hurt you."

I sit down, my wet shorts making me cold. "I know."

"If you know that...why are you so angry? I'm not angry anymore. I...look, what you did is wild, no doubt about it. Over-the-top. Just...like from a movie or something. But... it was flattering, too. And the really out-there thing is that it worked. I really fell in love with you, Randy. I told you things I've never told anyone, not even Brad, and I feel closer to you than anyone else in my life."

Some water drips from my hair onto the tent. Hudson sighs and reaches for his towel, and as he leans forward, I can see down his lower back to the top of his ass—he is definitely not wearing underwear. He throws the towel at me.

"Dry off," he says. "Change out of those wet things. I won't look."

He turns around and I strip and use his towel to get myself dry. The towel smells like him—that electric deodorant and the faint maple smell. I try not to think about it as I get in my sleeping bag. I throw the towel back at him. It lands on his head.

"That means I can turn around?" he asks.

I grin, then make my face angry again. "Yeah."

He turns around so we're both facing each other on our sides, naked in our sleeping bags, a wide space between us. I hate it, but my body is tingling. Maybe I don't hate it.

"So why are you so angry?" Hudson asks.

I shrug. "You don't like me. That makes me angry."

His eyes get large, sort of sad. "Why do you think that?"

"Because of everything you said. Everything you are." I sit up and gesture up and down his body. "Masc4masc, straight-acting only, all that."

"I just thought that people like that were...stronger," he says. "And safer. I could never bring someone back to my parents who wasn't...different, like me. Not a stereotype in their eyes. I could never hold hands with him on the street. So I just...didn't even look at them. That was wrong, I know. You showed me that. I'm not better than you, Randy. I'm not better than George or anyone else in the show." He pauses. "If anything, I'm worse."

"Worse?"

"You guys are just being yourselves." He sits up again, then lies down, unable to get comfortable. "I...I'm a character just as much as Del was, maybe. I don't know. I don't feel like I'm acting most of the time, but then...when Brad put on that nail polish, I was so jealous."

"Jealous?"

"Yeah. It was a cool color."

"Unicorn Trampocalypse."

He laughs. "Is that the name?" He turns to look at the ceiling of the tent, on his back but out of his sleeping bag enough that his stomach is exposed. "I like it. I wish I could wear it. I wanted to, in that moment. I wanted to be...more like me? Not that I think all gay guys have to wear nail polish to be themselves or anything. But it reminded me of my grandma, and painting her nails, and her sometimes painting mine and how happy that made me. I really loved it. Picking out the color, holding it up to the light, seeing it on me. Not just nail polish, either. Lipstick, eye shadow. I had so much fun putting makeup on Grandma, and wearing it. And then she would wipe it all off before my parents got home and tell me not to tell them. She was protecting me. So then, when she died, I started protecting myself because of..."

"What your mom did."

He nods. "But I think Grandma wanted to send me here because here is a kind of protection. Here I can...be myself. Right?"

"Like you've always said: You can be anyone you want," I say. "I kind of proved that."

He laughs. "Yeah." He turns back to me. "So, I want you to know, and, like, you don't need to say anything back, but I just want you to know, that I thought about everything— everything you said and did and...you were right. I do know you, Randy. Maybe not all the parts of you—I don't know about your love of musical theater, or your real fashion sense or anything like that. But I know the parts of you that make me laugh, that make me feel good about myself, that talk to me and make me feel special not because of what I'm not, but because of what I am. And, so...I still love all those parts."

I can feel my throat closing and force myself to take a deep breath through my nose. He reaches out his hand to me, but it doesn't close the distance, so he wriggles his sleeping bag closer, which makes us both laugh and then his hand is on my cheek and every part of me feels like it's filled with stars again.

"Wait," I say, pulling his hand off me.

"I want to know all the parts of you," he says. "I mean that. I want to hear all about the show and what you've been doing this week, I want to know about musical theater and clothes and...anything you want to talk to me about."

I smile. "Okay," I say. "But...I don't know you anymore."

"What?"

"Every summer, I've watched you, seen you inspire people—inspire me. You always made me feel like I can do anything...but it turns out what you meant was you thought I could be more...like you. And now, you're saying you want me to be me, but..."

"Randy," he says, looking straight into me, making new stars appear just with his eyes. "I do want you to be you. So, I know what I've said is...not, like, what you thought I meant. But...I like your version better. So...that's what I believe now." He shrugs. "You made me believe what you thought I believed this whole time. You're special. I think maybe...we're special."

Stars are born from explosions, and a thousand stars are born in me as he pulls my face close to his and kisses me.

When we pause, I pull back. "You want..." I swallow. "I mean, are we just picking back up where we left off, like nothing happened?"

"We are...trying," he says, and kisses me again. "But there's something I want you to do to me."

"Okay," I say, my voice a little breathier than I mean for it to be.

He scoots back over to his stuff and goes into his bag and pulls something out, then comes back over to me and shows it to me—nail polish. It's a deep purple color with dark blue glitter.

"Paint my nails?" he asks a little loudly.

I laugh. "Where did you even get this?"

"You're welcome, darling!" I hear George's voice shout through the rain.

"They set up their tent near ours," Hudson says with a sheepish smile. "George said I could use the nail polish as long as I let him know when it was happening so he could take credit."

Brad's voice comes in loud for a moment, over the rain, "Now can we—" The rain gets heavy again, cutting them off. Hudson and I laugh.

"So, will you paint my nails?" Hudson asks.

I nod, shaking the bottle. Hudson spreads his hands in front of me. I've held those hands a hundred times, linked my fingers through his, but I've never really looked at them before. They're delicate, more than I thought. They could use some moisturizer—they're a little rough—but the fingers are slender and graceful, and his nails, though short, are smooth. I take the brush and carefully spread it over his nails, trying to leave an even coat.

"I love this color," Hudson says. "It's so..."

"Regal?" I say.

"Yeah. Exactly. I'm like a king wearing this."

I smile, focusing on painting carefully, not dripping onto his skin or the tent. I go slowly, even though part of me wants to rush. Part of me knows what will happen next, when his nails are dry and his newly colored hands run down my body. I'm ready for it. I want it.

But also, I think, finishing his first hand, maybe this is stupid. I said I wanted Hudson in nail polish, and I'm getting him, but what does that even mean? How can this work when he's just coming out of his shell and I've only shown him part of me? Is that enough? Is one week left of camp enough?

I finish his second hand and blow on his nails.

"Shake your hands so it dries and I can do a second coat if you want."

"Can I do yours?"

I show off my hands. My nails are cropped short, and

bright pink metallic polish dots every finger. "Just painted them last night. But you can paint over them, if you want."

He nods, happy. "It'll be a cool effect," he says, starting to paint. He's a natural, too. All those years practicing on his grandma must have taught him well. He glides the brush in quick, precise strokes. He finishes faster than I did.

"I haven't done that in so long," he says. "It felt...nice." He looks up. "Thank you. I'm glad it was you."

I smile and blow on my nails and shake them in the air, wishing they would dry faster. He leans forward and kisses me again on the lips, then the neck.

"Stop," I say, "my nails are still wet."

"So you'd better not touch me," he says. "But mine are dry...." He puts his hand on my chest, then runs it down my stomach, and then he pauses, waiting for me to say something. I don't, and his hands go farther down in my sleeping bag. I gasp as he starts stroking me. I'm already hard—I have been since the moment I heard him take off his shorts.

"This is okay?" he whispers. I nod and kiss him again, then stop to frantically blow on my nails. "Relax," he says. "They'll dry." He unzips my sleeping bag and starts kissing down my neck onto my stomach until his mouth finds what it's looking for and...oh.

First blow job. That's happening now.

I look down and just the sight of Hudson doing what he's doing is enough to almost make me involuntarily end it prematurely, so I look away. I always thought it would be a bit like what I do in the shower when the cabin is empty, but it's very different from that. Much better. Should I do something, though? Do I put my hand on his head, or does that mean I want him to go deeper? I don't want him to do anything he doesn't want to do, so I carefully lay my hand on his head, like I'm patting a dog. No... this is not how it happens in porn. I grab his hair with both my hands.

"Ow," he says, stopping.

"Sorry."

He smiles and goes back to it. I let my hands rest in his hair and try to lie back and just enjoy it. And it feels... *amazing* is a cheap word for these sensations. I need some new word that makes me arch my back and makes my whole body feel like electricity is shooting through it—like my skeleton can feel things now.

I lose track of time, but also I'm aware of every moment of this. It's just that moments have no meaning, time wise, until I can feel that I need to stop him or else ask him if he's a spitter or a swallower.

"Wait," I say, panting. "I'm... not yet."

He lifts his mouth to mine and kisses me. "Your nails are probably dry by now," he says.

I laugh and touch one of them. Totally dry. I wrap my arms around him and kiss him, my body pushing against his sleeping bag, which I hastily unzip. He smiles and the space between us closes, our bodies knitting together, legs between legs, arms wrapped around bodies, hands running up and down. I pull away, enjoying myself too much.

"Do you want to?" He looks down at his own body.

I nod. "I've never." What do I do? I know no teeth. But is it like a lollipop scenario, or more of an ice cream cone?

"Just do what you think you'd like," he says, maybe seeing my panic. Which sounds well and good, but I just experienced it for the first time, so how do I know exactly what I like?

I'm not super sure how to do this, so I just open my mouth as wide as I can and go as far as I can. I must look like a fish. So sexy, Randy. I'm surprised by the taste. I thought it would be dirt-tasting and with an uncomfortable smell, but it tastes and smells like the crook of his neck. I use my tongue and lips and I smile when I hear him moan. I'm doing it, and doing it well enough—my first time giving a blow job. I try a few things, twisting my mouth, using my hands, going as far down as I can, which results in a very unsexy coughing fit that I try to hide and makes us both laugh. He starts giving me instructions, and that makes it easier.

"Like that. Slower. Don't press your lips together so hard."

He runs his hands through my hair and I stop for a minute to take a breath.

"You all right?"

I nod. "Am I doing it right?"

"Yeah," Hudson laughs. "You're a natural."

What surprises me most is how much I enjoy it. Not just for his sounds of pleasure, but because I want this. You always hear about how hot getting a blow job is, but never hear how hot it is to give one.

"Okay, okay," he says, after not enough time, pulling me back up to him. We kiss.

"I want you in me," he says. My eyes widen a little. "If you want."

"Are you sure?" I ask. "I mean, I could..."

He grins. "You're new to this. Let's start this way. If you want. We don't have to—"

I nod, cutting him off. "Yes," I say quickly. I'm not saying no to that. I'm checking every box I can on the virginity score card tonight. Is that a sports metaphor? Maybe I'm still a little Del after all.

He turns back to his bag, letting me admire the perky slopes of his ass, and pulls out several packets of lube and a condom.

"You'll have to show me," I say.

"Okay," he says. "Let's start with your finger."

I hold out my hand, and he opens a packet of lube onto his hand and mine, then he reaches behind himself. I test the lube between my hands. It feels...silly. Almost like rubbing Jell-O between my hands. I giggle at it, then look up and see Hudson biting his lower lip, his eyes rolling back as he fingers himself. All thoughts of Jell-O and silliness vanish.

"Can I see?" I ask.

He smiles and turns onto his stomach so I can watch him lube everything up and push his own finger into himself. He sighs deeply. Then he pulls it out. "You," he says, reaching for my lubed hand. Carefully, I push my finger into him. He stops me after a minute, pulling my hand out. "More lube," he says.

I grab another packet and try to open it, but my hands are already lubed up and it slips out, flying up and hitting the roof of the tent, then falling back down. Hudson laughs and picks it up, opening it with his teeth, and then pouring it over my hands. He rolls back over and guides my finger into him, farther than before. When he gasps, I stop.

"No, it feels good. Keep going. Slowly." I keep pushing in and he cranes his neck up so I kiss him on the mouth as I push. "Now in and out," he gasps. I follow his instructions, moving my finger as he makes noises that make every part of me stand on end. At his instruction, I curl my finger slightly, and the noises grow louder. He grabs my face close to him, kissing me hungrily. "Two fingers now."

I swallow and pull my finger out, and add more lube from one of the open packets before going back in with two fingers. I'm so glad I cut my nails before re-painting them yesterday.

"Wait," he says, and I stop as he takes a deep breath. "Okay." I push again, slower. When both fingers are nearly in all the way he gasps again, throwing his head down into the built-in pillow of his sleeping bag.

"Should I stop?"

"No," he says, his voice low and throaty. "It feels so good," he says half into his pillow. He looks up at me, his face both hungry and looking a little drunk and pulls me in for a kiss again. He rotates slightly, so our bodies are pressing together, my hand wrapped around his waist. "I'm ready," he says after some more kissing. "I want you."

I nod and he tears the condom open, rolling it down on me, which is much more fun than when I've practiced putting on condoms myself, and then he opens two more packets of lube and pours them over it.

"I'll start on top," he says, "if that's okay?"

"Anything is okay," I say, words not working quite right, so I kiss him. He smiles into the kiss, almost laughing, and then shoves me, so I'm lying on my back, and kneels over me. He slowly lowers himself, grabbing my body and guiding me, easing me into him. At first, the tightness is so intense it almost hurts, and I wonder if I've done something wrong, but his breathing turns heavy and he smiles, openmouthed, turning his head to the ceiling.

"Oh yes," he says, and starts moving up and down on me. It feels astounding. Different from the blow job. And much better than by myself in the shower. But even better than how I feel is watching Hudson, hearing the sounds he makes as he moves up and down on top of me.

He leans forward, kissing me, and I grab his ass, squeezing it as our tongues mingle, our bodies combine, then he throws his head back again, making more noises as I rock my hips gently up and down. He touches himself, his purple nail polish gleaming in the dim light. I love watching him; it's the sexiest thing I've ever seen. Here I am, finally having sex with Hudson, a man I've loved for years, who loves me, the real me, and it's like the world is applauding for me. Not like we're being watched—that's not something I'm into. I don't think. But it's like a standing ovation, but not from people, from the world itself. The world itself, the universe, the stars, all clapping for us, and saying, "What a wonderful end to a perfect love story."

"Want to try missionary?" Hudson asks. His hair is wet again, but now with sweat.

I grin. "Yeah."

TWENTY-SIX

ight pours in through the walls of the tent, kind of gray. The rain has stopped, but it's stuffy. I'm naked, on my sleeping bag, which is open and next to Hudson's, but Hudson is gone. The clothes he set drying are still there.

I take a deep breath. I'm not a virgin anymore. But I'm also alone. I want to replay last night over and over, but Hudson not being here is worrying me. I go through my bag for clean underwear and slip it on. Where did Hudson go? Is he regretting what we did, what he said, off somewhere trying to scrape away the nail polish? An image of him comes into my mind, scraping his nails until they bleed or come off, and I wince. If that's what he's doing, he's definitely done with me. Or maybe it was just an act, a new smooth routine from the Hal who carves his name in the tree every summer, a new conquest. Or a new flavor to try, which he'll now throw in the trash.

The front of the tent unzips and I try to cover myself with my sleeping bag as Hudson pokes his head in.

"Oh, you put on underwear," he says, disappointed.

I smile. "I can take it off again." Did that just come out of my mouth? One night of passion and suddenly I'm a femme fatale in a made-for-TV movie. I am doing this all wrong.

He steps into the tent and kisses me. "Maybe in a bit," he says. "I grabbed us breakfast. Bagels and cream cheese." He hands me a cold bagel, a mini packet of cream cheese, and a plastic knife. The same thing they send on the canoe trip every year. "Oh, but maybe..." He reaches into his bag and throws me a mini bottle of hand sanitizer, which I use.

He takes off his shoes and sits on his sleeping bag. He has his own bagel, already half eaten, which he finishes, smiling at me as I try to spread the cream cheese on mine. I start eating and he pulls his shirt off, putting it back in his bag. Then he strips his shorts off, revealing blue boxer briefs.

"It's stuffy in here," he says. "It's warm."

I nod, eating my bagel and watching him.

"So, the rain stopped. We can probably do stuff today. Karl says there'll be a lot of mushrooms out."

"Probably," I say.

"So, do you want to talk about anything?" he asks, tilting his head at me.

"I just..."

"You're not a virgin." He grins.

"That's part of it." I laugh, and then take another bite of my bagel. "But...I mean. What are we now?"

"Oh." His eyes widen. "I thought we were boyfriends again. If that's okay. Is that what you want?"

Is it? It's what I've always wanted. And...I love him. I think I do, at least. It's hard, peeling back these layers of Hudson and finding out how he feels about gay men, about himself, about what his parents taught him to hate, and what his grandmother tried to teach him to love. He's not the simple dream guy I thought he was. He's not just someone who's going to make me feel good because he believes in the best of everyone. His beliefs are changing. I'm changing them. I cut my hair and figured out I like the obstacle course, though, so he changed me first.

I look at his nails. They need a second coat. I should have done that last night.

"Randy?" he asks. I realize I've been quiet for a while.

"I was just trying to figure it out," I say. "Who you are. Who you think I am."

"I don't know if we can ever really know everything about each other," he says. "But I'd like to try. And like I said last night...I know enough of you to love you."

I smile. "I know enough of you to love you, too," I say.

"So, boyfriends?"

"Yes. Now get over here, because, sweetie, those nails need another coat."

He grins and takes out the nail polish, shaking it as I eat, then gives me his hands, and I carefully paint each nail.

The entire day is spent swimming in the river or helping Karl find dry wood and mushrooms and berries (which no one eats without checking with him first, since three summers ago when one of the girls from cabin twelve spent the day vomiting). And just like I slipped easily back into theater, I slip easily back into Hudson.

Not like that.

But it's like the fights and the last week never happened. No, they happened, but we worked through everything. We know more about each other now, and we love those parts of each other. So we walk hand in hand, matching nail polish and all. We sneak kisses behind trees and underwater when we're swimming. We lie on the sand of the beach together with George and Brad and Ashleigh and Paz and tell jokes and laugh and try to explain musical theater to Hudson, who says he wants to learn because I learned all about what he likes.

"So, we only have one week left," he says, holding my hand on the beach.

"Yeah," I say sadly. "We'll make the most of it."

"Right. So, I'm going to do theater for the last week."

"What?"

"You did all my stuff for two weeks. I can go a week without the obstacle course....Maybe I'll do some sports after lunch if I'm feeling like I have to move around, but only if it's okay with you, babe."

"You don't owe me anything," I say.

"All right, then even if it's not okay with you. But I'm joining theater. I will move stuff around, or...try to dance, or whatever."

I laugh. "How about you stop by when you can?"

"Okay. I just want to spend time with you."

"I know." I lay my head on his shoulder. "But the last week of rehearsal is always crazy. We literally call it Hell Week."

"So I won't see you?" He frowns.

"We'll make time," I say. "I promise."

He smiles and kisses me.

That night, we roast mushrooms and more hot dogs, but it's not raining, so there's no tarp and we don't end up living in a tent of smoke. Instead, we all sing and drink bug juice and tell jokes and watch the fire until it dies down. We all seem happy. We all feel like a family.

When the sun goes down, Hudson and I go back to our tent, kissing frantically before we even zip the door closed. You'd think finally having sex would calm me down, but it's only made me want him more, and I'm down on my knees undoing his fly in less than a minute.

"Maybe tonight," I say, pulling his shorts down and kissing his thighs through his boxer briefs, "you can top me?"

He laughs. "I'd love to, but not tonight. You're going to want a real shower before that."

I think about it for a minute before realizing what he means. "Right," I say, a little disappointed.

He kneels down next to me and kisses me. "But there's still plenty of other stuff we can do."

I grin, grabbing him by the waist and slipping my hands down the back of his underwear to squeeze his ass.

"Well, I guess if you insist."

The next day, after packing up and making sure we're leaving no trash behind, we row back to camp. We stay in the same canoes we came up in, but now the canoe with Hudson, Brad, and Sam glides alongside ours, all of us shouting jokes back and forth and singing together until Connie tells us we're too close and to get some distance, and we split up, and then get close again a few minutes later.

When we make it back to camp, everyone runs to the pool to bleach our bodies with chlorine and get the river stink off ourselves, before heading up to the cabins for a proper shower and then dinner.

After dinner, maybe knowing we're all a little overdosed on nature, is another movie night (*Love, Simon*) and Hudson and I hold hands and lean on each other as we watch. Then we make out a little next to the side of my cabin before I hear Mark call, "Lights-out in five," and we say good night.

"So, you finally get everything you wanted," Ashleigh

says when I come into the cabin and run for my toothbrush. "Plan executed. Happy ending."

"Endings," George says. "He had two nights in the tent."

I roll my eyes, but I smile. "Yeah, I guess it all worked."

And it did. And I should be happy. And I am. But I'm worried, too. The only time we have left is Hell Week, and then the summer is over and Hudson goes back to his parents, the real world, where he'll be constantly reminded that I'm not the right sort of boy for him to be with. That he can do better—not in the usual sense, because let's face it, he can't—but in the way he used to mean better. More straight-acting. More approved of. Safer. Has he really changed, or is it more like a constant battle where I'm fighting for him, and one where I'm not going to be in the picture for the next eleven months?

I look over at Mark, who is standing by the light switch, waiting for us all to get in bed.

"Okay, Randy?" he asks.

"I think so."

As always, Hell Week lives up to its name. Everything needs to be perfected and suddenly two dozen new problems pop up. A lighting gel melts, Jen inexplicably forgets all the lyrics to "Rosie," the chorus becomes entirely left-footed.

"Are we cursed?" Mark asks the theater one afternoon before stalking outside to call his therapist.

And yet, I'm loving it. The chaos, the energy. Maybe I'm the kind of drama queen that thrives on the chaos. Or maybe it's that Hudson is here, and every time I start to feel stressed, it's like he senses it, and he's suddenly next to me, his hand resting on my hip, telling me he doesn't quite get everything, but it seems pretty cool, or being amazed at how different colored lights change the tone of the set. Everything is new to him, and all he wants to do is be there for me. I'm really lucky.

And we talk, between scenes, during dinner. Really talk, with me as Randy, and he wants to know everything: about my love of musical theater (all-encompassing), why I don't wear eyeliner (I poke myself in the eye), the first time I wore nail polish (at camp, first week, after asking George if he'd do my nails; outside camp, at thirteen, I stole my mom's and when she caught me she laughed and said it was kind of weird to see a boy with painted nails, "But if it makes you happy..."). We talk about Randy things, and he listens and loves everything I tell him.

I tell him about our first week, the night we talked. He doesn't remember, but he says that he remembers that night, because it was the first week he'd slept soundly. And now he knows it was because of me.

Ashleigh gives me the photos from the underwater camera. All the underwater ones are blurry, but there's one of him kissing me on the cheek above water that I tape to the post of my bed, so I can look at it as I go to sleep.

He even starts helping out with the makeup for the actors in the show. It must be muscle memory or something, because he can apply one of the best cat's eyes I've seen, and fast, too. And he's made a few changes to the stage makeup that have everyone looking fantastic. I wonder if his grandma looked like everyone onstage at some point. If he'll see her when he watches the show, peeking out.

He even stole one of the blue eyeliner pencils and has started wearing it when he's around camp. Just a little cat's eye. Nothing too dramatic. But it makes me happy to know not only did he find his place in the theater, but it was like he was always meant to be there. Just like maybe I was always meant to direct (but not NOT act, of course. Direct in *addition* to acting).

I feel bad I don't have much time with him, though, and I feel especially bad that now that we're sleeping in cabins again, we can't get any alone time. On Thursday, he convinces me to sneak away after lunch to hike to our spot overlooking the camp, where we strip and don't spend any time at all admiring the view before rinsing ourselves off with water bottles and rushing back down to the drama cabin, where Mark rolls his eyes at us as we walk in late.

"I can't wait to introduce you to my parents," Hudson says to me over dinner, holding my hand. "I want to show them how happy you make me."

I smile so hard it hurts at that. "And you'll get to meet mine," I say.

I'm worried about Hudson's parents, though. I'm worried about what he said about how they might react to Brad's painted nails—by not letting Hudson come back next summer. I look down at our hands—still painted purple, but chipping. I love those nails, and his hands, holding them and seeing our matching nail polish. I love the feel of his hand woven into mine. But I also don't want that hand to get hurt.

After dinner, we go back to the theater to run a few more scenes. I sit next to Mark in the audience while Hudson is backstage helping put on people's makeup.

"Can I ask you something?" I say to Mark between scenes.

"It's really not the best time, Randy," Mark says. "But make it quick."

"Hudson's parents...they don't like him acting femme. Should I tell him to take off his nail polish before they get here? Should I take off mine?"

Mark snorts. "You should be yourself. And he should be himself. You've helped that boy come out of his shell, and he is clearly happier for it, and I'm very happy for you, but I don't know his family situation. My advice is to always be yourself, and not apologize for it."

I lean back in my chair. Right. That's true. That's good.

"Thanks," I say. He pats my leg, watching the stage.

"Still, you should talk to Connie. She knows his parents."

"Oh," I say, frowning that this isn't easy and decided. "All right. Can I go find her now?"

"Sure, sure, just...No, come on, the set needs to change faster than that, people! You did it twice as fast three hours ago. WHAT IS HAPPENING?"

I smile. Mark is too busy to give me much advice right now. But I get up and walk out of the cabin. The rest of the camp tonight is playing flashlight freeze tag, running around in the dark trying to catch each other in beams of light. Connie is one of the refs, so I find her standing to the side of the soccer field.

"Where's your flashlight, Randy? Or are you in the theater tonight? I hear the show is going to be good this year."

"It is." I nod, smiling. "But I wanted to talk to you about something."

"Sure," she says, turning away from the field and looking at me. "Everything okay?"

"I'm worried about Hudson."

"Why?"

"It's his parents. You've met them, right?"

Connie nods. "Yes. I've spoken to them at the end of the summer before. And I know a little about Hudson's home life from what he's told me."

"So you know Hudson and I are together, right?"

Connie laughs. "The whole camp knows, Randy."

I blush, happy the dark is hiding it. "Okay, but you've seen he's wearing nail polish and he's working at the theater."

"Yes. Young love can change a person. It's actually very sweet, I think."

"Will his parents think so, too, though?"

Connie sighs. "I was going to talk to him on Saturday," she says quietly. She sits down cross-legged on the grass and I sit down next to her. "I wanted to give him some more time being...here, you know? That's why we made this place. A place away from the world. You ever watch *The West Wing*? No, you're too young. Far from the things of man. That's what this place is. Except *man* meaning 'straight people.' It's a safe place. A place for you all to be yourselves and have a childhood that you don't get anywhere else." She takes a deep breath and exhales slowly. "But it's got an expiration date."

"Okay..."

"He needs to take the nail polish off," she says. "And if he's going to introduce you to his parents as his boyfriend, you need to take yours off, too. You need to be Del again."

"But isn't it better to just be yourself, and be proud?" I ask.

"Here? Yes. Absolutely. Out there? You have to keep yourself safe first. You're still just kids. Hudson needs his parents to feed him, clothe him, not kick him out or beat him or berate him or send him to a conversion camp. He needs them to let him come back here next summer. And that means he has to stay...what they want him to be."

"But they're his parents. They send him here."

356

"They don't like sending him here. I'm always happy when I see his name come in as a camper. I don't know how he convinces them, but they don't like this place." I know what it is. His grandma, guilting them from beyond the grave. "You'll see, on Sunday. Watch their eyes, like they're in enemy territory. We're not the same as them. We're not them. Maybe not even people. Hudson is, because he's their son, and because even with this one thing, he hasn't pushed himself too far outside their idea of what he should be: male, masculine . . . whatever nonsense words people put on behavior sets they approve of." She leans back against a tree, and her hands absently start pulling blades of grass. "I didn't come out until I was twenty-seven. You know that? I injured my leg, I knew my career was done, and it was a relief to me. Because now I could do it, now I could come out. Except I'd come out to my coach before that. Years before. Nineteen. He'd walked in on me one day in a hotel room, and I was wearing this skirt I'd seen and had to have. It was beautiful. Blue silk, dip dyed so it was lighter at the waist, flowed like a dream. He tore it off me. Ripped it to shreds. I tried to explain how I felt, how I'd always felt. But he told me that I couldn't be that. He said if I wanted to put on women's clothes in private, that was fine. But I couldn't do it in public. I couldn't be a woman, tell people I was a woman, do what felt right to me: longer hair, longer nails. . . . I had to show some restraint. Like an adult, he said. Everything else was . . . he called it 'bedroom stuff,' which I didn't understand at first, but then I realized he thought it was a sex thing." She pauses. "I should not be telling that to a camper."

"Mark says worse."

She snorts a laugh. "I know he does. Anyway, my coach told me if I came out, or even started to show signs I would, he would dump me, I'd lose all my endorsement deals, and I'd be banned from the sport. My life would be over. So I kept myself safe. Until my life kind of was over because of the injury. And then I finally got to be reborn."

"But is that the same?"

"No, no...nothing is the same. No coming out story is the same as another. And you're already out, Hudson is out. And gay is different from trans. Gender non-conforming is different from trans. You know that. But what I mean is there's out and then there's the sort of out people don't want you to be. I could know I was a woman in my mind, but not act on it. Hudson can know in his head he's a guy in nail polish and eyeliner who will kick your ass on the obstacle course and look fabulous doing it. There are different degrees of out...and you need to stick to the ones that are safe. Now, what's safe changes with where you are, and who you're with. I don't have that luxury. But I'm also an adult now. I'm not saying it's safe in the world for me, but my parents can't kick me out of the house. So Hudson has to find the degree of out that will keep him safe when he's around his parents."

I nod. "That...I think that's what I'm worried about." I lie back in the grass.

"I can talk to him. Convince him to take the nail polish off."

"No, I'll do it. It should be me." I don't want to, but it should be me.

"Just remember, Randy, he's your boyfriend, not your... camper. You're not responsible for... teaching him how to be gay."

I laugh. "I'm not teaching him that. There's no one way to be gay."

"You know what I mean. To be... himself."

"I know. And I'm not, I don't think. I'm just supporting him. Even if he weren't my boyfriend, that's what we're supposed to do for each other, right?"

"That's right," she says, standing up and brushing dirt off her knees. "You're a good kid, Randy. Let me know if you need help talking to him."

"Thanks."

I walk back to the theater, going inside just in time to watch a sandbag narrowly miss one of the new kids in the chorus as it falls to the stage with a thud loud enough that the whole theater goes quiet.

"Are we cursed?" Mark shouts. "Did one of you say the name of the Scottish play out loud or say it's going to be the best show ever or 'I bet no one gets hit by a sandbag this year' or 'I bet Mark doesn't have a stroke this year'? Well? Did any of you say that?" No one answers. "Everyone go outside and turn around three times and spit!"

I try not to laugh.

I find Hudson backstage, just sort of watching the panic in everyone's eyes, not sure how to help, and I take him by the hand and I lead him outside, where I kiss him and lie down in the grass.

"You have to take the nail polish off," I say. "Both of us do."

"No way, babe," he says, like he was expecting this conversation. "I don't care what my parents think."

I hold his face in my hands. He's so beautiful. And he's more beautiful now than he ever was.

"I'm glad you don't care, but you have to. We have to. Otherwise they might not send you back next year."

Hudson looks down at his nails. "But it reminds me of you." His voice is already shaky with tears. "Of us."

"We don't need nail polish to remember us, right? We'll have texting and video chat and I'm going to send you all the musicals on Netflix you should watch, because we need to improve your dramatic education."

He laughs, but only once, and it's sort of sad. "I feel like, now that I know who I am, or more of who I am, I don't want to hide it anymore. Such a cliché, right? But..." He holds his hands out, the nail polish glinting. "This is me. Every time I catch a glance of my hands now, I feel, like, this rush, like swinging across the Peanut Butter Pit, or making a goal. Every finger is like a victory, reminding me who I am. That I'm special. So I don't want to give that up."

I nod and stretch my own hands out, taking one of his. "If there's one thing I've learned this summer, it's that my wearing nail polish doesn't make me *me*. Sure, I see myself in my hands, and I feel more like me, I feel like I'm showing off who I am, like I'm proud of who I am...but even when I took it off, and called myself Del, I was Randy underneath. I don't think I could not be him even if I tried."

"I know," he says, squeezing my hand. "I fell in love with Randy."

"So, it's not really hiding," I say. "It's a role. For an audience of two—your parents. And you only have to play it around them. But you're still you. You have nail polish on underneath your nails, and eye shadow under your lids and the fiercest cat's eye...they're just under everything, waiting to come out. Which you can do with me. With me you always get to be whomever you want to be."

He takes my hands and our fingers wrap around each other.

"Okay, but not until Saturday. And you have to take it off. Oh...and there's one thing we have to do first."

Saturday night, when we don't have rehearsals—to give everyone a chance to rest up for tomorrow—Hudson and I walk to the tree in the woods where hearts and names are carved, and there, using an X-Acto knife from A&C, we carve our own heart, and in it: *Randy and Hudson*. Not HAL, not Del.

Hudson was very specific about that. We weren't those people anymore. And then, with our hands sticky with sap and bark, we walk up to the cliff, our cliff, and look out over the camp.

"Okay," Hudson says, his hand in mine, our legs dangling over the edge, staring at the camp below. "I'm ready."

With some cotton balls and nail polish remover that George lent me, we strip each other in a different way. Then we lie down in the grass, holding hands, staring at the stars, the chemical smell of the remover hovering in the air.

"I was thinking about sneaking out and buying makeup, practicing on myself in my room. I think I'd look cool in eye shadow."

"You'd look good in anything," I say. "But do your parents go through your room?"

"Yeah," he sighs.

"Your browser history?"

"I don't think so."

"Then find some videos. Makeup tutorials. Spend the whole year picking out your favorite colors and I'll bring them next summer."

He tightens his grip on my hand in the dark, like he's afraid to let go. I get it; I am, too. Above us, real stars sparkle like glitter on black velvet. A drag queen evening gown. They're miles away, I know, but it feels like we're wrapped in it.

"I'm afraid of being without you all year," he says. "I'm afraid of losing myself. Of turning back into..."

"You won't. I mean it. You can't suddenly wake up and say, 'I know this isn't who I am, but it's who I should be,' when you already know everyone is trying to trick you into thinking that."

"Are you sure?"

I'm not, but I don't say that. "I'll be there, whenever you need. Text or e-mail or even a phone call."

He lays his head on my chest. "I'm going to miss you so much, though."

"Me too."

TWENTY-SEVEN

When the curtain rises, I swear I can feel all my internal organs rising with it, trying to get out through my mouth and only failing because all of them get stuck in my throat at once. Every year before, I've been backstage, waiting in the wings, rehearsing my lines in my head, going over which face went with which lyric, my body shaking as I peek out to see the audience, wondering if I'll flub a line or miss a dance step or go flat.

This is so much worse than that.

I have no control, I realize. If I miss a dance step, that's my fault, and I can take responsibility for it. But this is everyone's dance steps. Everyone's acting and singing and if even one of them messes up, I know that's on me. For not directing them well enough. For not giving them what they needed to make it work. I look over at Mark, in the seat next to me in the front row, who is chewing on the edge of his thumbnail. A nicotine patch peeks out from under the arm of his counselor shirt.

"Is this how you feel every year?" I ask him. He nods. "No wonder you need so much therapy."

He barks a laugh and stops chewing his nail. "Thanks for that." He pats me on the leg. "It'll be fine, Randy. It'll be great."

I look over at my parents, who are watching this exchange with the usual look of "we don't understand, but we're proud of you, honey" that they wear whenever they come to camp. I love them for trying. Behind me is Hudson, and his parents, whom I met briefly and were exactly who Connie said they'd be—looking around like they were in enemy territory, their eyes always darting left and right, looking for exits, or maybe weak points. When Hudson introduced me as his boyfriend, his mother turned away to try to hide rolling her eyes and his dad's smile went hard and forced as he reached out to shake my hand. He had a tight grip, too, as he said, "Well, I guess you must be the girl, since you're shorter."

I wanted to tell him that's not how it works, but I smiled and pretended I hadn't heard it, instead. Because I didn't want Hudson to get in trouble. Hudson looked over at me, his eyes wide with amusement. It was easier than I thought, actually, the pretending to be Del again, or some variation of him, because I knew Hudson knows the real me, and I know the real him. It's like we were sharing a secret, one his parents will never know.

His parents felt more at ease when I introduced them to my parents, and they all talked while Hudson and I found a tree to hide behind and take kissing selfies with our newly returned phones. There's a great one where behind us you can see the tops of trees from underneath, and the shadows look like space and the light look like thousands of stars pressed together, and there we are, floating in space, kissing each other. I immediately made it my lock screen. We traded numbers and texted and settled everything we needed to stay in touch the rest of the year.

And then we all walked down to the theater and took our seats.

The whole show, I can feel Hudson behind me, like a reassuring presence, just as strongly as I can feel Mark's edginess, his involuntary winces at every almost-missed cue or whenever we come to a moment we'd been having trouble with. But nothing goes wrong. The show is amazing. Seeing it all together with the lights down and a full audience makes it different somehow. Now the actors get to work with someone—the people in the audience, play to them, play WITH them. You can see it in their eyes, the way they come to life when there's a laugh or people clap. And the way Mark directed—his vision, if you will—is stunning. It is the queerest I've ever seen one of his shows. *Bye Bye Birdie* is supposed to be about the war of the sexes, maybe. Kim's right to kiss

Birdie without making her boyfriend jealous. Rose wanting Albert to honor his promise to marry her. The fact that these men don't seem to respect these women enough to do what they promised or trust them. But with the cross-casting, a few lyric changes, and playing with the acting, it's become something different. Now it's about daring to be yourself, even when the world is telling you to be something else. Sure, Albert still won't commit to Rose, but now it feels like that's because his mother might be homophobic. Hugo still doesn't want Kim to kiss Birdie, but it's about the symbolism of their relationship in a different world. And George knocks it out of the park. He's a gay man now, but a family man, and one who maybe would have belonged to the Mattachine Society—one who believes it's best for queer people to blend in...until the Ed Sullivan number when he joins the rainbow choir. That's his moment of transcendence. Sure, he comes crashing back later, not understanding the kids and their new-fangled ways of looking at queerness, but in that moment, George gets to be all of us, finding our best selves through love.

I'm the first one up to give him a standing ovation, and he spots me in the audience and winks at me, and nods his head slightly. I turn around. I wasn't the first one up. Hudson was. And Brad was right behind him and then the entire audience rose as George and everyone else bowed.

"What a show." I breathe the words out as the curtain comes down.

"I think we did pretty good this year," Mark says, hugging Crystal on his other side, and then me. "Pretty damn good. Oh! Maybe we should do *Damn Yankees* next year?"

"Might be a bit adult," Crystal says. "And it's less of an ensemble piece."

"What do you mean less of an ensemble piece?" Mark says. "It's absolutely an ensemble piece!"

I turn away from them to my parents, who are beaming with pride and confusion.

"I loved those costumes, honey," my mom says. "Did you pick those out?"

"I helped," I say.

"So great, kiddo," Dad says, giving me a hug. "I didn't understand half of it, but I know good work when I see it."

"Thanks," I say, rolling my eyes. Behind me, Hudson's parents are already headed for the door, but Hudson is smiling at me.

"That was amazing," he says. "I don't know if I got all of it...but it was special. I could feel it was special."

"That's what I said!" my dad cried, clapping Hudson on the back. "I like him." He and Mom start walking for the exit, and Hudson gives me a hug.

"Thank you," Hudson says, his arms wrapped around me.

"You don't need to thank me. Thank you," I say. I can feel the tears coming. We're about to be apart for nearly a year.

"Babe, don't cry," he says softly. "If you cry, I'll cry, and if I cry, my parents will get mad."

I take a deep breath and break the hug, nodding. No crying. Not now anyway.

"We still have lunch first, anyway," I say.

He nods, and we go backstage to congratulate everyone on the show. Mark and Crystal are radiating joy, Ashleigh and Paz are dancing to music only they seem to hear, and George and Brad are making out in the prop closet. It really is the perfect end to a perfect(ish) summer.

"I'm going to miss this," Hudson says, squeezing my hand so tightly, I'm afraid it might come off. I squeeze back even tighter. "And you."

"It'll be here next year, waiting for us. And the year after that... we'll find the place in the world that's like this. Or we'll make it."

"Yeah," he says, putting his arm around me. "I like that. I think it won't be hard to make it, either. I think... wherever you are feels like camp now."

I pull his arms tight around me and take a deep breath. I can smell the grass and the trees outside, the hairspray and wood of the theater, the sweat of the actors and Hudson, that smell that I've given up trying to name, but that I know is him. All of it blends together and I can see a life extending from it in front of me, a future. Freedom, love ... no, it's better than that. It smells like home.

TRANSCRIPT OF L. C. ROSEN'S ACKNOWLEDGMENTS SPEECH FOR *CAMP*, GIVEN 5/25/2020

Oh my god, oh my god.

Rosen takes the mic on stage as applause dies down. He removes a piece of crumpled paper from his pocket.

I really didn't expect this at all.

Rosen unfolds paper, looks at the award, then looks back at the paper.

I'm going to try to go quickly, though.

To orchestra: Don't you play me off yet!

Rosen pauses, as though for laughter. There is none.

First of all, thank you to the Academy.

Rosen pauses—again there is no applause.

I'd like to start by thanking my family!

Rosen looks out at audience, in the direction of his parents.

My parents! I wouldn't be here without your support. I wouldn't even have tried writing without you. And to the rest of my family, thank you so much!

I, of course, need to thank my amazing agent, Joy, over at David Black. She's always looked out for me and believed in me, and look!

Rosen holds up the award statue and shakes it in the air. One person in the audience claps.

Look what we did! Thank you so much to the entire team over at David Black—David, Gary, anyone else I'm missing, and Lucy at APA—thank you for all the hard work you do!

And I couldn't have done this without Alvina at Little, Brown taking a chance on me and this project!

Rosen turns to Alvina in the audience.

Thank you so, so much. We make such a great team, and your constant guidance was inspirational! I really couldn't have done it without you.

Rosen turns back to the rest of the audience.

To all the aspiring young writers out there—if you get a chance to work with Alvina, do it! Best career decision you could ever make! And thank you so much to everyone else at Little, Brown: Victoria, Alex, Ruqayyah, Christy, Michelle, Marisa, Jen, Emily, Natali, Valerie, Karina, Angelie, Sasha, Olivia, I know I've forgotten some people, I'm sorry, oh no, the man in the orchestra pit is looking at me. No! Don't! Not yet! Just a few more names, I promise!

Rosen unfolds the paper again, revealing it to be even larger than it first seemed.

Thank you to my first readers! People who looked at

early drafts and told me I wasn't crazy: Robin, Adam, thank you! Couldn't have done it without you!

Oh! And the UK team! I love the UK team. They shouldn't be so far down the list!

Rosen looks up and shakes his head at this mistake, as though he hadn't written the whole thing out.

Ben! Ben, you took such a strong lead with this, and you were my rock. You helped me get through so much of this. Everyone, if you have a chance to work with Ben, work with Ben! And Simon. Simon hates it when I say nice things about him, but, Simon, working with you is always a dream. Michael, oh, Michael, you too! You're amazing. And Emma, Shreeta, Alice, and all the rest of the team at Penguin Random House UK, you are all a dream to work with, thank you!

Orchestra starts to play Stephen Sondheim's "Send in the Clowns."

To orchestra: No! Come on! We were working so well together!

Fine, I'll just talk over you, then!

Rosen yells over the orchestra.

And to my support system, my boys: Adam, Julian, Phil, Sandy, Adib, Caleb, Tom, Shaun, Cale!

Rosen beats his chest with a fist.

You are my everything—you keep me sane! And Lauren, Robin, Richard, Matt, Leslie, Theo, Staab, Skes, Molly, Laura, Desiree, Alexis, Ryan, Teri, T.S., Dahlia, Simon, Amy

Rose, Cori, and so many others! I couldn't keep doing what I'm doing without you!

The music begins to play louder. Behind Rosen, a man in a tuxedo steps forward. Rosen half turns and waves him away.

No! I still have more!

Rosen flips over the paper he's been reading from.

My mentor, Dan, and all my teachers! I know I'm forgetting people, but—

The mic cuts out. The man in the tuxedo takes Rosen by the elbow. Rosen shakes him off, but the man grabs hold again.

Fine! Fine! Just one more: Chris, for being Chris. Thank you all so, so much!

He is being pulled off stage as he shouts this. The music swells and the curtain closes to light applause.

AN ANNOTATED SELECTED PLAYLIST OF SONGS IN OR INSPIRED BY THE NOVEL *CAMP*

BY MARK ARYEH, THEATER COUNSELOR AT CAMP OUTLAND

You may start by asking yourself "Wait, how can Mark be writing an annotated selected playlist for a work of fiction in which he is a character? Is this some of that meta nonsense? Does Mark even know what he's talking about? Is he making this all up? Or is it that in the fictional world, all the stuff he's saying is true, but it's not true in my world? Is my world the real one? Is this really just the author putting on a voice?! WHAT IS AN ANNOTATED SELECTED PLAYLIST ANYWAY? Do I need to talk to my therapist about all this?" To which I respond, "TALK TO YOUR THERAPIST ABOUT EVERYTHING."

If you expect more of an explanation than that, look elsewhere, because from here on out, this is about THE MUSIC.

Now, *Camp* mentions over forty songs, musicals, singers, composers, and so forth, and you should be intimately familiar with all of them if you want to live the life of a decent human being with taste. But unfortunately, the tyrants over at Little, Brown Books for Young Readers won't give me the pages and pages necessary to teach you the history, significance, and MEANING of each mentioned musical reference. And so I've had to cut it down. To ten. It killed me to do it, let me tell you. I am writing this list in blood on the inside of my coffin because I'm dead and buried by the cruelty they inflicted on me by asking me to do this in so few words. My ghost is writing this! You're being haunted right now! And it's worth it—FOR THE MUSIC.

Pages 18-19
"ONE MINT JULEP (CHA-CHA TWIST)"
Performed and Orchestrations by Xavier Cugat and His Orchestra
Written by Rudy Toombs
When you think of music of the sixties, there are different ways you can go: early Cher, early Dolly, musical theater, some folk nonsense, or THIS kind of music. Randy doesn't name this song on page 18 (because he was making eyes at some boy instead of being inside the cabin listening to me announce the music) but describes it as "vintage doo-wop," and while he's

right about the vintage, I have no idea what he thinks doo-wop is, and I'm not going to acknowledge it by going into the history of doo-wop (again, TYRANTS at Little, Brown). Instead, let's talk about the history of this song and how it shows the way music changes from the fifties to the sixties! "One Mint Julep" was written in 1951 by Rudy Toombs for the Clovers. It was originally an R&B song, but fifties R&B was actually a move AWAY from doo-wop, RANDY, and more toward a Motown flavor. The song was a number one hit in 1951, and then AGAIN in 1961, when Ray Charles released a jazzier instrumental version of it with his big band, losing the lyrics about getting drunk. This is much closer to the version mentioned in the book; when Xavier Cugat decided to cover it, he added some of his signature style, which came from roots in Latin music, turning it into the "Cha-Cha Twist." This version is the one often used in movies, such as *Swingers* (1996) and *Down with Love* (2003). I chose it because it's SO sixties but also SO campy! It's the most musical theater version of the song! It makes you think of white girls in miniskirts twisting and grinning like maniacs! And that was the vibe I wanted my campers to feel.

Page 32
"HOW LOVELY TO BE A WOMAN"
From *Bye Bye Birdie*
Performed by Ann-Margaret
Music by Charles Strouse

Lyrics by Lee Adams

Orchestration by Don Ralke

There's going to be a lot of *Bye Bye Birdie* on this list! How could there not be?! But this one is special. While many of the songs will be from the original Broadway version, this is actually a bonus track from the soundtrack of the movie! It wasn't even featured in the film! Obviously the song was, but this version is not. That's because it was the SEXY version they recorded for the radio! Don Ralke, a music arranger with a talent for jazzing up musical theater, was brought in to modernize and popify the song, making it a real knockout for Ann-Margret. And he succeeded! Normally, the song is sweet. The joke of it is that Kim sings it as she gets out of her dress and into decidedly unwomanly pajamas (they can be boyish, like in the movie, or sometimes just childish). Kim has no idea what it is to be a woman, because she isn't one! She has no idea what she's singing about! But this version is much more WOMANLY, a word that is essentially meaningless, but here means MATURE. It's a little naughty; it's jazzy. This is Ann-Margret, sex symbol of the sixties, singing, not Kim. And Ann-Margret had her own music career, which started with her being sold as the female version of Elvis and went on to her being Elvis's leading lady. She was sexy, vivacious, naughty. This version of the song made sure no one forgot that, even as she played an innocent young woman. *Bye Bye Birdie* also launched her to superstardom, so putting out this version of the song was a smart way to keep her from getting typecast.

Page 87

"HONESTLY SINCERE"

From *Bye Bye Birdie*
Performed by Dick Gautier
Music by Charles Strouse
Lyrics by Lee Adams

I'm not going to leave out my ONE performance in the book! If the book wasn't following Randy around and had just focused on me, there would have been several others, as I sang to and with the campers, but I guess this is the only one I got, and I'm not letting my big number pass by. Another *Bye Bye Birdie* choice. This time I'm using the version from the original Broadway performance, where Dick Gautier shimmied up onstage, in an imitation of Conway Twitty more than of Elvis Presley. But maybe I should also include the movie version here because it's the movie version of the song that inspired the ENTIRE show at Camp Outland this year. When I was young, I used to watch the movie RELIGIOUSLY. It was my church, my god, my goddess, whatever. And though I was young and not completely aware of what a flaming homosexual I was yet, I remember there was one thing about this song that always struck me: The men fainted, too. This song, which doesn't do much to advance the plot except to tell everyone to be true to themselves (the THEME of the music, one might say, and also of this book you're holding). What it does to advance the plot is via the performance—here we finally see Birdie in action! We see

379

what it is about him that causes such overwhelming devotion. And we see the reaction people have to his music: They faint. And it's pretty clear they faint because his singing arouses a palpable desire that so overwhelms them they just can't stay conscious. I've been there myself. Or maybe that was dehydration. But in any case, we see people faint at Birdie's singing. First his fans. Then the mayor's wife and some older ladies. And then, by the end of the song—everyone is fainting, men included. Whatever effect Birdie has, it isn't strictly heterosexual. As a kid, that was fascinating to me. As a teenager, it was a relief to me. And as an adult, it inspired me to put on my super-queer production of the musical! After all, one of the original versions of the show is already queer! I was just bringing that out more. So I love this song. It's special and important, even if it's also a joke about how Birdie is kind of vapid. And of course in the course of this BOOK, it's important because I was telling Randy everything he needed to know, which he'd learn himself by the end of the book. Just THINK how it would have been if he'd just listened to me at the start, right? That Hudson kid wouldn't have been as happy, I'm sure, but I don't know him, and my therapist said if I get overly invested in one more camper, he's dumping me, so I don't WANT to know him.

Page 117

~~"LET ME BE YOUR STAR"~~
"THEY JUST KEEP MOVING THE LINE"

380

From *Bombshell*, the fictional musical from the TV show
Smash
Performed by Megan Hilty
Music by Marc Shaiman
Lyrics by Scott Wittman

I know, I KNOW, George auditioned with "Let Me Be Your
Star." And he didn't get the part he wanted! So what does
that tell you? "Let Me Be Your Star" is a fine song, the big
number they used to publicize *Smash* and all that, but there
are two issues with it: First, one of the performers on it has
since been revealed to be a Republican, so I would rather not
play any music that might give her money! Second, it's not
the best song in the show. That honor belongs to "They Just
Keep Moving the Line," performed by the divine LGBTQ+
advocate Megan Hilty! The fact that they even CONSID-
ERED Katherine McPhee to play Marilyn when they had
Megan Hilty staring them in the face is an affront to all that is
good and decent! Plus, Katherine auditioned with a pop song!
WHAT WAS THAT? If you don't know *Smash*, it was a TV
show that ran on NBC for two seasons from 2012–2013. It
was NOT a very good TV show. It was a VERY watchable
TV show, especially if you like theater. Strangely compel-
ling in a car-crash sort of way or if you're really into scarves.
So on some level, it was wonderful! It was just also awful—
you understand. It was, however, a TV show that had on it
a BRILLIANT musical called *Bombshell*. *Bombshell* was the
musical that was getting produced on the TV show (if that's

hard to follow I don't know how you've made it this far reading notes on a book from a fictional character IN the book). *Bombshell* was about the life of Marilyn Monroe, and throughout the seasons, we saw many musical numbers written, revised, and rehearsed. These musical numbers were ostensibly written by the on-the-show characters Julia Houston (Debra Messing, all anxiety and scarves) and Tom Levitt (Christian Borle, fussiness turned to 100). But in reality, they were written by superstar team Marc Shaiman and Scott Wittman. They also did *Hairspray*! But I prefer *Bombshell*, despite the shell game (see what I did there?) it takes to get to the actual musical. The music of *Bombshell* is astounding; it evokes classic Broadway music without feeling old, and the songs range from sexy dance number ("The National Pastime," "I Never Met a Wolf Who Didn't Love to Howl") to sexy bedroom number ("History Is Made at Night," "Our Little Secret") to genuine emotional numbers for Bernadette Peters ("Hang the Moon") and a plethora of catchy, fun, smart numbers that create one of the best scores of any modern musical. And there are also BALLADS. I'm not usually a ballad guy—I don't think a show needs more than two—but the ones in *Bombshell* are great, and the greatest, in my humble and correct opinion, is "They Just Keep Moving the Line." A song about Marilyn's inability to achieve real dramatic success and respect in the industry and how every time she proves herself, they...well...move the line, and yet she keeps achieving. But she's tired of it. She can't win; her successes turn to ash in her mouth! It's TRAGIC! It's POWER-FUL! It's BEAUTIFUL! I sing it in the shower at least once a week! If you don't know *Smash*, go find the videos of the songs online! Watch them! If you're feeling brave, find the whole show online! NBC.com! And definitely learn "They Just Keep Moving the Line"! If you audition with it, maybe you'll get the part you want.

Page 148

"YOUR DADDY'S SON"

From *Ragtime*
Performed by Audra McDonald
Music by Stephen Flaherty
Lyrics by Lynn Ahrens

AUDRA MCDONALD. She's mentioned on page 148 (Randy thinks he's soooo clever with this one, but the fact that Hudson didn't know who she was should have been a deal breaker right there, right then! I would have pushed that kid off me and marched directly back to the theater). But because she was mentioned, OF COURSE I had to include her. But it's just her name, no specific song! I need to choose ONE SONG to encapsulate her WHOLE career and talent?! IMPOSSIBLE. GENUIUNELY IMPOSSIBLE. I spent three hours on the phone with my therapist trying to work it out. It was useless. Now, if for some TERRIBLE reason, you, like Hudson, don't know who Audra McDonald is, she is A GODDESS come to earth to bless us with her beautiful voice! She has SIX Tony

Awards (maybe more by the time you're reading this!), three of which she won before she was thirty. She went to Juilliard to be an opera singer (because, she says, she didn't know that Juilliard didn't lead to musical theater, which was always her goal—HER DESTINY—and once she got in, she couldn't say no) but took a break from it when she got a role in *The Secret Garden* at age twenty-one! She went back, finished at Juilliard, and then a year out, landed the role in *Carousel* for which she'd win her first Tony. And then her career just got better and better. I could write a book about her! (But those TYRANTS at Little, Brown say they only publish books written by ACTUAL HUMAN BEINGS.) She has operatic voice training but also grew up with musical theater, so she can make her voice do anything from lyric soprano to jazz belt. But more than her actual vocal ability, the thing that makes Audra special is her emotion. Every GODDAMNED NOTE that comes out of her mouth is not only perfectly placed and rich, but it vibrates with feeling. "Your Daddy's Son" shows all her skill off: The vocal skill is palpable because of the ease with which she sings, the craft of her voice, but the real power comes from the emotions in the way she sings. I dare any one of you to close your eyes and listen, really listen, to her singing. If you don't feel anything, congratulations, YOU'RE A CONFIRMED MONSTER. My therapist says that's not a real test, but he is WRONG. This song makes me cry every time! I'm crying right now just thinking about it! Go listen. Go listen to every song Audra has ever sung. Maybe you'll say I should have chosen another song to encapsulate her! That's FINE! There are NO WRONG CHOICES when it comes to Audra.

Page 149

"FINISHING THE HAT"

From *Sunday in the Park with George*

Performed by Mandy Patinkin

Music and Lyrics by Stephen Sondheim

Again, part of Randy's LACK OF PREPARATION for his role is he didn't have a favorite book. So he told the truth and chose Stephen Sondheim's autobiography, *Finishing the Hat*, named for the song in *Sunday in the Park with George*, one of his greatest musicals. Who am I kidding? THEY'RE ALL GREAT. Sondheim is one of the GREATEST modern musical theater composers and lyricists. He has changed the face of musical theater by melding traditional melodic Broadway music with modern and postmodern composition. He's created music that, when performed right, is not just complicated and intelligent but emotional. If I had to choose just ONE song like I did with AUDRA, I would have a BREAKDOWN! Luckily, Steve chose one himself when he titled his autobiography. "Finishing the Hat" is sung by George Seurat, the painter and titular star of *Sunday in the Park with George*. Seurat was a pointillist painter, and so Sondheim has taken the idea of pointillism—of using dots of primary color on the canvas, blended by the eye, not the brush—and converted it to music, using dots of music to create a greater painting of song. The song opens with almost unrelated beats of music that, as George gets working, all blend together into a beautiful song about the act of creation and what an artist has to give up to make art but how it's still worth it. No wonder Sondheim chose it for the title of his autobiography. As the song goes along, the dots of music start grouping together in ways that sing. Above it all, the voice soars! Sondheim is an actor's writer—he needs actors, like Audra McDonald, who can really emote in their voices. Mandy Patinkin is a classic example of this, so it's no wonder he was such a collaborator with Steve. He's no Audra, mind you—no one can compare there—but he's good. If you're unfamiliar with Sondheim, GO EDUCATE YOURSELF. Listen to *Sunday in the Park with George*! Listen to *Company* and *Into the Woods*! Listen to all of it! I won't say every song he's ever written is a work of incomparable genius, but every song has thought in it, every song is doing something. And that something is CHANGING THE FACE OF MUSICAL THEATER!

Page 206
"FLY ME TO THE MOON"
Performed by Astrud Gilberto
Written by Bart Howard
Written originally in 1954 and performed by Kaye Ballard under the title "In Other Words," the most famous version of this song came a decade later, when Frank Sinatra covered it, and it became the theme of the 1960s Space Race. You've

probably heard that version. It was arranged by Quincy Jones, who boosted the tempo and made it very classic Sinatra. Swinging, masculine, jazzy, a big change from the sweeping romantic ballad it was originally. Gilberto's version was also recorded in 1964, same year as Sinatra's, though they'd both been singing it for a while. I'm not sure whose came first, but they both upped that tempo. The difference is that Gilberto's version has more bossa nova, more of the swinging sixties that wasn't about masculinity and fedoras, but that was about bikinis and fashion! Or, to put it another way, her version was more feminine, in the way that our HETEROCENTRIC society defines that word. In the movie *Down with Love*, there's a wonderful juxtaposition using her version and Sinatra's, showing a man and woman getting ready for a date, the song switching versions depending on who we're focusing on. It really shows the different gendered spheres of the sixties—the man all conquering, the woman all romance. So it's NO WONDER this is the version I played for my campers. We will have NONE of that TOXIC MASCULINITY in my cabin! This version is romantic but still sexy, bringing in the vibes of the original version's longing but making it dance like it's the sixties. Which it was! Gilberto herself was a Brazilian singer of bossa nova, samba, and Latin jazz, probably most famous for "The Girl From Ipanema." Her voice is like chiffon, satin, silk. You can feel it breeze over you and float down. Randy says the song makes him think of posing in silk robes, and that's not just the arrangement, it's her voice, soft and melodic.

Page 250–251

"HYMN FOR A SUNDAY EVENING"

From *Bye Bye Birdie*
Performed by Paul Lynde
Music by Charles Strouse
Lyrics by Lee Adams

GEORGE WAS PERFECT FOR THIS ROLE. I know, I know, he wanted Kim. Kim is cute and sweet and one of the leads, and in the movie she sings the opener. But Kim isn't that funny. Her humor comes from her being very sure of herself about very stupid things in the way teenagers are. But the humor from Harry requires more nuance—this song being the peak of that. While the rest of the time he might be an exasperated father yo-yoing between disappointment and anger, here he is actually captured by the idea of his own potential fame—it's literally a religious experience for him, as shown by the title of the song, the music, and in the case of the film and some stage productions, the actual choir robes he and his family don. George could do this nuance better than anyone else. I knew I wanted this moment to be about queerness in our show, a moment about embracing your own big gay dreams, even if, say, you're a little older than a teenager, maybe in your forties, maybe things aren't going the way you thought they would and you're not a big Broadway star and instead you're a chorus boy on cruise shows and direct teenagers at a camp musical in the summer. THAT DOESN'T MEAN YOUR DREAM ISN'T COMING! And I wanted to make sure it was the same dream that Kim had—to kiss the idol you love most. For Kim, it's Birdie. For Harry, it's Ed. Putting all that into one song that is also a hymn and a religious experience and a love song and making it funny? Only George could do that. I REGRET NOTHING. This song is an important moment in the musical, showing that we all have dreams of meeting our celebrities, of being a celebrity, and that Kim is no different from her father. I made it even bigger than that. Plus, it's just a wonderful hymn. Beautifully written, it's religious but also still sounds like musical theater. I'm so proud of the way George made my admittedly difficult vision come alive. Here's a bit of trivia: Ed Sullivan himself, upon hearing the song for the first time, said, "Sylvia and I sat there with our friends staring at us. I only wanted the floor to open up and swallow us both."

Page 274
"BYE BYE BIRDIE"
From *Bye Bye Birdie* (the movie)
Performed by Ann-Margaret
Music by Charles Strouse
Lyrics by Lee Adams
The opening number of the film is probably the most famous, both musically and visually—Ann-Margaret in a yellow dress against a blue background singing her heart out. But it's not in the stage version! It was written specifically for the movie. This was mostly to really launch Ann-Margaret's career. The

director and producers had a sexy new young singer, and they wanted to showcase her. They didn't film the opener and closer of the film until after everything else was filmed, and it cost them another sixty grand to do so (a lot back then, movie-wise). They wanted to give her more songs! (They also cut down Rosie's part and cut her song "Spanish Rose" from the movie, but considering Janet Leigh was playing it, and she's not in any way Spanish, that was probably a good idea.) And they weren't wrong about it! It did launch Ann-Margaret's career, and both the song and the visuals of her performing it are ICONIC! The way she acts to the camera without any other context but her voice! The dress, the wind, the way the camera interacts with her! It's electric! No wonder she became a star!

Page 312

"THE SHOOP SHOOP SONG (IT'S IN HIS KISS)"

Performed by Cher

Lyrics by Rudy Clark

Rudy Clark was an R&B songwriter who had several number one hits during the sixties. "It's in His Kiss," though, took a little warming up to get there. First the Shirelles rejected it, then when Merry Clayton used it as her first recorded single, it didn't hit the charts. It wasn't until Betty Everett recorded the song a year later, in 1964, that it finally found success—and then just kept finding it! This song has been covered by SO MANY artists over the years: Ramona King, Linda Lewis, Linda Ronstadt, Aretha Franklin, and finally,

CHER. She recorded it for the soundtrack of her movie *Mermaids*, and it quickly became a huge hit—in fact it was Cher's first SOLO hit since she'd split with Sonny. It topped the charts all over the world, and it's OBVIOUS WHY: IT'S CHER! Not much has changed in the arrangement since the original; it's just a GREAT SONG, and CHER IS A GODDESS. The perfect combination!

And now I'm out of words, according to THE TYRANTS AT LITTLE, BROWN, so I'm going to wrap it up. But there are MANY, MANY more songs mentioned or alluded to in *Camp*, and I'm putting them all in one big playlist on Spotify with some bonus songs, too. So if you have a Spotify account and want to listen to all this and more, check it out: **https://tinyurl.com/campoutland**

If a singer, band, musical, or composer are mentioned in the book, I put a song by them on the playlist! Often more than one! (But sometimes just one. Who mentioned *Peter Pan*?) They're not in any order past these first ten! IT'S VERY RANDOM. You should probably hit shuffle! But I recommend you give it a listen!

I know you've loved learning about music as much as I've loved teaching you! Now go take in some musical theater! Give to Actor's Equity! LOVE THE ARTS.

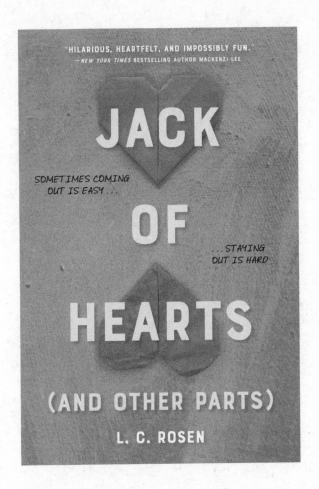

1

My reputation for sluttiness is only partially deserved. Yeah, I was kissing that guy from St. Jude's, sure, and then I kissed that guy Zack, who maybe was a friend of Jessica Lauter's, but mentioned being president of his GSA, so I don't think he was there with her. Although, maybe, I guess? I didn't ask. He should have said something. There wasn't a fourth guy. There was a big mirror in the bathroom, maybe that's what Tori saw. But yeah, that's me. Jack. I don't love being called queeny, but I do have some fantastic tank tops and a love of eyeliner and black nail polish. I also have some great button-downs with mesh insets and tight jeans with tears so high up you have to go commando in them. I talk with my hands a lot, too. So, sure, call me "queeny" if you're feeling nasty. I won't hold it against you, as long as it's said with love.

I don't know if Kaitlyn, Ava, and Emily know that the vent in the girls' bathroom means I can hear everything they're saying from the boys' bathroom. But on Mondays, I like to come in here for my second-period break, smoke a cigarette (the only time I do, mostly), and hear about what I did over the weekend. It's scandalous.

So, true story: Yes, we were in the downstairs bathroom at Hannah Ling's party, and yes, I maybe kissed both of them, one after the other. Yeah, with tongue. And it was pretty hot. They were going to kiss each other next. But we all had our clothes on, and we weren't going to strip down and have a threesome right there. I mean, we would have gone back to my place, or someone's place or something.

But then Tori walked in and gasped, really dramatically, and the guy from St. Jude's blushed and took off and Zack started laughing. We made out a little more after that, but then he had to go home and study or something. I think he wasn't so into me as he was into the idea of the threesome, which is fine, because the feeling was mutual.

So I didn't even get laid, much less have my first three- or foursome, but somehow, it seems I had a hot-tub orgy. My rumored life is so much more fun than my real one. I bet rumor-me doesn't have a history quiz next period. Or if he does, he already has an A on it for giving Mr. Davidson a blowjob.

I toss the cigarette out the window and hop down from the counter where you can hear the best, check my hair and makeup in the mirror, then leave. I leave before they do, because I think if they came out of the bathroom the same time as me, they'd just explode with giggles or embarrassment or . . . something. Better to just let them have their fun.

I'm not big on confrontation. I walk by the guys who mutter "fag" under their breath. I know, it seems like I should be that guy who screams at them, calls them homophobes. But why start something? Just . . . try to be likeable. That's my motto. Not, like, pretend to be someone you're not, obviously. Just be likeable. Don't cause drama just because people who won't talk to you in class talk about you naked when they think you can't hear.

What is there to get mad about, really? They think I'm hot and want to lady-jack-off to the idea of me getting pounded by three guys. It could be worse, so I tell myself not to think about it. Private school in New York City is liberal and cool, generally. It's not like I'm in Arkansas, forced into the closet and getting beaten up every day for just saying the wrong thing, my wrist being too limp. I've seen the "It Gets Better" videos. I know what it can be.

I mean, I do wonder what it is about my sex life, even active as it is, that attracts their attention. Other people have sex without becoming the stuff of legend and gossip. I guess I'm just special. Lucky me.

At my locker, I take out my history book to cram, but a note falls out when I open the door. A pink piece of paper, folded origami style into a triangle. It lands on the floor louder than I think paper should land. I pick it up and unfold it.

You are so cute. ♡

I smile. A secret admirer? That's sweet. Or creepy, maybe? I
look up and down the hall, but no one is looking at me, waiting
to see my reaction. I look back down at the paper. Black marker.
Bad handwriting. I doubt it's any of the other out boys in school.
Ben is one of my closest friends and I am not his type. He likes
bears—big hairy guys—usually older. I'm definitely not in that
particular gay subset of wildlife (on Grindr, I unhappily checked
the twink box, because I'm seventeen and hairless and slim—
but muscled, from running track—why isn't that a box?). And
Jeremy Diaz thinks I'm a whore who gives queers a bad name,
and Don Caul is way too focused on getting into Yale to take
the time to write a love note. Maybe some new freshman? Or
maybe someone still in the closet? Is this Ricky Gavallino's way
of finally trying to inch his way out? Oh god—what if it's a girl?

"Hey," Jenna Rodriguez says from behind me. I stuff the piece of paper in my pocket and turn around.

"Hey," I say. She raises an eyebrow at me, barely visible under the tangle of long half-bleached hair.

"What was that?"

"Nothing."

She purses her tea-painted lips like she doesn't believe me, but then shrugs, deciding she also doesn't care. That's why I love Jenna. If I want to keep something private, she doesn't pry.

"So, I had this idea," she says, sitting down. I sit down next to her, our backs against the lockers, her dark skirt pooling on the floor. "For the blog."

Jenna was kicked off the school paper for, in the words of Principal Pattyn, "pursuing an agenda of aggressive anti–Parkhurst School spirit." That was after she reported that Mr. Botts had crashed his car driving drunk one weekend. So she started her own blog—website, I guess—called The Private Line, writing about the stuff the school doesn't want us to know. All the schools, really—the private schools. It's not a gossip blog, like Famke Stein runs, with all the hookups and breakups and rumors. (I don't feature on it as much as you might think—Famke is way more interested in the more popular boys and girls. But I do have my own tag.) The Private Line is actual, newsworthy sort of stuff. Local news. Teachers getting fired for whatever, department budget crises. Her mom is a reporter—the kind that travels the world and visits war zones and interviews dictators, so Jenna holds herself to a high standard of reporting. But lately she's been trying to branch out. And for some reason, she wants me involved.

"Okay," I say, opening my history textbook to the chapter I didn't read last night.

"I want you to do a column."

"I'm not a reporter."

"I know," she says. "An advice column. Sex advice."

"Oh god," I say, bringing the textbook up to cover my face. "Why? What did you hear?"

"Well, I did hear you found a guy on Grindr who looks like Tom Blackwell's dad and you invited him to the tennis match last week and made out with him in the stands opposite Tom so he'd play a lousy game."

"I don't know Tom," I say, dropping the book. "I wasn't even *at* the tennis game." I know it's not the end of the world, but I wish I could fuck around without any commentary in the girls' bathroom. I guess I could stop listening…but that's not going to happen.

Jenna shrugs. "Just own it. Use it. For this column."

"No."

"Please?" she says in a slightly begging voice. "You can use it on your college applications."

"How is that going to look? 'Told people how to suck dick.' That's some serious Harvard material."

"Okay, so not a sex column. Like, a relationship advice column. We can call it Jack of Hearts." She makes a headline in the air with her hands.

"Right. And other parts."

"I like that," she says, hitting me on the shoulder. "We can call it that."

"I haven't had a boyfriend who lasted more than three weeks."

"So what? You know what makes people tick. You'd be good at it."

"I'd be a disaster." I turn the page in my history book without having read it.

"Do it once." Jenna clasps my arm with both her hands, her tawny fingers warm but her pewter-painted nails digging in sharply. "Please? I need a little spice. People aren't as interested in the backroom politics of the teachers' union as they once were. Famke's kicking my ass with that story about the Miller twins at Edgemont dating the same guy without him knowing."

I sigh. We both know I'm going to give in. "I just have to answer questions?"

"Yeah. I'll give you a stack, and you pick one out and you answer it. Easy."

"I'll do one," I promise. "But only because you're my friend. Not because I want to."

"You never know," she says, reaching into my bag and taking out my phone. She knows the password and has it open in two seconds. "You might like it." She hands my phone back to me—there's a new mail app on it. I tap it open to see I have a full mailbox waiting.

"You already have the questions?" I swipe through the emails. There's a little over fifty of them, but at least a dozen are just calling me a fag.

"I may have used the rumor mill to spread the idea that you were going to be doing this last week. . . . That way I'd know if there was interest before asking you to do it. And I set up a special server that anonymizes the senders' information. People feel more secure asking questions that way."

"Thinking ahead," I say, deleting the fag emails.

"A reporter's job. Anyway, I didn't filter them. So a lot are just like 'How do you know you're gay?' and 'Doesn't anal hurt?' stuff, but there are some good ones in there. But if you want to talk about anal, that's okay, too."

"Good to know what people think of when they hear my name," I say flatly.

"Live it up," Jenna says. "Better than not being known at all, right?"

"Sure," I say, though anonymity sounds delightful. I know lots of kids want to be famous, and yeah, I like attention, but I'd much prefer it for things I do—like dress amazing and say witty things—than *who* I do.

"It's like a public service," she says in the voice she used when she ran for class president freshman year. "They don't teach gay stuff in sex ed."

"I can take a few days with these, right?" I ask, shaking the phone.

"Take until Thursday. Email me your question and response. I want to post your first column a week from today—Monday. And then the second one the Thursday after that. Then we'll decide on weekly or twice weekly, depending on how people react."

"I'm just doing one," I say as firmly as I can.

She leans her head on my shoulder and rubs my knee. "No," she says. "You're not."

"Not what?" Ben asks, coming down the hall. He plops down on my other side and takes out his history textbook, looks at what page I'm open to, and opens his to match. "Oh, I read all this already," he says, flipping ahead. "You're in trouble, girl."

"Thanks."

"Jack is going to write a column for my blog," Jenna says. "Relationship stuff."

"Oh, I bet that'll be popular," Ben says, without a trace of sarcasm. Ben doesn't do sarcasm. Ben Parrish is like a beach ball—short, bouncy, round, and somehow always radiating happiness. The shaved head and round red glasses add to the effect. He also wears yellow a lot. His skin is really dark, so he pulls it off well.

"Right?" Jenna says, pushing me slightly in a "told ya" way.

"Is it going to be erotic?" Ben asks.

"No," I say. "It's advice. How is advice erotic?"

"Like, 'How to spice things up in the bedroom!' or 'Ten great kissing tips!'"

"No." I shake my head and turn to Jenna. "Right?"

She shrugs. "It's whatever you want it to be. Erotic is fine." She smiles, like she thinks that's what it's going to be anyway.

"Come on," I say, standing up, "let's go fail a quiz."

"Later, fellas," Jenna says, taking out her phone.

"I'm not going to fail," Ben says, walking next to me. "I studied."

"I studied...some," I say. I look sideways at him. "Hey, you didn't slip a note in my locker, did you?"

"A note?" Ben sounds confused. "What, are we in one of those old John Hughes movies we watched in our film history class?" He pauses. "Because I would love that."

"There were no gay people in John Hughes movies," I say. "Or black people."

"I could break ground! Or it could be a modern reboot. I look extra pretty in pink."

I snort as we get to Mr. Davidson's classroom. It's empty and the lights are out—class isn't for another ten minutes. I don't turn them on, just plop down in my seat next to the window and open my textbook again.

"Wait," Ben says, apparently oblivious to my attempts to cram that last chapter in before class. "Did someone slip a note in your locker?"

"Never mind, I need to study."

"Let me see!"

"I threw it out already." I don't know why I don't want to show him, but there was something so weird and intimate about it.

"Was it a love note? Like, a secret admirer?"

"Can I study?"

"Why would you think I would write you a love note?"

"It wasn't a love note. It was...nothing." I point at the textbook. "I don't want to fail."

"Mmmhm." Ben crosses his arms and juts his chin out at me.

"Fine, keep your secret admirer secret. But if you figure out who it is, you better tell me."

"I don't think I want to know," I say, before focusing on the history book again. The start of World War I. I know the whole wrong-turn-led-to-an-assassination story—that's fun. But the actual reasons for the assassination are a little fuzzier than they should be. Luckily, Ben lets me go over them for the next few minutes as the other students trickle in. Then Mr. Davidson comes in, makes us put our books away, and hands out the quiz. Quizzes aren't so bad. They're quiet, which I like. And I can focus on the questions I know the answers to—which is about the first half.

But then there's a question I don't know, and suddenly that pink note is burning a hole in my pocket. Who writes notes anymore? Is it sweet or creepy? Or both? I guess it depends on who sent it. I mean, if it were like, Dylan Vandergraff, then it's sweet, because I fantasize about him pretty regularly. He's got blond hair but darker stubble, and he's on the swim team, with thighs that could crack walnuts. I would love to be between those thighs. So if he wrote the note, then that's delicious, and he can call me cute all he wants, and we're going to live happily ever after.

But if it's someone else—and let's be honest, it probably is— then maybe it's less cute.

"Ten minutes," Mr. Davidson says. I turn back to the test and fill it out best I can. The perfectly folded triangle of the note presses into my leg like a branding iron.

L. C. ROSEN, also known as Lev Rosen, has written several books for adults and children, including the young-adult novel *Jack of Hearts (and other parts)*. His books have been featured on numerous Best of the Year lists and nominated for several awards. He lives in New York City with his husband and a very small cat.

MORE FROM L. C. ROSEN

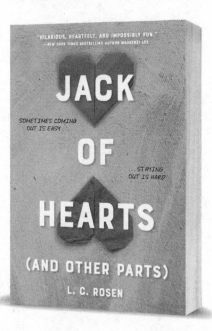

"HILARIOUS, HEARTFELT, AND IMPOSSIBLY FUN."
—NEW YORK TIMES BESTSELLING AUTHOR MACKENZI LEE

JACK OF HEARTS
(AND OTHER PARTS)

SOMETIMES COMING OUT IS EASY...

...STAYING OUT IS HARD

L. C. ROSEN

PUTTING THE "OUT" IN THE GREAT OUTDOORS

CAMP

L. C. ROSEN

BOB995

"Bold. Unfiltered. Funny. Boundary-shattering."
—Dahlia Adler, author of *Under the Lights*

"Joyful, exuberant, incisive, and terrifically queer."
—Adib Khorram, author of *Darius the Great Is Not Okay*